STONE PROMISES

samantha christy

Books Publishing Group

Saint Augustine, FL 32092

Copyright © 2017 by Samantha Christy

Cover design © Sarah Hansen, Okay Creations

ISBN-13: 978-1542579568

ISBN-10: 1542579562

This book is dedicated to all the readers who have reached out to me. I will never tire of hearing from you.

Books by Samantha Christy

Be My Reason
Abstract Love
Finding Mikayla

Purple Orchids (The Mitchell Sisters Book One)
White Lilies (The Mitchell Sisters Book Two)
Black Roses (The Mitchell Sisters Book Three)

Stone Rules (The Stone Brothers Book One)
Stone Promises (The Stone Brothers Book Two)

STONE
PROMISES

CHAPTER ONE

Chad

"Is it true you only have one testicle?" someone shouts.

I look up, only to be blinded by dozens of camera flashes. *Damn it!*

Even with the private entrance, secure hallways, and VIP lounges, we still have to go through TSA security like everyone else. And now pictures of me removing my belt while Courtney was conveniently draped over me like a cheap fucking suit will be tabloid fodder for days.

I look over my shoulder at my publicist. "Kendra?"

She nods knowingly. "I'm on it," she says, depositing her phone into a security bin. "As soon as we get through the line."

Kendra has proven to be worth her weight in gold. She probably works harder than most publicists out there considering my less-than-ideal past. She's only been with me for a few months, since the pre-release screenings of *Defcon One* started last December. That was when the studio pretty much told me if this film doesn't shoot me straight to A-list, nothing would.

As soon as we're on the other side, being escorted to our private lounge in LAX, she's chatting away on her phone trying to

1

do damage control on what the press will surely twist into some kind of torrid ongoing affair between Courtney and me. And that's exactly how Courtney would like it. Ever since I tossed her to the curb when I found out she was using, she's tried her best to be connected with me every chance she gets.

Not that anyone seems to mind except Kendra and me. Hell, the studio and even my own manager drool over it. Everyone wants to see the leading man and woman get together. Sex sells. And off-screen sex sells even more.

After being secretly boarded through a side door into our first-class seats, I snag a seat by the window, wanting to get some shuteye on the five-hour flight to New York. Courtney sits down next to me and I roll my eyes and let my head fall back onto the seat as I reach for my earbuds.

"Courtney," Kendra says, coming up to stand beside her, "I really need to borrow Thad for a while. I have tons of interviews to prepare him for. Would you mind?" The two women participate in a stare down.

Courtney huffs and picks up the small bag she had tucked under the seat in front of her. "Fine." She looks around for an empty seat, finally taking the one next to Hayden, the actor who portrayed my arch enemy in the movie, but who is probably the closest thing I have to a true friend at this point. With the exception of Kendra maybe, but I'm paying her so she doesn't really count.

I think back to the last time in my life I had genuine friends. Friends who liked *Chad* Stone, the kid who liked to play basketball. The kid who shaved the neighbor's cat as a practical joke one Halloween. The kid who didn't have an eight-figure bank account thanks not only to a random discovery by a talent scout in a

2

shopping mall of all places, but also to inheriting a shitload of money from his grandparents.

Nine years. That's how long it's been since I haven't had to question the motives of anyone who speaks to me. That's how long it's been since I've had a best friend who doesn't share my last name. Ethan and Kyle, my two brothers, became my best friends when I was sixteen, after I left the only two people I'd never be able to replace when my parents moved me across the country. But my brothers both reside back in New York City now which makes it hard to see them as much as I'd like. And knowing I'm on my way there, that the Manhattan premiere of *Defcon One* will allow me to hang out with them for two straight weeks, almost makes having to put up with that bitch, Courtney, worth it.

Every time I think of my brothers, I long for the normalcy they have. The practicality of a nine-to-five job that doesn't hang in the balance if they say the wrong thing, do the wrong thing, or put on a few pounds. A job that allows them to go to the goddamn grocery store without being mobbed by paparazzi and psychotic fans. Don't get me wrong, I love the fans—most of them. It's the fans who have put me where I am today, and it's the fans who will decide if I stay here. But some of them just go too far and ruin it for everyone.

I love acting. It's a job I never dreamed of pursuing. Hell, I'd only ever acted one time in a sappy play back in high school. For all I knew, I was going to teach high school history. Or maybe college. I hadn't decided yet. But acting? No, that was Mallory's dream—not mine.

Mallory. I close my eyes and sigh. I try not to think about her anymore. She represents everything that was ever normal in my life. Everything that is the opposite of who I've become. The man who is *Thad* Stone. Sometimes the line between Thad and Chad becomes blurred. Sometimes I wish I could just become that history teacher who goes home to his wife and kids at the end of every day. But I know it's not possible. First, because I do enjoy my profession—if you take away the rabid fans, the overbearing press, and the general upheaval of normal existence. And second, because there is only one person I could ever see myself coming home to and she wrote me off years ago. Who can blame her after all the things I've done? After the mess I've made of my life.

"You okay, Thad?" Kendra asks, touching my forearm in a motherly way even though she's only five years my senior.

"Yeah," I say, shaking off unproductive thoughts of the past. "Thanks for saving me from the queen bitch of the universe again. Have I told you lately how much I love you?"

"Ha! I wish," she says.

I laugh off her comment. "You do not. I think Todd would have something to say about that."

She shakes her head in amusement, her beautiful short auburn hair bouncing around her chin.

"What?" I ask.

"Do you know you're the only one of my clients who even knows my husband's name?"

"Get the fuck out of here," I say.

"Really," she says, nodding.

I ponder it for a second before saying, "Do you know you're the only publicist who would give me the time of day last December?"

"Actually, I did know that," she says, shrugging. "But I'd been following your career since *Malibu 310* and saw great potential there. I also saw a kid thrust into the public eye who didn't have the first clue about how to deal with it. People make bad choices, Thad, but that doesn't make them bad people."

I nod, pretending to agree with her. But I know better. The things I've done follow me around like stink on shit, and Kendra is a saint to deal with all of it. She took a chance on me. I know that. And I don't plan on letting her down. I'm different now. I know the studio and the fans see Thad Stone as the ultimate bad boy of Hollywood, but that hasn't been who I am for a long time now. And they will all have to fucking deal with it.

"So, you're not staying at The Waldorf with the rest of us?" she asks. "Paul said you'd be staying with your brother, Ethan. You know the ramifications, right?"

"You can bet Paul made sure I knew the studio would only provide security if I followed their strict guidelines. Don't worry, Cole is flying in later today. He'll be here in time for the premiere."

"Good. I'm glad to hear that."

"Hear what? That my manager tore into me—again. Or that I hired my own bodyguard?"

She laughs. "Thad, Paul tearing into you is nothing new. If he went one day without reading you the riot act, I would think he had developed a fever or something. I'm glad you decided to hire Cole. He's good. Better than studio security for sure. Are you going to make it permanent?"

"I'm not sure yet. This is still all so new to me. I mean, back when I did *Malibu*, everything was different. The fans were different. Not so goddamn scary."

"That's because they were all adolescent girls," she jokes. "And that's the difference between the small screen and the silver screen."

I nod. "I guess I'm not quite ready to completely give up my independence. This could be a one-time thing, you know."

Kendra looks at me like I'm crazy. "Thad, you saw what happened at the L.A. premiere. And the London one. And you've already signed on for the sequel, and then there is *Blind Shot* which everyone is saying will be just as big as *Defcon One*. And then next year, *Dark Tunnels*—they *gave* you that role, Thad. Things like that don't happen to B-listers. You no longer have to audition for parts. When are you going to realize that you've made it to the big time?" She pats my hand. "It's time to talk to Cole about making it permanent. Besides, I hear Greyson James uses him, too. You need to beat him to the punch if Cole is who you want."

"I'll think about it," I say to placate her. But deep down, I believe all the craziness surrounding the *Defcon One* release will die out. Then I'll be yesterday's news. Just like after they canceled *Malibu*.

"So, how is that adorable nephew of yours?" she asks. "Eli, right?"

I proudly whip out my phone and show her the latest pictures of Ethan's three-month-old son. "You know, I could say the same thing about you," I tell her. "You are the only person working for me who knows the name of everyone in my family."

She smiles. "It's my job to know that stuff, Thad."

"I suppose," I say, nodding to my phone. "But it's not your job to pretend to be interested in them."

"Pretend?" she asks, abhorrently. "I was going to ask when I could get my hands on the little guy."

"Really?" I furrow my brow at her.

"I love babies," she says.

My face falls. She sees my expression and laughs. "Don't worry," she says. "Todd and I are very happy with the status quo. Between our burgeoning careers, we are in no position to have kids any time soon. You're stuck with me for at least the next five years or so. If you want me, that is."

I feel a huge sense of relief. Kendra is the only person in this business who truly seems to care about me and not her own status or bank account. "Thanks," I say. "Maybe I could arrange for you to have dinner with us at Ethan's penthouse one night."

"That would be fantastic," she says, handing me a pillow the flight attendant brought by. "Here, get some rest, you're going to need it. The next week is going to be crazy—starting with tonight."

~ ~ ~

I'm still on a high from the premiere. Still reeling over the fact that it was me up on that screen. I was used to seeing myself on TV when I did *Malibu*. But this—watching the premiere of my movie, seeing my name first up on that screen instead of fourth, ninth or twenty-second as in the three previous films I've done—this is surreal.

Walking the red carpet to the third premiere of *Defcon One* was even more insane than the previous two. With each subsequent screening, the film has garnered more attention, the fans have come out in bigger droves, the paparazzi presence has quadrupled. I was grateful not only for the studio security, but for Cole Wilcox, who dropped everything to fly out and be part of my entourage for the next few weeks.

Now, as Ethan, Kyle and I exit the limo to be escorted into the after-party at a famous Manhattan club, I look down the sidewalk to see screaming fans twenty deep, and I think maybe Kendra is right. Maybe it is time to talk to Cole about coming on full-time.

I see some girls holding out pictures of me, begging me to autograph them. I send Ethan and Kyle inside and turn to my bodyguard. "Cole." I nod to the fans.

He speaks into the small microphone attached to his cuff, presumably telling the rest of the security team our plans. Then he walks me over to the girls. "Mr. Stone will sign a few autographs and pose for some pictures as long as you remain orderly."

Girls scream my name and trample each other to get closer to me. So much for remaining orderly. I purposefully only choose the ones who aren't being aggressive. I quickly sign my name to a few dozen photos, a couple of shirts, even one lady's bare arm. Cole grabs a few of the phones being shoved at me and takes some pictures of me with various girls.

The local police do a good job of not letting anyone past the barriers on either side of the club entrance. One of my biggest fears is being mobbed with no place to go. I think the phobia stems from when I was filming inside a cave for several weeks. I've been somewhat claustrophobic ever since. Now, the crush of fans triggers that same feeling. I've seen fans get downright violent, ripping clothing to shreds to get a small piece of something belonging to an actor without any concern for the safety and sanity of the object of their obsession.

My breathing speeds up and sweat trickles down my brow on this cool evening. Cole has only worked for me a few times before, but he can already sense when I've had enough. "Thank you all for coming out! Mr. Stone is needed inside!" Cole yells into the boisterous crowd.

I turn to wave goodbye to the crowd when I catch a glimpse of some disturbance beyond the first few rows of screaming women. I think my eyes have betrayed me. I have to squint to make sure I'm seeing what I think I'm seeing. There is a girl caught up in the crowd who looks like she's trying to get farther away when everyone around her is trying to get closer to me. She looks lost, the sea of women around her swallowing her small body whole as she tries to escape what looks to be the last place on earth she wants to be. When she looks over at me and our eyes meet, my fucking heart slams into my chest wall.

It's her. I know it's her. It's been nine years but I'd know her anywhere. I know every curve of her face, every location of every freckle on her arms. I know because I counted them all one day when I was eight years old. I told her she must have a hundred. She doubted that was true, so I sat her down on the curb in front of my house and counted them. One hundred and twelve freckles on her arms if you count the ones from her fingers up to her shoulders. "Mal?" I say, more of a question to myself because she'd never hear me over the screaming crowd.

I think she must be some kind of aberration. A dream I conjured up on the plane ride over. But then her lips move, and I think she says my name. My real name. Not the name she made up for me when she was six years old. Not the name I use to this day as my stage name. No, I could swear she says, "Chad."

And then, probably because I'm frozen in place and people see it as an opportunity, girls start to jump over the barricade, police being overcome by dozens of them as Cole swiftly moves me towards the door and out of harm's way. I work against him, trying to get over to Mallory, or to the person I believe to be her, because I never thought in a million years I'd see her again. Not after the shame I brought upon myself. Not after I let her down so horribly by becoming the person I was. But Cole outweighs me by a good fifty pounds and could probably bench press me for pure entertainment. So despite my best efforts, I'm no match for his professional training and he's able to wrangle me indoors.

Once I'm safely inside the club, Cole lets me go and Kendra runs over to me, apparently having watched the entire debacle. "What just happened out there, Thad?"

9

The whole scene replays in my mind and I realize what Kendra is asking. I'm sure I was caught on camera looking like a deer in headlights. *Oh shit.* I wonder if anyone realized who I was looking at, because if so, I may have just put her in danger.

"I thought I saw someone," I tell her.

"Who?" she asks. "Who do you think you saw that would make you react that way?"

I close my eyes and sigh, and then I tell her the truth that I've only ever admitted to myself. "The only girl I've ever loved."

CHAPTER TWO

Mallory

Melissa and I get pushed aside by a cocky teenager with an attitude. "Don't you know anything? His name is *Thad*," the girl says. "Go get a life, loser."

I turn to my friend, ready to complain about today's youth to get my mind off what just happened. When I see Melissa's face, however, her mouth agape and her eyes glazed over as she stares at me, I realize I might have a bit of explaining to do.

"*That's* Chad?" she asks, pointing at the now empty sidewalk in front of the club.

I nod and look to the ground.

She grabs my hand, pulling me away from the bustling crowd to a quieter location. She nods back to the commotion we walked away from. "*That's* the Chad you grew up with? As in the boy who lived next door? As in your childhood best friend? As in the guy you never got over?"

My eyes snap to hers. "Who said I never got over him?"

"You might not have ever admitted it, but the way you talk about him—it's obvious you had a huge thing for him. And, geez, now I know why." Her head tilts to the side and her eyebrows

11

shoot up. "You knew him before he was famous, Mal. How cool is that? Oh, my God, did you play doctor? Did you see his wee-wee? Oh, shit, was he your first? Please tell me he was your first. Ahhhhhh!" she screams. "I need details!" Then she swats my arm. "How is it I've known you for five years and you didn't tell me about this? I mean, Thad Stone? The star of *Malibu 310?* The guy who is most likely *People Magazine's* next hottest man of the year?"

I shake my head, not wanting to acknowledge how some of what she just said is true. I don't even admit to myself that I had a thing for him. "That is not the boy I grew up with," I say, nodding in the direction of the club. "Far from it. The boy I grew up with didn't do drugs. Or . . ." I cringe. "Or use women. The boy I grew up with is nothing like that man." I stare at my friend who is majorly fangirling at the moment. "See this," —I motion to her face— "*this* is why I don't tell people."

She sighs. Her expression immediately changes from obsessed fan to supportive friend. She grabs my elbow and walks us down the street, pulling me into a small neighborhood bar. We slip into a booth in the back and Melissa orders us each a glass of white wine.

"For the duration of our drink, I promise not to fangirl," she says. "You obviously need to talk to someone about this, so talk."

Even just thinking about it, it's hard to keep the tears from falling. I grab a napkin from the dispenser and wipe my eyes. Melissa is right, I need to talk about it. But I'm afraid it will just stir up feelings I've repressed for nine years.

What are the odds of this even happening? Of Mel and I walking back to her place after dinner and coming upon a swarm of people outside a club? It's not an unusual thing for New York City. We've seen some pretty big stars on occasion. So we figured, what the hell, we'd stick around to see what all the fuss was about. Never in a million years did I think it would result in a face-to-face meeting with Chad. Well, eye-to-eye anyway.

"Do you want me to call Julian?" Melissa asks, knowing how close we are. "Wait. Julian grew up with you. Oh, my God, he knew him, too? How is it that neither of you has ever said anything?"

Chad is a closely guarded secret I've kept locked up inside. Only my dad and Julian know the real story of my childhood. Julian was there. He lived it with me. We were inseparable, the three of us. That is until Julian went to Brazil the summer before his junior year. And then of course when Chad left me. Left us.

Julian and I have never talked about it. I think he was as hurt by Chad's departure as I was. Well, not so much by his departure, but by his blatant and total removal of his presence from our lives when he became a star.

"Call him," I say.

After explaining to Julian what happened and where we are, she puts down the phone. "He will be here as soon as he can. Do you want to wait for him?"

The waitress brings our wine and I take a sip. I shake my head. "There isn't anything I could tell you about Chad that Julian doesn't already know." *Well, except that one little thing about me being in love with him back then.*

"You guys were really close," she says. It's a statement more than a question.

"We were," I say, remembering fondly some of the good times we had together. "I was six when Chad moved in next door. Wait, have I told you this story before?"

"Maybe," she says. "But I want to hear it again. Somehow, it's different now."

"Well, he moved in the day before school started. I was going into first grade and he was going into second." I run my tongue over my teeth. "I hadn't grown into my very large front teeth yet and some older boys at our bus stop were teasing me. Chad stood up to them even though he was younger than them. Even though he was the new kid."

"He was a hero even then," she says with an audible sigh.

I shoot her a scolding look.

"Sorry," she says. She presses her lips together, forming a thin line before she twists her fingers over them and mimes throwing away a key.

"From that day on, we were practically joined at the hip. And when Julian moved into a house down the street a few months later and was bullied by the same fourth-grade jerks at the bus stop, we became the three musketeers. Julian was a year older than me as well. They both became my protectors; the older brothers I never had. Other kids were jealous of what we had. Of the indescribable bond we shared. We didn't even have to talk to each other to communicate. It's like we were connected in some other-worldly way. Of course, that's why the teasing continued. When we reached adolescence, our classmates were downright mean. They accused us of being a threesome. They accused Julian and Chad of being gay and me of being a slut. It furthered our separation from other kids and solidified our bond with each other. It was us against the world."

"Wow," Melissa says. "So what happened? How could you be that close and then let geography destroy your friendship?"

"It wasn't geography that destroyed it. It was Chad's sudden rise to fame," I tell her.

She gets a sour face. "He just dropped you like a hot potato when he became famous? That bastard." She shakes her head in disgust. "He has definitely just lost his godlike status with me, the jerk. Who does that?"

"It wasn't quite that sudden. We still talked a lot the first year he was on *Malibu 310*. He even came back here over the holidays to visit us and his older brother, Ethan. But after that, he changed."

"Changed?" she asks.

"When we would talk on the phone, our conversations seemed forced. He wasn't as much at ease with me, and for the first time in our friendship, I couldn't tell what he was thinking.

"Julian would say similar things about his phone calls with Chad. He thought maybe he was on drugs or something. I didn't believe it. Chad was the poster child for the 'Just say no' campaign at our high school. He would fight kids who offered us drugs."

"But then Hollywood happened," Melissa says, supportively touching my hand.

I nod. "Yeah. It became more evident each time we talked. Even his emails became disjointed. Sometimes I questioned whether he realized who he was writing to. Then one day, into the second season of his show, I got an email that was obviously not meant for me. It was meant for Julian. It was disgusting. It gave explicit details about his latest sexual conquest. And in that moment, I realized Chad was gone and all that was left was Thad. He even signed his name to the email that way. I was more than a little hurt. Not just because I secretly had a crush on him since I was six and was jealous of him being with other girls, but I truly grieved for the friendship that was dying. I replied back to 'Thad' telling him I never wanted to hear from him again. And I didn't. I never wanted to hear from Thad. I wanted Chad back."

"Oh, Mal, I'm so sorry," Melissa says, tears of sympathy balancing on her lashes.

"He tried to call me once after that, but I let it roll to voicemail. It was a drug-induced attempt to smooth things over. He was incoherent. He was pathetic. It broke my heart. I deleted the voicemail. Then I deleted his contact. Then I blocked him on social media. I cut all ties, never seeing or hearing from him again until tonight."

"And Julian?"

"Julian was a little more tolerant of him. Their friendship went on a while longer. That is until my mom died."

"What happened when your mom died?" she asks.

"Julian never gave me the details about it, but I'm pretty sure he called Chad to let him know she had died. I think Chad blew him off or gave him excuses or something. Julian told me Chad couldn't get away mid-season, making it impossible for him to attend the funeral. But I could sense he wasn't telling me everything. And I never heard from Chad again. Never got a condolence card. Never got a call from the boy who once loved my mother almost as much as his own. I think it was the last straw for Julian. After that, he cut Chad out of his life like I had."

Melissa downs the rest of her wine, all but smashing the glass back down on the table. "That little shit. If he weren't protected by that Goliath without a neck, I'd kill the insensitive prick with my bare hands." She shakes her head in confusion. "But it doesn't make sense."

"What doesn't make sense?" I ask.

"The way he looked at you tonight."

"What do you mean? I'm not even sure he recognized me."

"Recognized you? Mallory, he looked like he wanted to eat you alive. He said your name for Christ's sake. Of course, I was just reading his lips, for all we know he could have been saying 'Mel' and not 'Mal'," she jokes. "Do you think Steve would mind if I had a one-nighter with a mega-star?"

I stare her down, unamused.

"Right," she says. "Too soon for sarcasm." She gives me a sympathetic look. "Maybe you should get in touch with him. Clearly, he was affected by seeing you. The guy's world seemed to stop as soon as he made eye contact with you."

"Contact him? God, no." I shift uncomfortably in my seat.

"Why not?" she asks. "People change. I read he went to rehab a while back. Maybe he's better now."

"He hasn't changed, Mel. It seems every other week he's got a different girl on his arm. Anyway, I think he's with the co-star of the movie."

"Courtney Benson? That girl doesn't hold a candle to you."

I raise my brow at her. "You're a little biased, don't you think?"

"Just saying it like it is, sister. What could it hurt, calling him? You know, just to get closure if that's what you need."

I shake my head again. "No. It just hurts too much. The drugs. The women. The promises he broke."

"What promises did he break?" she asks.

I trace the circular base of my wine glass. "All of them."

At that moment, Julian comes through the pub door, saving me from further explanation. I watch him walk towards us, pain evident on his otherwise swoon-worthy face. Besides Melissa, he is my best friend. He has been since I was six, with the exception of those three years after *he* broke my heart, too.

Julian could give Chad a run for his money in the looks department. Both are devilishly handsome but almost completely opposite. While Chad has light-blonde hair, blue eyes, and a permanently sun-kissed complexion, Julian's hair is dark, his eyes matching my green ones and his skin fair. We've often been accused of being brother and sister.

He slips into the booth beside me and puts his arm around my shoulder. I lean into him. Much like when we were kids, words aren't always necessary. He kisses the top of my head.

"Let's go get our girl drunk," he says to Melissa. "She can crash at my place again."

"Steve and I really don't mind when she sleeps on our couch," Melissa says.

"Of course you don't," he says. "But you know how she gets when she's drunk. She might want to talk shit out later."

I raise my head off his shoulder. "*She* is sitting right here, guys. Don't I have a say in this?"

"No," they both say together.

Melissa slips out of the booth and motions to the door. "Come on, let's go find a club, dance our asses off, and remind you who your real friends are."

CHAPTER THREE

Chad

"Anything?" I ask Kendra.

"Nope," she replies through the speaker of my cell phone.

Both of us are busy on our laptops trying to figure out if Mallory was photographed last night. I breathe a huge sigh of relief as I page through the tabloid and news magazine sites. There are plenty of pictures of me and the cast at the premiere. Several cell phone photos from the after party. Loads of pictures pairing Courtney and me together through blatantly doctored-up photos. We'll deal with that shit later; anything else has become a minor annoyance compared to what could happen if my royal fuck-up ends up costing Mal her privacy.

"Look up for a second please, Mr. Stone," the makeup artist asks, obviously annoyed that I'm trying to work while she is.

"I'll be there in five," Kendra says. "Interviews start at one-thirty, that'll give me enough time to vet the questions."

I check the last few sites before putting away my laptop, making my makeup artist happy. A few minutes later, she hands me off to the stylist who puts crap in my hair to make it look like I just got out of bed. Why does it take a paid professional to create that look? I swear she spends ten minutes on one chunk of hair, making sure it is positioned just so over my forehead.

"Perfect," Kendra says, walking through the door. "But then again, you'd look great having actually just rolled out of bed."

"Ha! Exactly what I was thinking," I say. Then I shrug at my seemingly conceited words. "I mean the rolling out of bed part, not the looking great part."

She winks at me, patting my shoulder. "I know what you meant, Thad. If there is one thing I've learned about you these past months, it's that you are the least vain person in show business."

"You should have seen him five years ago," Ethan pipes up from the corner of the room.

Kendra walks over to greet him. "Hi, Ethan. Nice to see you again. We didn't scare you off last night with all of the craziness?"

"Not a chance," he says. "I just took my little brother out to lunch. He asked me to keep him company for a bit before I have to head back to work."

"You're a private investigator, right?" she asks.

"That's right."

"That must be a very exciting job."

"It can be at times, but mostly it's boring as hell. Sitting around waiting for people. Blending into the background. Asking questions. Averting crises."

Kendra laughs. "Sounds a lot like what I do."

I raise my eyebrows. "Your job is boring as hell?"

"Uh . . . no." She looks embarrassed. "God, no. I love my job, Thad. And you are anything but boring."

"I was only kidding, Kendra." I turn to Ethan. "Don't let her fool you, she hardly sits around. She must be one of the hardest-working publicists in the business."

"I don't doubt it," Ethan says to her. "And you're doing a great job. My brother's image is almost squeaky clean as of late."

I wad up my disposable makeup bib and throw it at him. "That's because I *am* squeaky clean, you pain in the ass."

"Well, thank God for that, brother. It was a long road, but we're all proud of you."

I brush off his compliment. I don't deserve it. If it weren't for all the trouble I caused, there wouldn't have been a long road to travel. I brought shitloads of shame and embarrassment down on my family. Some days I still don't understand why they didn't disown me.

"Kendra, my brother tells me you are enamored with my son," Ethan says.

"Oh my gosh, yes," she says, her eyes brightening. "What's not to love? He is absolutely adorable."

"Well then you must come meet him in the flesh," he says. "How about dinner tonight? My wife, Charlie has become a fabulous cook and we'd love to have you."

"I'd be honored, Ethan. Thank you," Kendra says, looking particularly pleased. She glances at her watch and turns to me. "Thad, we'd better get started on prepping you for the interviews."

"I hate media junkets," I mumble under my breath.

"That may be so," she says. "But it's media junkets that sell tickets."

I roll my eyes at her. I know it's necessary. But it's always the same dance, different city. We get ushered from room to room in some hotel, spending fifteen minutes at each location before getting whisked off to the next only to answer the exact same questions for a different interviewer.

She shoves a piece of paper at me. "Here are the list of questions you may be asked. They are pretty much the standard fare. Although I'm sure some will ask about the latest picture of you and Courtney, so be prepared for that."

"You mean, don't confirm or deny it," I say with a long face.

"Thad, you know I don't always agree with Paul and the studio. But you have to admit, *Defcon One* does get a lot more hype when fans think you and Courtney are together."

"Fine," I say, getting up out of the hairdresser's chair. "Come on, let's get this over with."

~ ~ ~

Kendra and I arrive at Ethan's penthouse, exhausted from hours of interviews. Against my better judgment, my manager, Paul, talked me into doing an impromptu photo shoot with Courtney at the hotel. Well, talked me into is an understatement. More like threatened me with life and limb. I suspect he had it planned all along but made it look like it was the brain child of the very popular magazine photographer who just *happened* to be at the hotel when we were.

Needless to say, Paul didn't get an invitation to tonight's dinner. The less time I have to spend with him, the better. He's been great for my career, but he has the personality of a pet fucking rock and the heart of a serial killer. And the funny part is, he's an upgrade from the previous manager I had. I've come to understand talent managers are all assholes and part of being in the business is putting up with them.

Which is why I consider myself lucky as hell to have Kendra as my publicist. For the most part, she takes my side when it comes to arguing with Paul. And it's refreshing to have someone in my court for a change. I can see that she doesn't take very well to Courtney either, and I suspect it bothers her to no end to have to tell me to go along with the rumors for the sake of box office bankability.

My cousin, Jarod, answers Ethan's door. "Hey, cuz," he says, pulling me in for a hug.

"Jarod, I'm glad you could make it. Sorry you had to miss the premiere last night." I step aside, allowing Kendra to pass before I shut the door. "This is my publicist, Kendra Riggs."

"Hi, Kendra," he says, shaking her hand. "Nice to meet you."

Ethan's wife comes over to greet us. "I'm Charlie," she says to Kendra. "I'm so happy to finally meet you. Chad has great things to say about you."

Kendra shakes her hand. "The feeling is quite mutual, I assure you. Thank you so much for having me." She studies Charlie, her eyes taking in her long red hair and tall stature. "Wow, it's uncanny how much you resemble your mother. I was truly sorry to hear of her passing."

"Thank you," Charlie says politely, even though it's become obvious to me that she didn't have a good relationship with her famous mother. In fact, I think she hated her. But it's not something she talks about.

The front door opens behind us and Kyle bounds through carrying a few bottles of Cristal. He puts them on the kitchen counter as Kendra trails behind to talk to him. "I'm sorry we didn't get much of a chance to talk last night. You're the doctor, right?"

"The almost-doctor," he says. "I'm in my last year of med school."

"Impressive," she says. Then she turns to Jarod. "And you are a waiter at what I've been told is one of the best restaurants in the city. Thad promised he'd take me there this week."

Jarod laughs. "I don't think I'll ever get over hearing people call you Thad, cuz."

"And yet to me, *Chad* sounds strange," Kendra says.

"Speaking of nicknames and childhood friends who created them, care to tell us any more about what happened outside the club last night with Mallory?" Ethan asks me.

I regret even mentioning to him that I saw her. In my defense, I'd had a drink and was a bit loose in the lips.

"Wait, what? You saw Mallory?" Charlie perks up, stepping away from the stove to corner me. She turns to scold Ethan with her eyes. "Ethan didn't tell me anything about this. You saw her? The girl who started calling you Thad? Your childhood friend?"

I shoot a traitorous stare at my older brother but he blows me off, busying himself filling champagne glasses.

"Dude," Kyle says. "You saw Mallory? Why didn't you tell me?"

I look around at five sets of eyes, begging me for answers. I motion around to all of them. "This is why. I didn't want to go dredging up shit from the past."

Charlie looks guilty for making such a big deal about it. I know she's been through a lot of crap in her life that she keeps under wraps. "I'm sorry, Chad," she says. "I didn't mean to open a can of worms."

I put my hands on her shoulders and reassure her. "It's okay, Charlie. You didn't know. Anyway, it was Ethan who brought it up, not you. It's fine. Really."

She nods, shuffling back over to remove some casserole dishes from the oven. *Shit.* Now I feel bad because she feels bad. I take the champagne glass Ethan offers me and down a healthy sip. Then I notice all eyes are still on me. "Jesus, fine," I say, walking over to the couch to take a seat while everyone grabs a glass and follows me.

I start telling the story mostly for Charlie and Kendra, as they are the only ones here who've never heard it. "The girl at the premiere was Mallory Schaffer. She was my best friend growing up. When I was seven, we moved into the house next door to hers. When we were introduced to her family, my mentally-challenged older brother here, was going through a phase where he put everyone's name into that rhyming song, you know the one that goes 'Chad, Thad, bo-bad, banana-fana, fo-fad . . .'?"

A few laughs go around the room at the recognition of the catchy tune.

"Yeah, well, Mallory started calling me Thad, and for some reason I didn't have the heart to tell her it wasn't my name."

"You mean the balls," Kyle adds, earning him a swift slap on the back of the head.

"Awe, that is so sweet," Kendra says. "How long was it before she figured it out?"

"It was a while. Months I think. I mean, Ethan called me 'dip shit,' and Kyle called me, uh" —I turn to him— "what was it you called me when you were six?"

"Buzz?" he says with scrunched brows. "I think that was my Toy Story phase."

"Right, Buzz Lightyear. And my mother called me sweetheart or some shit like that. And Mallory wasn't in my grade, she was a year behind me, so she pretty much never heard anyone else call my name."

"So she was in Kyle's grade?" Charlie asks, now seeming less guilty and more curious about the whole thing. She turns to my younger brother. "Were you her friend, too?"

"Kind of," Kyle tells her. "Sometimes we would all play tag and stuff together, but Mallory and I never connected like she and Chad did. I'm pretty sure I thought all girls were yucky back then."

He turns to Chad. "It was your birthday party when she finally figured out your name, right?"

I nod, remembering the day fondly. It was the worst birthday party I'd ever had. But it was one of the best memories I have of Mal. "We were at my party and my mom brought out the cake right away. I loved cake and insisted we eat it even before presents and playing. Everyone sang to me, and when it came time to sing my name, Mallory sang *Thad* when everyone else sang *Chad*. She was the only girl there, so her voice was very discernable. Needless to say, some of the other kids in attendance starting teasing her about it, saying she was a stupid first-grader with a lisp. She looked at my cake with horror on her face, the bold icing confirming the correct spelling of my name. She was so embarrassed that she ran out of the house."

"Oh, the poor thing," Kendra says. "What happened after that? Did she ever come back?"

"No, she didn't. And neither did I."

Ethan laughs. "Boy was Mom pissed. She had to entertain eight second-grade boys for two hours until their parents came to pick them up. She sent Kyle and me to scour the neighborhood for you but we never found you. You were gone the rest of the day. I think you were grounded for a week after that."

"Where did you go?" Charlie asks. "Did you find Mallory?"

Everyone is on the edge of their seats, even the ones who pretty much know the story. They're acting like this is more interesting than my latest blockbuster movie. "There was only one place I knew she'd be. In the treehouse her dad built for her. Nobody else knew that was where she went when she was sad. I found her up there crying and I laid down next to her on the sleeping bag she kept there. We fell asleep and didn't wake up until after dark. Dozens of people were looking for us." I turn to Ethan. "I think I was grounded for a lot longer than a week."

"So what happened then?" Kendra asks. "Did Mallory just keep calling you Thad? I mean, obviously the name stuck with you or you'd never have chosen it as your stage name."

I shake my head. "No, she started calling me by my real name. But as we got older, every once in a while she would call me Thad as a joke." I can't help but break out in a huge smile when I tell the rest of the story. "When I was fourteen, she played an elaborate practical joke on me. It was my first day of high school and when my teachers called role, they all called me Thad. I had no idea what was going on. How could every single one of my teachers have gotten my name wrong? I had to explain to them it wasn't my name but they didn't believe me. One of them even showed me her class roster that she said came directly from the student database. The school ended up having to call my mom so she could bring my birth certificate to prove my name."

Everyone on the couch is laughing. "She was hilarious," Ethan says. "Man, I loved that girl."

Yeah, me too.

"I like her already," Kendra says. "Sounds like she's got spunk. How did she manage to pull it off?"

"It took me weeks to get her to admit it. And it wasn't until I heard her mom talking about how she had volunteered to teach a CPR class at the high school over the summer. Her mom was a nurse . . ." My head falls back against the couch as it dawns on me once again that she died and I wasn't there for Mal. Just one more crappy thing I did in my life to the people I loved.

"So Mallory was at the school with her mom and somehow changed your name in the database?" Charlie asks.

"Pretty much," I say, picking at a thread on my jeans.

27

"And you moved to California a few years later and never saw her again until last night?" Kendra asks.

"Well, I came back for a visit once after moving, and that was the last time I saw her until yesterday." I grab my glass off the table and down the rest of my champagne. "Hey listen, if we're all done with this little trip down memory lane, how about we get some grub?"

Charlie gives me a sad smile. She gets that there are some things you just don't want to talk about. "Come on, it's time to eat," she says, heading to the kitchen.

Eli's cries are amplified through the baby monitor as we take our places at the table. Charlie laughs. "Every time," she says. "I swear that child knows exactly when we sit down to dinner."

Kendra's face lights up. "Could I? I mean, if you think he wouldn't mind a stranger holding him through dinner."

"He's three months old," Ethan says. "He wouldn't care if Charles Manson held him."

"Oh, no," Charlie says, being the perfect hostess. "I couldn't ask you to hold him during dinner."

"You aren't asking," Kendra says. "I'm offering."

"She pretty much flew three thousand miles across the country to see Eli," I tell Charlie. "She drools over the pictures I show her. No offense to your cooking, but believe me when I say she'd be more satisfied holding your kid than eating your meal."

Kendra swats me on the back of the head. "Be nice," she says.

"Come on, Kendra," Charlie says, motioning to the hallway. "Let's go introduce the two of you."

Dinner is incredible. And to my surprise, Kendra is expertly able to maneuver a baby in one hand and a fork in the other.

Afterward, the champagne is flowing freely and my cousin and brothers are getting noticeably drunk. I stopped at two glasses myself. It's always my limit. Alcohol was never my problem, but addiction isn't picky about choosing its vice so I don't want to tempt fate.

"You should call her," Kyle says, slurring his words.

I shoot him a venomous stare. "And you should lay off the sauce, doctor."

He holds up his hands in surrender. "I'm just saying, I know you never got over the girl. Those first months in Cali were fucking torture, bro. It was always *Mal this* and *Mal that*. It was nauseating how much you talked about her. Don't you at least want to know what became of her? Doesn't it interest you at all? And didn't you guys have some kind of pact that if neither of you were married by thirty, you'd get hitched? What happened, Chad?"

"Shut the hell up, Kyle, and mind your own fucking business," I say, leaping off the couch to walk over to the windows so I can pretend to admire the view.

"Kyle, don't," Ethan says.

"What?" Kyle asks. "Someone has to pull his head out of his ass. She was there last night. That has to mean something."

I shake my head. "She wanted to be anywhere but there, I could see it in her eyes. She doesn't want to see me. She hates me."

"Are you one-hundred-percent sure of that, brother?" Kyle asks, coming up beside me, putting a hand on my shoulder. "If there is even a small chance she wants to see you, don't you think you need to explore that? You have to be the one, Chad. Contacting you these days is harder than putting a call through to the fucking president. There is no way for her to get to you. Will you be able to live with yourself if you don't at least try? Because if you don't, you'll always be living under the shadow of what could have been."

I turn and stare at my drunk little brother who's still in full doc mode. "You pick your specialty yet? Because with all that bullshit you just fed me, maybe it should be psychiatry."

Everyone laughs. Even me. Because it's better than admitting everything he said is true. But the thought of contacting her scares the living shit out of me. Maybe it's just better to dream about what could have been rather than to see what actually is.

CHAPTER FOUR

Mallory

I'm finding it hard to concentrate on work today. And you can believe the twenty-one fourth graders in my classroom are taking advantage of that. They are particularly unruly today and I just don't have the energy to deal with it. Sleep has not been my friend the past two nights. Every time I close my eyes, I see him. Every time I fall asleep, I dream of him. Every waking hour, I try to forget him.

Melissa was right. The way he looked at me—it's not the way you look at someone who you don't want in your life. But then why has he never contacted me? Does he think I don't want to see him? Maybe he's right. Maybe I don't. He hurt me in more ways than one and I'm not sure I could ever trust him not to do it again. He damaged me. Making friends after he left was not easy. I was afraid to let anyone get close. I didn't want to risk it happening again. I was grateful for Julian, but then when *he* hurt me, I was left completely alone. Best-friendless. That is until Mel and I met in college.

You forgave Julian, I tell myself. Was what Chad did to me any worse than what Julian did? Can I even blame Chad for what happened? After all, he was only seventeen when his life went into a tailspin. I often wonder what would have happened if it had been me and not him who was catapulted into sudden stardom. Should he be held responsible for how he behaved when his life was so out of control?

Yes, he should. I mean, underneath it all, we're still human. I just think the least he could have done was call me when Mom died. But by then, I'd told him I never wanted to hear from him again. I guess he took me at my word after I didn't acknowledge his pathetic attempt to make excuses in the voicemail he left me.

"Ms. Schaffer?"

I look up to see that the dismissal bell is about to ring and Billy Green is trying to get my attention. "Yes, Billy?"

"Uh, you haven't given us our homework assignment yet and it's almost three o'clock."

I glance around the classroom to see all of my students packing up for the day. This is unlike me. I'm organized. I plan everything out down to the minute. I usually write homework assignments on the board while the kids are at recess.

"No homework tonight," I announce to the cheers of my class. "But I still want each of you to read for thirty minutes." They grumble about that, but I can tell they are still happy for the most part.

"Are you okay, Ms. Schaffer?" Kim asks, swinging her lighter-than-usual backpack onto her shoulder.

I nod in reassurance. "Yes, Kim. I ran into an old friend the other day and I guess I was just daydreaming or something."

"How old was she?" Kim asks.

I laugh. "It was a *he*," I say. "And he's not old as in age; he's an old friend meaning I used to know him when we were kids."

"But you don't know him anymore?"

"No. Not really," I tell her.

"But you dream about him?" she asks.

All the time. "Daydream," I say. "Daydreaming is kind of like thinking about something when you're awake. And you think about it so hard, sometimes you forget where you are or what you are doing."

She nods in understanding. "Oh, I get it. Like Billy and Justin during math section."

I giggle. "Yeah, kind of like that. You'd better get going or you'll miss the bus."

"Bye, Ms. Schaffer."

"Bye, Kim. See you tomorrow."

I spend the next hour going over tomorrow's lesson plan. I'm not even sure what I taught today. I hope the kids actually got something out of whatever I said. My door swings open and Melissa walks through.

"Are you about done? I'm ready to get to the gym," she says.

I put away my planner and gather my things. "Yes. The gym is exactly what I need today."

~ ~ ~

Kate, another teacher at our school, joined us at the gym and then we decided to go for dinner after, so the sun is setting by the time I get home. As I pull into the driveway, I wonder whose SUV is parked out in front of our house. Dad didn't say anything about company. He never has company. I park in the garage and reach into the passenger seat to get my leftovers. I hope Dad hasn't eaten dinner yet because the meal I ordered was amazing.

Melissa keeps trying to talk me into moving to the city, but I can't get myself to leave. At first, I stayed to save up money for my own place. But after that, as the time came closer for me to move, I couldn't pull the trigger. My dad all but stopped living after my mom died seven years ago. He still works at the local hospital as an orthopedic surgeon, and that has become his life. Work and me. So I cook for him a few times a week. He cooks for me a few times a week. The rest of the time, I'm with my friends or we get take out. Every so often he'll ask me about my savings and when I think I'll have enough to move out. I always give him the same answer, 'go big or go home—so I'm staying home until I can go big.' He smiles every time I say it. He also offers me money to reach my goal. I never accept it and he never argues. We have a symbiotic relationship. Or an enabling one. I'm not sure which. He needs to get on with his life. I need to learn to live on my own. But what we have works for both of us.

Before the garage door closes, I see a man leaning against the hood of the SUV, looking at his cell phone. It's kind of creepy because it's getting dark. I take out my phone and pull up the dial screen, ready to call 911 if I need to. I quietly step into the mudroom and put down my teacher bag.

I hear my dad laughing in the kitchen and I breathe a sigh of relief. For two reasons. One: the man outside is probably not a serial killer; and two: my dad has company, which never happens.

Then I hear the other voice and my heart flips over. Actually, my heart leaves my body, travels around the corner into the kitchen, does flips and then returns to me, although not in its proper place. It seems to be currently lodged somewhere in the vicinity of my throat.

What the hell is Chad Stone doing here?

I head toward the kitchen. Then I turn around and head toward the garage. Then I turn back around. I change my mind so many times, I make myself dizzy. Then I bump into the coat rack, dislodging my purse, sending it thumping onto the floor. *Shit.*

"Mallory, is that you?" my dad asks.

Shit, shit, shit.

I close my eyes and take a calming breath, trying to control the pace of my heartbeat which is pounding so hard I feel like I'm still on the treadmill at the gym. I hold my head high and walk around the corner.

When I see Chad, smiling and sitting with my dad, two beers on the table in front of them as if they are old friends themselves, it guts me. Here he is after nine years, back in my house, looking all gorgeous and not at all nervous. Looking like he didn't rip out my heart when he left. Looking all regal like the rich bastard he's become. Looking like he doesn't even care about the shit he left in his wake to get there.

"Uh, okay," I say, looking at them. I don't know what to do or what to say. Did he come here to see my dad? They got along back then, and his folks were good friends with mine. Maybe he's just here to see him. Should I join them? Walk past them and go to my room? Turn back around and go to Mel's? I bite my lip pondering my choices.

Just then, my dad scoots his chair out, finishes his beer and puts the empty bottle in the trash. "I'm sure you two have a lot of catching up to do. I think I'll turn in early." He offers his hand to Chad. "Nice to see you again, son. Don't be a stranger."

"I don't plan to be, sir," Chad says, shaking my dad's hand.

My dad walks out of the room with purpose, loudly climbing the stairs so there's no mistaking where he's going, and then he shuts his door heavy-handedly. I roll my eyes at his unnecessary performance.

I realize I'm still standing in the doorway to the kitchen, not having moved since seeing Chad in my house. I search for something to say. But what do you say to the boy who left you high and dry when he went on to make millions on a TV show before getting fired for drugs and gambling and fighting, who then went on to make movies, hobnobbing with mega-stars who only need one name like Zac, Liam or Brad?

He doesn't seem to know what to say either. Maybe he's nervous after all. He probably thinks I'm going to hit him or something. Maybe I should.

I clear my throat. "Um, so the guy outside. He's with you? Your driver?"

He nods. "My bodyguard."

"You have a *bodyguard?*" I ask, reeling over the fact that my one-time friend is so uber-famous that there is a huge man perched against a big black SUV outside my house to protect him.

He shrugs, seemingly embarrassed by my reaction. "Well, not all the time, but for premieres and stuff."

All of a sudden, I find myself becoming protective of my old friend. "Has someone threatened you? Do you have a stalker?"

"No." He huffs out a strained laugh. "Not this week anyway."

My heart sinks. He's had stalkers? It must be awful not to be able to go where you want to go and do what you want to do because some wacko is out there.

He nods to the chair my father vacated. "Are you just going to stand there all night, or do you want to sit?"

"Uh . . . " I look at the bag of leftovers I'm still holding. I walk to the fridge and deposit it inside, grabbing myself a beer before I shut it. I may need a bit of liquid courage to get through this conversation. I sit across from him. He reaches over to open my beer for me. Our hands touch. I try to ignore the shooting sensation that travels through me, piercing my heart. "Thanks," I say, pulling my beer away from his hand. I motion to his drink. "I thought you didn't drink. Weren't you in rehab?"

He laughs awkwardly. "Direct much?" he says.

I take a drink of my beer. "I never censored myself with you when we were kids, why start now?"

"I know. It was one of the things I loved about you. You always said it like it was. And, yes, I was in rehab. Not for alcohol though."

"Isn't it all the same?" I ask. "Can't you just replace one addiction with another?"

"Yes, some people can become cross-addicted. I don't seem to have a problem with alcohol. My issue was with cocaine. But it's an unforgiving drug, so I don't ever drink enough to lower my inhibitions and make bad decisions. I find that as long as I limit myself to just a drink or two, I'm good. I still like to have fun. Just not crazy doped-up fun."

"Oh." I'd read countless articles about Chad's partying early on. I've seen too many pictures of him and half-naked women looking gorked out. Eventually, I stopped looking. I stopped reading. I even tried to pretend I had stopped caring.

He nods in the direction of the stairs. "So, you still live here with your dad?"

I look around the kitchen that is the only one I've ever known. My parents bought this house when my mom was pregnant with me. "Yes. It'd be such a big place just for him, you know?"

He looks down at the table, nodding reluctantly. "I'm really sorry about your mom. I should have called."

"You were a little busy back then," I say, trying to keep bitterness from lacing my words.

Samantha Christy

"That's no excuse. I should have come back for her funeral. She was like a second mom to me. And you . . . " Guilt washes over his finely-chiseled features as he traces a bead of condensation on his bottle. "I just should have done something. I was in a bad way back then. It's no excuse, I know. But it's all I have."

"It was a long time ago," I say.

"You were only seventeen. You needed your friends. I fucked up. Will you ever forgive me?"

I study him for a minute. He wants my forgiveness? Is that why he's here, to exonerate himself of guilt? But he looks sincere. Sad even, like he feels he lost a piece of himself when he cut off those he loved. Maybe Mel was right. Maybe he has changed. Still, if it's my friendship he wants, it may be too little too late. "Why are you here, Chad? Uh, can I even call you that anymore?"

"Yes, please call me Chad. Thad isn't who I really am. Not anymore. My family calls me Chad; I want you to as well."

I think back to when he had just gotten discovered and his agent told him there was already an actor by the name of Chad Stoner, so he had to pick a new name because his was too similar. I was so excited that he chose Thad. The name that had so much meaning, but only to the two of us. It was a name that connected us in a way nobody else would ever understand. I somehow thought it would tie us together forever. Instead, it eventually ripped us apart, and now—well I'm glad he's okay with me calling him Chad, because that other name is nothing more than a dirty word in my book.

"I'm sure you know I saw you at the premiere the other night," he says. He sighs deeply. "My life has been a little bit crazy lately, to say the least. What is happening now is ten times worse than when I was on *Malibu*. Sometimes it feels like my life is not my own anymore. And I hope you don't take this the wrong way, but when I saw you, it was like seeing a lifeline to normal again. There were hundreds of screaming fans on that sidewalk, and then there was you. And you were the only one who wasn't trying to get close enough to get a piece of me. It was like a breath of fresh air in the chaos."

"I didn't know it was you at the club. Well, not until I saw you," I tell him. "My friend, Melissa, and I were on our way back from dinner when we stumbled upon the crowd. We hung around to see what all the fuss was about."

For a second, Chad's face falls. He looks dejected. This gorgeous, mega-rich, up-and-coming superstar looks like a kid who just had his candy swiped from him. "You didn't know I was going to be there?" he asks.

I shake my head.

"I guess that makes sense," he says. "It looked like you were trying to get away."

I'm not sure what to say to that. *Sorry, Chad, I don't follow your career because I think you are a self-centered prick who drops friends at the first hint of something better?* I take a sip of beer instead of speaking.

"Your dad tells me you're a teacher," he says, filling the uncomfortable silence.

"I am."

He stares at me with a smirk.

I roll my eyes. "Yeah, the irony is not lost on me."

Chad used to say he wanted to teach high school history. And I was the one who was going to be an actor. I starred in every middle and high school theater production. I even got Chad to audition for one of the particularly time-consuming plays so we would be able to spend more time together. The play that should have resulted in our first kiss. And our second and third. It ran three nights. But we never rehearsed the kiss, and we ended up chickening out, hugging each other instead. Our lips never even touched. Not then; not ever.

"Why didn't you pursue acting?" he asks. "You were so good at it."

"I did. But not everyone can walk into a shopping mall and get discovered," I say.

"Are you still interested? I could pull some strings if you want to try it out. I think you'd be amazing."

I vehemently shake my head. "Oh, no. I love my job. Plus, I wouldn't want that career anymore, not after seeing what it did . . . uh . . ." I try to remove my very large foot from my very big mouth.

He nods knowingly. "After seeing what it did to me."

"Sorry," I say. "I don't mean to be disrespectful. I know you've worked hard to get where you are."

He takes the last sip of his beer and puts the empty bottle on the table between us before standing up. "Please thank your dad for the beer. It's been great seeing you again."

And just like that, Chad Stone walks out of my life as quickly as he walked back into it.

CHAPTER FIVE

Chad

Mallory stays seated at her kitchen table as I walk through the house and out the front door. She doesn't need to show me the way. I practically lived here when I was younger. I guess there isn't much else to say. She wasn't at the premiere party because of me. She's obviously still pissed at me. And she has every right to be.

God, she's beautiful. She was always pretty. But now, she's fucking gorgeous. Those green eyes of hers are even darker than I remember, her fair skin even creamier. And Jesus, she's a school teacher. Is there anything sexier than that? What the hell was I thinking not keeping in touch with her? *That you didn't want her to see what you'd become, you damn fool.*

Shit. I didn't think to look at her left ring finger. I assume she's not married since she still lives with her dad. But who's to say she's not spoken for? A woman who looks like that must have men beating her door down. Richard didn't say anything about a fiancé or a boyfriend. But then again, other than him telling me where she worked, we didn't talk about her, we only talked about me. I think Richard wanted it that way. I'm sure he knows how Mal feels about me and he didn't think it was appropriate to give me any personal details about her life.

I descend the four porch steps to the front walk where, tucked under a corner shrub, a ceramic frog still keeps watch over the front yard. I lean down and pick it up, looking underneath it. The house key is still taped to the bottom where it always was. The strong tape is weathered and torn and I wonder if they even remember the key is here. I put him back in his spot and walk to the driveway, glancing at Cole who has been waiting patiently for me.

Then I notice the old, rusty basketball hoop that is attached to the house over the garage door. Most of the netting is torn, as it was back then. It had seen hundreds of games of HORSE. Thousands maybe. I smile thinking of the times Mal and Julian and I spent out here. Immediately, my eyes go to the driveway hedge on the left side of the garage, lighting up when they spot an orange ball. It's almost as if I were meant to find it.

I hold up a finger to Cole, alerting him I'll be a bit longer. Then I pick the ball up out of the concave indentation that had become its home over the years. I press it firmly between my hands. It feels decently inflated. I dribble it a few times, happy to see it come back up to meet my hand each time.

I take a few steps back and take a free-throw shot. I miss of course. After all, it's been nine years since I played. I dribble the ball around and take several more shots, making some now that the familiarity is coming back. I start to get into it, announcing my own fantasy game as if I were playing in the NBA finals. "And, Lebron fakes to the outside, but cuts in, spinning away from his defender and, wait, he's going for three" —I jump up and make a sloppy-yet-effective three-pointer— "aaaaaaand, it's nothing but net as the crowd goes wild." I kiss my fingers and wave them to the pretend crowd as I take my victory lap around the driveway all but knocking over Mallory when I run up near the sidewalk. "Uh, sorry," I say, shocked to see her watching me.

She's laughing at me and I think it's the best sound I've ever heard. "I heard the thumping of the basketball and came out to see what it was," she says, putting her arms through her coat sleeves.

I back away from her, dribbling the ball. I nod to the net. "How about a game of HORSE? You know, for old times' sake?"

She looks at the net and then at me, her eyes turning sad. She shakes her head. "I don't think so. It's pretty late."

I look at my wrist as if there is a watch on it. "Oh, come on, Mal. It's barely dark outside. I'm sure your dad will let you play a little longer, even if it is a school night," I tease.

She looks back up at the house, just as the outside lights magically turn on, illuminating the entire driveway. I catch a glimpse of a curtain closing in the living room. I smile. Richard may think she hates me, but it appears he's rooting for me anyway.

I bounce the ball on the ground, passing it to her. "Come on," I goad as she catches the ball. "You know you want to. I'm a little rusty so you will probably kick my ass."

She snickers. "That's nothing new, Chad. I always kicked your ass."

"Ouch!" I cover my heart with my hand. "That hurt, Mal. My ego is very fragile."

"Ha!" she cries. "Somehow I doubt that." She throws the ball at me. Hard.

I pass it right back to her. "Think fast!"

She catches it and dribbles it expertly behind her back. I raise an eyebrow. "You've been practicing," I say.

"My dad and I play sometimes."

"Shit," I say. "You really are gonna kick my ass. Come on, you go first."

She rolls her gorgeous green eyes at me. "Fine." She walks to the middle of the driveway, about three feet away from the basket and she lobs a shot up and over the rim.

"Going easy on me, Schaffer?"

She shrugs.

Even though it's been a few years, I still make the shot easily from this distance. I throw the ball back to her. "You're going to have to come up with something better than that."

"Okay." She walks back a few steps. "Eyes closed this time." She shoots and misses.

"Yes!" I say, with the enthusiasm of an adolescent boy. I scoop up the ball and position myself where the free-throw line would be and I take a shot. She follows my lead, easily making the basket.

Next, I try to trip her up with a left-handed shot, but I miss it myself. "Back to you," I say, handing her the ball.

She walks beyond the driveway crack that was our unofficial three-point mark. She throws the ball in the air, swooshing it into the basket. I walk up the driveway to retrieve the ball and then plant myself in her spot and attempt the shot. I miss. "Shit. That's an 'H' for me."

I give her back the ball and she bites her lip in thought. Then she moves up four steps and says, "Bank swish." And just as she intended, the ball hits the backboard and falls through the basket touching nothing but net.

I'm mildly impressed. She smirks as she hands over the ball. I shoot and miss. Well, I don't miss, but it touches the rim so it doesn't count. "Crap!" I shout. "There's my 'O.' Where the hell is Julian when I need someone to look like more of a loser than me?"

She laughs. "Julian used to kick your ass, too," she says. "I think all the fame has gone to your head and you're having delusions of childhood grandeur."

"Julian used to beat me, too?" That I don't remember. Maybe because I was always so focused on *her*.

She raises her eyebrows, nodding.

"Oh, hell. I really was a loser, wasn't I?"

"You weren't a loser, Chad," she says, right before shooting an easy jump shot, probably to take pity on me.

"So, do you still keep in touch with him?" I ask, taking and making the jump shot.

"Who?" she asks.

"Julian. Do you still talk to him at all?"

I see something flicker across her face. Guilt? She quickly turns away from me and walks over to retrieve the ball.

"What is it, Mal?"

"Yeah, we still talk," she says, running up to the garage from the other side of the driveway to do a lay-up. "He's one of my best friends, in fact."

She throws the ball to me but doesn't make eye contact. I hold the ball and stare her down, trying not to be jealous that Julian has remained in her life all these years. "You're not telling me something. What is it?"

"You're stalling the game, Chad. Take the shot," she says.

I narrow my eyes at her and then turn away, focusing on the basket as I run up to it. Halfway into my lay-up, something dawns on me and I trip myself up, missing horribly as I fall to the ground, landing on my ass.

"Are you okay?" Mallory asks, running over to me when I don't get up right away.

"I'm fine." I drape my arms across my knees, looking up at her. "He's your boyfriend, isn't he?" When she doesn't deny it, I shake my head in anger. "That little shit. He promised."

She looks surprised by my outburst. "What do you mean he promised?"

I stand up and walk over to sit on the bench next to the driveway. "He never told you?"

"Told me what?" she asks, sitting down on the other end of the bench.

"That we made a pact before he went to Brazil."

"You made a pact? About what?"

I sigh. Then I laugh at myself. We were sixteen back then. Of course he didn't keep his promise. Plus, I guess I gave him an out by moving across the country. I'd never know if he broke it and there wasn't anything I could do about it if he did. "I think Julian was afraid I'd make a move on you back then. He was getting ready to leave for Brazil for the summer and he made me promise I wouldn't touch you."

Mallory guffaws. "Why would he say such a thing? That's silly. We were all best friends."

I stare her down. "Oh, come on. You must know both of us had a major crush on you."

"W-what?" she asks, looking at me like I'm ten cards shy of a full deck.

"Seriously? You didn't know?" I ask.

She shakes her head, her mouth hanging open in disbelief.

"It wasn't just a one-sided promise," I tell her. "It was a pact. We made it sound as if it would ruin our friendship if one of us acted on our crush, but in reality, neither one of us wanted the other to have you." I push off the bench and go over to collect the ball. "I guess it only makes sense that you'd end up with him. He's a lucky guy, Mallory." I throw the ball to her. "Your turn again."

"Left-handed hook shot from the elbow off the backboard," she says, with a sly grin.

"No fucking way," I challenge her.

She makes it of course.

"Just gimme the goddamn 'S'," I say.

She giggles. "He's not my boyfriend, you know. Not anymore."

All in a matter of two seconds I feel relief. Then jealousy. Then anger. But I think relief wins the battle. "Anymore?" I ask.

"Long story," she says, taking the ball from me and I get the idea the subject is off-limits. "Three-pointer. Backwards." She lines up the shot perfectly then misses.

"Sweet!" I shout, plotting my next shot. I grab the ball and spin around twice before shooting, surprising myself by making the basket. "So, is there one? A boyfriend?"

"Not at the moment." She motions for the ball. "Piece of cake," she says, spinning around and shooting, only to miss the rim by a good two feet. "Aw, darn it. That's an 'H' for me."

I can't help but laugh at her version of a swear word. "You still can't say it, can you?"

"Say what?" she asks.

"Fuck."

"Ugh. I can say it," she whines.

"Then say it."

"No. It's not the same if I just say it out of context."

"Okay." I try to think of how she can use the word. "How about this—why don't you ask me why the fuck I stopped emailing you and calling you? Ask me why I was the worst fucking friend of all time. Why don't you ask me that, Mallory?"

"Because I'm sure you had your reasons," she says, pulling her coat tightly around her.

I go back over to reclaim my spot on the bench, leaning forward to rest my elbows on my knees. "Nothing short of a lobotomy could excuse everything I did."

"Do you want to talk about it?" she asks, resuming her seat next to me.

"There's not much to talk about. Shit happened. A lot of shit happened. But that was then and this is now." I look up and stare into her stunning eyes. "And I really like now."

I could swear I see a blush creep across her face. Either that, or she's freezing on this cold night. "I guess we all have skeletons in our closet," she says. "Yours are just a little more on display for the world to see."

I cringe wondering just how much she knows about the things I've done. But that feeling is trumped by another one—curiosity, and maybe guilt, knowing she has skeletons, too, but that I wasn't here when she might have needed me. "*You* have skeletons?" I ask. "Squeaky-clean Mallory Schaffer?"

She elbows me in the side. "Maybe not so squeaky-clean anymore. And maybe not skeletons as much as regrets."

There's that feeling again. A pressure from within, gripping my chest like a vise. She has regrets. Regrets over Julian? Over some other guy, perhaps? "I'm sorry," I say, scooting closer to her so I can put my hand on top of hers. "Maybe someday we can share our secrets like we used to. I'd like that, you know."

She looks down at our hands and then up at my face. She looks at me like she can see my soul and extrapolate my secrets without me having to say a single word. Her eyes burn into mine. The soft flesh of her cold hand takes me back to old times. Times when we would sit for hours in her treehouse, barely saying a word yet always knowing what the other was thinking. Life seemed so much simpler back then. When we had each other's backs through thick and thin. When it was us against the world.

Suddenly, she jerks her hand away from mine, sitting up to wrap her arms around herself. "It's getting cold just sitting here, let's finish our game."

I spend the next twenty minutes getting my ass kicked in basketball by a girl. Not just any girl. *The* girl. I came here not knowing what to expect. But I'm leaving knowing exactly what I want. I want her. I've always wanted her. I'm just not sure what price I'm willing to pay to get her. Or better yet, what price she would have to pay to be with me.

CHAPTER SIX

Mallory

My phone vibrates in my pocket, alerting me of a text during my math lesson. I worry it might be an emergency because nobody I know would text me during school hours. I turn my back on the students and walk to the whiteboard, taking a peek at my phone. It's a number I don't recognize, so I slip it back into my pocket.

I'm a little more here today than I was yesterday, although I'm still distracted by thoughts of last night. I'm still not exactly sure why Chad showed up on my doorstep. Maybe he didn't know I lived there anymore and came to see my dad but felt obligated to hang out with me. Maybe after he saw me at the club, he felt the need to tie up loose ends.

But the thing is, it didn't feel like loose ends to me. Some of the things he said about him not being a stranger and about how he'd like us to share our secrets 'someday,' made me feel like maybe he wanted to rekindle our friendship. Which is ridiculous. He lives in L.A. and I live here. He's famous and I'm a school teacher. Our lives are polar opposites. We'd have nothing in common anymore.

After I walk the kids to the cafeteria for lunch, I head to Mel's classroom to eat with her. Along the way, my phone vibrates again, reminding me of the earlier text I need to read. I reach Melissa's classroom before she does, so I get out my turkey wrap and start munching on some grapes as I read my missed messages.

310-555-0186: Can I take you to dinner tonight?

I don't recognize the number and I have no idea who it is, although part of me knows who I want it to be. A very reluctant part of me. There is another text from a few minutes ago from the same number.

310-555-0186: Is that a no or are you making me sweat it out? I was hoping to do a little more groveling over say, pizza? It's still your favorite, right?

I smile. It must be him. And the fact that he's afraid I'll refuse his invitation is mildly endearing. I find it amusing that his area code matches that of the show he once starred in—*Malibu 310*. Guess that's where they got the name. I tap out a text.

Me: Who is this?

I quickly program his phone number into my contacts and put my phone away, knowing a busy guy like Chad probably doesn't have much time for chitchat.

Melissa walks in the room, complaining about having to meet with a parent of a misbehaving student. She immediately stops rambling when she looks up at me. "Why the cheesy smile?" she asks.

My phone vibrates and I can feel my smile widen even further. I resist looking at it straight away. "Just happy to see you," I say.

"Bullshit." She sets her salad down, eyeing me skeptically. "You are still reeling over last night, aren't you?"

As soon as Chad left, I was on the phone to Mel, spilling every last detail of what happened as we analyzed each conversation I had with him. I swore her to secrecy of course. Not that I needed to, she'd never use my past with Chad as a way to get attention. Luckily, I've been blessed with friends who are anything but attention whores. Well, maybe I have *one* friend who is an attention whore, but whether or not we are friends anymore remains to be seen.

"He texted me today," I tell her, popping another grape into my mouth. "Asked me to dinner."

Her squeals bounce of the classroom walls. "What? Oh, my God, Mal, he asked you out?"

I shake my head. "No. He asked me to dinner."

"Same difference," she says. "Oh my God, you're going to be on TMZ. You'll be famous. And I can say I knew you when."

All of a sudden, a sick feeling washes over me. I didn't even think about that. What would happen if we were seen in public together? Every woman he's seen with becomes his reported girlfriend. I'm sure he doesn't want that—to be seen with a teacher, a nobody. And I don't want that either. He has a bodyguard for Christ's sake. He's that famous. Why would he even want to risk his reputation by having dinner with me? "It is not the same, Melissa. He just wants to get together and talk."

"Where is he taking you?" She holds her hand out to silence me before I say anything. "No, let me guess. Eleven Madison Park? Or maybe Masa? Jesus, you're lucky."

"First off, I'm not accepting his invitation. And second, really?" I stare her down as she bounces around on her chair like one of her second-grade students.

She stills in her seat. "Sorry. I forgot that he's an insensitive prick and that we hate him."

"Well, maybe hate is too harsh a word," I say. "But the jury is still out."

I pull out my phone and check the new message.

> **Chad: Should I be concerned that you might have more than one random guy asking you to dinner? It's Chad.**

Without thinking too much about it, my fingers start tapping out a text.

> **Me: Oh, Chad! You mean the guy whose butt I kicked in HORSE last night?**

> **Chad: One and the same. I want a rematch by the way. I've been practicing.**

> **Me: You've been practicing? Since last night?**

> **Chad: Hells yeah. Ethan took me to his gym this morning. So watch out, I'll be ready for you next time.**

Next time? I can't help the smile that extends from ear to ear. *Wait—do I want a next time?*

Melissa squeals again. "Oh, my God, you're texting him right now, aren't you? You are sitting here just nonchalantly texting Thad Stone. Hearts are breaking all over the world right now, you realize that?"

"Shut up, Mel. It's not like that at all."

She leans over to read our texts. "Not like that, my ass. The man wants in your pants, Mallory."

My smile quickly fades. My friend has put it all into perspective for me. Of course he wants in my pants. He wants in everyone's pants. Why should it matter that I'm not famous? Either way, I would just be another notch on his bedpost.

> **Me: Thanks for the invitation, but I have plans tonight. BTW, how did you get my number?**

"Plans? Are you crazy?" Melissa asks.

"I'm volunteering tonight. It's Tuesday," I remind her.

Every Tuesday I volunteer at a place called Hope For Life. It's a shelter for pregnant teens who've been kicked out by their parents and have nowhere to go. I've been going there for years.

"I think the girls can go one night without you," she says.

> **Chad: Sucks for me. Pizza for one it is. About the number - do you want the real answer or a less-stalkerish one?**

Mel squeals again. "He's stalking you. You are being stalked by a superstar! Oh my God, you have to go out with him. Do not let that man eat alone. Or send me in your place."

I shoot her a traitorous look. "Steve would not appreciate that very much."

She scoffs at the mention of her husband. "Steve who?" she says, laughing.

Me: I'll go with real for one hundred, Alex.

Chad: LOL. When your dad hit the bathroom last night, I saw your cell phone bill on the kitchen counter. I may have peeked inside.

Me: I thought my dad gave it to you.

Chad: Richard was pretty tight-lipped about you.

Me: He's just being protective. Lunch break almost over. Gotta go.

"Liar," Melissa says, looking at the clock on her wall.

Chad: How about tomorrow night?

"Christ Almighty, he's begging," Mel says, fanning herself. "Will you just put the poor man out of his misery already?"

Me: Aren't you busy promoting your movie?

Chad: That's mostly during the day, interviews and stuff.

Me: Oh. Can I get back to you on that?

Chad: Always. Have a great day, Mal.

Me: Thanks. You too.

"Are you crazy?" Melissa asks. "Do you know how many people would kill to be you right now?"

"Stop being a fangirl for two seconds, Mel, and think about it. I'm not going to be his New York booty call. What else could he want? He's only in town for a week. If he really wanted to reconnect with old friends, he'd be contacting Julian, too."

She puts down her fork, looking guilty. "God, you're right. I'm so sorry. I'm such a bitch. I promise to only be supportive from now on."

"No more fangirl?" I ask with raised brows.

"No more fangirl." She picks up her fork and starts eating again. "So, can I tell you about the hot single dad of my new student?" she asks around her mouthful of salad.

~ ~ ~

"How was it at Hope today?" Julian asks me at our late dinner.

"It was good I guess. But we had a thirteen-year-old go into labor tonight." I shake my head still in disbelief. "Thirteen," I repeat. "She's only a few years older than my students and she's having a baby. It's so sad. Babies having babies."

He leans over and puts his arms around me. He knows how much this stuff gets to me. "What's going to happen to her?" he asks.

57

"Same as a lot of the others, I imagine. She wasn't going to keep it, so she'll probably end up going back to her family, into the same abusive situation she was exiled from four months ago when they found out she was pregnant. I just wish there was more I could do."

"You're doing everything you can, Mallory. You being there to support them, it's helping them in ways you will probably never know."

"Thanks," I say. "I hope so."

The waitress brings our food, putting the large pizza down on the table in front of us. It makes me wonder if Chad is eating pizza tonight as well. Pizza for one. Surely not. There are probably a hundred people he could eat with. Courtney Benson seems like she'd be first in line. I wanted to ask him about her last night. I should have when he questioned me about Julian. It would have been the perfect opportunity. But maybe I didn't want to know if the rumors are true.

"Has he contacted you?" I ask Julian.

"And by *he*, I assume you mean Chad?"

I nod.

"I was wondering when his name would come up. No, he hasn't." He studies me. "Wait, has he contacted *you?*"

"Yeah. He came to the house last night," I tell him, reaching for a slice of pizza.

He drops his jaw along with the food in his hand. "He came to your house?"

"I know. I had the same reaction. He was there when I came home from dinner. Just sitting at the table having a beer with my dad like they were old buddies."

"He was drinking?" he asks, concern evident in his voice.

"That's what *I* said. Apparently, his issues were with cocaine, not alcohol. He told me he doesn't drink that much."

"Hmm," he mumbles. "What did he want?"

"I'm still not sure. Forgiveness maybe?"

"You didn't give it to him, did you?"

I shake my head. "No. But we did play basketball for an hour."

"Basketball? What the hell, Mallory? The guy walks back into your life and you just forget about how much of a dick he is?"

I try not to get defensive. After all, Julian is kind of right. "I haven't forgotten. But he did seem like he needed a friend. He said his life was crazy and he needed a little bit of normal."

"What does that even mean?" he asks.

"He said when he saw me outside the club Saturday night, he saw me as normal or something so he looked me up."

"You are anything but normal, Mallory," he says, plucking a pepperoni off his pizza and popping it into his mouth.

"Yeah, well, I think he meant it as a compliment. He really hasn't contacted you?"

"Nope." He narrows his eyes at me in thought. "Did you tell him about us?"

"I didn't tell him, but he guessed," I say.

"Did you tell him why we broke up?" he asks, looking guilty.

"I didn't think it was any of his business."

"Good. It's not. None of it is. He lost his right to our business when he became the dick that he is."

"He was actually pretty nice, Julian." He looks at me like he's going to spit out hateful words, so I put up my hand to stop him. "We're not BFFs again or anything, so don't get your panties in a wad. I just think maybe you should give him a chance."

"Is that what you're doing, giving him a chance?"

I'm not sure why Julian is so upset about this. I mean, he stayed friends with Chad far longer than I did. "I didn't say that. After all, I turned down his invite to dinner so I could be here with you."

He looks slightly placated. "You did?" he asks, smiling.

"Yes, so eat up before it gets cold." I take a drink of my wine and start on my second piece of pie.

"He won't call me, you know," he says, with his mouth half full.

"Why not?"

An expression of extreme satisfaction crosses his face. "Because I dated you and he didn't."

I laugh. "Is this about that silly pact you guys made?"

"You knew about that?" he asks with wide eyes.

"Not until last night." I lean over and swat his arm. "You never told me you both had a crush on me."

"Would it have made a difference?" he asks.

I chew my food, thinking about it for a minute. "I guess not. I mean, we had a good thing going and two of us hooking up would have ruined that."

"Exactly," he says. "But I wouldn't be surprised if he tried to get into your pants now. You know, just to one-up me."

"*One-up* you?" I ask.

"It's what guys do," he says, washing his bite down with wine. "Especially arrogant movie stars who are jealous of childhood friends."

I roll my eyes at him.

"We fought over you back then," he says. "Even when we were in middle school. I'm just not sure we ever realized why we were doing it."

"You did?"

He nods. "Remember the one Halloween when you wanted to be Beauty?"

"Belle," I say, smiling at the memory. "I loved that costume. I was ten and I wanted you guys to dress up as characters from the movie."

"That's right. Well, we both wanted to be the Beast. Chad said he should get to do it because he was bigger than me. I told him that because I had dark hair, it should be me. His mom walked in and found us fighting about it. She called my mom and together, they conspired to make us outfits that would go with yours."

"So that's how you ended up as the teacup, Chip," she says.

"Yup, I was the stupid little teacup and Chad was that geeky candlestick dude. It was humiliating."

"Lumiere," I say, remembering it fondly.

"Whatever. And remember our high school trip to the amusement park? Man, we fought all day over who would sit with you on rides. Didn't it ever occur to you that not once did you sit alone even though there were only three of us?"

I try to think back on that day. "I don't know. I guess I thought you were just being chivalrous or something, not letting a girl ride alone."

"I could go on all night with these kinds of stories," he says.

I put up my hand to stop him. "Please don't," I say. "Oh, wow, now I'm questioning my entire childhood existence."

He laughs. I love Julian's laugh. His whole body participates in it, making it almost impossible for anyone near him not to feel happy. "Don't," he says. "We worshiped you and the ground you walked on. You should appreciate the fact that you had us completely under your spell."

We spend the rest of dinner reminiscing about some of the great times we had together—the three of us. And I can't be certain, but by the time we say goodbye at my train stop, I could almost swear Julian might be amenable to a reunion.

Pulling out of the parking garage, I feel my phone vibrate with a text. After I get home, I read it.

Chad: Well?

I look around the car as if someone might be able to explain his text.

Me: Well, what?

Chad: You said you'd think about it. I gave you almost twelve hours. Are you going to have dinner with me tomorrow?

I take stock in the night I just had. Julian is great. I love him like a brother. I trust him. And he knows me better than anyone. He's just trying to protect me from getting hurt again. And he's probably right. Nothing good can come of seeing Chad again. He'll be gone in a few days and life will go back to normal.

Normal.

Me: I don't think it's a good idea. But thank you for asking. It was nice seeing you last night.

A minute goes by and I think maybe he's pissed at my rejection so he's not going to text back. It's probably for the best. I quietly make my way into the house and up to my room. It's late and Dad is sleeping. I set my alarm for six in the morning, knowing

I'm not going to get a full night's sleep because once again, Julian and I lost track of time.

Right before I doze off. My phone vibrates.

Chad: I'm sure you know about a lot of the shit in my past. I mean, who doesn't? My post-Mallory past. My drug-induced idiotic past. My womanizing past. But I want to assure you, that's not me anymore. Please give me a chance to prove it to you. I've been sitting here wondering why you won't see me again. And if I were in your shoes, I'd shoot me down too, because I would think you only wanted me for a quick lay. I miss you, Mal. I miss the trouble we'd get into and the talks we used to have. I miss sneaking over to your house late at night to watch SNL. I miss your laugh that almost got us busted by your parents more than a few times on those occasions. So please, I'm begging you, as the friend you once knew, give it a little more thought.

I read the text. I read it three times. Did the man take charm lessons in acting school? He was rather charming last night, too. I'm afraid to see what would happen if I actually went to dinner with him. And for that reason alone, I know it's a bad idea. I start to type in my response, but then decide to wait. I'll squash his hopes tomorrow.

CHAPTER SEVEN

Chad

Hayden and I wait in the green room of the morning show 'Wake Up America.' Yesterday, they interviewed the women from *Defcon One*, today it's our turn. I wasn't happy with the spin Courtney put on our relationship. She insinuated we are still together, feeding into the frenzy that already exists out there.

"You still pissed at Courtney?" Hayden asks.

"I just wish she would quit embellishing the truth," I say. "I saw the clip. She was talking about having dinner with me. The dinner she failed to mention was a work function. And then she had to go and make it seem like breakfast the next day was a goddamn extension of some date we had, not a cast meeting to discuss the Vancouver junket."

"Is it really that bad?" he asks with a smirk. "I mean, it's not like you have an *actual* girlfriend who would get jealous over it."

I pick up a croissant and toss it at him just as we're called to head on set. We're quickly situated on an L-shaped couch next to Tanya Weathers, co-anchor of the show. We exchange a few pleasantries during the commercial break and she reminds us that they will show a clip of the film and then she's going to start with

Hayden and then move on to me, keeping the entire segment at about nine minutes. I glance over at Kendra, who is standing behind one of the cameras. She gives us a thumbs up.

After what only seems like thirty seconds of airtime, Tanya turns her attention from Hayden to me. "So, Thad, or should I call you Lieutenant Cross?" she says, fanning herself with her note cards. "You are just about the hottest thing since sliced bread if the crowd outside our studio is any indication. We haven't drawn a crowd this big since the Pope was here."

I try not to show my apprehension over the hordes of people outside. And once again I find myself glad Cole is with me. I laugh it off. "For me? Nah, I think I saw the Teletubbies going into the studio next door. Heck, after we're done here, I might go wait in line for some autographs myself."

Tanya pastes on a big smile. "You've had premieres in L.A. and London and now here. Where to next?"

"Vancouver is our last stop; we go there in ten days."

"Are you going to be in New York until then or will you be heading back to the west coast?" she asks.

"I'm not exactly sure yet. My commitments here end this weekend, but I have family here so I may hang out a while longer."

"I'll bet you just made a lot of the women of New York City very happy," she says. "Then again, with all the photos of you and a certain leading lady floating around, is it safe to say you're off the market?"

I shift around in my seat. "What leading lady would that be?"

She laughs. "That's right, you have a history of dating your co-stars going all the way back to Heather Crawford on *Malibu 310*. I even heard a rumor that you and Ana Garner may have broken a few hearts on the set of another movie you filmed late last year."

I shake my head. "Don't believe everything you hear, Tanya."

"So you and Ana didn't date? Was it because you and Courtney Benson have a long-standing relationship? Or maybe you are dating both of them," she asks, with a rise of her brows.

I resist the urge to fire a counter attack and mention the rumor of Tanya's husband cheating on her with her nanny. Instead, I reply, "Let's just say I'm enjoying life right now and I don't plan to put a ring on anyone's finger anytime soon."

"Did you hear that?" Tanya asks, cupping her hand around her ear. "That's the sound of the collective cheers of every woman between the ages of thirteen and sixty."

"Sixty?" I feign a look of disappointment. "I must be losing my touch."

She goes on to ask me a few questions about *Defcon One*, doing her best to bring Hayden into the conversation. As well she should. I was not the only star of the film and it bothers me when I get treated as such. Hayden's character was an integral part of the story and he nailed the part.

"Did it bother you to have to film in that cave?" she asks. "I heard the conditions down there were deplorable. Cold and wet and very close quarters."

"I didn't think much about it." *Hell yes, it bothered me.* "It's all part of the job, Tanya. I try not to let anything phase me."

"Really? So would you say you're a hard man to surprise?" she asks.

I look at Hayden, confused by her question. He shrugs. "Uh, I guess so," I tell her.

She discreetly motions to someone offstage. "You seemed awfully surprised by something the night of the premiere," she says, pointing to a screen behind us that is now displaying a picture of me outside the club Saturday night. And yes, I look very, very surprised.

Uneasiness washes through me. "I thought I saw someone I knew in the crowd. Uh, my father," I say awkwardly. "And it was unexpected since he lives back in California."

She smiles innocently like the cat that ate the canary. "Is your father a beautiful brunette, say mid-twenties?" She again motions to the screen, and when I see the photo that's plastered across it, my stomach knots up.

There on the screen is a picture of Mallory. You can't see her face, and for that I'm grateful, but it's her. I shoot a glance at Kendra who looks pale. This was not on the list of agreed topics. "I suppose that woman is beautiful, but since we can't see her face, it's kind of hard to tell, wouldn't you say? And there were hundreds of beautiful women there who caught my eye."

They split the image, putting the first one of me looking surprised next to the side-view of Mallory. "Please tell your father he's never looked better," she jokes. She turns and speaks into the camera. "Thad Stone and Hayden Keys, folks. You can see them in *Defcon One*, opening in theaters everywhere on March 23rd."

They go to commercial and Tanya quickly thanks us before being whisked away for her next segment. Kendra comes up behind me as we are escorted back to the green room. "Don't worry about it, Thad. The picture is vague. Nobody can tell who she is. You played it off very well. There won't be any fallout from this."

"Played it off well?" I rub the tense muscles in the back of my neck. "Why didn't I just say I thought it was my mother, or a cousin maybe? Now it looks like I'm hiding something."

"You're in show business, Thad," she says. "Who *isn't* hiding something?"

Cole comes to escort us out of the building into the car waiting in the underground parking garage. On our way to drop

Kendra and Hayden back at the hotel, I wonder if Mallory watched the show. I think she was probably at work by the time my segment came on. But the picture is out there now. Will the press continue to dig, or will they drop it? I should probably tell her about this before she finds out some other way.

I pull out my phone and see I've gotten a text from her that she sent earlier this morning.

> **Mal: I miss all that stuff, too. But things are different. We are different people now and there is no going back. I'm glad you've changed and I wish you all the best in your career. I know you will do great things. Bye, Chad.**

Bye, Chad? She's blowing me off. She really doesn't want to see me again. This won't do. This won't fucking do at all. After we drop the others off, I tell Cole, "Change of plans."

~ ~ ~

I walk up to the desk and talk to the lady behind the counter who has a phone to one ear and a stack of folders in her hand. "I'm here to see Mallory Schaffer."

She barely glances up at me. "Do you have an appointment?" she asks. "It is the middle of the school day, you know. Are you a parent?"

"No. I'm not a parent. I just need to see her," I say.

She holds a finger out to me as she finishes her conversation with whomever is on the other end of the phone. She places the handset in the receiver and drops her folders. "Shoot," she says, crouching down to pick up the strewn papers. "Are you on the approved volunteer list?"

Shit. There's a list? I look around at all the signs on the walls and see one in particular. I get an idea. "I'm here for career day," I say.

"That's not until tomorrow." She looks up when someone comes through the door behind her. "Don't open that!" she yells as a student walks through, toppling more stacked folders onto the floor. "Oh, gosh. I'm sorry, I don't normally run the front desk, but our secretary called in sick today. I'm the assistant principal." She finally looks up at me. "What did you say your name—" Her words trail off and her mouth slowly forms the shape of an O as she once again drops the papers in her hand. "Uh, you're . . . um, you're . . . who are you here to see?"

I reach my hand over the desk. "Thad Stone. I'm here to see Mallory Schaffer, Mrs. . . . ."

"*Ms.* Blanchard," she says, shaking my hand with her trembling one. "Call me Carly."

"Nice to meet you, Carly. You seem awfully young for an assistant principal," I say to the middle-aged woman, hoping flattery will get me beyond the front desk. "Ms. Schaffer invited me for career day. I must've gotten the days wrong." I look down at the floor in sadness. "Darn. I'm leaving for L.A. shortly. I was hoping to get to talk to her great group of fourth-graders. She can't say enough about them. And this school. Man, she really does love working here. Well, my bodyguard is waiting for me outside. I guess I'll go tell him the bad news. It was really nice meeting you, Carly."

I turn around and take a slow step when she says. "Mr. Stone?"

I smile before looking at her over my shoulder. "Call me Thad, Carly."

She blushes. "Okay, Thad. I'm not supposed to do this without you being on the volunteer list." She looks over her shoulder to see the student walk out the door, leaving us alone in the front office. She writes my name on a visitor's badge and peels the backing off before handing the sticker to me. "But seeing as you're only in town today, I would hate to deprive Ms. Schaffer's class of meeting you."

She buzzes me through the door to the back. "That's very kind of you, Carly. Thank you."

"I'll show you the way." She presses a button on her phone. "Can you please cover the front desk for a minute, Martha?"

Martha comes out of another door and smiles at me. Martha is about seventy-five years old. She doesn't recognize me. It's refreshing.

Carly asks me all about *Defcon One* as she escorts me to Mal's classroom. I'm happy to answer her questions. After all, she's doing me a solid. We come to a door that is decorated with several different-sized paper cutouts of shoes. The shoes lead to a sign at the top that reads 'Step into learning.' Mallory's full name is on a nameplate next to the door.

I laugh to myself. I can't believe she's a teacher. I remember her as the fifteen-year-old girl who would cut class with me to get ice cream. And now she's a grown-up with a real job. A normal job. And I find myself jealous of someone who probably doesn't even make in one year what I make in one week.

Carly peeks in the window next to the door. "Good, it looks like we caught them at a good time." She knocks once and then opens the door. She goes in first. "Ms. Schaffer, you have a visitor."

71

"Oh?" Mallory looks up, probably confused as to why her class is being interrupted. She sees me and freezes. She looks at her students and then to Carly and then to me again. "Uh . . . hi." She walks over to me and I have to keep myself from laughing. The expression on her face is priceless. She has no idea why I'm here. She's scared. She's confused. She's excited. Yup, even after all these years, I can still read her like an old familiar book.

"What are you doing here?" she whispers through her pasted-on smile.

"He's here for career day," Carly says. "He mixed up the days a bit, but since he's going back to L.A. tomorrow, I told him he could go ahead and talk to your students today." She turns to walk back out the door. "I'll leave you to it then."

"Thank you," I tell her. "I appreciate your help and I trust you can keep this a secret?"

"Can I get a picture with you on your way out?" she asks shyly.

"Of course."

"Then consider my lips sealed," she says with a huge smile before closing the door.

Mallory and I are left standing at the front of the classroom, her jaw still agape that I'd have the gall to show up. "Why are you here?"

I shrug. "You wouldn't answer my text," I say quietly.

"I answered you this morning," she whispers.

"It wasn't the answer I wanted."

"Chad, you can't just show up unannounced."

"I didn't. Ms. Blanchard announced me." I wink at her. "Plus, I've heard sometimes you have to make a grand gesture in order to get noticed. And I'm not Chad today." I motion to her students. "I'm Thad."

"A grand *what?*" Her forehead forms these adorable wrinkles as she questions me.

I glance at the students who have all been very quiet as they watch us. I take it they aren't used to visitors. "Well, come on, teacher," I say. "It's career day, are you going to introduce me or what?"

She looks over at the kids as if she forgot they were there. "Uh, okay. Class, this is Thad Stone. Thad is an actor and he's going to talk to you for a little while about what it means to have a job like his."

A boy raises his hand before I can get a word out. "Yes, Billy?" Mallory asks.

"You're in that new movie, right? The one about the world ending? I've seen you on TV, only your hair was shorter and you were a lot dirtier."

I laugh. "What you saw was called a movie trailer. That's where they take bits and pieces of the movie and show it to you so you'll want to come see it in the theater. Although it's rated R, so I don't think any of you should go. But if your parents want to go, that would be great. And all that dirt on my face and clothes is called makeup. Do you know it took a makeup artist an hour to make me look like that?"

"That's cool," Billy says. "Did you really jump out of that plane?"

"No, I didn't. That was a stuntman. But they made him up to look like me, and in the movie, you can't tell the difference. Sometimes I do my own stunts, like I had to rappel down the side of a mountain for another movie. It took me two weeks to learn how to do it. That's part of the fun in acting. You get to do so many things and pretend to be a lot of different people."

All the kids raise their hands. Mallory points to a girl in the back. "Yes, Jessica? What's your question for Mr. Stone?"

"How many movies have you been in?" she asks.

"Five. But only three of them have been released so far. The other two have been filmed but aren't in movie theaters yet. That's why I'm here in New York, to promote the fourth film I did, *Defcon One*. My first movie was called *Red Sky Rising*. I had a very small part. I played the son of the main character, but I was only in three scenes. My next two movies were called *I Never* and *Last Week*. They were romantic comedies."

"Like where you kiss girls?" Jessica asks.

I nod. "Yes, but I didn't get to kiss any because I wasn't the main character."

"Yes, Ryan?" Mallory asks, pointing to a kid wearing a SpongeBob SquarePants shirt.

"What's a main character?" Ryan asks.

"It's the most important person in a movie." I motion to his shirt. "Kind of like SpongeBob. He's the main character of that TV show. In my new movie, *Defcon One*, I'm kind of like SpongeBob, but in the movie, *Last Week*, I was more like Squidward, who's called a supporting actor."

One by one the kids ask questions and I patiently answer every one as Mallory learns more about me than she would ever ask. I'm a fucking genius. She's getting insight into the man she thinks she doesn't know anymore. She's getting to hear all the good stuff, and not just what the press thinks is a newsworthy story. She's getting see my job is just like any other job, only I do it in front of millions of people. And as each minute passes, I see her become more and more relaxed.

But as time wears on, I realize I'll have to leave soon and I'm not exactly sure what is supposed to happen next. I never got that far in my head. If I leave here without her commitment to see me again, I'm as good as yesterday's news. She could just blow me off with another text. I've got to up my game. Hit her where she'll feel it. Get her students on my side. I look around her classroom for ideas.

I spot what looks to be a fundraiser poster on the wall. One of those pictures of an empty thermometer and as they raise money, they color it in from the bottom up. It looks like they are pretty close to reaching their goal. "I have a question for one of you." I look around the room, carefully choosing my subject as they all wonder who I'm going to pick. "SpongeBob, can you tell me what 'Wishes for Kids' is?"

Ryan's face lights up when I choose him. "We collect money for kids who can't come to school like us. Kids who have cancer and other bad stuff and sometimes they live at the hospital. They get to take trips to Disney World and stuff because they are sick."

"Ahhh, I see." I look around and pick another kid. "Jessica, right?" She nods shyly. "Can you tell me how much money you've raised?"

She walks up to the poster and points to the amounts down the side. "We have almost eight hundred dollars."

"Wow, that's great," I say.

"I guess, but Ms. Ellison's class is going to win the party," she says with a frown.

"Jessica," Mallory says. "Fundraising is not about winning. It's about giving to others."

"Yes, Ms. Schaffer." She returns to her seat.

"Well, wait a minute," I say. "Why can't it be about giving to others *and* winning?"

"What do you mean?" Mallory asks me.

"Can anyone tell me how much money you need to get the party?"

The boy in the blue shirt, whose name I can't remember, says, "My friend Joey said that Ms. Ellison's class has almost a thousand dollars. That's a lot."

"And can someone else tell me when the fundraiser is ending?"

They all look at each other and shrug. Mallory says, "Friday. It ends this Friday."

I reach into my pocket and get my wallet. I count my money. Five hundred and twenty-three dollars. I pull out everything but twenty-three and hand it to Mal. "You have a great class here and I'd hate for them to miss out on the party."

She shakes her head at me, mouth agape as I stuff the money in her hand. "See now, I feel better already. I love helping people, don't you guys?" The students all agree. "Doesn't it feel good to help people, Ms. Schaffer?"

"Yes, it does," she says.

"And sometimes when somebody does something nice for you, you want to do something nice in return, isn't that so, Billy?"

He nods fervently.

"Well then, I have a little problem and I need some help," I tell the class. "I have to go to this dinner tonight see, and I'm supposed to bring someone with me because everyone else who will be there will bring someone with them and I don't want to be the only one who goes alone. I was hoping that Ms. Schaffer here would help me out. Do you guys think she should help me out? Don't you think it will make her feel good to do that?" All the kids nod and tell her she should help me.

I look at the daily schedule on the wall and see it's almost time for their lunch. "I've really enjoyed my time here with you guys. I hope you learned something about being an actor and maybe one day, some of you can become actors too."

"Please thank Mr. Stone for coming to speak with us today," Mallory says.

All the kids do as she asks. "You're welcome," I say. "Thank you for having me, Ms. Schaffer. Pick you up at seven?"

We have a stare down. She bites her bottom lip the whole time. Then she rolls her eyes and blows out a sigh. "Fine," she says.

I walk out the door, closing it before I jump up, pumping my fist in the air. Then I turn back around only to see Mallory peeking out her window after me. I give her a sailor's salute and go on my way.

Samantha Christy

CHAPTER EIGHT

Mallory

I look around my bedroom at all the clothes strewn about. I must've tried on twelve different outfits. We're just going to his brother's house, so I decide not to dress up, finally settling on a nice pair of jeans and a light-green blouse that's just tight enough to stress the buttons without showing too much cleavage. I finish the outfit with my favorite black ankle boots.

I look at myself from every angle in my floor-length mirror. Casual yet flirty. *Do I want to look flirty?* After all, I would never have agreed to this if he hadn't strong-armed me in front of my class by making that generous donation. I roll my eyes thinking back on this morning. I never heard the end of it from Carly. She cornered me at lunch, wanting every detail about what happened in my classroom after she left. She showed me the picture of her and Chad that she took on his way out. I asked her to be discreet about it and she promised she would, but she also said that some of the mothers who were coming in to help with lunch had recognized him and their phones were clicking and videoing as he walked back to his car.

I hear a car door shut outside and all of a sudden, my stomach is in my throat. I feel sick. I haven't been this nervous since the first day of my teaching job. That's not true. I've never been this nervous. Will he think this is a date? I need to make it very clear upfront that it's not.

I put on my pink lip gloss and grab my purse before heading down the stairs to find Chad talking to my dad. They both look up at me when they hear the heels of my boots click across the hardwood floor. Chad stops talking mid-sentence and his mouth hangs slightly open as he silently watches me descend the stairs. I can't help feel a bit of an ego boost having him look at me this way. After all the women he's been with. Beautiful actresses. Models. Yet he looks at me the way he is.

This is not a date, Mallory, I remind myself.

"Hi," I say, reaching the bottom step.

"Hi, yourself," he says back. "Wow, you look great, Mal."

For a moment, I wonder what his reaction would have been if I'd worn the little black dress I tried on earlier. "Thanks, you look nice, too." He's wearing jeans as well, paired with a simple blue t-shirt and Doc Martens. The shirt he's wearing brings out the color of his eyes, making them seem a shade brighter. His blonde hair is a bit unruly as if he'd recently run his hands through it. And despite the four-inch heels on my boots, he towers over me. I can see the allure. He looks like a movie star. My stomach does twists again. *He is a movie star, Mallory.*

"Nice to see you again, Mr. Schaffer," Chad says, shaking my dad's hand.

"Please, call me Richard. You're not sixteen anymore."

Chad laughs, looking me over again. "That I'm not." He motions to the front door. "Are you ready to go?"

"Sure," I say, grabbing my coat from the closet. Chad takes it from me and helps me put it on. "Bye, Daddy."

"Bye, sweetheart. I won't wait up," he says with a wink.

I shoot my dad an angry glare. Then I don't miss the smirk on Chad's face. Once out the door, I tell him, "This isn't a date, you know. Just one old friend helping out another."

"Not a date," he repeats. "Got it."

We get to the car and I see the same guy who was here the other night. His bodyguard. He steps forward to open the back door, but Chad waves him off. "I got it," he says. "Mallory Schaffer, I'd like you to meet Cole Wilcox."

Cole offers me his gargantuan-sized hand. "Nice to meet you, Ms. Schaffer," he says in a baritone voice that matches his size.

"It's just Mallory," I say, shaking his hand. "Nice to meet you, Cole."

"The pleasure is all mine, Mallory." He walks around to the driver's side and gets in as Chad situates me in the back seat.

Then, to my surprise, Chad walks around the car and joins me in the back rather than sitting up front with Cole. He smiles at my reaction. "Ethan is stoked to see you again," he says.

"I'm excited to see him, too." He was several years older than me, so we didn't hang out much, but Chad looked up to him and sometimes he would sneak us into R-rated movies.

"He's married now. Has a kid and everything," he says. "He's happy."

"I'm really glad to hear that. He deserves to be happy after everything he went through." I shudder remembering the funeral of a girl taken far too soon and how much it wrecked Ethan.

"Kyle will be there, too," he says.

"Really? Did he come with you for a visit?" I ask, wondering what it will be like to see the three of them together again after all this time.

"He lives here. He moved back to go to college and now he goes to med school at NYU."

My jaw drops. "Kyle is going to be a doctor?" I ask. "Kyle—the kid who threw up at the sight of my blood when I fell off my bike and ripped my arm open?"

Chad laughs, his eyes lighting up at the memory. "I had forgotten all about that. We teased him for months," he says. "Ethan and I would taunt him every time we got so much as a scrape." He turns on the backseat light, nodding to my right arm. "Can you still see the scar?"

I push up my sleeve and hold my arm out so he can see the long, curvy, faded scar. He holds my arm up to the light as tingles race through me from his touch. He examines it from several angles. He traces the scar with his finger, making me catch my breath as the tiny hairs on my arm stand at attention. "I can still see the faint lines where some of the stitches were. Nine, right?"

My eyes shoot to his, surprised that he'd remember something that happened when I was eleven years old. "That's right. What about you?" I motion to his foot. "You had me beat with your thirteen stitches. Can you still see yours?"

He puts down my arm and removes his left shoe and sock, showing me the jagged scar that was the result of a shoeless skateboard accident. I stare at his faded scar, longing to reach out and touch the soft skin on the top of his foot. *What is so darn sexy about men's feet?*

"Interesting, don't you think?" he asks, putting his shoe back on.

"What's interesting?"

"How we both remembered exactly how many stitches the other had."

I shrug. "Well, it was kind of traumatic for us. I mean, you *were* only nine when you had your accident."

"That's right, I was. And you were eleven when you had yours," he says smiling. "And I remember asking my mother if you could go with me to get stitches because I knew if you were there it wouldn't be so bad."

"That's why you wanted me to go with you?" I ask. "I thought you needed me to tell the doctors what happened."

"Nah." He shakes his head. "I just wanted you there with me. I always wanted you there."

Feeling a bit uncomfortable with how he's looking at me, I change the subject back to Kyle. "So who's Kyle bringing tonight?" I ask. "Is he married, too?"

Chad snorts. "Married to his job, maybe. As a fourth-year med student, he pretty much spends all of his time at the hospital."

"But you said everyone going tonight was bringing someone."

"Shit," he says, looking guilty. "I guess you got me there. I may have embellished the truth a bit. But in my defense, there will be three other guys and three other girls there, so I didn't want to be the odd man out."

"So who's the girl you paired with Kyle?"

"My publicist, Kendra. She's great. You'll love her. In fact, I think you'll get along with all the women there."

Rather than be pissed that he lied to me, I'm relieved that not everyone else there is part of a couple. Makes this whole 'not a date' thing more plausible. "Who else is going?" I ask.

"Ethan's wife's best friend and her husband."

The car comes to a stop and Cole gets out to open my door. Chad exits the car behind me. "We'll be several hours, Cole. Go get yourself some dinner and I'll text you when we're ready."

I look up at the tall building on a very nice street in Midtown as the car pulls away from the curb. "Cole doesn't need to come in with you?" I ask.

"We're good. The building has security," he says. Then a group of girls passing by see Chad and start screaming.

They run up to him, completely ignoring my presence. "Thad! Thad! Oh, my God. I heard you were in New York."

"Can I get a picture, Thad? I love you!"

"Oh my God! Thad Stone! Can you sign this?" one says, shoving a piece of paper at him.

A few more people hear the screams of the girls and stop to see what's going on. In a matter of ten seconds, a small crowd has gathered, all wanting a piece of him.

He turns to me, guilt on his face. "I'll just be a minute," he says, motioning to the door of the building. "I'll meet you inside."

The doorman lets me inside and I turn to watch Chad spend the next few minutes posing for pictures and signing autographs. He smiles at them, but it's not authentic. It's strained. Not like the smile I remember when we were kids. Not like how he looked at me when he saw me tonight. More people come up the sidewalk and he quickly ducks into the building, looking a bit frazzled.

"Can you take care of that?" Chad asks the doorman.

"No problem, Mr. Stone," he says, going out to disband the crowd.

I motion to the growing crowd. "Looks like you may need Cole after all."

"I can't even walk from the fucking curb to a building anymore? It's getting goddamn ridiculous." He shakes his head in disgust. "I didn't mean to blow you off out there. I just didn't want anyone bothering you or taking your picture."

"It's perfectly fine, Chad. I understand. And I think it's nice that you took the time to do what you did for your fans. A lot of actors would have just ignored them."

He laughs. "A lot of actors aren't as stupid as I am."

"Not stupid," I tell him. "Just kind."

"Come on, let's go up before anyone tries to come in after us." He leads me to the elevator and presses the button for the penthouse.

I look at him with inquisitive eyes. "The penthouse?" I ask. "Did Ethan win the lottery or something?"

"If you call my grandparents dying and leaving us all their money winning the lottery, then yes."

My hand comes to cover my mouth. "Oh, Chad, your Pap and Nana died? I'm so sorry." I remember them fondly. We would often go out to their house in The Hamptons in the summer. They had a fantastic pool that had a separate pool house. We would pretend it was our house and we were a king and queen. When Julian would come, they would take turns being the prince.

"Thanks," he says. "It's been about six years now."

"I wish I would have known, I'd like to have attended their funerals."

He nods. "I'm sorry, I know you would have. My parents asked if I wanted to call you. But I couldn't."

"Why?"

"Pap died first," he says, hooking his thumbs into his front pockets. "It was about a year after you stopped talking to me. My life was a mess. I couldn't get through the day without drugs. I didn't want you seeing me like that. I knew I had become a disappointment to you."

"Why would you think that?" I ask, knowing it's true but finding it surprising he'd thought it.

"Because you stopped taking my calls. You stopped emailing me. You cut me off all social media." He shakes his head and sighs. "And because when your mom died and I didn't come back for her funeral, Julian tore me a new one, telling me how much you hated what I'd become. It's true, right? That you hated me?"

I take a step back and lean against the elevator wall. "I wouldn't say I hated you. I just missed my friend, Chad. He was gone and it made me sad."

Chad pushes himself off the wall and cages me in, his hands on either side of my face. "I'm so sorry," he says, staring intensely into my eyes. "You'll never know just how much. But I'm me again. I'm Chad. That other selfish prick is gone."

The elevator doors open and he backs away, allowing me to breathe again. He helps me off with my coat when we reach the penthouse door.

When we walk through, Ethan comes over, ignoring Chad as he pulls me in for a huge hug. "Little Mallory Schaffer," he says, releasing me to look me over. "You look wonderful. It's so nice to see you again."

"You too, Ethan. Thank you for having me." My eyes quickly take in the massive great room lined by floor-to-ceiling windows overlooking the city. "Hey, can I borrow a hundred-dollar bill to scrape the gum off my shoe that I stepped on in that deplorable contraption you call an elevator? I mean, seriously, this building should be condemned."

"You always were a smartass, Schaffer. I'm glad to see some things haven't changed." He takes my elbow and escorts me into the kitchen. "Mallory, this is my wife, Charlie."

She looks familiar. About my age, maybe a bit younger. I wonder if we went to college together. "Nice to meet you, Charlie."

I extend my hand to her but she hugs me. "It's nice to meet you, too. I've heard a lot about you this week."

She has? "You have?"

"Oh, yeah," she says, nodding. "My brother-in-law here has you on a pretty high pedestal."

Ethan clears his throat. "You'll have to excuse my wife and her unfiltered mouth."

Charlie swats him. "You love my mouth," she says.

He pulls her in for a kiss. "Very true. Must be that Stone men love smartass women."

"Must be," she says, her striking red hair flowing around her shoulders.

Pedestal? Stone men love smartass women? Am I missing something here?

I can't get over the feeling I know Charlie from somewhere. "You look so familiar; did you go to Berkeley?"

"Nope, I skipped college and went straight to life," she says.

"Charlie's mom was Caroline Anthony," Ethan says. "Caroline was an actress and Charlie looks a lot like her, that's probably why she looks familiar." The way he says it is like he's said it a thousand times before, matter-of-factly, but in a protective kind of way.

Oh, geez. She's Caroline Anthony's daughter? Charlie looks a bit perturbed by the mention of her mother, so I don't ask her about it. Maybe she feels the same way I did when Melissa was bombarding me with questions about Chad.

"Mallory, this is my best friend, Piper Mitchell," Charlie says, indicating the woman sitting at the bar. "And this is her fiancé, Mason Lawrence."

I look at the stunning couple, immediately recognizing Mason as a professional football player. What, is *everyone* here famous or uber-freaking-rich? Suddenly I feel very insignificant. And very out of place. "Uh, hello. Nice to meet you." I shake Piper's hand and then Mason's. "My dad is a huge fan," I say with a shaky voice. "He will be beside himself when I tell him I had dinner with you." I feel a little faint and quickly take a seat on the couch as everyone falls into comfortable conversation.

Chad sits next to me on the end of the couch. "Are you okay, Mal? You look a little pale. Can I get you something?"

I shake my head. "I'll be okay," I whisper so only he can hear. "I mean, as if you being a movie star isn't enough, but now—this penthouse, the daughter of an Oscar-winning actress, a guy who plays football for the Giants? I guess I'm just a little overwhelmed, that's all. And way out of my league."

"We're all just regular people like you, Mal," he says.

I look at him like he's gone off his rocker. "Right," I say. "Just ask those girls downstairs, or the hundreds of people that swarmed you at the club the other night."

"That's just part of the job," he says. "It's not who we are. We want to get together and have a good time with our friends, just like everyone else. That's all this is, a good time with friends. Okay?"

I look around at everyone. I guess he's right. Watching them talk and drink and laugh, they do all seem fairly normal despite the fact that the collective wealth in this room could eliminate a big chunk of the national debt.

I see a woman come down the hallway with a baby in her arms. She walks up to Charlie. "He's all clean. Thanks for letting me change him," she says.

"Are you kidding?" Charlie hands the woman a drink, leaning down to kiss the baby. "You can have that job whenever you'd like. You're a lifesaver."

Chad stands up and holds his hand out to me. I let him pull me up off the couch. He walks us over to the woman, not letting go of my hand. It reminds me of the times he held my hand when we were young. Only with more sparks now. "Mallory, this is my publicist, Kendra."

"Hi, Mallory," she says, smiling at our entwined hands. "Sorry, I'd give you a hug, but my hands are kind of full."

"Here, let me," Chad says, taking the baby from her. I'm surprised at the emptiness I feel when he pulls his hand from mine.

Kendra gives me a hug. "So, you're the one," she whispers in my ear.

I have the feeling tonight is some elaborate hoax that everyone is in on but me. Maybe I'm being punk'd. I look at Kendra as she releases me and she gives me this incredible, ear-to-ear smile. "Doesn't he look like a natural?" she asks, motioning to Chad.

"I think Eli has my nose," he says, admiring the tiny baby in his arms.

"Eli has *my* nose," Ethan shouts from the kitchen.

The front door slams shut. "You're both crazy, he has *my* nose. And he's damn lucky because you two have beaks that belong on pelicans."

"Kyle!" I race over to hug the youngest Stone brother. "Oh my gosh, I've missed you."

"Hi, Mallory." He holds me at arm's length, looking me over from head to toe. "Jesus, you look incredible. I never had a teacher as hot as you in fourth grade, that's for damn sure."

I'm surprised he knows I teach fourth grade. But before I can ask, Chad comes up beside me, draping a possessive arm over my shoulder. "Go get your own hot teacher," he says. "This one's mine." He leans down to place a kiss on the top of my head, causing goosebumps to line my arms.

Mine? He wants me to be his? His what—friend, one-night-stand, New York booty-call?

"Dinner's ready," Charlie calls from the kitchen.

I extract myself from Chad, happy to have an excuse to get away from him for a minute so I can breathe again. Piper, Kendra and I help Charlie carry plates of food from the kitchen to the dining room.

Dinner is surreal. I hear all about what professional football players do in the off-season. Ethan and Charlie entertain us with tales of some of the strangest cases they've had at their P.I. agency. Kendra regales us with stories of her most diva-like clients—minus the names, of course. She is their publicist after all. And Kyle grosses us out by telling us about the latest cadaver he got to dissect. My tales of teaching don't even begin to hold a candle to the rest of the dinnertime chatter.

"What about you?" I ask Chad. "Do you have any funny stories to tell?"

He shakes his head. "Nope. My life is hardly interesting."

Chad gets pelted with rolls thrown by his brothers. He takes one and rips at it with his teeth, throwing it back to Ethan and then does the same to Kyle.

"Do *not* have a food fight in my house, boys," Charlie says with the conviction of a tried-and-true mother. "Play nice or I'll cut you off." She stands up and retrieves a bottle of wine, making her way around the table to refill all the glasses. Chad puts his hand over his glass and waves her by.

Is he doing that just for me, because he told me the other night he doesn't drink much? Or has he really changed his ways? He's only had one glass tonight when everyone else has had at least three. But then, who's counting?

I should quit analyzing everything about him. Every look he gives me with those ocean-blue eyes. Every chair he pulls out for me. Every flutter of my heart when he touches me innocently.

He's so much like the boy I remember. At my house. At the school. Tonight. He's nothing like the movie star the press makes him out to be. Nothing like the womanizing drug-head I thought he was. In fact, he's the kind of man I could see myself with. Then again, he is an actor. By profession, he lies to people, getting them to believe he's something that he's not.

Kendra slurs her words ever so slightly when she asks, "I want to hear about the missing ball."

All eyes at the table turn to her. "The *what?*" Ethan asks.

"It's been driving me crazy for a few days," she says. "I dug into it and there are some records of hospital employees violating HIPPA laws by talking about your case, so what I want to know is" —she looks at Chad— "and please don't fire me for this, but how in the hell did you lose a testicle at the Santa Monica Pier?"

Kyle chokes on his wine, sputtering some across the table. "Oh, hell yes," he says. "Tell them the story, bro."

"I'm not telling shit," Chad says, looking embarrassed as he rolls the stem of his empty wine glass between his fingers.

"I was there, I'll tell it then," Kyle says.

"Whatever," Chad says, stiffening in his chair. He chews on his inner cheek. Nobody else seems to notice that he's bothered by this. But I can read his body language. I've always been able to.

I look around to see that everyone is done with dinner. "Chad, I'd really like to see the view," I say. "Will you show me the balcony?"

He looks at me and sighs. He thanks me with his eyes. He's happy I saved him. But it's no big deal, really, it's what we've always done. Saved each other. Except for the one time when I couldn't.

He stands up and takes my hand, leading me away from the table as Kyle begins to tell his story.

CHAPTER NINE

Chad

Mallory is beautiful as she leans over the railing to see the street below. I tried my best not to stare at her throughout dinner, but I couldn't help it. I swear her eyes have gotten greener. Her hair, that was always long when we were kids, has gotten even wavier. Her breasts . . . Jesus, my dick still thinks I'm a hormonal sixteen-year-old kid.

"This is incredible," she says, enjoying the awe-inspiring view. "How far up are we?"

"Twenty-five floors," I tell her. "So almost three-hundred feet I'd say."

"Do you have a place like this out in L.A.?" she asks.

"I used to. But not anymore."

"Why not?"

"I sold it along with three of my cars."

She gasps. "You had three cars?"

"Four," I tell her. "I kept one of them."

It's hard for me to keep my eyes focused on her face. It's chilly out here and her nipples are standing at full attention under the thin fabric of her blouse. "Uh, do you want to go back inside, it's pretty cold out here."

"It's nice. I like it," she says, blowing out a deep breath that turns to smoke as she exhales. "So why did you sell your high-rise apartment and three of your cars?"

"Because I've changed." I walk up next to her and join her taking in the stunning view. It's one of the things I had taken for granted during those years. Watching her look wide-eyed at the city below is fascinating. She sees it like a little girl who's looking over the city for the first time. "I went wild those first few years. I bought everything money could buy. And when I got my inheritance, things just got worse."

She turns to me, holding my eyes with hers. "You keep saying you've changed. But what do you mean exactly?" I see her shiver and she wraps her arms around herself. "And what was it that made you want to change?"

I position myself behind her so that we're both looking over the city. It's truth time and I'm not sure I want her looking at me when she hears it. I rub her arms to try and keep her warm. "When I got signed for *Malibu*, my life changed in ways I could have never imagined. I was seventeen—just a kid. I wasn't equipped to handle it. Money was rolling in. Everyone wanted a piece of me. Hollywood doesn't care how old you are, it just cares *who* you are. Booze, drugs, women—they were all thrown at me like it was no big deal. My parents tried to keep me grounded, but there was only so much they could do. They worked all the time and I was good at hiding things from them early on. And then when I turned eighteen, I moved out, giving them no say at all. That's when things got really bad."

She nods. "That's when I got that horrible email from you, when you were eighteen."

"What email?"

"The one that wasn't meant for me. I think you had intended for Julian to get it. You wrote about sleeping with one of your co-stars. You wrote about it graphically. I sent you an email back, don't you remember it?"

I close my eyes, absorbing the words she just said. And for the millionth time, I berate myself for the asshole I became. I can't imagine how horrible that must have been for her. "God, Mallory, I'm so sorry. I wish I could say I remember it, but there is a lot of stuff I don't. Things that were important to me like friends and family just stopped being a priority for me once I started doing drugs. The only thing that mattered was when I could get my next high."

She turns around, our bodies so close I can feel the heat radiating from hers. "What happened to change all that?"

"You mean, what was my rock bottom?"

She nods.

"You might hate me if I tell you."

"I'm willing to risk it," she says.

"Maybe I'm not." I walk away from her and sit down on one of the lounge chairs. "This week has been one of the best I've had in years, Mal. Seeing you after all this time, it's better than I imagined. I feel like a kid again."

She takes the seat next to me. "You say you want to be friends again, Chad?"

"I do. More than anything."

"Then help me understand you," she says. "Because you hurt me back then. And I need to know it won't happen again."

"I hurt a lot of people back then, Mallory." I sit forward and put my elbows on my knees. "I'd like to say hurting you was what I regret the most, but I can't. I've done worse. And I promised myself I would never do anything like that again." I look up and our eyes meet. "I promise you I'll never hurt you."

"Well, that's the thing, Chad. You've broken so many promises before, I don't know if I can trust you."

I nod in agreement. "I know. I'm sorry."

"You say you'll never hurt me. You promised that once before, you know, that you'd never let anyone hurt me," she says. "Do you remember that? I was six and you were seven and those bullies at the bus stop were making fun of me, and then I ran away and tripped over my own feet. You helped me up and then you stood up to them. They towered over you by a foot and you stood up to them and then you promised me you'd never let anyone hurt me again. But the irony is, you are the one who hurt me most of all."

I nod regretfully. I remember every promise I ever made to her. "I also promised I'd never leave you."

"Yeah, well in your defense, you couldn't help breaking that promise. You were only sixteen when your parents moved. It's not like you had a choice in the matter."

"No, I didn't," I say. "But just because I left you geographically, didn't mean I had to leave you emotionally." *But I couldn't bear for you to see me like that.* "Do you remember the other promise? The one we made at your aunt's wedding?"

She laughs. "I had forgotten about that one," she says, bashfully.

Mallory was fourteen and I was fifteen when we went to her Aunt Marie's wedding reception. There were a lot of single middle-aged people there getting drunk and hitting on each other. We thought it was pathetic and we promised we'd never let it happen to us. We made a pact to get married if both of us were still single when she turned thirty. I pretend to check my watch. "If I'm correct, I have about six more years to fulfill that promise."

"You can't say things like that, Chad," she says, getting up and walking back to the railing. "I'm not even sure we qualify as friends anymore." She waves her hand around at our surroundings. "This is all just a favor."

"Do you want to know why I wouldn't tell the Santa Monica Pier story in there?"

She stares blankly at me and then shrugs a shoulder.

"I wouldn't tell the story because I *couldn't* tell it. I don't remember it. I was cranked out of my mind. All I know is what Kyle has told me. And it involves something about a Ferris wheel and me sneaking in after closing to scale it. So if you don't mind, I'd like not to ruin what has been a pretty great night by telling you other stories about how badly I fucked up back then and the other people I hurt."

She looks down at the ground. "Fair enough," she says. "Maybe we've shared enough for one night."

"You look like you're freezing." I stand up and offer her my hand. "Let's get you inside."

Mallory looks appalled when we join the others. "I'm a terrible guest," she says to Charlie, eyeing the cleaned up table. "I'm sorry for not helping you clear the dishes."

"Don't be," Charlie says. "The guys took care of it." She pours Mallory another glass of wine. "So you teach fourth grade. That sounds very rewarding."

Mallory's eyes light up. "Oh, yes. It is. I love teaching. But my most rewarding job is the one I don't get paid for. I volunteer at a place called Hope For Life."

I ignore my brothers as I listen intently to the conversation the girls are having. Mallory tells her all about her charity work.

Not that I'm surprised. Mal was always helping people when we were kids. She would run a lemonade stand and give all the profits—all twenty dollars of it—to some cause benefitting underprivileged kids.

"Would you mind if I tag along with you one night?" Charlie asks her. "I'd love to see what kind of work you do there."

"Really?" Mallory asks, surprised. "I mean, yes, of course they'd love to have you." She pulls a piece of paper out of her purse and scribbles something on it. "I volunteer every Tuesday night. Call me if you want to go sometime."

I look at the clock on the wall, disappointed because I know the night must come to an end. Mallory has to get up early for her job. "I'd better get the teacher home," I tell the group. "It is a school night, you know."

I pull out my phone to text Cole. Mallory questions me with her eyes. "I'm asking Cole to bring the car around."

"Does he go everywhere with you?" she asks. "Will he accompany you to Vancouver?"

I'm amused she knows where I'm headed after New York City. Maybe she follows my career after all. Or maybe she just heard Kendra talking about it. "No, he doesn't go everywhere with me, but Kendra thought I'd need him here in the city. She wants me to hire him permanently."

"I think that's a good idea," she says.

"Why?"

"I like knowing you're safe."

I can't help the smile that overtakes my face. She knows where I'm going next. She wants me safe. I feel like I've won the fucking lottery and Mallory is the grand prize.

We say our goodbyes and then Kendra joins us in the elevator for the ride down to brief me on tomorrow's schedule, reminding me of my meeting with my manager first thing in the morning. The elevator doors open and we walk out, only to find said manager standing in the building lobby. "It looks like someone can't wait that long," I say to Kendra. "What brings you here this late, Paul?"

He looks at Mallory as if she's an annoyance. "What brings me here?" He pulls out his iPad and shows me a picture. *Shit*. It's a picture of me leaving Mallory's school today. The school name is clearly visible in the background. "Care to explain this?"

Kendra takes the iPad and examines the picture, reading the article underneath that says something about me making a surprise visit. "You visited a school today?"

"Does *she* have anything to do with this?" Paul asks, finally acknowledging Mallory.

"She has a name, Paul." I turn to Mallory. "Mallory Schaffer, this is my manager, Paul Quinn."

"Nice to meet you, Paul," she says.

"Mmmm," he gruffs, dismissing her. "We need to talk, Thad."

"We have a meeting tomorrow," I remind him. "Can't this wait until then?"

"No. This can't wait. When one of my clients goes rogue, we have to do damage control immediately."

"Damage?" I ask, skeptically. "What fallout could there possibly be from me visiting a local elementary school?"

Cole walks in, asking me if we're ready to go. Paul answers him. "Why don't you take Valarie home. I need Thad here."

"It's *Mallory*," I say, irritation pinching between my brows. "And I'll be escorting her home."

"No, it's okay," Mallory says. "I'll be fine. Have your meeting."

I grab her arm and pull her to the side, away from the others. "Mal, I brought you here, I'm taking you home."

"Chad, this is your job. Your manager needs to talk with you. It's okay. I don't mind Cole driving me home. I had a lovely evening. Thank you for having me." She starts walking over to Cole.

"Wait . . . uh, I want to see you again," I say, pissed that I'm having to say goodbye to her in front of an audience.

She turns back around. "I thought you were leaving town tomorrow."

"I've decided to stay in New York until I have to go to Vancouver late next week."

"But you told Carly you were leaving. When did you change your mind?"

I shrug innocently. "As soon as I saw you walk down your stairs tonight."

I watch as a blush works its way up her face. She looks over at Kendra and Cole who are both smiling. She looks at Paul, who's scoffing. She looks back at me. "I'll think about it," she says.

"I know a bunch of nine-year-olds who think you should."

She laughs. "We'll see. Bye, Chad. Thanks again for tonight."

She walks away with Cole and I'm left brooding because my bodyguard gets to take *my* girl home. The girl I wanted to walk up her front steps and kiss. It's the kiss I've been dreaming about since I was fifteen. The kiss I've fantasized over but never thought was possible after all the shit I've pulled. Maybe my luck is changing.

~ ~ ~

Back up in Ethan's office, I sit behind his desk, Kendra and Paul occupying the chairs on the other side. "What's this all about, Paul?"

"What the hell do you think, Thad?" he asks, motioning to his iPad. "You can't just make public appearances without clearing it with me first."

I ignore his question and ask, "Kendra, is Mallory's name on any of this?"

She shakes her head, still going through tabloid sites. "I don't think so. There isn't any mention of the teacher you went to visit."

"Good. Then what's the problem?" I ask Paul.

He scowls furiously. "The problem is you can't do that shit without my approval."

"Do what exactly? Go see a personal friend of mine at her place of employment?"

"This article says you talked to a group of kids about being an actor. I'd say that falls exactly under the umbrella of making it my fucking business," he scolds me.

I shoot an apologetic look to Kendra. I feel guilty I didn't warn her about this. "Listen, I didn't even know I was going there until I was there. I just wanted to talk to Mallory and it ended up turning into some career day gig. Then I made a small donation to some charity fundraiser they were doing."

"Oh, this is good," Kendra says. "I can totally work with this. Thad Stone talks to local kids about acting then makes a charitable donation. Great human interest piece. I'll release it right away to thwart off any rumors about why you were there."

"See," I say to Paul, motioning to Kendra. "No harm done. It's really no big deal."

He puts down his iPad and looks me square in the eye. "Who is this Valerie anyway?"

"Cut the crap, Paul. She's an old friend of mine. One who I hope will be in my life for a very long time. So you'd better get used to it and learn her goddamn name."

He blows out a frustrated breath. "Kendra tells me you plan to stay in New York until the Vancouver junket, is this true?"

"It's only a week. We didn't have anything planned for the break between cities anyway."

"What about *Blind Shot* looping?" he asks, referring to voice-overs for the movie I filmed last fall.

"Done. Finished last week and I got an email two days ago that confirmed the studio got what they needed. You should know this, Paul."

"Don't you need to prepare for Vancouver?" he asks.

"I can do that from here. What's your problem?" I stare him down. I can see him searching his brain for arguments when it dawns on me. "Oh, I get it. Mallory is not Courtney Benson." I shake my head in disgust. "I really don't give a shit if it's not good for box office sales for me to be seen with her."

"You just don't get it, do you?" he asks. "You think you can act for nine weeks, collect a huge paycheck and sit on your ass until the next one? You have a lot to learn, kiddo. Acting is more about promoting. More about making the public fall in love with you off camera as much as on."

"Funny, you don't seem to care when the press brings up all the shit from my past. You don't care if they pair me with ten actresses, as long as one of them is my leading lady."

"It's all about image, Thad. Where's the Hollywood bad boy in dating a boring old school teacher? Hollywood bad boy sells tickets. Hollywood bad boy pays for your lunch."

"Uh, Paul," Kendra interrupts. "Although I agree with some of what you are saying, I'm not so sure Thad dating a school teacher is as deplorable as you might think. His female fans might appreciate the fact that he would date someone who's not an actress. The girl next door so to speak. Someone who could be them. Who knows, it could have quite the opposite effect."

"That's ridiculous," Paul says. "Nobody wants to see you with a school teacher."

I stand up, almost knocking my chair over in anger. "This meeting is over. As my manager, I realize you have a say in my professional life. But I draw the fucking line at you thinking you can tell me who I can and can't date. Remember that when your contract comes up for renewal, Paul. Remember that you are replaceable."

He laughs a cocky laugh. "If I were you, I'd remember who got you to where you are today, Thad. You've been on top for exactly ten minutes. Replacing you with the next up-and-coming wouldn't be hard. You'd be forgotten by next Christmas. Trust me."

"Okay, you guys. Nobody is getting replaced," Kendra says, trying to smooth things over. "Let's adjourn this meeting and regroup tomorrow at nine at the hotel. Paul, I think you're making too much out of this. Thad was just taking a friend to his brother's house for dinner. Thad, you'll be leaving in a week and you may not want to start something you can't finish. Please, let's all sleep on this."

"Fine." Paul flashes me a mutinous stare before he gets up in a huff and lets himself out.

"Thad," Kendra says, pulling me aside before leaving herself. "Mallory is absolutely lovely. I see the way you look at her. I know you have a lot of history together. But you'd better be sure this is what you want. You can't take a girl like that down this path unless you truly mean it."

"I'm sure, Kendra," I say without so much as a hint of doubt. "I've been sure since I was seven years old."

Samantha Christy

CHAPTER TEN

Mallory

Teaching is hard today. I can't keep my mind focused and away from last night. The way he looked at me. The way he touched me. It was almost like fifteen-year-old Mallory hanging out with sixteen-year-old Chad, but with serious sexual tension. Then there are the texts he's sent today. He hasn't asked to see me again; they've just been funny and casual. Letting me know he had a good time last night; he and his one testicle. Telling me he hopes I'm having a good day.

I find myself disappointed come the end of the school day that he hasn't asked me out, and I wonder what that means. Do I want him to ask me out because I want to be with him? Or just because I want to feel like I'm worthy of the superstar he has become?

I lost a lot of sleep last night wondering if I can even blame him for everything he did when he was under the influence of drugs. I mean, yes, I blame him for getting involved with drugs, but once someone is physically addicted, do they have control over their actions? And is what he did to me really that bad in the overall scheme of things? It's not unusual for friends to move away and lose touch.

Maybe I'm just making excuses so it's easier for me to justify seeing him again.

Then a sick feeling washes over me. The person who killed my mom was drunk. He ran her off the road and right into a telephone pole, killing her instantly on the way home from her overnight nursing shift. *He* was held responsible for his actions. He was an alcoholic who went to jail for three years—not nearly long enough to make up for the time we'll never have with her. Damn right he should be held responsible. Nobody forced the guy to drink. Just like nobody forced Chad to use cocaine.

I decide to visit my mom's grave in the cemetery on the way home. Ask her what she thinks about all this. She loved Chad like a son. She loved all the Stone boys, but she had a sweet spot for Chad. Everybody did.

When I arrive home, there's another strange car in the driveway and my heartbeat quickens. I want it to be him. I want it to be him more than I've ever wanted anything. But in some strange way, at the same time, I don't. But there's no Cole standing next to the car. I peek in the car windows before closing the garage, just to see if I can get a clue as to who is visiting. But when I go in the house, I can hear exactly who it is.

I walk into the living room. "Hi, Kendra. Nice to see you again."

"You too, Mallory. I was just telling your dad that you have a lovely home."

"Thank you. Did you come to see where Chad grew up?" I motion to the front door. "I'm sure the neighbors won't mind if you want to see his old house."

"I came to see you, Mallory."

"Me?"

She nods. "Is it okay if we sit for a while?"

"Uh, yeah." I look at my dad and he shrugs, giving me no indication of why she's here. "Can I get you a drink first? Water, coffee?"

"Thanks, your dad already offered. I don't want to take up much of your time." She nods to the couch. "Is here okay?"

I walk over and sit down.

"Nice to meet you, Kendra," my dad says. "I'm going to start dinner, Mallory. Take your time."

"It was a pleasure meeting you, Richard." She sits next to me. "Your dad seems great. And he's a doctor. Impressive."

"Yeah, he's pretty great," I agree.

She points to a family picture on the mantle. "And your mom, what does she do?"

"My mom died seven years ago," I tell her. "It's just us now."

Kendra's face falls into a frown. "I'm so sorry. I lost my mom at a young age as well. I know how hard it must be for you."

"Thanks. Sorry you lost yours," I say.

"We have a lot in common," she says, followed by a deep sigh. "I have a feeling one of those things is loving Thad . . . uh, Chad."

Two things happen at once. My jaw drops. And my heart breaks. She loves him? Of course she does. She's here to shoo me away. But it doesn't make any sense, given what she said to me last night.

Kendra starts laughing at my reaction. She scoots closer and puts her hand on my arm. "Oh, gosh, that obviously came out the wrong way. No, no, I love him, but I don't *love* him. I'm married." She shows me her ring and then studies me for a second. "But if your face is any indication, I believe I've hit the nail on the head."

"Huh?" I ask, still fazed.

"You care for him, don't you?" she says with a motherly smile.

"We grew up together. We went through a lot back then. So, yeah, I guess I do. But I don't know him anymore. Things are different."

"I don't disagree that people change, Mallory. And I won't try to defend his past actions. I've only known him for three months myself, and of course, I didn't know him back when you did. But I can tell you this—if I had a daughter, there isn't anyone I'd rather see her with than that man." She shakes her head laughing. "Let me clarify. Not that I'd necessarily want my daughter dating a star, but the man he is inside—the huge heart he has—that's the kind of guy I would wish for her."

"Back when we were kids, he was like that," I tell her. "He was always protecting me. Helping me. Helping our friend Julian or his brothers. He didn't have a mean bone in his body. Well, unless you were hurting someone he loved. Then, all bets were off."

"Sounds like the same guy I've come to know and love," she says. "I get that you see him as the star he is today. The bad-boy persona that is plastered all over the news. Maybe that was him for a few years when he lost his way, but not anymore. It's the press who keep trying to make him fit that same mold, twisting everything you see and read to make it look like that is still who he is. But I'm here to tell you it's not. Don't believe everything you hear. That's rule number one of Hollywood, listen with deaf ears."

"What about Courtney?" I ask.

"What about her?"

"Well, aren't they sort of dating . . . or whatever?" *Probably a lot of whatever.*

"Is that what you think?" She shakes her head vehemently. "I told you, Mallory, don't believe everything you hear. Pairing them as a couple is good for the box office. He's told not to deny it."

I look up at her, surprised. "What?"

She nods. "It's all part of the game," she says. "You really should be asking Chad about this. However, I will tell you that they did date briefly around the time of filming, but it didn't work out. There were a lot of pictures taken of them during that time. They keep resurfacing. And if you ask me, Courtney likes it that way."

I pick at a spot on the couch. "So they're not . . ."

"Not for a long time," she says.

I feel a huge sense of relief; like I'd been holding my breath since he walked into my life, but now I can come up for air. "What you whispered to me last night, about me being the one, what does that mean?"

"You must see the way he looks at you, Mallory. It's the same way my husband looks at me. The man is completely smitten. I haven't seen him so much as look at another woman since he saw you outside the club on Saturday."

"But there are so many of them. Why me?"

She gives me a scolding look. "Why not you, Mallory? You are nice. You're beautiful. You have a history together that nobody can even come close to."

I eye her skeptically. "Did Chad send you here to get me to go out with him?"

She guffaws. "Lord no. And to be honest, Mallory, I'm not sure if I'm here to encourage you to date him or to warn you away."

"Warn me?"

"Yes. Listen, I love Chad to death, but you need to know that dating a celebrity comes at a hefty price. You'll lose your anonymity. Some of your freedom. As soon as the press finds out about you, every facet of your relationship will be plastered across tabloids, internet and entertainment TV. You may develop a fan base of your own. You may even get hate mail."

I take in a sharp breath. "Hate mail?"

She nods reassuringly. "You have what others want."

"I don't *have* anything," I tell her.

"Oh, but you do. You have that man's heart."

I find myself tearing up at her words. I wanted him for so many years. I think I fell in love with him when I was six, the minute he stood up to those bullies for me. Every boy in my life— every man—has been compared to him—the younger version of him—and none have measured up. I tried like hell to erase him from my life back then. I did stupid, destructive things. But no one has ever been able to take his place. Strings of failed relationships plagued me until I just gave up and stopped dating. I thought the problem was me, but maybe it was Chad all along—or the fact that he'd had *my* heart, making me unable to truly give it to anyone else.

Kendra takes my hand. "I know this is a lot to take in. And it's unfair to you. You shouldn't have to deal with all the crap that comes along with him. New relationships can be hard enough as it is. But it's a package deal if you want to be with him. And it's already started, you know. There is a picture of you out there."

I'm completely caught off guard. "A picture of *me?*"

She nods reluctantly. "From the night of the premiere. It's only your profile. You can't even tell it's you. But after Chad's reaction to seeing you that night, some photographer took your picture and it ended up on the morning show Chad did yesterday. I'm assuming he didn't tell you about it because he didn't want to alarm you. And it's not a big deal. Not yet anyway. But it will be. With him going to your school and then you showing up together at his brother's residence—it won't take long before the press put it all together."

I sink back into the couch cushion trying to figure out how I feel about all of this.

"I'm not telling you this to scare you away," she says. "But I do want you to think long and hard about it. If you don't think you can handle it, please don't get his hopes up any more than they already are. I don't want to see him get hurt, Mallory. And I think you may be one of the only things in this world that can truly hurt him."

I take in a shaky breath, still trying to hold back my tears. "It—it's a lot to think about."

She pulls a business card out of her purse and hands it to me. "I'm his publicist. It's my job to know everything that's going on with him so I can put out fires and get as much good press out there as I can. If you ever have any questions about what you see or hear, call me. Don't jump to conclusions. Nine times out of ten what you see is not true, or at least it's a twisted version of it. But woman-to-woman and not publicist-to-girlfriend, you can trust me to be straight with you."

Girlfriend? My head is spinning.

"I like you a lot, Mallory. I think you'd be great for him. And to be honest, I think you'd be great for his career. People seeing him with someone who's not an actor might be a benefit. Tone down that bad-boy persona and all."

I fold my restless hands together in my lap. "That's not what his manager thinks."

"Who, Paul?" she scoffs with a rebellious look. "Don't pay any attention to that stick in the mud."

"But he's not the only one who would disapprove," I say. "His fans. Courtney Benson. God knows who else wouldn't want him with me. I feel it would be an uphill battle."

She nods. "It may well be. And you need to figure out if it's worth it. If *he's* worth it."

My eyes snap to hers as I absorb the words she's said. She gives me a sympathetic look as she stands up and slings her purse over her shoulder. "You *do* have a lot to think about. But remember this, just because he's a celebrity does not mean his heart can't break just like everyone else's."

After she leaves, I head into the kitchen and sit at the table, eyeing the spaghetti dinner my dad has prepared for us. I try to get myself to eat, but find I'm mostly pushing food around on my plate.

"You're awfully quiet," Dad says.

I nod. "Sorry."

"Did Mom ever tell you the story of how she and I got together?" he asks.

"You were a resident and she was a new nurse, right?"

"That's right," he says. "Residency is just this side of being in hell. Your life does not belong to you, it belongs to the hospital. You have no time to date. No time to do anything but learn. Your fellow residents become your family. They are who you spend all your time with. It's no joke what you see on TV about residents sleeping together in on-call rooms. It happens. It happens because there's just no time to do it anywhere else."

"Then how did you have time for Mom?" I ask.

"I didn't, that was the problem." He gets up to put his plate in the sink, coming back with a bottle of beer for each of us.

I smile when he puts mine on the table in front of me. When I was younger, he'd set out milk and cookies when he wanted to have a talk. How times have changed.

"I was a new resident and your mom had recently started her nursing career. Neither of us knew what we were doing and both of us were trying to impress our supervisors. But as doctors, we're supposed to know more than nurses. Especially new nurses."

He settles into his seat and takes a sip of beer. "One day, a man was brought to the hospital for a supposed panic attack and none of the residents could figure out what was going on with him. Your mom was standing in the corner of the room and made a comment under her breath. Our attending physician heard her and made her repeat what she said. Her face turned red. Her hands were shaking. But she stepped forward and told us that maybe we should check his thyroid levels because based on his symptoms it sounded like he could be in hyperthyroid crisis." He laughs, shaking his head at the memory. "Turns out she was right. This young, wet-behind-the-ears nurse put four residents to shame by diagnosing our patient. And she taught us all a lesson, one that our attending never failed to keep reminding us of—to think outside the box. Men rarely present with thyroid disorders. Especially younger men as that one was."

I smile, proud of the mother I only got to know for seventeen years. "Is that why you started dating her?"

"Oh, no. I think we all hated her for embarrassing us in front of our boss. But she did earn my respect. And I can tell you, from that day on, I looked at nurses differently. It wasn't until a year later that I'd really noticed her. I was leaning towards orthopedics as my specialty and she happened to have transferred to that department so we kept crossing paths. My schedule was still hectic. I knew I wouldn't get to see her much if we dated, but I took a chance and asked her out anyway. She turned me down for months."

I look up at him, surprised. "She did?"

"Yes. She knew my schedule. She knew how second-years were tied to the hospital. She also knew I'd had a reputation for hanging out in the on-call rooms."

"Dad, really?" I ask, my mouth hanging open.

He nods bashfully. "Sorry, did I just ruin my chances for Father of the Year?"

I laugh. "Of course not, that was before you dated her." *Oh, God, at least I hope so.* "It *was* before you dated her, right?"

He pats my hand reassuringly. "From the moment I asked her out, I never even looked at another woman."

I smile, thinking of how Kendra said the same thing about Chad. "So how did you get her to go out with you?"

"It wasn't easy," he says. "I basically stalked her at the hospital. I'd show up in the cafeteria when she was eating lunch. I made friends with the nurse manager who would put your mom on some of my cases. I'd leave funny notes in patient charts knowing she'd see them."

"So you finally wore her down," I say, amused to be hearing the story of my parents' courtship. Especially since we rarely talk about my mom. It causes him too much pain.

"I did, but it didn't come without challenges. She had a lot to overcome. My schedule. The demands of my job. My past indiscretions." He finishes his beer and takes my plate over to the sink.

"So why do you think she did it?" I ask. "Why did she put up with all of that?"

He turns around and leans against the sink. He looks me square in the eye. "I guess she thought I was worth it."

My eyes become misty for the second time tonight. "You were listening?"

He pulls on his earlobe. "Ears of a dog," he says.

I get up from the table and walk over to hug him. How does he always manage to do that—give me advice without it being so obvious? As I hug him, I smile. I smile because I realize he's just had the most wonderful conversation with me about my mother and it didn't make him sad. In fact, from the look on his face, he enjoyed those memories. Maybe he's finally healing. "Thank you, Daddy. I love you."

He hugs me tightly, kissing the top of my head. "I love you too, pumpkin."

CHAPTER ELEVEN

Chad

Mallory has turned me down twice since last night. Making excuses about being busy and how I'm only in town for a few more days. I don't care if I'm leaving in two days or two years, I want to take her out on a proper date. I've always wanted to do that, ever since I was little. I'm just not going to beg.

That's not true. I probably would beg. But I'm not quite there yet. No, I've got something else in mind.

I dribble the ball around her driveway, working on my trick shots. I've been to Ethan's gym every day this week practicing for this moment.

I smile when I hear a car turn into the driveway behind me. And even though she shot me down, I'm pretty sure I see her smile through the windshield of her compact car. I step aside so she can pull into the garage. She exits the car, arms piled high with folders. I run over to help her out before she spills them all over the garage.

"Hi. Thanks," she says, willingly letting me take the load from her.

I nod to the heavy pile of papers in my hands. "How much homework do you give those kids? I thought you'd be one of those cool teachers who doesn't pile a ton of work on your students."

"First off," she says, scolding me with a hot-teacher look that has me needing to adjust my pants, "Cool teachers *do* give homework. And second, I've been a bit otherwise occupied this week and haven't had a chance to grade these papers yet."

"Otherwise occupied?" I ask, looking down at her with raised brows. "I only occupied you for two nights. Whose ass do I have to kick for occupying the other two?"

She rolls her eyes at me. "No one's," she says, walking towards the door to the house. "Come on, you can put those down in the kitchen."

I follow her in, happy to have my foot in the door so to speak. I put her things down and turn around to face her. "Why won't you go to dinner with me?"

She sighs, shaking her head. "It's not a good idea, Chad. Someone could see us. I don't want to cause a stir. And you're leaving soon."

"You keep saying I'm leaving soon. But why does that mean we can't be friends?"

She stares at me. She stares at me hard. Her eyes tell me everything she's thinking.

"Shit," I say, finally realizing the obvious. "I'm not going to do that again, Mal. I promise to stay in touch this time. I'll even come back. Or you can come see me. Don't shut me out. Please?"

Okay, so maybe it is time for begging.

"I don't know," she says, leaning against the counter. "It's just all so complicated."

"It doesn't have to be," I tell her.

She sighs again. She's going to say no, I can feel it.

"Let's play for it," I say, nodding towards the garage.

"You want to play HORSE to get me to go to dinner with you? You do realize you never win, don't you?"

My lips curve into a devious smile. "I've never been this motivated before," I say. "Plus, I've been practicing. And I'm starving. I haven't eaten all day, so can we hurry this along?"

Her eyes go wide. "Tonight? You want to do dinner *tonight?*" She looks over at the pile of papers on the counter. "I can't, Chad. I have so much to do."

"First, it's Friday. You have all weekend to grade papers. Second, if you really need them graded that badly, I'll help you."

She gives me that scolding hot-teacher look again. Damn, she has to quit doing that. "*You'll* grade papers?"

"It'd be fun," I say. "I always wanted to be a teacher you know."

"Yeah, I know. I know everything about you." She looks down at the floor, frowning. "Well, I used to."

I step up next to her. "You can again, Mal. Just give me a chance." I nod to the door that leads to the garage. "Come on. Let me try to win that date."

She shakes her head. "Not a date," she says. "Just dinner. *If* you win."

"Game on, Mal." I take her hand and drag her behind me out to the driveway.

~ ~ ~

Mallory stares at the orange ball as it rolls off the driveway and lays to rest in the bushes. "I can't believe you won."

"Believe it, baby," I say, smiling from ear to ear. Although if I'm being totally honest, and I hope I am, I'd say she had something to do with it. I look at my watch. "You have exactly one hour to get ready. Now find me a red pen so I can play teacher."

For the next sixty minutes, I transform into Chad Stone—school teacher. I have a ball grading dozens of papers that are dated all the way back to Monday. Was she really so distracted by me that she hasn't been able to do anything since then?

For a while, I wonder what life would have been like for us if I'd have stayed here and followed that dream. Would we still live in this town? Maybe even in one of these houses? Life would be so simple. So perfectly normal. No. I love what I do. I just don't always love the crap that comes along with it.

I hear her heels click on the hardwood as she comes downstairs. I put the papers away, happy that I've made a good dent in them for her. When she comes around the corner, my heart stops. "Uh, Mal . . . if you don't want this to be a date, don't wear shit like that."

My eyes travel the length of her from head to toe. She has another green blouse on, this one darker than the one she wore to Ethan's. It makes her eyes stand out. But tonight, instead of jeans, she's wearing a black skirt. A *short* black skirt. I can see her shapely legs. Legs that beg to be wrapped around a man. And that man better bloody well be me.

"You didn't say where we were going, so I hope this will do," she says.

I tamp down my boyish fantasies about fourth-grade teachers in sinfully short skirts. "You're gonna kill me, Ms. Schaffer."

Mallory rifles through the papers I graded, smiling as she flips from one to the next.

"What?" I ask. "Didn't think a college drop-out could grade a bunch of nine-year-olds' math problems?"

She shakes her head laughing. "It's not that." She flips one of the papers around and points to the upper corner. "I just didn't think a big movie star would draw smiley faces on them."

"Well, I didn't have any of those gold star stickers. Do they still use those?"

"Not so much anymore, we use stamps and, um . . . smiley faces," she says, rolling those gorgeous emerald-green eyes.

"Ha! See—I'm *so* an awesome school teacher. I missed my calling."

She straightens the pile of papers and puts them back in a folder. "No, you definitely did not miss your calling."

Now I'm the one smiling. "Oh, really? Are you telling me you've seen my movies, Ms. Schaffer?"

"Don't call me Ms. Schaffer, it's kind of pervy."

I laugh. "Answer the question, Mal." I walk over and stand in front of her. "Have. You. Seen. My. Movies? Simple question."

"Not the new one," she says, still refusing to outright admit anything.

"So you have? And what about *Malibu*? I know you watched season one, but after . . . did you watch the others?"

She looks anywhere but at me.

"Come on, Mal."

She scrunches her nose, putting a cute-as-hell wrinkle in it. "Okay, fine. I watched them. All seventy-two episodes. Are you happy now?"

She pouts, heading for the door but I grab her hand and pull her back to me, landing her so close, our faces are only inches apart. I get a good whiff of her incredible scent. God, she even *smells* like a school teacher—fresh and clean and innocent, yet so damn sexy. "What's the name of your perfume?"

She narrows her eyes at me. "It's called 'Desire Me'. Why?"

Of course it is. I repeat it over and over in my head so I don't forget the name. *As if.* I'll need to know it later, for when I send her a gallon of it. "Just curious, that's all. It's nice."

"Thanks, I like it, too. Are you ready to go? I thought you were starving."

I open the door for her and eye her legs as she walks through. "Yes, I absolutely am."

We load up in the backseat of the car and I tell Cole where to take us. "The Pizza Garden on 5th, please."

He punches it into the GPS as Mallory squeals. Good, I was hoping that was the reaction I'd get. "Still your favorite place?" I ask.

"Are you kidding? I think they've gotten even better since you lived here." She squirms happily in her seat. *Lucky fucking seat.* "Wait until you taste it," she says. "You'll go nuts."

"I'm looking forward to it."

"Wait. We can't go there," she says, looking disappointed. "It's Friday night. It'll be packed."

"Don't worry about it," I tell her.

"Don't worry?" She looks slightly panicked. "One of us has to, Chad. You shouldn't be seen out with me."

She doesn't realize what I have planned, but her comment pisses me off anyway. The way she said it was self-deprecating. Like she was somehow worried about what it would look like if I were to be seen with 'someone like' her. "Why the hell not?"

"Isn't it obvious?" she says, holding out her arms and looking down at herself.

"Jesus, Mallory, would you quit that shit? You are gorgeous and smart and generous, and any man would be honored to be seen with you. You were never self-conscious when we were younger. Why now?"

"Oh, let's see," she says, looking around the car. "Maybe because when we were younger you didn't have a bodyguard-slash-driver. Or maybe because you weren't a gazillionaire movie star. Or maybe because you weren't dating beautiful actresses or hobnobbing with famous athletes. Should I go on?"

"Gazillionaire?" I mock. "Is that even a word?"

"Whatever. I mean, come on, Chad. You have to admit, this is all pretty intimidating for someone like me."

"It shouldn't be. You should have everything that I have. You should have it and more. I want to give it to you."

She stares at me in the darkness of the back seat. "You can't say things like that."

"I can say whatever the hell I want, Mal. I've never censored myself with you and I'm not about to start now. I want to see you. I want to take you on a real date. And at the end of that date, I want to kiss you. I want to kiss you until your knees go weak. I want to kiss you so long and so hard that any other kiss you've ever had with another guy will seem inconsequential. I'm not going to hide how I feel, and I'm sure as shit not going to feel badly about it."

Mallory is frozen to the seat, speechless. I glance at Cole, who has been witness to the entire conversation. He catches my eyes in the rearview mirror and smiles. Cole doesn't smile.

"I—I'm just a little overwhelmed, I guess," she says, straightening her skirt. "This is all so new to me, Chad. You've had years to get used to the money and the fame and this new life that goes with it. You can't expect me to accept it all in six short days. Can we take a breath, please? Can we have dinner and talk about things like we used to? Can we just be friends tonight before we make any decisions?"

I get what she's saying. I do. But once you've made a decision about your life, you want to get on with it and start living. "I've already made mine," I tell her. "But yeah, we can just have dinner and talk. Being with you tonight is all I wanted. The rest can wait."

She takes in a deep breath and lets it out slowly. I can see the tension leaving her as we drive through the city. Cole pulls into the alley in the back and knocks on the rear door to the restaurant.

Mallory looks sideways at me. "Sneaking in the back, are we?"

"It's all part of my plan to seduce you," I tease. "Nothing screams sexy like wading through dumpsters and homeless people to impress your girl."

"You're terrible," she says, swatting my leg.

I trap her hand on my thigh and hold it there until Cole opens the door for us. The best part about it is, she lets me.

"Everything set?" I ask Cole.

He nods. "Just like you asked." He escorts us the ten feet from the car to the back door of the restaurant. "I'll park it and be close by if you need me."

"Welcome, Mr. Stone," says the small Italian man with a heavy accent who greets us at the door. "I'm Mario, the owner of this establishment. Anything you want, just ask. Follow me. I set a good table for you in back. Far from the windows. No one will see."

He walks us into the main dining room. It's dark and quiet, with candles in the center of each table providing just enough light so we don't trip over anything. He points to a large table in the back corner. It's set with a red-and-white-checkered tablecloth.

Mallory takes in the barren dining room, looking from one empty table to the next. She questions me with her eyes as we make our way to the table with the most candles. There is already a bottle of champagne chilling and a glass of her favorite beer on the table.

At least I think it's her favorite. It's the kind she had at her house when I shared one with her dad. Maybe it's only her dad's favorite. *Shit*—there is so much I need to learn about her. I just hope she'll let me.

She thanks Mario for seating us and then turns to me with a hard stare. "Where is everybody?"

"I didn't want us to be bothered. Sometimes this is the only way."

Her jaw drops. "You rented out the whole restaurant for the night?"

"Not the whole thing," I say. "They still do delivery. Don't worry, the people of New York can still have their favorite pizza tonight."

"That must've cost you hundreds, or maybe thousands. Chad, you shouldn't have."

I'm not about to tell her it cost me over ten grand. "Don't worry about it." I can see she's about to argue the point, so I add, "I didn't do it to impress you, Mallory. I did it for me. I just wanted one night where I could go out and feel normal. Go to a regular place like everyone else and enjoy dinner like everyone else does, without cameras going off every ten seconds. Without having to pretend I don't mind being interrupted twenty times when I'm trying to eat. Without having to worry about every goddamn facial expression and mannerism because they could end up plastered all over TMZ. This was our place, Mal. I wanted to bring you here for a normal dinner. Please don't make me feel bad about it."

She closes her eyes and takes a breath. Then she looks at me with a sad smile. "I'm sorry. I didn't even think about what it must be like for you to have a night out. Of course you should be allowed to go to your favorite places without being mobbed. I don't know how you do it." She looks around the old familiar place we used to come to on special occasions. "Thank you for bringing me here. It looks the same, but somehow different."

My eyes don't leave her face. "I completely agree."

She takes a drink of her beer, smiling at the taste. "You got my favorite," she says. Then she nods at my glass of ice water. "You're not drinking? Does it bother you that I am? I don't have to."

"It doesn't bother me at all, Mal. I want you to enjoy yourself." I point to the ice bucket next to the table. "I'm saving myself for the good stuff."

She laughs. "Pizza and champagne. Now I know I've died and gone to heaven."

That laugh. This girl. I'm the one who's in fucking heaven.

CHAPTER TWELVE

Mallory

He watches me take another drink, almost like he's jealous of the glass. "Wait a second," he says. "You said this place looks the same but different. I thought you said you'd been here since we were kids. In the car, you said the pizza is even better now."

I shake my head. I haven't stepped foot in this place since he left. It didn't seem right. It was *our* place. "I haven't been inside since we were kids. But my friend, Melissa, lives a few blocks over and sometimes we get takeout when I crash there."

My phone rings. Darn, I forgot to shut off the ringer. "Sorry," I say, switching the sound off. I notice Julian is trying to call me. *So* not a good time.

A waitress arrives, putting a hot loaf of sliced cheese bread on the table. She fumbles with it, almost spilling it in my lap, obviously nervous about serving the famous Thad Stone. "You really can't get away from it, can you?" I ask after she leaves the table.

He shrugs. "Sometimes I put on a ball cap and glasses and go out and walk the streets, just to feel anonymous for a little while."

I shake my head at the thought of it. "You have to disguise yourself just to take a walk? I have to ask, is it worth it? Is making movies worth all the lost freedom? I mean, you have enough money without it, so why do it if you don't like all the attention?"

"Why did *you* do it?" he asks me. "Why did you act in all those plays in middle school and high school?"

I think about his question as I pick at a piece of bread. "I don't know, I guess because I liked pretending to be something I wasn't. Because I liked making other people happy when they watched me. And maybe because I thought I was good at it."

He nods. "You were *great* at it, Mal. And that's why I do it— for all those reasons and more. It's the most rewarding thing I've ever done. It's something I can be proud of. I'd do it even if they didn't pay me for it."

My phone starts vibrating across the table. Chad motions to it. "Someone really wants to get a hold of you. You should answer it."

"Okay. I'll make it quick." I pick up my phone and look at the screen. Darn, it's Julian again. I shoot a guilty glance at Chad before I answer it. "Hey."

"Hey to you, too," Julian says. "What's up?"

"Not much. Just getting a bite to eat." I peek at Chad who is munching on a piece of bread.

"Having anything interesting? Or any*one?*" He laughs.

I shift uncomfortably in my seat. This is not the time to tell him I'm out with Chad. "Uh, no, it's just me." I hate lying to him. But I don't have time for him to give me a lecture.

"Want to meet up tonight? There's a band I've been wanting to see that will be playing at Gringo's later."

"I can't. I have to grade papers." I look anywhere but at Chad. He's stopped eating and I can feel his eyes burning into me.

"It's Friday, Mallory. Can't those wait?" Julian pouts.

"I know it's Friday, but I have so much work to do. It's just not a good night, Julian. Listen, I have to go, I'll call you tomorrow, okay? We'll make plans then." It's such an obvious blow-off, I expect him to argue, but he doesn't.

"Fine. Talk to you tomorrow then," he says, disconnecting the call without saying goodbye.

Could he know what I'm doing tonight? No, it's impossible. I didn't even know what I was doing tonight until a few hours ago. I put my phone away so there will be no more interruptions. "I'm sorry about that."

"Julian?" Chad asks. "He wanted to go out with you?"

"He wanted to see a new band."

"Why didn't you tell him you were with me?"

I pause, taking a thoughtful drink before I answer him. But instead, I ask a question of my own. "Why haven't you called him?"

"Because he's had something I've always wanted." He stares at me in the dim light of the restaurant. Even in the relative darkness, I can read his eyes. And I'm pretty sure they are telling me all the things I wanted to hear when I was fifteen. All the things every girl wants to hear. But is it too little, too late? "That's my excuse," he says. "What's yours?"

"Uh . . ." Like in the backseat of the car, it seems he's rendered me speechless. "I guess I didn't want to stir things up."

"He knows you've been talking to me though, right?"

I nod.

"And he's not happy about it," he says.

"He thinks you'll hurt me again," I tell him.

"I'm not going to hurt you, Mal. I promise."

"He's just watching out for me like always."

Pain washes across Chad's face. I know I hurt him when I say things like that. But he needs to remember that I can't just forget the past. He needs to know life went on without him and he can't simply waltz back into my life and pick up where we left off.

"Will you tell me about you and him?" he asks. "You know, like when did you start dating and for how long?"

"There's not much to tell," I say. *Except for maybe that he cheated on me, ruined our friendship, and further broke the trust I placed in men.* "We got together after my mom died. He helped me through it and I guess I was at the point where I needed something more. But we only dated for a year."

"What happened?"

It's too soon to reveal all my secrets to the boy who abandoned me. "We just wanted different things, I guess."

"But you stayed friends. That's good."

I nod. "It took a while to rebuild our friendship, but we got there. And now he and Melissa are my best friends."

Chad's eyebrows shoot up. "So there's a chance for you and me after all, huh? I mean, if you rebuilt your friendship with Julian . . ."

And therein lies my dilemma. Julian cheated on me. He did one of the worst things a boy can do to a girl. How can I forgive him for that and not forgive Chad for merely forgetting me when his parents moved him away? *Maybe because losing Chad felt so much worse than losing Julian.*

"Maybe," I say. "But there is so much I don't know about you anymore."

He spreads his arms wide open, leaning back in his chair. "What do you want to know? I'm an open book for you, Mal."

I really want to know what sent him to rehab. What horrible thing happened that made him realize he needed to get clean? What life-changing event prompted him to sober up? The thing he said would make me hate him. But I don't ask. I don't ask because I fear it might have to do with another woman. One who gave him an ultimatum perhaps. One who he loved so much he got clean for. The thought of him being in love hurts my heart. It physically causes my chest to constrict and my throat to tighten.

Our server arrives, placing a large pizza on the table. I look at it and then smile at Chad. "You remembered?"

He leans over to get the champagne out of the ice bucket, waving off Mario when he rushes over to help him. "Of course I remembered. I remember everything about you. I remember you like spinach on your pizza. And that you don't like red M&Ms. And that you prefer your water without ice because you think your body will have to work too hard to get it back to body temperature." He turns away from me, popping the cork in the other direction, laughing at me when I plug my ears. "And that you hate loud noises that sound like gunshots."

He pours us each a glass and then raises his. "To . . . possibilities."

I hesitate before raising mine. He frowns. "Come on, Mal. Throw a guy a bone here. I'm really trying."

I think about everything he's done for me this week. Coming to my house and talking with my dad. Showing up at the school. Ethan's dinner. Tonight. And then I think about the fact that all week long, he's done everything right. He's been nice, funny, chivalrous, generous. And those eyes, I swear I could get lost in them. I raise my glass. "To possibilities," I say.

"So, open book," he says, serving me a slice. "Shoot."

"Okay. Tell me about Courtney Benson."

He brings a hand to his neck. "Going right for the jugular, eh?"

"We have to start somewhere." I take a huge bite of my dinner, never losing eye contact.

"See, that's what I love about you. You're very direct. And you aren't afraid to eat in front of me, even when you get spinach in your teeth."

I use my free hand to cover my mouth. "Oh, fudge. I have spinach in my teeth?"

He laughs. "No, you don't. But I'll give you a thousand bucks right now if you say the word fuck."

I feel the heat cross my face. It's not that I haven't said the word. I've said it plenty of times. Like when I stub my toe in the middle of the night walking to the bathroom. Or when I failed my first calculus exam. But for some reason, I can't say it to him. *Maybe it's because you've always wanted to do it to him.*

"You don't actually have a thousand dollars with you, do you?" I hold up my hand before he speaks. "Wait, don't answer that. I really don't want to know if you have more in your pocket than I make in one week."

He finishes his slice and then refills my glass and only my glass. "So, you want to know about Courtney." He puts the bottle back in the ice bucket and wipes his hands. "As I'm sure you already know, we dated for a while last year. We met during *Defcon One* pre-production, hit it off and were together most of the summer and throughout filming. I broke it off when I found out she was using drugs. I tasted it on her one day and it scared the shit out of me. What if just kissing her would get me hooked on it again? It wasn't a chance I was willing to take. I don't think she's a hard-core user like I was, but it was a deal-breaker for me."

"And what about the others?" I ask, as long as he's given me carte blanche. "Heather Crawford and Ana Garner? That Tanya woman said you have a history of dating your leading women."

"You saw the show, huh? I was wondering if you did. I didn't want to say anything to freak you out and send you running for the hills so soon."

"I saw it." I don't tell him that Kendra was the one who told me about it and that I had to search my TV for past episodes until I found it.

He holds up two fingers. "Twice I've dated a leading lady. Not *every* time like she made it out to be. I dated Heather way back when. Then there was Courtney. It was bullshit what Tanya said about Ana. Ana and I are friends, but we never dated." He chews on his lip in thought. "I took Lila Knox out for dinner a few times, she had a supporting role on *Malibu*. Other than that, I've dated some random women. Would you like me to compile a list?"

"I'm not sure we could come up with enough paper," I joke.

His hand covers his heart. "Ouch, Mal. That hurt. In any case, that falls under the 'shit from the past' category, okay? That's not me anymore."

"Not anymore, huh?" I ask skeptically. "Then tell me, who is the last woman you slept with and when?"

His jaw drops at my temerity.

"You said open book, Chad."

I can see he's at war with himself on how to answer the question. *Oh, God, please don't let it be this week.* I take a very large sip of my champagne, draining the glass.

"That I did. Okay then, it was late last year. Her name was Nikki and she's the daughter of one of the *Blind Shot* producers. She lives here in New York, so anytime I was here last fall, she would be my date. We hooked up a few times but it was casual. Courtney was my last relationship."

He refills my glass for the third time. "Do I get to ask you the same question?"

My answer comes quickly. "No."

He frowns and looks at the table. "Please don't tell me it was this week, Mal."

I can't help but smile that his words matched my very thoughts. I laugh. "No, not this week. *So* far removed from this week it's downright embarrassing."

Now *he's* the one smiling. Smiling a little too big if you ask me. But it doesn't last long as his face turns somber and he runs a hand through his hair. "I'm not sure I want the answer to this, but was Julian your first?"

I look down at the table, not very fond of remembering that low time in my life. "No. Julian and I never—"

"Wait," he interrupts. "*Never?* You dated for a year and you never . . . not once?"

I shake my head. "It's complicated. And you don't have to look so darn happy about it."

"Never," he whispers under his breath, looking at me in disbelief as the smile returns to his face.

"What about you?" I ask, not missing an opportunity to quid pro quo. "Who was *your* first?"

He closes his eyes and shakes his head. When he opens them, he looks directly at me, holding my stare with his like a tractor beam. I fear he's going to tell me something I don't want to hear because I see so much truth behind those blue eyes. He reaches over and puts his hand on top of mine. "Someone who should have been you."

For the third time tonight, his words slay me and all I can do is stare at him. Take in his golden-blonde hair that is longer than he kept it when we were younger. Take in his handsome face that has grown more manly over the years. Take in his hand on top of mine and the intense feelings plowing through my body from his simple touch. And I realize in this moment that even though my mind is telling me it's a bad idea—even though my heart may never survive another beating from him—even though all odds are against us, I know that I want this man more than I've ever wanted anything. And right here, right now, I decide that yes, maybe the boy I grew up with is worth everything I've endured and everything I'll have to go through to get him. I blink, sending tears rolling down my cheeks.

He reads my bleeding eyes. He knows every thought that crosses behind them. He always has. He moves his chair closer to mine and wipes away my tears. "Mallory, I want this. I want to give this a chance. More than anything. But being with me comes at a price. One you might not want to pay. I need you to understand what you are in for."

I nod, sniffing back more tears. "I know, Kendra told me."

"She *what?*" he raises his voice, clearly upset by the revelation.

"She came to see me yesterday." Chad looks like he might blow a gasket so I quickly add, "Don't be mad. She's the reason I'm here. I wasn't going to see you again, but she reminded me about all of your good qualities. I really like her."

"I'm going to double her salary," he jokes. "Seriously though, Kendra is great at what she does, but there is only so much she can bury. Eventually, this will come out. And probably sooner rather than later." He nods to the kitchen where servers have been peeking out at us all night. "See them? They could be taking pictures or video. Even with the non-disclosure agreements I had them sign, things always get leaked."

My jaw drops. "You had them sign non-disclosure agreements? Do you do that everywhere you go?"

"No, but I needed to tonight. I had to do everything I could to make sure your face didn't get plastered across every news magazine. Because that's what will happen, Mal. And it won't be long before they find out your name. And then after that, reporters and paparazzi might show up at your house or your school. A lot of people will be nice about it, but there are always those who will hate you for being with me." He takes the last swig of his champagne, looking pained. "There are so many reasons why you shouldn't want to be with me. And every one of them is valid. But I'm asking you to be with me anyway. I'm asking you to risk everything to see if we can get back what we once had and more."

I realize his hand hasn't let go of mine, and now he's threaded his fingers through my fingers. Our hands are entwined as if they were made to be this way. As if my hand was crafted solely and specifically to fit with his and no other.

He gives my hand a squeeze. "What do you say, Mal? Are you willing to risk it? For me? For us?"

His blue eyes sparkle as candlelight reflects off their glassy surface. He's got tears in his eyes. Tears that mirror mine. He wants this as badly as I do. Maybe if we both want it so much, we can make it work. Even though everything is against us, maybe the ten years we spent together will trump the nine years we spent apart. Maybe the bond we made back then can't be broken, just weakened. "I wasn't," I tell him. "I was ready to have you walk out of my life as quickly as you came back into it."

"And now?" he asks, hopefully.

"You've been nothing but a gentleman, Chad. You've treated me like a queen, and I'm not talking about the money. I could care less about that, I hope you know that. I watched the person you became after you moved to L.A. and I see the person you are now—there is no comparison. I might be willing to give this a shot. But I can't make any promises."

"Well, *I* can," he says. "I promise I won't let anyone hurt you, Mal. Including me. *Especially* me. Before, when I made you that promise, I was seven years old. I'm twenty-five now. My promises are worth more. The stakes are higher. And I'm telling you, you can count on me to be the best goddamn boyfriend anyone ever had."

Boyfriend. Chad Stone could be my boyfriend. Never in a million years did I think I'd be in this position. It's surreal. I find myself wanting to call Mel and Julian and tell them about it. But after all that's happened, I'm not sure they will support me; not Julian anyway. And then I think that maybe they won't fit into Chad's world. Would he expect me to choose his friends over mine? Would he expect me to give up all the things that make me who I am? *He's a superstar, of course he would.* My heart falls into the pit of my stomach and I feel sick.

"Mal? You're starting to scare me." He takes both of my hands in his. "If you have any reservations, just tell me. If you agree to be my girlfriend, none of that other shit matters. The only things that matter are what you and I want. Everything else will work out. Believe me."

I nod reluctantly. "Okay," I whisper.

"Okay?" he practically yells, his eyes full of joy like a kid on Christmas morning.

"Yes. Under one condition," I say.

"Anything," he says. "You can have anything you want."

"I want you to meet with Julian."

CHAPTER THIRTEEN

Chad

I feel like I'm auditioning for a part. To be Mallory's boyfriend. And it might just be the most important audition of my life. Her friends are everything to her. I know that from firsthand experience.

I sit across the table from her two best friends. Melissa, whom I've just met; and the guy who was once *my* best friend. The third musketeer. My partner in crime during some damn good years. But now, it's hard to see him as anything except the guy who stole my girl. Logically, I know that's not true. In fact, I pretty much handed her to him on a silver fucking platter. But that doesn't make it any easier to think of the two of them together. My only solace is he didn't sleep with her. Thank God. I'm not sure I could sit here and play nice if he had.

When Julian walked into the small private dining room at The Waldorf, we sized each other up. I half expected us to circle around each other and then pounce, fighting to the death to defend what we think is ours. Instead, we both pasted on smiles, shaking hands, unsure of the feelings we have for the brothers we once were.

"What do you expect her to do when you leave?" Julian asks, pushing his salmon around on his plate. "Just sit back and watch as you parade around with other women?"

"Of course not," I say. "I'm not going to be with anyone else, Julian. I've made a commitment to Mallory."

He turns to her. "Do you really believe he's going to forgo all of that for you? Have you not seen the news? Even since he's been here. While he's been seeing you this week—he's still been seeing Courtney Benson."

"He's not seeing her, Julian," Mallory says. "They work together. They have to make appearances together. The press, the paparazzi, they twist things around to make it look like a more interesting story. And because they dated last year, there are a lot of old pictures that give the stories credibility."

I try not to look like I'm gloating as she defends me. But on the inside—there's a party going on. And as the night progresses, I see her becoming more invested in this. In us.

"And you're okay with that?" he asks her. "With him traveling around the world doing God knows what with someone he used to go out with?"

"How is that any fucking different than Mal being friends with you, Julian?" I ask. "The two of you go to dinner. You hang out all the time. Hell, she even crashes at your apartment sometimes." I turn my attention to Mallory. "We will have to trust each other."

"So what, you're going to swing into town when you need a booty call?" Julian asks. "What the hell is she supposed to do the rest of the time, sit here and wait until you decide it's convenient to see her?"

"Julian," Melissa scolds him. "That's not fair. It's not like he can just give up his career or anything."

Melissa Connelly is Mal's best friend from college. I invited her to join us because I need Mallory to see how I can fit into her life just as much as she can fit into mine. I know she's expecting me to ask her to give things up for me. That couldn't be further from the truth. I'm willing to do almost anything for her. "I'm not saying things will be perfect," I tell them. "We have a lot to figure out. And, no, I'm not going to just blow into town when it's *convenient.*" I give Julian a reprimanding stare. "I have commitments, schedules I have no control over, but outside of those, I'm free to go where I choose."

Julian keeps trying to pour me more wine. I've already had a glass and don't intend on having more, but he doesn't seem to take no for an answer. When he tries for the third time, I lose it. "What's your problem, man? I said I don't want any more."

"He's a recovering addict, Julian," Mallory reminds him. "Don't push him. Please."

Julian holds up his hands in a gesture of innocence. "What happens when someone else does, Mallory?" he asks. "What happens when he has that second or third glass at a cast party? I mean, he shouldn't be drinking at all." He puts down the bottle and looks me in the eye. "You're reckless. Mallory doesn't need that in her life."

If it weren't for the fact that I'm so fucking pissed at him, I might actually respect him. After all, he's standing up for her. Making sure she's safe. "Maybe I was reckless once, but I'm not anymore. That was a long time ago, Julian. I won't make excuses for what I did back then. There are none. But it's been three years since I was that person. I know you may not believe that because of how they make me look in the news, but it's true. But you know what? You aren't the one I need to convince of that. *She* is."

I want to reach over and take Mal's hand. Put up a united front. Mark my goddamn territory. But I don't. They have a history together, one I have to accept and respect.

"Okay, boys," Melissa says, trying to reign both of us in. "Can we all just agree that every relationship has its complications and yours won't be any different? You guys will have to figure out a lot of stuff if you want to be together. But we certainly don't need to hash it all out now." She gives Julian a biting stare. "Do we, Julian?"

He scoffs, shaking his head.

"Has Mallory told you how we met?" Melissa asks me.

"She just said you met at school."

She looks at Mallory. "Can I tell him?"

Mal shrugs. "I guess. It won't be the first embarrassing thing he learns about me."

"Wait," I say. "This isn't worse than when you went to the wrong house to babysit, is it?"

Julian laughs. "Oh, my God, that was hilarious." He turns to Melissa, telling the story. "Chad and I were at my house, which was down the street from the two of theirs. We were hanging out in my yard when Mallory walked down the street to the babysitting job her mom got for her. So she sees the kids out front and starts playing with them."

Mallory covers her eyes in embarrassment. It's so damn cute. "She even picked up the smallest one, who was about four years old," I say.

"Oh, shit, yeah," Julian says, shaking his head in amusement. "That was when the mom came out and started yelling at Mallory to put down her kid."

I start laughing at the memory. "Mallory was completely freaked out. After all, she thought that's why she was there."

"Chad and I rushed over when we saw that something was wrong. It took a few minutes, but we were able to figure out she went to the wrong house. The mailboxes were next to each other and when she saw the kids out front, she just assumed that was the house."

"Hey," Mallory interjects. "It wasn't all that bad. Mrs. Jenner ended up hiring me to babysit those very kids. I made a lot of money that summer."

"That was a great summer," I say.

Julian nods. "It was, wasn't it?"

It was the last summer we all spent together. The next year, Julian spent the summer in Brazil so it was just Mal and me. And then I moved.

The waiter comes to clear the table and show us the dessert tray. The girls fawn over the chocolate delicacies and decide to split one. I want to tell them it's not necessary, but I don't need another lecture from Julian about how I choose to spend my money. So what if I rented out the private dining room? I only did it to protect Mallory. He should be thanking me, not reprimanding me.

"Okay, Melissa," I say. "Let's hear it. How did you two meet?"

She looks excited, rubbing her hands together and then settling into her chair like this will be a long story. "Okay, so it was freshman year and Mallory was rushing a sorority, Delta—"

"Wait." I hold up my hand to stop Melissa as I turn to Mallory with wide eyes. "*You* rushed a sorority? You—the girl who organized a protest sophomore year when the student body president wanted to make every Friday spirit day. You didn't want anyone telling you what to do or what to wear. *That* Mallory joined a sorority?"

"Just let her finish the darn story," Mallory says, rolling her eyes.

"So she was a few weeks into the pledging process," Melissa says. "Hazing wasn't technically allowed, but they still got asked to do some pretty outrageous stuff. I found her standing in the middle of campus by herself, wearing a cheerleader's outfit from a rival school. She was shouting that cheer 'two, four, six, eight' . . ."

My brain is still stuck on Mallory in a cheerleader's uniform. Holy God I'd like to see that. I glance at Mal to see her taking a large swallow of wine as she tries to hide her mortification.

"She got heckled by students, of course," Melissa says. "That was the point. To teach humility or some crap like that. But some of the students were downright mean, even when they knew she had to do it as part of pledging. By the time I came upon her, I guess she'd about had enough, because she ripped off her sweater and skirt, threw them down, stomping on them and then she marched over to some girls from her sorority that were videotaping her from behind a tree. She told them to take their sorority and go fuck themselves."

My jaw is almost on the table. "You stripped in the middle of campus?" Then it hits me. "Wait. You said *fuck?*"

She laughs, shrugging innocently. "I had a tank top and shorts on underneath."

Melissa laughs. "Don't let her fool you. She stripped. Her 'tank top' was a cami and her 'shorts' were those underwear things cheerleaders wear so you can't see their crotches."

"Shit. I wish I had been there to see it," I say.

"I'm pretty sure it exists out on YouTube somewhere," Melissa says. "It was epic. I followed her and offered her the t-shirt and yoga pants I had in my workout bag. We hit it off and the rest was history. We've been Mal and Mel ever since."

"What made you want to join a sorority?" I ask Mallory.

"I didn't have any friends there," she says. "I thought pledging a sorority would be a quick way to change that."

I turn to Julian. "Didn't you go to Berkeley?" We always talked about going there together, the three of us, even though Julian and I would go there a year before Mallory could.

"Uh, no. I went to Penn State," he says, looking guiltily at Mal.

I wonder if that had anything to do with their breakup. I assume it did, but now isn't the time to get into it. Obviously, the three of them know things I don't and it pisses me off. I've been replaced. It used to be the three of us—now it's the three of them.

"Anyway, it was Melissa who got me into teaching," Mallory says, smiling over at her friend in an attempt to stave off the awkwardness from my previous question.

"And you are great at it," Julian says, proudly. "Did she tell you she won an award in her district for being the rookie teacher of the year?"

I watch the way he looks at her. It's with more emotion than how one friend looks at another. He's revering her. Hell, he's worshiping her. I know this because it's the same goddamn way *I* look at her.

"No, she didn't. That's great, Mal," I say. "I'm not surprised, however. I knew you'd be great at whatever you chose to do." I turn back to Julian. "So, Penn State, huh? Where did that lead? Mallory hasn't said much of anything about you."

I get a little kick under the table from Mal for that remark. I know it was a dig. But if he's going to look at my girl that way, he'd better be prepared for me to push back.

"I'm an investment banker," he says. "For Walters and Leeman."

"Shit, really?" I shake my head in awe. "You must be one smart dude, but then I always knew you were. Good for you."

I catch Melissa whispering something to Mal, but Mallory brushes her off, quietly asking her not to bombard me with silly fangirl questions. "It's okay, Mal," I say. "Let her ask. Personal questions from friends are different than personal questions from fans." I turn to Melissa. "What do you want to know?"

Melissa looks to her friend for approval and Mal gives her a reluctant nod. "Mallory told me you got your big break in a shopping mall," she says. "Can you tell me what happened? Did they have auditions there? Was it like a massive American Idol audition but for actors?"

My eyes dart between the two girls. "Mallory hasn't told you any of this?"

"No," she says. "Mallory never told me about *Thad*. All I knew was she had a best friend, Chad, who moved away when she was in high school. I never even knew the boy she grew up with was the same person as Thad Stone until she saw you last week at the club."

I have conflicting emotions over her statement. On one hand, I think maybe I wasn't important enough to her to tell her friends about me. On the other, I'm flat-out impressed Mal never resorted to name-dropping like most people would have done. Julian, too. I shake my head in wonder before answering Melissa's question.

"No. It wasn't an audition," I say. "It was a total fluke. I was in the food court waiting for my little brother, who was fifteen at the time, when he came racing out of a store looking terrified. Two security guards were running up behind him. Kyle said he snatched something from the store and he begged me not to let them put him in jail. Apparently, I gave the performance of a lifetime, sweet-talking the guards into letting it slide. I fed them so much bullshit, I'm surprised they didn't drown in it.

"After the security guards left, a man came up to me, telling me he saw the whole thing. I thought he was a cop, but it turned out he was a talent agent. He said he was impressed by my improv and my confidence and that I had what he was looking for. I told him I didn't have any acting experience other than a play I did in high school. He didn't seem to care. He said I had the right look or some shit like that. He gave me his card. On a dare from Kyle, I called the guy a week later. The next month, I was cast in *Malibu 310*."

"Wow," Melissa says. "How lucky were you?"

Sometimes I wonder. I wonder if it was the best thing that ever happened to me, or the worst. It did, after all, separate me from who I was. And from Mal. But then again, it also led me back to her. And now here we are, right where we should be.

We are served dessert and spend the rest of the night reminiscing about old times. Despite the awkwardness with Julian, I don't want the night to end. Mainly because Mallory came with Melissa and not me. She thought it'd be more neutral that way. She didn't want it to seem like we were teaming up on him. But it means when we say goodbye, I won't see her for two days. I've got plans with my cousin Jarod and his family tomorrow, and the next night she does her volunteer work. It was bad enough not seeing her for the entire day yesterday, I can't imagine going two days without seeing her now that I know we can finally be together. It makes me dread Thursday, the day I leave for Vancouver. I've got commitments for the next two weeks. Two weeks where she can change her mind. Two weeks for Julian to talk her out of it. Two weeks for her to meet someone else who doesn't come with all my baggage.

The girls get up to use the bathroom before we leave. I watch Julian follow Mallory out the door with his eyes. And then he and I are left sitting alone for the first time tonight. "You're in love with her," I say.

It's not a question.

He smirks. "Looks like we're right back where we started then, aren't we?"

That's no lie. I think we both loved her even then. Before he dated her. Before I came back. "Yeah, but you had your chance, Julian. Now it's my turn."

He nods reluctantly. "I know. But I'd be remiss if I didn't threaten to kick your ass if you hurt her."

"Duly noted," I say. "If I hurt her, I'll be the first one to let you."

The server comes to clear the table, our cue to leave. Julian gets out his wallet. "No," I tell him. "It's already been taken care of. You can get the next one."

I put on my baseball cap as we head out into the lobby. I managed to sneak in without notice, so I hope my luck holds. Cole sees me and heads out to get the car. The ladies find us waiting for them and come over to say goodbye. I hold my hand out to Julian. "It's been good seeing you again. We should hang out sometime when I'm in town."

He pulls a business card out of his pocket. "Sure. Give me a call."

I try to judge his sincerity. Does he really want to try and be friends again? Or does he want to keep tabs on me? Keep your friends close and your enemies closer and all that shit. I read his business card. Maybe he just wants my money. It really fucking sucks not knowing what people's true motives are when your face is plastered on billboards and buses.

"It was nice to meet you, Melissa. I hope we can do this again sometime." I give her a kiss on the cheek.

She blushes. And squeals. "Holy shit, Thad Stone just kissed me."

"No," I tell her. "Mallory's boyfriend did."

I take Mallory by the elbow. "We good?"

She looks in my eyes. She knows exactly what I'm asking. She smiles up at me, nodding.

I lean down and kiss her on the head. "Good. I'll see you soon, then."

I head out the front door, tapping out a text as I wait for Cole.

Me: The next time I say goodnight to my girlfriend, I'm going to kiss the fucking shit out of her. Just sayin'.

I peek back inside and watch Mallory pull her phone out of her pocket. Then I watch a huge smile overtake her face. Then I can't help my celebratory fist pump.

CHAPTER FOURTEEN

Mallory

As I wait for Chad to pick me up, I page through the texts he's sent me over the past few days. Texts a boyfriend sends to a girlfriend. Texts about wanting to kiss me, hold hands with me. Texts that reference a future he wants me to be a part of.

I'm teeming with excitement that we are even considering a future together. I thought the door on that was shut nine years ago. But at the same time, I'm wary. Julian brought up some valid points. When are we even going to have the time to see each other? I teach and he has so many appearances, interviews, upcoming movies to promote, new films to make. Will either of us be happy with a significant other we can only see once a month or whatever? Will he be able to resist all the temptations that go along with being who he is?

Then I think about all the nice things he's done for me since he came back into my life. And I know in my heart that even seeing him once a month would be a hundred times better than seeing some other guy every day of the week.

Take Monday night. A courier arrived at my door when I got home from work. He delivered a huge box along with a beautiful vase of flowers. Inside the box was a copy of *Defcon One* on Blu-ray. It hasn't even been released to theaters yet, not until next month. He sent me my own private copy. Also in the box was everything you'd need for a night at the movies—popcorn, jujubes, and an uber-comfy pillow and blanket for me to cuddle up with. And darn it if they didn't smell like him. I think he must have spritzed his cologne on them before boxing them up. He included a card.

> Here's the next best thing to actually being with me. Me—I'll have to rely on the memory of your incredible smell and the picture I took of you last night. Counting the hours until tomorrow evening.

I curled up on the couch and watched as Lt. Jake Cross stole my heart almost as much as Chad Stone has. He's a phenomenal actor. Truly gifted at his craft. It almost makes those years we spent apart worth it. If he hadn't moved away, he never would have been discovered. And I'm convinced nobody could have played the part of Lt. Cross as well as he did. I'm a firm believer that everything happens for a reason. That there is a butterfly effect and everything that happens influences what will happen next. Even my mom dying. I mean, what if she hadn't been on the road at that very minute in that very spot? Instead, what if it were a young family, or a pregnant woman in labor being rushed to the hospital? Maybe that drunk driver running into *her* saved other lives. And maybe one of those lives that was saved is someone who will go on to discover how to prevent cancer. Or global warming. Or nuclear war.

Maybe everything that's happened in my life and in Chad's has led us to this moment—the time when we can finally be together—the time we were always *meant* to be together.

The doorbell rings and my heart pounds. This is it. Our first official date. I'm going out with Chad Stone. I smooth my hands down my dress and open the door.

I watch the reaction on Chad's face as his eyes rake over me. It's everything I imagined and more. His mouth hangs slightly agape as his gaze travels from my hair, that I pinned up with loose tendrils framing my face, to my little black dress that fits well in all the right places, to my stocking-clad legs and then down to my heeled sandals. And then he slowly works his way back up again.

By the time he gets to my face, I feel like I've been thoroughly made love to yet he hasn't touched me at all. My insides coil, my legs start to shake, my breathing comes quickly. Oh, Lord, how am I going to make it through an evening with this man?

"Holy shit, Mal," he says, finding my eyes once again. "I've never seen anything as beautiful as you are right now."

I don't even know what to say. And I couldn't say it even if I did. He's rendered me speechless once again. I tug my lower lip into my mouth.

His eyes close briefly. "Oh, God. I was wrong." He reaches over to touch my lips. "This is even better." He shakes his head as if intentionally ridding it of wayward thoughts. He runs his hands through his hair as he backs up out of the doorway, putting him on the other side of the threshold. "We'd better leave now if I want to keep my gentlemanly status."

I laugh, grabbing my coat. He helps me put it on after I lock the front door. I pull it tightly around me. It's brisk tonight on this late-February evening.

As we walk down the sidewalk towards the waiting car, Chad nods at the basketball in the bushes. "I wonder what we could play HORSE for next?" Then his blue eyes take hold of my green ones. *Oh. My. God.* Shivers run down my spine. And not because of the freezing temperature.

I'm going on a date with Chad Stone.

He opens the door for me and I slide over on the black leather seat to let him get in beside me. Before I can settle myself into the seat by the window, he captures my hand, keeping me in the middle seat as he entwines our fingers.

I'm holding hands with Chad Stone.

With his other hand, he reaches across me and pulls the seatbelt over my body, all the while I'm smelling him and it reminds me of his movie that I watched the other night. I open my eyes to see his face mere inches from mine as he clasps me in. The brilliant smile on his face tells me he knows exactly what he's doing to me.

I'm being strapped in by Chad Stone.

I think he's going to kiss me, but he doesn't. He sits back in his seat and puts on his seatbelt one-handedly, all the while, the aforementioned smile still glued to his face as if he's doing a toothpaste commercial.

"Hello again, Mallory," Cole says from the front. "Nice to see you."

"You too, Cole. Thanks for keeping the car warm."

"Of course. Are you all set?"

"Ready," Chad says.

"So where are you taking me?" I'm a bit nervous. We haven't yet talked about what will happen if we're seen out together. Am I supposed to go into the building while he signs autographs, like at Ethan's? What happens if people ask who I am? What am I supposed to say? What if they take pictures of us together? Has he cleared this with his publicist? His manager? Does he even have to do that?

I realize there is still so much I don't know about him and his lifestyle. I'm not sure I'm ready just yet to be thrown into it so unprepared.

"Relax," Chad says, squeezing my hand. He senses my tension. "I'm not taking you to the Golden Globes or anything. Not yet anyway. We're going on a picnic."

I'm not sure which shocks me more, the fact that I may one day get to walk a red carpet with him or that it's thirty degrees outside and he's taking me on a picnic. I look down at my black dress—the one that barely covers my thighs. Even with my coat on, I'd still freeze to death. I scissor my stocking-covered legs to make a point. "Uh, I wish you had said something."

He laughs. "Don't worry, you'll be fine. I've got it covered. Hey, how was your dinner with Charlie last night?"

Ethan's wife, Charlie, accompanied me last night during my shift at Hope. Then we went to dinner. What happened there was surreal, but I gather it's only a taste of what I'm in for if Chad and I stay together. "It was great. I really like Charlie a lot. We've already made plans to go shopping this weekend."

He smiles again. He's glad I'm making friends with his inner circle.

"Did you know what she was going to do?" I ask.

"What do you mean?"

"The donation," I say.

His eyebrows shoot up. "Charlie made a donation?"

He didn't know. Somehow that makes me happy. "Donation is an understatement," I say. "More like a miracle. She wrote a check for a million dollars, Chad." I shake my head remembering how she nonchalantly handed it over to me like she was paying a thirty-dollar dinner tab. "Who does that? After only one visit?"

"Well, her mom died last year, leaving her quite a bit of money. And it's no secret she and Ethan are well off. He told me a few months ago she was looking for a good cause—I guess she found it. You must have impressed her the other night, Mal. She's been researching the charity ever since. She grilled me for information, but I wasn't much help. So, what made you get involved with that particular organization?"

"Uh . . . " I shift awkwardly in my seat. "Well, a lot of things I guess. Do you remember Penny Garrison? She was in my grade."

"Yeah. Blonde hair. Big . . . teeth." He winks at me. "Slutty."

I nod. That's how most people remember her.

"She got pregnant after you left. Senior year."

He snaps his head to me, looking surprised. "She did?"

"Yeah. And her parents kicked her out. She literally had nowhere to go. No friends. No relatives. She would have been out on the street if it weren't for Hope For Life."

"And you were always helping people, so when you found out about it . . . Makes sense; I always knew you'd end up doing something like that."

"It's not much," I tell him. "I only volunteer one night a week. It's not like I gave them a million dollars or anything."

"Don't sell yourself short, Mal. You give your time. That is incredibly valuable. If it weren't for people like you, organizations like that couldn't exist." He squeezes my hand. "My girlfriend— teacher of the year, philanthropist . . . Are there any other hidden talents you have that I should know about?"

I blush in the darkness at his insinuation. I shake my head. "I still can't get used to it. You calling me your girlfriend."

"Well, get used to it, Mal. Because it's true. But the world might have to wait a little longer to find out about it."

I can't help the sigh of relief that escapes me when he says that.

He laughs at the relief rolling off me in waves. "Tell me how you really feel, Mal." He shifts in his seat so that he's facing me. "Listen, I know this will be an adjustment for you. For me, too, believe it or not. So let's just try to keep it to ourselves for a while. I just got you back. I don't want to share you with anyone quite yet."

"That sounds good to me," I tell him. "More than good."

"We're here," Cole announces from the front seat. He parks the car, but keeps it running, talking to a man outside who trades places with him in the driver's seat as we exit the back.

When I see where we are, I'm confused. He wasn't kidding. We really are going on a picnic. He's brought me to Central Park. I look down at my clothes again. "Uh . . ."

Chad holds his hand out to me. "Trust me, Mallory."

I take his hand and we follow Cole through the winding sidewalks of the park. I'm glad it hasn't snowed recently or I'd be sloshing through it in my brand new heels. It's already dark out. That's probably the only reason why Chad hasn't been mobbed yet.

We don't walk far, maybe a few blocks, when we come upon a large tent. It's completely enclosed on all four sides, its white fabric walls illuminated from the inside. A beautiful woman sees us coming and hurries to carry a few more items inside the tent. She emerges a minute later and greets us. "Mr. Stone, nice to see you again. Everything has been set up as requested." She hands him her card, pointing to the phone number on it. "If you need anything, I have a team waiting in the catering van just outside the park. Just text me at this number. Anything you need."

I take a peek at the card. It reads: **Mitchell's NYC Catering**. "Thanks, Skylar. My friends call me Chad." He motions to me. "And this is Mallory Schaffer."

Skylar shakes my hand. "It's really nice to meet you. Charlie told me all about you." She hands me one of her cards as well. "We do girls' night a few times a month and it would be great if you'd join us. Give me a call sometime."

"Uh, okay. Thanks." I slip her card in my purse. Does Chad know *everyone* in this city?

As she walks away, Chad explains, "Skylar is Piper's sister. You remember Piper Mitchell from Ethan's dinner? Skylar manages Mitchell's. Best restaurant in the city. I met her last fall and ever since, I haven't missed a chance to dine there when I'm in town. She insisted on being here herself instead of appointing one of her catering managers. They have another sister, too, Baylor. Charlie practically grew up with them. Great bunch of girls. You should go to girls' night. Take Melissa."

I shrug. It would be nice to get to know some of the people in Chad's life. "Maybe I will."

Cole sets up outside the front of the tent, putting a large thermos of coffee on a table next to his chair.

Chad holds the fabric door for me and I walk through, surprised to be met with a wave of heat. I look around and see what he's done. There are a few of those tall propane heaters scattered throughout the tent enclosure. At one end of the tent there is a couch and coffee table with a bottle of champagne chilling in an ice bucket. In the center, a well-appointed dining table for two. Strings of white lights like tiny Christmas lights line the entire ceiling, and ornate candles illuminate the dining and coffee tables. Off to the far end, there is what appears to be a smaller tent-within-a-tent. I question him with my eyes.

"Port-o-potty," he says. "Damn nice one. Toilet flushes and everything, you should check it out."

I can't help myself, I walk over and peek into it. It's nicer than my bathroom at home. I laugh at the absurdness of it all. I feel like I've walked into someone else's life. Part of me wants to chastise him for spending so much money, but I know it's not just for me. It's for him, too. To keep what we have private. At least for now.

"Can I interest you in a drink?" Chad asks, motioning to the couch.

It's so warm in here, I start to remove my coat on the way and he helps me, hanging it on a coat stand by the door. Who thinks of stuff like that? A coat rack inside a tent with a port-o-potty in the middle of Central Park?

He pours me a full glass of bubbly, but only a half for himself. He raises his glass. "To new beginnings."

I smile, thinking of how my life may never be the same. I hope it won't anyway. I hope I'll never have to live another day without him in it. "To new beginnings," I say, clinking my glass to his as one side of his mouth turns up in a sexy smile.

CHAPTER FIFTEEN

Chad

It's a good thing we're in the middle of Central Park where Cole or Skylar could walk in at any minute, because the way she looks in that dress, if we were at her house—or Ethan's—all bets would be off.

Those legs. She's wearing pale black stockings and when I reach my hand over to hold hers, placing them to rest on her thigh, I swear I can feel the outline of a garter through the fabric of her dress. *Fuuuuck me.* She's wearing garter belts.

I try to think of something to get rid of my rising problem. "I'm going to need you to clear something up for me," I say. "I need to know why you and Julian didn't work out."

She looks around the room, stalling like she's pondering what or how much to tell me.

"Come on, Mal. I'm leaving tomorrow. I'm leaving you here with him—again. I know you are close and, yeah, it makes me jealous as hell, but I'll deal with it because I have to trust you as I'm asking you to trust me. But I need to know. You said you wanted different things. What does that mean exactly?"

She looks down at our entwined hands and nods. She blows out a deep sigh. "It means he wanted to screw his philosophy TA because I wouldn't sleep with him, and it means I wanted to kill him because I wasn't exactly okay with that."

"Oh, shit, Mal. He cheated on you?" Warring emotions are raging through my head. Part of me wants to beat him bloody for hurting her. The other part is happy he was such a douche and she ended things. "That's a pretty low blow. How is it you're still friends?"

"It took a while," she says. "I didn't see him for three years after we broke up. But it wasn't hard to avoid him, he was away at Penn State."

"You said you started dating after your mom died. So you were a junior and he was a senior?"

"Yeah. It was right before summer break at the end of my junior year when we got together. But as soon as he went away to college, everything changed. We never should have dated. We were much better as friends."

"Why didn't he go to Berkeley like we always said?"

She gives me a sad smile. "Why didn't you?"

"Right," I say. "Things change. So how did you end up friends again?"

"Funny story, actually. Or maybe ironic," she says. "Melissa and I were out at a club. She went up to the bar to get us some drinks. She came back mooning over some guy she met there who had just grabbed her out of nowhere and kissed her. Right there in the middle of the bar, some guy kissed a complete stranger. She invited him and his friends to sit with us. I about died when I saw it was Julian. He'd just graduated and was back in town interviewing for jobs. Apparently, he'd just gotten a great offer at Walters and Leeman and he was so excited, he started kissing random girls." She smiles and I'm glad she can think about that time without being upset. "Once Mel realized who he was, she quit salivating over him. And it didn't take long to realize we could still be friends; that we should have never tried to be anything more. That was three years ago."

Twice now she's said something that resonates with me. "That's not how you think of us, is it? That we're better as friends?"

"I've thought about that a lot over the past week," she admits. "Back then, when it was the three of us, and even when Julian was in Brazil that summer and it was just you and me—I think it would have been a mistake. I think we might have ruined a great friendship. But now, well, we have all this distance. Nine years of it. There's nothing to ruin. I mean, yes, I want to be your friend again, but I think there's a chance we could be good at more now."

A triumphant smile travels up my face. "I think there's a hell of a lot more than just a chance. I'm betting on it being a sure thing. Do you know how difficult it was for me to keep my hands off you back then? I was a horny teenager and you were this beautiful, smart, kind girl who knew everything about me. I basically walked around with a perpetual hard-on because of you."

She almost spits out her champagne, putting a hand over her mouth as she swallows it. "You did not," she says.

"It's true. And some things never change." I wink at her.

Her eyes quickly scan my lap and then she blushes when she sees I've caught her looking.

"Do you remember all those times we spent in your treehouse?" I ask.

She nods. "That was a lot of fun. I think about those times often."

"My fantasies were pretty much centered around you and that treehouse and what I would do to you on the sleeping bag you kept up there."

"Oh, my God, really?" she asks, her face taking on an even deeper shade of red than before.

"I spent a lot of time in my bathroom those days." I laugh as she drains her glass and holds it out for more. I fill it and then I get up off the couch, holding my hand out to her. "We'd better eat before the food gets too cold. They've got warmers on it, but still."

I put my hand on the small of her back as I walk her across the room. Heat radiates between us through the thin material of her dress. Something else radiates as well. Desire? Passion? Whatever the hell it is, I haven't felt it in nine years. That's not true, I haven't felt it *ever*. Not like this. I hold out the chair for her and then I serve her the salad from the cooler. She smiles up at me. "I think I like this, you serving me. Must be a novelty for you, huh?"

"I don't have servants, Mal. I hate the fact that I have to be driven around like a little kid, but sometimes it's a necessity of the job. Maybe there was a time when I thought people should serve me, but I was a stupid prick. Not anymore. Never again."

"Speaking of Cole. Are you going to hire him full-time?" she asks, her eyes filled with hope.

I nod. "Already did. Offered him the job yesterday. Damned if I'm not going to have security around when *you* are with me. You are my top priority, Mal. I mean that."

We finish our salads and I get the main dish out from the propane warmer. It's some kind of chicken and pasta with asparagus. I pretty much let Skylar set the menu. I'm not too picky when it comes to food.

"This looks delicious," Mallory says when I put it down on the table. She closes her eyes and takes in the aroma of the dish in front of her.

God that's sexy. It's the same thing she did to me in the car when I leaned over to put her seatbelt on. Makes me a bit jealous of her dinner. "I've never had a bad meal at Mitchell's," I tell her. "You should go there sometime."

She takes a bite of her food, rolling her eyes toward the heavens at the taste of it. "Oh, wow," she says around her food. "I totally will."

My pocket vibrates twice in quick succession, it's the special code alerting me to a text from Megan. I recently set Mal up with *her* own special code so I don't miss a text from her either. *Damn*. If it were anyone else, I would ignore it. But it's Megan. I have to check it.

I pull my phone from my pocket and nod to it. "Sorry," I say. "I just need to answer this text. I'll just be a second." I tap out a response to Megan and send it.

"It's okay," Mallory says, politely. "Is it your manager?"

Shit. Why did she have to ask? I don't want to lie to her.

"No," I say, tapping out another quick text. "It's a friend from L.A." I put away my phone. "There, all done. No more interruptions."

I can tell she's disappointed by my non-explanation. But Mal wouldn't understand. And I can't risk ruining our first date. I quickly change the subject. "Save room for dessert," I say. "It's your favorite." Then I frown. "Or at least it was."

"You had them make me dirt cake?" she asks, eyes wide in surprise.

I shake my head. "No, I didn't have *them* make it," I tell her. "*I* did."

She freezes, her fork halfway to her mouth. *"You* made dirt cake for me?"

I smile with pride. "Of course I did. I told you, I'm here to serve."

She laughs. "I can see it now," she says. "The famous Thad Stone crushing up Oreos and mixing chocolate pudding and whip cream. Wait . . . you didn't get gummy worms did you?"

"Hell yes, I got gummy worms. What kind of dirt cake doesn't have gummy worms?"

She puts her utensils down on her plate, ending her meal that was only half eaten. "Who needs this drivel when we can have some of that? Bring it on."

Now I'm laughing with her. I clear our plates and dive back into the cooler to bring out the individual portions of dirt cake I made earlier today.

"Oh, my God!" she squeals. "You even put them in miniature flower pots. I love it! Thank you, Chad."

Her smile. This girl. Shit, I'll make her dirt cake every damn day if it makes her this happy.

After our bellies are full, we move back to the couch and I turn on some music from my phone.

"Are we ever going to talk about it?" she asks.

I know what she's asking just by looking into her eyes. "You want to know where we go from here. What happens next, right?"

She nods. "I know you have a lot of things on your plate and that my job seems insignificant in comparison, but I have commitments too."

"Of course you do," I say. "I wouldn't ask you to give those up."

"I pretty much have to be here Monday through Friday every week," she explains. "Except summer, but that's a long way off. How are we going to have time to see each other?"

"We'll make the time," I tell her. "*I'll* make the time." I pick up my phone and pull up my calendar. "Let's schedule something right now so we know what's next. So we have something to look forward to."

She smiles, getting her phone out as well. She pages through her mostly blank calendar as I peek over her shoulder. She tosses her phone back into her purse, laughing. "Who am I kidding," she says. "My life is boring as hell."

I put my hand up on the back of her neck. "You are anything but boring, Mal. I promise you that." I pull her face towards mine and rest our foreheads together. Her lips are close, so close I can almost smell the lip gloss she had on earlier. I want to taste those strawberry lips. I want to feel her tongue with mine. I want to do all that and more. But the build-up is so much fun, so I release her neck and pull away. I swear I can hear a faint mewl down in her throat and I have to hold back my chuckle.

I turn my attention back to my phone. "I'll be in Vancouver for a week on a press junket and then I have to go to L.A. for the Academy Awards ceremony. I might be able to squeeze in a weekend after that, but then I have to be back in L.A. for some pre-production meetings for the *Defcon* sequel. We start shooting this summer."

Mallory is so quiet I have to look up from my phone to see why. She takes a deep breath and blows it out. "Sorry," she says, shaking her head in disbelief. "I think I've finally been hit with the enormity of all this. I mean, Academy Awards ceremony? Pre-production meetings? Shooting a film? You're a movie star, Chad.

Are you sure we can even make this work? I mean, I'm just a teacher."

"Would you please quit saying that? Being a teacher is what you do, it's who you are. I happen to love that it's who you are. And yes, we can make this work. So get your calendar back out and pencil me in for two weeks from Friday."

She pulls up her calendar again and smiles. "Oh, that's a long weekend. I have that Friday off."

"Great, then I'll come Thursday." I add it to my calendar and then type out a text.

She raises a brow at me. "Friend in L.A. again?"

Shit. She *was* bothered by that. "I just texted my travel agent. Told her to fly me in that Thursday afternoon until Sunday night. You okay with that?"

"You can do it just like that?" she asks. "Don't you have to clear it with your manager or Kendra or somebody?"

I laugh. "I know it might not seem like it sometimes, but they work for me, not the other way around as Paul would have everyone think."

She studies me for a minute. "You're not actually winning an Oscar, are you?"

I laugh at the mention of it. "Not even close."

"I bet you will for *Defcon One*," she says. "It was a great movie. You were stunning. I was thoroughly impressed."

I beam with pride at her compliment. "Thanks. That means a lot coming from you. But no, I won't win for that. Apocalyptic movies rarely get nominated for Oscars."

"Oh, well they should," she says.

I grab her phone from her and block out all three days with my name. She looks at it and smiles. Then she bites her lip. Damn, if I only knew what she was thinking right this second. Because if it's the same thing I'm thinking, that weekend might just turn out to be the best fucking weekend of my life. Pun intended.

Mallory falls asleep on me in the car on the way home. I guess the problem with me not drinking much is that I tend to give others too much to make up the difference. I wrap my arm around her and let her head sink into the crook of my neck. I inhale the scent of her hair, memorizing it so I can remember it later when she's not with me. I know she thinks that because I'm rich and make movies and have fans that she's not enough for me. She couldn't be further from the truth. Not only is she enough, she's the *only*.

"Wake up, baby; you're home." I contemplate carrying her up to her house, but I know if I did—if I had her in my arms that way, I wouldn't be able to let her go. But she's had too much to drink. I won't be the guy who takes advantage.

"Sorry," she says, embarrassed that she dozed off. "I didn't mean to ruin our last few minutes together."

I squeeze her hand. "Are you kidding? I've been wanting you to sleep with me for years."

Cole opens my door and I get out, helping her out after me. "I'll just be a minute," I tell him.

I walk her up the porch stairs and she pauses as we reach the door. "You don't want to come in?" she asks with a sad smile.

"That's a loaded question, Mallory Kate." I motion to the door. "I want to come in more than you can imagine. I want to come in and take you up to your bedroom and make slow incredible love to you. I want to hold you in my arms and stare at your beautiful face until the sun rises. I want all that and more." I put my hands on her cheeks and stare at her full lips. "But you're drunk and your dad would probably kick my ass, so I'm not walking through that door. But I am going to make good on the text I sent you the other night."

I wind my hands around her neck and pull her to me, our lips inches apart—so close the air between us warms with our quickening breaths. "I've waited my whole life for this," I say, just before my lips come crashing down on hers. Her lips are soft and supple and I work them gently with mine, tasting and memorizing them before I pry them apart with my tongue. When her tongue mingles with mine, doing a perfectly choreographed dance, it's like a well-rehearsed scene coming together as if we'd practiced it a dozen times, except that it's our first time.

A sultry noise escapes her throat, fueling my need for her as we devour each other. I press her back against the door, trapping her with my body as I lean into her, showing her just how much this kiss is affecting me. Her hands come up and work through my hair as mine find her arms, her shoulders, her ribs, moving from one body part to the next, studying each with nimble fingers.

When we are starving for air, my mouth escapes hers only to find its way to her neck, savoring every inch of skin between her exposed collarbone and her ear. She tastes like heaven. When I suck on a spot on her neck, a muffled cry escapes her. I smile against her skin as I record the exact location of the area for future reference.

My mouth finds hers again and our tongues resume roaming, tasting and licking like this is the first kiss either of our lips have been allowed to have. Ever. My hands travel under her coat, around her back and down to the perfectly-rounded globes of her ass. I pull her against me, grinding myself into her. Her hands grab my shoulders and she supports herself on me as if her knees have become too weak to hold her.

The headlights of a passing car remind me we're still standing on Mallory's front porch. I give her one last kiss, reluctantly pulling my lips from hers. I look into her eyes that are drunk with passion if not alcohol. "Jesus, Mal, that was so much better," I say.

Her fingers come up to wipe her swollen lips. "Better than what?" she asks, breathily.

I cup her chin with my hand. "Anything I ever imagined."

She smiles brightly, her eyes dancing in agreement.

"I'm warning you right now, I'm going to fall in love with you, Mallory Kate. And I'm going to fall hard." I press her languid body back against the door so she won't fall down when I release her. "I may already have."

I walk down the steps and head out to the waiting car. I turn around and shout, "See you in two weeks!" Then I watch her fall through her door and into the house.

CHAPTER SIXTEEN

Mallory

I didn't know how hard it was going to be. I didn't realize how he'd become such an integral part of my life in the short time he was here. But being without him these last two weeks—it's like being without air.

Our daily texts and phone calls have kept us going, and the occasional reminders he's sent to me from afar have been my beacons of light. Part of me loves that he has all this money yet he chooses to send me a simple bouquet of roses. Or the greeting cards he took the time to handwrite and mail. Or the pizza and champagne he had delivered from The Pizza Garden.

I can barely contain my excitement knowing I'm going to see him in just a few minutes. He texted me when his plane landed, saying he'd be here shortly.

Although the past two weeks have been hard without him; they've been anything but lonely. Between shopping with Charlie, a girls' night with her and the Mitchell sisters, and endless cross-examination during dinners with Julian and Mel, I've had little time to myself. I even went to dinner at Ethan's and got to catch up with him and Kyle a bit more. My life has become so much richer since Chad came back into it, and it has nothing to do with the enormous bank accounts of all my new friends.

On the flip side, news has gotten out that the hot star of the upcoming release, *Defcon One*, has a new lady. A mysterious woman who appeared in the crowd, who accompanied him to dinner, and who was seen walking with him one night in the park.

Fortunately, all pictures of me are obscured. Someone snapped a photo of me through the glass doors of Ethan's building. Another person used cellphone video to tape us at the pizza place—just as he warned would probably happen. Thank goodness it was dark there. Stories of the mystery woman with long brown hair have been plastered over the tabloids, with headlines screaming of how Thad Stone has stepped out on his leading lady. There have even been rumors of him and Heather Crawford rekindling their relationship. Courtney has denied every allegation and continues to drape herself over Chad anytime a photographer is around.

It's been difficult, me being here and seeing his face with Courtney's all over the media. He's been good about calling me to prepare me every time they get photographed by the paparazzi—or 'papped' as he calls it. And I've been doing my best to avoid entertainment news and grocery store newsstands because I know it's inevitable, them ending up on the cover. After all, their movie release is coming up soon and they were together in Vancouver for an entire week.

I'm glad my dad is still working. I'd hate for him to see what a wreck I am waiting for Chad to show up. I changed three times. I shaved every place that needed shaving. I plucked. I moisturized. I've paced around the house for an hour. I wonder if this is how his fans feel when they get to meet him.

I hear a car door shut in the driveway and my heart surges, beating a thousand times in quick succession. Then I hear the thump-thump-thump of the basketball, and suddenly, I'm not scared anymore. A few minutes ago I was wondering what it would be like to see him again. After that incredible date. After he said the things he did at my door. After our time apart. But now, I realize there's nothing to be scared of. He's just Chad, and I'm just Mallory. Like it used to be. Like it always should have been.

I rip open the door to get to him. I have to refrain from running down the porch steps and jumping into his arms. Because that is exactly what I want to do. And by the look on his face when he sees me, I'm positive he wouldn't mind in the least if I did. Instead, however, he throws me the ball as I step onto the driveway.

No kiss. No hug. Not even a word of hello. "HORSE?" he asks, with a sinful smile.

"What are the stakes?" I answer, nonchalantly as if my insides aren't imagining all the possibilities.

"I win, you pack an overnight bag," he says.

A warm shiver runs down my spine, all the way to my toes. "What if *I* win," I ask, trying not to let my voice crack with sheer desperation.

"Well, you can have whatever you want," he says.

What if I already have it?

When I don't speak, he says, "You don't have to tell me now. It can be like a secret wish you can save for later." He winks.

"I'll go first," I say, not pulling my eyes from him as I take a shot and miss.

He laughs, letting the ball roll into the bushes as he strides over and wraps his arms around me. "Hi," he says, smiling down on me.

"Hi," I say, right before he kisses me.

His hands pull me to him by the small of my back, pressing our bodies together as our mouths explore each other. He tastes even better than I remember. Two weeks of separation has heightened my senses. Every touch has my skin on fire. Every caress is like a crescendo of waves. Every murmur from his lips is a spear to my thundering heart.

We break apart, lips swollen but not nearly satiated. "I forfeit," I whisper.

We both break into laughter as he picks me up and twirls me around. Free—that's how I feel. Free to finally feel for him what I wanted to all those years.

~ ~ ~

An hour later, Cole pulls our car up in front of a very nice hotel. I turn to Chad. "We're not going to Ethan's? I thought that's where you always stay when you come to town."

"Not anymore," he says, reaching down to pull something from his bag. He hands me a baseball hat and sunglasses. "Here, put these on."

I watch as he puts on his own Yankees hat and aviator sunglasses, making him look every bit the movie star that he is, albeit somewhat camouflaged. He shrugs. "Why ruin a good thing?"

He's right. I don't think people seeing us going into a hotel together is the right way to announce our relationship. I like having this secret that only we know. And as Kendra pointed out, as soon as the cat's out of the bag, everything we do will be scrutinized. I twist my hair up into a bun and put it under my hat.

Chad looks at me with his trademark sexy smile, shaking his head back and forth. "What?" I ask. "Do I look that silly?"

"Silly?" He reaches up and puts his hand behind my neck. "I was just thinking about what I'd like to do to this beautiful neck of yours." He pulls me close and kisses me on a spot that makes my whole body tingle.

Cole clears his throat from the front seat and Chad pulls back, laughing. "Sorry, buddy. I can't help myself around her."

I smile and put on my glasses. He has beautiful women throwing themselves at his feet but it's *me* he can't help himself around. It's quite a heady feeling. What millions of women wouldn't do to be in my position.

A concierge opens the door for us and retrieves our bags from the trunk. Cole hands over the keys to the valet and we all head into the hotel. At the desk, we stand back as Cole checks us in. "Rooms for Mr. and Mrs. Grape."

I shoot a funny look to Chad. Only he can't see it through my glasses. Cole pays with a credit card and we're escorted to the elevators. The bellman carries our bags for us. "Mr. and Mrs. Grape," he says. "Your suite is right this way." He nods to Cole, pointing at a door down the hall. "Yours is right over there."

After our bags are placed in the bedroom, Chad tips the bellman, sending him on his way. "Do you think he recognized you?" I ask, worried about our cover being blown.

He shrugs, removing his hat and glasses. "Hard to say. They are used to having celebrities stay here."

I look around the lavishly decorated suite that is so out of my price range I doubt I could afford the wallpaper. "Wow," I say. "Do you always stay in places like this?"

"Sometimes. When you travel a lot like we do, it's nice to have room to move around."

177

I frown. "It must be hard being away from home so much."

He nods. "Yeah, it gets to the point where you forget which city you're in."

"Does it ever end?" I ask him. "Do you ever get a break from it all?"

"Not really. Not yet anyway. If I take a break now, I might stop getting offered the big roles." He sees my look of trepidation. "It's not that bad," he says. "I do get weeks here and there. Like now, I'm here with you. And I'm all yours."

All mine. More tingles work their way across my body. "So, what's up with Mr. Grape?"

"Mr. and *Mrs.* Grape," he corrects me with a snarky smirk. "Linda—that's my travel agent—she's always booking me under names that have to do with food. I've been Mr. Burger, Mr. Linguini, Mr. Pita. I've heard she also books her clients using names of clothing, cities, and marine life."

"But don't they all know who you are when you go to pay with your credit card?" Then I remember it was Cole who paid. "Or does Cole always use *his?*"

He gets out his wallet and shows me his credit card. "Cole uses one of my cards. It's only got the name of my business on it for that very reason. But a lot of the time, they know who we are, especially if people like Courtney want special treatment."

I read his Visa card. "Treehouse Enterprises?"

"Yup. That's my business name. I use it for travel and purchases. Makes things easier sometimes."

"How long have you used that name?" I ask.

"A few years I guess."

Years?

He sees the surprise on my face. "I told you, Mal. Boyhood fantasies die hard."

I feel the blush cross my face and he chuckles.

"So, Cole doesn't have to stay in the suite with you?" I ask, wondering about the bodyguard/guardee dynamic.

"Occasionally we'll get a two-bedroom suite and he'll take one of the bedrooms. But now is not one of those occasions." He smiles at me suggestively. "But speaking of Cole. I'd like to go over a few things with you."

He motions to the couch and I sit. "Oh, okay."

He points to a door on the far side of the living room. "Cole's room is on the other side of that connecting door. He's been instructed that whenever I'm with you, he's to protect the both of us, not just me."

"What?" I ask, incredulously. "Why would he need to protect me?"

"Because I need you safe," he says. Then he shakes his head in disgust. "And because there are some sicko people in this world." He holds his hand out. "Can I see your phone, please?" I hand it to him and watch over his shoulder as he programs Cole's number into my contacts and sets it on my favorites screen.

He smiles up at me. "I'm on your favorites screen?"

I nod, embarrassed.

He whips out his phone and taps it a few times. "And you're on mine," he says, proudly showing me his phone.

I read his list of favorites. Ethan. Kyle. His mom and dad. Me. And then there is a girl named Megan. I look up at him and he shifts uncomfortably. He's obviously forgotten to wipe an old girlfriend or something. He cringes. "Sorry," he says. "Haven't cleaned it out in a while."

I want to ask who the hell Megan is. Because I'm pretty sure he claimed Courtney was his last girlfriend. But I fear Chad has a lot of skeletons in his closet and I'm just not sure I want to know about all of them. After all, does it matter what he did before me? I try to push aside my jealousy of a girl who may only exist as a memory on his phone.

He clears his throat. "Uh, anyway, call him anytime you need to. Even when we're not in town. He will always know where I am in case you need me."

A horrid grumbling sound comes from my stomach. "Oh, my gosh. Sorry about that," I say. "I haven't eaten since breakfast."

He looks at his watch. "It's nearly six o'clock, Mallory. Why didn't you eat lunch?" he scolds me.

"I wasn't hungry then. I guess I was . . . uh, nervous."

"Nervous?" He laughs. "Mal, you've seen me take a dump in the woods before. Why would you be nervous after that?"

I cover my mouth as I erupt in giggles. "I had forgotten all about that. I didn't actually watch you, you know. I did turn my back. I mean, gross."

We start reminiscing about old times, sinking into the couch, holding hands and talking until my stomach growls again.

"That's it, I'm feeding you, woman." He goes over to the desk and retrieves a menu. "Room service okay? It's not a picnic in Central Park or anything, but it means I get to keep you all to myself."

"Room service is perfect," I say.

He quickly calls in our order, not even bothering to ask what I want. He orders two cheeseburgers, medium rare. One without pickles. He also gets fries. And chocolate shakes. Because what good are fries if you don't have chocolate shakes to dip them in? I love that he knows all this about me.

And despite the fact that there's a huge dining room table in the suite, we sit on the floor and eat our burgers at the coffee table. I smile, thinking this was something we would do when we were kids. "In case I forgot to tell you, that picnic was the best picnic I've ever had in my entire life."

He ignores his half-eaten burger and catches my eyes. "Better than the one we had over in Greyson County when we saw all those horses and Julian tried to ride one bareback?"

I laugh at the memory. "Better," I tell him.

"How about the one we had out at my grandparents' place that summer when we made s'mores on the beach?"

"Better." I smile because he remembers. He remembers all of it.

"And the one at the lake, when your bikini top came off—that was a pretty damn great picn—"

"Nope," I interrupt. "It was the best, Chad. The best one ever. I'll never forget it."

He beams with pride. Then he startles me by reaching over me, grabbing me by the hips and lifting me on top of him. I'm straddling him as he stares up at me. "This," he says, wiping mustard from my lip with his thumb and then putting it in his mouth to clean it. "I'll never forget this or any other moment I get to spend with you. They are the best of my life, Mal." He puts his hand on my neck and pulls me to him, mashing our mouths and bodies together.

He tastes of ketchup and salt and chocolate. I don't even mind that he tastes of pickles. I feel him grow hard beneath me and my body takes over, undulating on top of him as we explore each other with our mouths. "God, Mal," he whispers, as his lips find my earlobe. "I've missed you so much."

"Me too," I say, my head falling back to give him more room to work.

"I think I missed you more these past weeks than the nine years we were apart," he says against my skin. Then he suddenly pulls away from me, looking guilty. "Not that I didn't miss you then. Because I swear I did. I thought about you all the time. But after that kiss two weeks ago. Jesus, do you know how hard it was to get on that plane and fly away from you?"

"I know what you mean," I say smiling down at him. "I feel the same way."

His head cocks to the side and he studies me. "You do?" he asks, tracing the ball of his thumb across my cheek. "I mean, do you really? Or are you just saying that? Because I'm not shitting you, Mal. These past weeks were torture. I'm not sure what I'm even going to do after . . . "

His eyes do all the talking after his words stop. I get it. I know exactly what he's saying. How are we going to be apart after this weekend? If we do all the things I think we are going to do. After spending three days together. If being apart from him after just one kiss was that hard, I can't even imagine what being apart after making love will feel like.

I put his face between my hands and caress his cheeks with my thumbs. "I'm not just saying it, Chad. It's true. Being without you these past weeks, it was horrible. And I know you're only here for a few days. But that's okay. Because if a few days is all I get, I'm willing to take it. I'll take whatever you give me."

He pulls my lips to his. "Everything," he whispers into them. "I want to give you everything."

CHAPTER SEVENTEEN

Chad

I pick Mallory up and carry her back to the bedroom. This is it. This is the moment I finally get to see her—finally get to *have* her. I place her down on the bed and lie beside her. I trace the outline of her face with my fingers. I want to remember every curve, every placement of each freckle, every nuance of her heated expression.

My heart thunders beneath my shirt. My hand shakes as it works its way down her shoulder. I realize I'm fucking terrified. I've been with a lot of girls. So many I don't even remember all of their names. But this time is different. I shake my head and snort a laugh before capturing her eyes with mine. "Now *I'm* the one who's nervous," I admit.

"You?" She tilts her head with a questioning gaze. "Why?"

I stare into her gorgeous green eyes. "You're so beautiful, Mallory. I want this to be perfect. I want to live up to your expectations. And, well, I might be a little worried about any preconceived notions you might have given that I'm, uh . . . "

"A famous movie star that girls drool over who has a reputation of being good with the ladies?" she asks, smirking.

"Ugh," I groan, burying my head in the crook of her neck. I wish I could take it all away. Turn back the clock and erase all the stupid shit I did.

"Chad." She runs her fingers through my hair and I look up at her. "Don't you think I'm nervous, too? Not because of who you are now, but who you *were*. I'm lying in bed with the boy I had a crush on all those years. We were perfect together then. This will be perfect, too. Because it's us."

Man up, Stone.

I climb on top of her, supporting my weight on my elbows as I hover over her lips. "Damn right it's us. It'll always be us, Mal." Then I claim her mouth as if it has always belonged to me. As I kiss her deeply, the nerves I felt disappear and turn into something else. Pure hunger for this woman. Every kiss with her is better than the one before. Every touch has us exploring new, uncharted territory.

I press myself into her, grinding our clothed bodies together in simulation of what is yet to come. A soft, mewling sound comes from the back of her throat. It's sexy as hell. I sit up and straddle her, fingering the hem of her shirt, visually asking for permission to remove it. She smiles. I don't hesitate another second before pushing it up her body, past her black lace bra and over her head. I don't even know where I throw it because all of my attention is focused on her breasts. Holy God, they're incredible. I put my hands on her, molding each breast into one of my hands. They fit perfectly. Warm and soft and oh, so natural.

My fingers find the front clasp of her bra and when I snap it open and take in her bare chest, I'm sure I've died and this is heaven. "Jesus, Mal. You are so beautiful."

Her hands pull at my shirt, begging to find what's underneath. I reach behind my head and pull it over me, depositing it next to the bed. Her hands on my chest feel incredible. But that's not what sends ripples of pleasure through me, it's the way her eyes take me in. She doesn't look at me like other women do; like I'm a prize they will get to brag about to their friends; like I'm a conquest to add to their accomplishments. No, Mallory looks at me in awe and with complete reverence, like she's seeing the Mona Lisa for the first time. Like she's unearthed some secret that is only known to her. And I swear to God it's better than any high I've ever gotten from drugs.

We take slow and careful pleasure exploring each other, learning one another's skin inch by silken inch. My fingers come upon a small raised scar several inches from her belly button. I get off her and position myself next to her as I lean down to examine it, running my finger carefully along it.

Mal shivers from my touch. "Appendix," she says. "I was twenty."

I frown, thinking of her scared and having an operation. For the millionth time, I scold myself for not being there for her. I bend over and kiss her scar, my tongue taking the same trail across it as my finger had. My hungry mouth works its way up her stomach, tasting every inch of her as I blaze a path to her breasts. Her nipples are stiff and they pucker further under my tongue. She groans as I lick and suck them, arching her back as her chest pushes into me. The sultry noises she's making have my dick straining painfully against the fly of my jeans.

As if reading my mind, Mallory's hand works its way between us, caressing me through the denim. I push into her, craving every stroke she gives me. Her dexterous fingers make easy work of unbuttoning my jeans, and when she slips her hand beneath my boxer briefs and touches my bare skin, I shout out, "Mallory, Jesus!"

I'm living my boyhood dream. Mallory Schaffer has my dick in her hands. And just like a boy, I'm not going to last very long unless I get a grip. Her hand slips from my jeans as I resume my spot on top of her. I watch her face as I unzip her pants. One look from her gives me the green light, so I work my way down her body, pulling off her pants and shoes in the process.

As I climb back up her legs, my mouth finds her smooth calves, then her knees, then her thighs, as she squirms beneath me. Her alluring musky scent hits me as I hover over her black lace panties. I push them aside and run a finger down her soft trail of curls to find her soaking wet. My dick dances in my jeans as I slip a finger inside her, then two.

"Chad," she says, breathlessly, pushing herself into me.

She fucks my fingers with her body and I can hardly stand it. I want to be inside her right now, but I need to go slow. Take my time with her. Make this an experience she will never forget. It's already the best sexual encounter I've had and yet she's only touched me for maybe thirty seconds.

I remove my fingers from her and she protests with a squeaky sigh that makes me chuckle. But I need to get rid of her panties. I pull them down her legs, kissing the sensitive skin along her inner knees as I go. When I return to the apex of her thighs, I hold her stare as she looks down on me when I press my mouth to her. Damn, that's hot—her watching me when I do this. My tongue runs slow circles around her clit as my fingers resume their expedition inside of her. Another minute of this has her eyes closing and her head falling back and lashing against the pillow as her thighs tighten around me.

"Oh, God!" she shouts at the ceiling as she pulsates around my fingers. I watch her taut stomach convulse as waves of pleasure shoot through her. It's got to be the hottest thing I've ever seen in my whole damn life.

As she recovers, I quickly remove my jeans, pulling a condom from my wallet before I deposit them on the floor. I lie next to her on the bed and show her the small square package. I didn't want to presume that she'd let me make love to her tonight, but I sure as hell was going to be prepared. I raise my eyebrows in question.

She smiles. "Yes, please," she says softly. Then she takes it from me. "Here, let me." She tears it open and carefully rolls the condom onto my rock-hard length as I try not to think about how many times she might have done this before with some other guy.

"I've always wanted to do that," she says with a shy smile.

Fuck. If she only knew how much better she just made this for me. As I kneel next to her, I take a moment to stare at her naked body and I wonder what the hell a guy like me ever did to deserve a woman like her. "Have I told you how beautiful you are?"

A blush works across her face and she nods. "Once or twice," she says, smiling.

"Well get used to it," I say. "Because it's true and I'm never going to let you forget it."

I climb on top of her and position myself at her entrance. I shake my head at the unbelievable reality that I'm about to make love to Mallory Schaffer. As I start to push inside her, I lean down and whisper, "This is everything I've ever wanted." And then I kiss her as our bodies join together for the very first time.

We moan into one another's mouths as I fill her completely. The feeling of being inside her is like no other. She's soft. Tight. Safe. And as I make love to a woman for what feels like the first time in my life, I find emotion flooding through me. I lock eyes with Mallory and see her experiencing the same thing. A tear escapes her eye and rolls back into her hair. I lean down and kiss the wet trail.

"God, Mal," I whisper in her ear, as I continue my long, soft strokes inside her.

Her hands glide over every inch of my back and then find their way down to my ass. She pushes me deeper inside of her, bringing her hips off the bed to meet mine with increasing speed. "Chad," she says, my name flowing off her lips like a prayer, "please."

I rise up on an elbow, changing my angle in hopes of finding that sweet spot that'll send her toppling over the edge. With my free hand, I grab her breast, kneading the soft mound, pinching her stiff nipple.

"Uh . . . Oh, God . . . Yes," she murmurs.

I can feel her begin to stiffen beneath me. Her thighs tightly embrace me and her fingers dig into my ass cheeks. She shouts my name as she bucks under me, her walls clamping down on me as I witness what is no doubt the eighth wonder of the world. Watching her orgasm has me quickly chasing my own. My sac tightens and waves of painful pleasure shoot through me as I empty myself into her before her aftershocks cease. "Unnnnngh," I cry, biting down on my lower lip as I pulsate inside her.

I collapse onto her, our slick bodies languid as we replenish our lungs with much-needed air. I can feel her racing heartbeat underneath mine. I stay on top of her until it calms; until our breathing slows and I find myself capable of purposeful movement.

I wince as I pull out of her, moving to her side before I wrap her tightly against me. "Jesus, Mal. I've never . . ."

"Me either," she says, craning her neck to look at me. We stare at each other for long drawn-out seconds. We don't need words to tell each other what just happened. That in these past minutes, our lives have forever changed. That never again will we accept anything less than what we just had. That we've become connected by a bond that cannot be broken.

I touch her face with my hand, her shimmering eyes mirroring mine. "I love you, Mallory Kate."

She closes her eyes, squeezing tears from them before looking at me again. "I love you, too, Chad Christopher."

I embrace her, needing to remember every detail of this moment until the day I die. I hold her until our bodies cool down, still slick from sweat and now becoming chilled from the movement of warm air circulating from the room's heating system. I lift her up and pull down the covers so we can climb in under them. Then I lay my head down on her pillow, inches from her radiant face. "I've loved you forever," I tell her.

"When did you first know?" she asks, tracing the outline of my ribs with her finger.

"Did you ever wonder why I didn't kiss you when we were in that play?"

She shakes her head. "I assumed because you were nervous. We both were."

"I had psyched myself up for it. Even Mr. Spencer told me it would seem more real if we kissed for the first time on opening night. That's why he didn't have us rehearse it. But right before I was supposed to kiss you, I realized I didn't want it to happen on that stage. I wanted our first kiss to belong only to us, not a few hundred other people. And that's when I knew. I was only fifteen years old, but I knew right then that I was in love with you."

Her eyes glisten once again. "Thank you," she says. "Thank you for not kissing me back then. Now it belongs only to us. Well, and maybe Cole. And my dad, if he was peeking out of the curtains."

I laugh along with her. "What about you? When did *you* know?"

"The night of your premiere, when I saw you at the club," she says. "When you made eye contact with me, I just knew. I knew instantly what I had denied for the past nine years. And that's why I had to get away. I was in love with a memory. A man I could never have. And I feared the rest of my life would be lived under the shadow of what could have been."

"Wait," I say, rising up on my elbow. "You knew then that you loved me but you made me work my ass off to get you to see me again?"

"Can you blame me?" she asks. "You do come with a little baggage, Chad."

I blow out a long sigh. "Yeah, I guess you're right. I'm glad you could get past all that. The only thing that matters from here on out is you and me."

She frowns. "I'm not sure I *am* past it yet. There's still so much we don't know about each other."

"We have forever to figure it all out, Mal. All you need to know is that I'm with you and only you. And if you tell me the same, that's all I need to hear."

She nods. "Of course, Chad. It's only you."

"Good." I kiss her on the tip of her nose and jump out of bed. "I'm going to clean up. Do you need anything?"

"Nope." She lays her head lazily on the pillow. "Everything I need is right here."

There's that look again—better than drugs.

I get rid of the condom in the bathroom. Then I go grab a few bottles of water from the minibar in the living room. My phone vibrates across the coffee table so I pick it up on along the way. I plant myself back in bed and Mallory rests her head on my chest as I peruse my missed messages. There are a few from Paul, wanting me to look at some new scripts when I get back. Another from him begging for me to lay low and not make a big deal over anything. That's code for: don't let the press photograph you with Mallory because it'll be bad for ticket sales. Ron, my lawyer, wants to sit down and tie up a few loose ends over my *Defcon* sequel contract before pre-production meetings. But it's when I read Kendra's text that my entire body stiffens.

"What is it?" Mal asks, raising her head off my chest to look at me. "Your heart rate just went through the roof, Chad. Is everything okay?"

I shake my head in disgust and put my phone on the bedside table. I put my arms around her. "Just some of that baggage we talked about."

"Can you tell me about it?"

I nod. "You're not going to like it."

"Will you tell me anyway?" she asks.

I close my eyes and steel myself for her reaction. "Some girl is claiming I'm her baby daddy."

Mallory shoots up in bed, drawing the covers around her. "What? I thought you said you hadn't been with anyone in a while."

"I haven't." I sit up too, taking her hands into mine. "She's not pregnant *now*. Claims the two-year-old kid she has is mine. Listen, it's not all that unusual for people to come out of the woodwork and make accusations like this, especially considering my reputation. It's not true, Mal. But you better believe the media will drool over the story."

She takes in a shaky breath. "But, how do you know it's not true?"

"For one, I always wear condoms. Always."

She narrows her accusing eyes at me. "How can you be so sure, Chad? I mean, you didn't even remember losing a testicle at the Santa Monica Pier. How can you be absolutely sure you used a condom every single time you slept with someone?"

Shit. She does have a valid point. "Because I know, Mallory. I've taken a lot of risks in my life, but that's one thing I didn't mess around with. Plus, the timeline doesn't hold water. It's been over three years since I got clean. I've only been with a handful of girls since then. She doesn't have a leg to stand on. Who knows, maybe I did hook up with her once, long ago, and now she's looking to cash in on that because of *Defcon One.* Kendra's doing damage control, but one way or another, it'll get out there. And people will believe anything once it's in print."

I can tell Mallory is very upset by this. I squeeze her hands in assurance. "Baby, it's not true. You have to trust me. Do you know how many other girls have made the same claim? Five. She's the sixth one. And every one of the six is a lie."

She closes her eyes. "The thought that you could have a kid out there somewhere . . ."

"I don't, Mal. If I did, I assure you I'd take responsibility. But that isn't going to happen. These girls are liars. Con artists. Sluts who made their damn beds and now they have to lie in them."

Mallory pulls away from me and leans her back against the headboard, drawing her legs up to her chest. "I'm one of them."

"One of who?"

A tear rolls down her cheek. "One of the sluts who made their bed and had to lie in it."

"What the hell are you talking about, Mal?"

She pulls the sheets up to her chin, almost as if using them for protection against what she's going to tell me. "Do you remember when I told you about Penny Garrison?"

"Yeah, that she got pregnant and had to go live at Hope For Life because her parents kicked her out?"

She nods. "I'm the one who told her about the place," she says.

My heart rate shoots through the fucking roof. "How did *you* know about it, Mal?"

She inhales deeply through her nose, closing her eyes as she releases a painful sigh. "Because I thought I might have to live there, too."

She got pregnant? I lose my breath as much as if the wind got knocked out of me. I don't know what to say. There is nothing *to* say. My heart is in my throat and I feel helpless. "What? . . . How? . . . When?"

"I kind of went wild after you left," she says. "I know I still had Julian and all, but it wasn't the same. I guess I went looking for the attention I was no longer getting from you." She covers her eyes with her hands, her head shaking as she reveals her secret. "I slept with several guys in a short period of time, and . . . and I ended up pregnant. I was sixteen."

"Oh, Mal." I scoot up the bed and situate myself next to her, leaning back on the headboard like she is. I don't touch her. I'm not sure she wants to be touched right now, when she's telling me the ugly truths of her past. "Will you tell me about it? Please?"

"There isn't much to tell really. I was reckless and stupid and then one day at school I threw up for no reason so I peed on a stick and it turned blue. I was sure my parents would disown me. They went to church every Sunday. The dragged me to youth group and instilled their values into me. I was terrified of what they would do if they found out. But I also couldn't dream of having an abortion, so I didn't know what to do."

She had a fucking baby? Oh, my God.

"So I did my research and found a place where I could go to have the baby if my parents made me leave."

"But you didn't have to go there, right? I knew your parents, Mal. There is no way they would kick their only daughter to the curb. I don't care if they were the right hand of God, there is no way they would abandon you." I think of Mallory, sixteen, helpless and alone living at a shelter because she'd already been abandoned by one person in her life. "Please tell me they didn't."

She shakes her head. "No, they didn't kick me out. Quite the opposite, in fact. They were very supportive. They even said they would help me raise the baby."

I'm confused. Surely she would have told me by now if she were a mom. There was no evidence of a child at her house. No mention by her friends or Richard. "What happened?" I ask. "Do you have a child, Mal?"

"No," she says. "I had a miscarriage at seventeen weeks." She looks down at her stomach, bereft. "I know it was for the best."

"I'm so sorry." I put my arm around her and pull her close as she sinks into my side. "It's all my fault. I should never have left you."

Her eyes snap to mine. "It was *not* your fault, Chad. And I won't have you thinking it was. Your parents moved you away and there was nothing you could do about it. It was on me. I missed my best friend and I handled it poorly. I guess we both did stupid things in our past. You turned to drugs to fill whatever void you felt and I turned to boys."

There's so much truth in her words. More than I ever realized. She's right. There was a void. She was missing from my life as much as if I'd lost a piece of myself. "I wish I could have been there for you," I say. "But I'm glad Julian was at least."

She shakes her head. "Julian didn't know."

"About the guys or about the baby?" I ask.

"The baby," she says. "I suspected he knew about the guys, but we never talked about it. I think he was in denial. I'm actually kind of surprised he didn't tell you about them since the two of you talked long after you and I stopped."

"He never said a word," I tell her. "So nobody knew about the pregnancy except you and your parents? What about the father?"

She shakes her head. "I wasn't even sure who it was. And before you ask, you didn't know him . . . or them. It wasn't anyone from our school. Nobody else knew about any of it. It wasn't until Julian and I broke up that I decided to tell him."

"Why tell him then?"

"Because he called me a tease; said it was why he had to sleep with someone else. He never understood why I went and hooked up with those guys after you left but wouldn't sleep with *him*. Then when he cheated on me, I finally told him why I hadn't been able to be with him. I didn't want to risk another pregnancy. I wasn't ready for that kind of responsibility yet."

"God, Mal, I'll bet he felt about as low as a guy can feel after that."

She nods. "He did. But feeling that way didn't exonerate him. He should have ended things with me first."

"Guys are dicks," I say. "We can be stupid bastards, can't we?"

She turns to me, begging me with her eyes. "Don't be a stupid bastard with me, Chad. I'm not sure I could take it after tonight."

"Never," I promise her. "Never again." We sink down into the bed and I spoon her from behind as she falls into sleep. I rub my hand across her flat stomach. I don't tell her that no way in hell would I ever get a girl pregnant. Not ever. Not unless that girl was her.

CHAPTER EIGHTEEN

Mallory

Forty-eight hours we've been holed up in Chad's hotel suite. Forty-eight incredible, romantic, blissfully happy hours. We've christened every room and every surface. My body is so deliciously sore, I may never recover. I didn't know it could be like this. I never even had an orgasm at the hands of a man until this weekend. And now I've had ten. He's so proud of them that he's keeping count.

Tonight, however, we're having company. Julian is going out to dinner with us. It was Chad's idea. He's determined to get his support for our relationship. Quite frankly, I'm not sure why Julian is being so negative about it. I get that he doesn't want to see me hurt, but it's kind of hypocritical coming from him seeing as *he* hurt me. But deep down, even if Julian had never cheated on me, I know it wouldn't have worked out. It never felt right. Being with *any* guy never felt right until now.

Julian arrives right on schedule, his head shaking in disapproval as he enters the Presidential Suite. "Seriously?" he asks Chad. "Show off much?"

"Let's get something straight right fucking now," Chad says, closing the door behind Julian. "I've got money, Julian. Lots of it. I inherited ten million from my dead grandparents; and as of late, I'm making half of that for every film I do." He motions his hand around at our surroundings. "This is nothing to me, a drop in the bucket. I'm sorry if you think I should be staying at a goddamn Motel Six, but that's not going to happen. This isn't to show off. I'm not playing any games here. So get over yourself and deal with it."

I try to pick my chin up off the floor. Oh, my God. I knew he was rich, but hearing him spell it out like that, it's more than I can even fathom. I make fifty-eight thousand dollars a year. He probably makes that in interest alone every month. My head is spinning.

"So if you are going to belittle me for something," Chad says to Julian, "there are a whole lot of other things you can choose besides my portfolio." He walks over to the minibar. "Now do you want some ridiculously overpriced champagne or don't you?"

"Sure." Julian shakes his head, laughing as he walks over to greet me. "Hey," he says, pulling me in for a hug.

I peek at Chad to see his jaw twitching at our embrace. *Boys.* That man has nothing to worry about. He branded me as his from our first kiss a few weeks ago. He's ruined me for anyone else.

Cole knocks on the connecting door and sticks his head through as Julian and I get handed glasses of champagne. "A word, Thad?"

"Make yourself comfortable," Chad says, motioning to the couch. "I'll only be a minute." He walks through the door to Cole's room, closing it behind him.

"Are you staying here with him?" Julian asks, cutting right to the chase.

"I am, yes."

"So you're sleeping with him." He sucks in air between his teeth, producing a hissing noise. "Boy, that didn't take long. Not even *close* to a year, huh?"

"That's not fair, Julian. Things were different then and you know it. I'm twenty-four now and perfectly capable of making responsible decisions."

"Have you told him why we broke up?" he asks.

"I've told him everything. I don't have any secrets from him."

He snorts. "Has he told *you* everything?"

"We're getting there," I say. "He has a lot more to tell than I do."

"So that's a no," he says, punctuating his words with a swig of his drink. "What are you going to do when everyone finds out about this? There's already buzz about some mystery woman in his life, but the press still keeps printing stories about him and Courtney Benson. Is he with you or not?"

"Yes. Of course, he's with me. I . . . I love him, Julian."

He runs a hand through his dark hair. "You *love* him? It's only been a few weeks, Mallory. You're setting yourself up to get hurt."

"A few weeks and ten years," I remind him. "It's not like I met him yesterday, Julian. And he loves me, too. This thing is for real."

"Then why doesn't he have the balls to admit it in public?" he asks. "Why is he keeping you a secret? If it were me, I'd be shouting it from the damn rooftops. What does that even tell you?"

"He's trying to protect me," I say. "Once we go public, our relationship will be scrutinized. People will want my picture or an interview. He doesn't want me to have to deal with that."

"Hmmm," he gruffs.

"You need to give him a chance, Julian. He hurt me back then. He hurt you, too. But his parents moved him across the country. He had no control over that. Can we really blame him for losing touch? Is that really worth holding a grudge? Haven't worse indiscretions been forgiven?" I raise my brows at him, giving him an accusing stare.

He looks guiltily at the ground. "You're right. I know you're right. It's just hard for me, Mallory. You have to know that. It's hard for me to see you with *any* man, let alone Chad."

What? "What are you saying, Julian?"

"I'm saying that I was a royal douche and I should have never cheated on you. I didn't know a good thing when I had it."

I cock my head to the side, absorbing his words. "Oh, Julian." I had no idea he still felt that way about me. He's dated a lot of women these past few years, but none have stuck. Is that why? Now I'm the one who feels guilty, parading Chad around under his nose. Talking about him endlessly whenever he and Mel and I have dinner.

"It's fine," he says, downing another long drink. "Well, it's not fine, but I'll get over it. Eventually. I know you don't see me that way anymore. It's my issue, not yours. But he's still got to prove himself before I can trust him with you."

I nod my head. "He will. He is." I put my hand on his arm. "Please give him a chance. Get to know him again."

The connecting door opens and Chad walks through, his disapproving stare honing in on my hand that is touching Julian. He looks at me and I try to reassure him with my eyes that he has nothing to worry about.

"Change of plans," he says, walking over to join us. "Someone at the restaurant blabbed and word got out that we were coming. There's a mob of people there now." He turns his attention to me.

"I know you're probably feeling claustrophobic by now, but I didn't know what else to do. I arranged for the hotel to cater our dinner up here in the suite. That's what took me so long."

"That's fine, Chad. Of course, we should stay in. Shouldn't we, Julian?" I shoot him a pleading look. "We don't need a crowd watching us eat dinner and spreading rumors. Didn't we have enough of those when we were teenagers?"

The two of them laugh as we start reminiscing about how everyone accused us of being a threesome. By the time dinner arrives, I feel Julian may actually be coming around. It still makes me sad that all this time, he's felt that way about me and I didn't know. Not that it would have changed anything. Even when I was *with* Julian, I had a hard time seeing myself with him.

We get through dinner, enjoying a delicious spread of surf and turf, without any more fighting or animosity. And after, Chad asks me if I would mind if he takes Julian out for a drink. All I can do is smile. He's making a real effort with him.

I say goodbye to Julian and Chad at the door, but as I turn to walk away, Chad catches me by the arm, spinning me up against his chest. "I'll be back in one hour," he says to me privately. "I want you naked in my bed when I return."

Heat spreads between my legs at his words. I look up at him and whisper a tease. "A bit bossy, aren't we?"

He grabs me behind my neck, pulling me to him as he whispers back, "*You're* the boss tonight. Anything you want—you get." He kisses the tip of my nose before closing the door, leaving me a mushy pile of hormones. The next sixty minutes will seem like an eternity.

~ ~ ~

Sunday evening has come all too quickly. The thought of him leaving me after what we've shared this weekend has me straining to hold back tears as Cole drives us back to my house.

"You're awfully quiet," Chad says, squeezing my hand.

Of course I am. This is the moment I've dreaded since he picked me up Thursday night. What happens next? We didn't talk about it at all this weekend. What if he doesn't have any time for me? What if this is all I get for now? Can I live with that?

"Sorry," I say. "I had such a great time this weekend. I guess I just don't want it to end. Thank you for everything."

He chuckles. "Mallory, you didn't set foot outside the hotel room for three straight days, you call that fun?"

"The best," I say, remembering all the different ways we showed our love for each other.

His face breaks into a triumphant smile. "Thank you," he says. "It was the best weekend I've ever had, Mal."

I nod, looking up at him as a tear trickles down my cheek. He wipes it with his thumb. "Hey, none of this. Don't you know this is not the end? It's only the beginning, Mallory. The first of so many more great times to come."

I sniff back more tears as Cole pulls up to my house after a drive that didn't last nearly long enough to say goodbye. Cole exits the car but doesn't open my door. I look at Chad and he smiles, pulling a small package out of his carry-on bag.

"You got me a present?" I ask. "When did you have time to do that?"

He shrugs, nodding at the package. "Open it."

I tear off the ribbon and open the package. Inside is a piece of paper. It's an airline itinerary. Dated three weeks from now. From JFK to LAX. And it has my name on it. *He's bought me a ticket to L.A. for my spring break?* I want to be happy, but I can't. I've already got plans with three other teachers from school. We're driving down to Myrtle Beach to stay in a rental house.

"Oh, Chad." I look out the window trying not to cry.

"Don't you want to know how I knew when your spring break was?" he asks.

"How?"

"I called Melissa last night when I was with Julian. I cleared it with her. She said she even knows another teacher who would be willing to take your place on the trip. It'll be great, Mal. You can come see where I live. Hang out with my parents. Meet some of my friends." Then his smile turns into a frown. "Oh, shit," he says. "That is unless you'd rather go to the beach with your friends." He takes the itinerary from me, folding it up and placing it back into the box. "I overstepped my bounds, didn't I? I'm sorry. I shouldn't have assumed you'd drop everything to be with me. I'm being selfish. And right after I promised you I wouldn't be a stupid bastard."

I snatch the box out of his hands. "I would love to come visit you, Chad. And you aren't selfish. You were actually very considerate to clear it with Melissa first." I can't help the smile that overtakes my face. "A whole week together?"

"Not just a week. Nine days," he says. "You're flying out right after school on Friday and I'm keeping you until the next Sunday night. It won't be exactly like this weekend. I'll have to work a little; we have pre-production meetings for the *Defcon* sequel. But the rest of the time, I promise I'm all yours."

"All mine?" I say, biting my lower lip. "I like the sound of that."

He runs a finger across the lip I was biting. "Quit that or I'll be riding to JFK with a painful hard-on." He leans over to kiss me, but instead, I climb onto his lap, pressing my mouth to his as I grind against his growing erection.

"Good luck with that," I say, giggling between kisses. Spring break is three weeks away. Three weeks of not being able to see him. Kiss him. Touch him. I need to remember what he tastes like. I need to remember everything about him. Two weeks without him was torture. Three will feel like forever.

"I am, you know," he murmurs into my mouth.

"You are what?" I ask breathlessly.

"I'm yours, Mallory Kate," he says, pulling back but keeping our lips only inches apart. He frames my face with his hands. "In a way, I always have been, I just didn't know it. But now, after this weekend, I can't imagine myself with anyone else. I'm yours—for as long as you'll have me."

Tears stream down my face as he holds my eyes with his. I've never seen more truth in them than I do right this second. "What if I say I want you forever?" I ask with a thick voice.

"I'd tell you I'm the luckiest son-of-a-bitch to ever walk the earth." He pulls me to him, crashing our lips together one last time.

~ ~ ~

"How are you holding up?" Kyle asks after hugging me as we walk into Mitchell's restaurant for dinner.

"I'm good," I say. "You don't have to babysit me, you know."

He flashes me a look of annoyance. "I'm not babysitting you," he says. "I'm catching up with an old friend."

"Did he ask you to check up on me?"

"No," he says, looking over to catch my questioning eyes. "Okay, yes, but I was going to call you anyway. I feel bad that we've lived so close and haven't been in contact."

"Me, too. I've missed you." We get seated at our table and when the hostess leaves, I ask him, "Why did you ask how I'm holding up, Kyle?"

"Because if you're even half as love-sick as my brother, you are miserable being so far away from him."

I can't help my smile. "He's miserable?"

He laughs. "You don't have to look so happy about it. But yes. He's been away from you for two weeks and quite frankly, I'm surprised he hasn't hopped on a plane back here to kidnap you and take you with him."

Part of me would love that. But the logical half of me knows I have responsibilities here. My job. My volunteer work. My dad. Not to mention Mel and Julian. "He's been really busy," I say.

With the national release of *Defcon One* last weekend, he's been flying all over the country doing interviews. Between that and meeting with his manager, the studio, his lawyer, his publicist; not to mention preparations for the film he's going to shoot this summer, he's been booked solid. I'm surprised he finds time to call and text me every day. But he does, and it's become the highlight of my existence. I'm pathetically love-sick. I'm counting down the hours until I get to see him on Friday.

Skylar Mitchell sees us and comes over to say hello. We've become good friends; she and her sisters have been very welcoming to me, making me a part of their close-knit family. I stand up to hug her around her baby bump. "How long is it now?" I ask.

"Eight more weeks." She rubs her belly. "So, how's our movie star doing? I saw him on the news last night," she says, sympathy washing across her face.

She must have seen the story about him and Courtney. Once again, the buzz is that the two of them are still together. There was even video of them being ushered through the Miami airport, Courtney tugging Chad by his hand. Of course, the cameras zoomed in on their hands, not bothering to show how he pulled away from her. And even though I know the story is made up, it still hurts to see him with her. They're always being thrown together and there is no end in sight. After all, she's his leading lady in the sequel to be filmed this summer. "He's fine," I say. "Don't believe everything you see on TV, Skylar."

"I know," she says. "Still, I know it's hard for you. When Griffin is away on photo shoots with glamorous models, it's hard for me not to feel jealous. But it's part of the job. That man loves you, Mallory. Everyone can see that."

"Not everyone," I say, looking down at the table. I know it's stupid to wish our relationship was public knowledge. I realize as soon as that happens, everything could change.

"Everyone who matters," she says, before running off to deal with a kitchen crisis.

We order dinner, Kyle and I falling into comfortable conversation like no time has passed since we were kids. What is it about the Stone brothers that makes them able to charm their way into the hearts of all women?

"I really am sorry I never contacted you," he says. "I guess I just didn't know what to say to you back then after Chad just left you hanging. But there really wasn't much to say. He was lost to drugs. He was in his own world and he wasn't himself. We were all scared to death that we'd get a middle-of-the-night phone call saying he was dead. It was that bad, Mallory."

I shudder thinking about what my life would be like without him. Tears flood my eyes at the thought of living in a world where Chad doesn't exist.

"You really love him, don't you?" he asks.

I nod, using my napkin to dab my eyes. "I think I always have."

"He never shut up about you in the beginning, you know. When we first moved to L.A., you were all he talked about. Getting that job on *Malibu 310* was the best and worst thing that ever happened to him. It all happened so fast and he didn't know how to handle it. And when that Heather bitch got him hooked on drugs, he became someone else entirely." He runs a hand through his hair in obvious frustration over the memory. Then he studies me. "Oh, shit. I never really put it together."

"Put what together?" I ask.

"Heather Crawford. She looks a lot like you. Same color hair. She even has green eyes and freckles." He shakes his head. "No wonder he latched onto her. I guess he was trying to hold onto to you through her or something."

"*She's* the one who got him doing drugs?" I hate her. I hate her more than I've ever hated anyone because she took him from me. From his family.

He nods. "That was when it all started. The gambling, the fighting, the . . . women." He cringes when he says the last word.

I stare blankly at Kyle. Chad hasn't yet let me into the entirety of his painful past. I only know bits and pieces and what I've seen in the news.

"He hasn't told you everything, has he?" Kyle asks.

I shake my head. "But that's okay. I'm not sure I want to know the details. He's not that person anymore."

"He's not," Kyle says. "But that doesn't mean you won't have to deal with a lot of crap, kiddo. The stuff he did in the past, it follows him around like stink on shit. Bookies still contact him, trying to lure him back in the game, even after all this time. He's got some pending lawsuits stemming from fights he got into. Hell, do you know he even stole from our parents, before he was eighteen and got control of his *Malibu* money?"

I gasp. I knew he was messed up, but it was even worse than I thought. "Why wouldn't he tell me that?"

"Probably because he thought you'd run," he says. He reaches across the table and pats my hand. "Listen, Mallory, none of this should make you nervous. He's very committed to you. But it is a lot to take in and it's a lot you might have to deal with."

"I'm glad I didn't know everything," I admit. "I think it would have scared me away a few weeks ago. But things are different now. And we've all done things we're ashamed of. We shouldn't be defined by them."

"You're just as awesome now as you were when we were kids, Mallory. My brother doesn't deserve you," he says.

"I feel like I'm the one who's undeserving, Kyle. It's hard for me to see him as that deviant bad boy celebrity now. He's just regular old Chad to me. He's the guy who came in to fix my dad's leaky faucet when he brought me home one night a few weeks ago. A movie star, who could have easily called a high-priced plumber, crawled under our sink and got his hands dirty just because he wanted to feel normal. He's the man who, when he took me out to dinner, ordered a pizza for the homeless guy out back, and then stuffed a roll of bills into the pizza box. He does so many selfless things, how can I not see him as anything but wonderful?"

Kyle smiles with pride as our dinner arrives; and we eat, talking about old times. Laughing about the trouble we'd find ourselves in.

"What about you?" I ask. "Is there someone special in your life?"

He shakes his head. "There's no time. The last year of med school is crazy. I'm busy working in the hospital and when I'm not there, I'm studying pretty much all the time."

"Why do you do it?" I ask. It's the same question I asked his older brother. "I mean, Chad told me what he inherited from your grandparents. I assume you got the same. My dad has told me many times how grueling med school and residency can be. Why go through it all?"

He shrugs. "I guess it comes down to wanting to help people," he says. "I donate to several charities, and I always keep cash on me for when I see people in need, but sometimes giving money isn't enough. These people need someone to care about them. To go that extra mile. Too many doctors these days are in it for the paycheck. They see indigent people as a nuisance. I see them as a quick turn of fate—something that could have happened to any of us given certain circumstances. Eventually, I want to run a clinic for those people. One that doesn't just 'treat 'em and street 'em.' I mean, if I could just help one person's life turn around for the better, it would all be worth it."

"Wow," I say.

Kyle narrows his eyes at me in question. "What?"

"You Stone boys sure know how to make a girl swoon, don't you?"

"Swoon?" he asks, laughing.

"Yes. You are all inherently good people. Well, when you're not doped up on drugs," I say, wrinkling my nose.

"We have incredible parents," he says.

"I know you do. I can't wait to see them when I go to L.A."

He signs the check and escorts me to the train station around the corner. Along the way, we pass a newsstand and my whole world changes in the blink of an eye. It changes because I see myself plastered across the cover of a tabloid magazine. I jump behind Kyle, using him as camouflage. "Kyle, oh my God, look." I point to the magazine.

Kyle quickly snatches up every copy, throwing a wad of cash at the proprietor. Then instead of walking me to the train station as planned, he hails me a cab. "It was bound to happen sooner or later, Mallory." He hands me one of the copies as he puts me in the back seat. Then he gives the driver some cash. "Call his publicist, she'll tell you how to handle this. It's not going to be as bad as you might think. Things like this blow over quickly."

I nod, hoping he's right. "Thanks for dinner, Kyle. Let's do it again soon." I try to keep the terror out of my voice.

"Next time we might even let Ethan come," he says, winking at me.

As the cab takes me back to where I parked my car just outside the city, I study my picture on the front page. It's a pretty clear picture of me. In a robe. Next to a half-naked Chad in the living room of his hotel suite. One of the room service team must have snapped the picture. My heart sinks. Everyone who knows me will recognize me. What will my colleagues think? My students? The article claims Thad Stone has stepped out on Courtney Benson, having an affair with a local New York City resident on the side. They claim this is typical for the star, leaving scorned women in his wake. The only solace—there is no mention of my name. They haven't found that out at least. But I'm sure it won't be long.

I pick up my phone to see a few missed texts from Chad and one from Kendra since I'd had my phone off during dinner.

Chad: Call me, Mal.

Chad: Someone took a picture of us in the hotel. You look hot, BTW. But it's out there now. They haven't identified you yet. Hopefully, they won't before you come here. I don't want you dealing with that shit without me.

Chad: Mallory, are you okay?

Kendra: Hi, Mallory. Give me a call re: the tabloid photo.

I roll to voicemail trying to get Chad so I call Kendra. "Hi, Kendra, it's Mallory Schaffer."

"Hi, Mallory, how are you?"

"Things could be better," I say.

"So, you've seen it?"

"Yes."

"And you are wondering what you should do about it?"

"Yes."

"Well, they haven't found out your name yet, but I imagine it won't take them long. We don't want to make a statement until that happens. So for now, my best advice is for you to do nothing."

"What do you mean, make a statement?" I ask.

"Have you and Chad not talked about this?" she asks, sounding concerned.

"No, why?"

She sighs into the phone. "We've had a few meetings about this subject over the past two weeks, Mallory."

"Meetings? About *me?*"

"About your relationship, more specifically. Chad's manager and the studio don't want a serious relationship being front page news. They think it will hurt box office sales of the new release. They want the illusion of the leading man and lady having a love affair. Especially as they prepare to film the sequel."

I close my eyes. "What does Chad say?"

"I think this is a conversation you should be having with *him*, Mallory," she says. "Chad loves you and wants to keep you safe. I think he would prefer to go public with your status, but he seems to be acquiescing to the higher powers that be. He still has a job to do. This is all part of it."

My heart sinks into my stomach. Keeping me hidden is part of his job. Maybe Julian was right. "So, I'm the other woman?" I ask. "The slut who he's cheating on Courtney with?"

"No. Of course not," she says. "Our official statement will be that you're a childhood friend and you've recently rekindled your friendship. End of story."

"Oh, come on," I scoff. "Did we look like friends in that picture?"

"I can't tell you when or if that position will change, Mallory. We'll deal with it as we have to, but for now, that's what we'll say."

"And I'm to go along with it?" I ask in defiance.

She sighs into the phone. "I'm not going to tell you what to say, Mallory. But it would be best if you could put up a united front. Listen, aren't you flying out in a few days? We can sit down and talk about it then. Maybe we'll be lucky and your name won't become public before you get here."

The whole way home I wonder if it's worth it. I love him, but am I willing to be labeled the friend, at best? At worst, the other woman? People will hate me. And it looks like Chad might just be okay with that.

CHAPTER NINETEEN

Chad

The past few days have been horrible. Not just because I miss the hell out of Mal, but because our conversations seem strained. Ever since her picture came out in that tabloid magazine, she's been standoffish. I've told her everything will be okay, that we'll deal with it together. But all she says is we'll talk about it when she gets here. It scares the shit out of me, quite frankly. I've been wondering if she's going to break up with me but didn't want to do it over the phone. Maybe it's all too much for her to deal with.

I can't even go into the airport to meet her. Neither can Cole. He's become well known as my bodyguard now and the pap knows that where he is, I'm not far behind. It would cause too much of a stir if either of us showed up to collect her, so I sit here in the back of a limo, not knowing my fate, while Kendra goes inside to get her. I know Mal will think it's pretentious, me getting a limousine. But I didn't want our first meeting in three weeks to be witnessed by anyone else. Plus, if she *is* breaking up with me, I didn't want anyone to see me get on my knees and beg.

The back door opens and Mallory gets inside. Our eyes lock. A million emotions pass between us. But thankfully, one trumps all the rest. The love I have for her grows stronger each time I see her. She becomes more beautiful every time we're apart. Her eyes tear up and spill over. I reach out to her. "Mal, what's wrong?"

She sniffs, wiping a tear with the back of her finger. "I . . . I was starting to think this was a bad idea," she says, tucking her face into my shoulder. "But just now, with the way you looked at me, I can't imagine being without you."

I wrap her face in my hands, forcing her to look up at me. "Were you?" I ask, my heart hammering in my chest. "Imagining being without me?"

She nods reluctantly as I feel the car pull away from the curb. "I didn't want to," she says. "But with the photo and you not wanting to admit to our relationship. I wasn't sure . . ."

"Not wanting to admit to it?" I say, incredulously. "Mal, I want to put up billboards announcing to everyone that I fucking love you. Don't you know that? It's Paul. The studio. They think it's a bad idea. He's my manager, baby. I have to trust he knows what's best for my career. It doesn't mean I don't love you. I do. I love you so much. I've only ever loved you."

"I know. I'm sorry," she says. "I guess it just took me seeing you again to understand that."

"Well then, there's no way in hell I'm going three weeks without seeing you again. I don't care if I have to fly to New York for two hours and fly back. I'm not giving you another chance at second thoughts."

"You'd do that for me?"

"You have no idea the depths of what I'd do for you, Mallory Kate."

"Right now, I'd just like you to kiss me," she says with a sultry smile.

She doesn't have to ask me twice. I shift her up onto my lap, pulling her head down until her lips meet mine. She tastes exactly like I remember. Strawberries and mint. I put my hand on her thigh, a low growl escaping me at the feel of her bare skin under her skirt. "I like this," I murmur against her lips. "Easy access."

"It was a little chilly in New York," she says, allowing my lips to explore her neck. "But I was hoping it would be seasonable out here and I was right."

"We should have great weather this week," I say. "I'm going to be able to give you that beach vacation after all." My fingers travel up to the apex of her thighs, being met with her damp panties. I push them aside and slip a finger inside her as she gasps. "Jesus, Mal. I'm not sure I can wait. Want to live dangerously?"

Her eyes widen as she looks at me in surprise. Then she looks at the closed partition separating us from Cole and Kendra. "Don't worry," I say. "I may have mentioned to them not to bother us unless the damn car was on fire."

She looks back at me and smiles. *Holy shit.* I never really thought she'd agree. I waste no time at all shifting her on my lap so she's straddling me. Then I push up her skirt and, taking care not to dig into her skin, I rip the panties right off her.

"Caveman much?" she asks, laughing.

I cup her breasts through her shirt, not wanting to expose her just in case there actually *is* a fire in the limo. She feels incredible under my hungry hands. She's been with me all of five minutes, and already I'm rock hard beneath her. Hell, just the thought of her gets me hard. These past weeks, I've felt like a teenage boy again, needing to get my rocks off frequently or else walk around with a constant hard-on.

She untucks my shirt and puts her hands underneath it, exploring my chest as I continue to explore hers. She unbuttons my pants and I remove my hands from her just long enough to lower them to my thighs. She takes my hard length in her hand, watching herself give me long, slow strokes. She's taking control and it's hot as hell.

I feel the car slow and I know we're getting off the highway, meaning we don't have a whole lot of time. I'll take my time with her later. Right now, I just need to be inside her. "I'm not going to last very long, Mal. And neither is this drive." I push two fingers inside her, circling my thumb around her slick clit. She's so ready. I reach underneath me to get a condom out of my wallet, putting it on in mere seconds. She lifts herself up and slowly sheaths me with her tight walls.

"Oh, God," she sighs as I fill her.

Hearing what this does to her brings me right to the edge. I do everything I can to hold off. I want her there with me. I whisper things into her ear, hoping my words will heighten her arousal. "You're so beautiful, Mallory. I dreamed about your perfect breasts. Your soft skin. About tasting you. You can't imagine how much I want to taste you. And I will . . . later." I put a hand between us and rub slow circles on her clit. "I want to make you come so hard you can't see straight. The way you make me come. Even when you're not with me, you make me come that hard. Only you, baby."

Her breaths come in shorts spurts as she works herself up and down on me with increasing speed. I feel my muscles tighten. "That's it," I say. "Jesus, you feel so good. So tight. Come with me, Mal."

"Uhhhh . . . Oh, Chad." She bites down on my shoulder to keep herself from screaming. The sensual pain sends me right over the cliff with her and I grunt loudly, pumping myself inside her as her walls squeeze and pulsate against me.

The car comes to a stop and I hear voices. We must be at the gate to my neighborhood. I help Mallory situate herself next to me and then I take off the condom, roll down the window and chuck it into the passing bushes.

Mallory giggles. "You can be fined up to a thousand dollars for littering, you know."

"Worth every penny," I tell her with a wink.

We pull up to my house and Cole opens the back door. Mallory gets out, embarrassed to even look at him as she says hello. She's flushed. And I think I might have yelled. It's more than obvious what we were doing back here. But Cole is a professional. However, not so much that he doesn't fist-bump me behind Mal's back.

Cole takes her bag and puts it inside the house before leaving to take Kendra back and return the limo. Mallory looks around at the houses surrounding mine before returning her gaze to my humble abode. The place I chose to live after rehab is not ostentatious or flashy. It's a two-bedroom cottage on a half-acre lot, flanked by similar sized houses lining my street.

"Wow," she says. "I'm impressed, Mr. Stone."

"What's to be impressed by?" I ask, looking around the middle-class neighborhood.

"Exactly. Is your house any bigger than the Presidential Suite?" she asks.

I laugh. "Barely."

As we walk through the door, I lean down, annoyed as I pick up some cards left on my doorstep. It's getting worse. Today it's only letters, but sometimes they leave packages and stuffed animals. What do they think I'm going to do with all that shit? Fucking gate guard, the guy will let anyone with big tits in. I need to get Cole to have a talk with the head of security. Mallory may be here alone at times and I don't want her exposed unnecessarily.

Mallory looks at the cards in my hands. "Love notes?" she jokes.

I shrug and then nod.

"Really?" she asks. "I was only teasing. I thought it was your mail."

"Sadly, it's not. That gets properly delivered to my box. The minimum-wage gate guard is not very vigilant about who he lets pass." I open the waste basket to deposit the cards.

"Wait!" She stops me. "Don't you at least want to read them?"

"They're all the same," I tell her. "*'I love you, Thad.' 'Marry me, Thad.' 'Have my baby, Thad.'* And those are the good ones."

She nods to them. "May I?"

"Don't you want a tour of the place?" I ask, slightly perturbed.

"I can pretty much see it all from here," she jokes. "Come on. Let me see them. I mean, you get fan mail, Chad. Isn't that unreal? People love you so much they take the time to tell you in writing."

I guess I used to think it was cool. When it first started back when I was on *Malibu*. "Fine." I hand her the half-dozen cards and watch over her shoulder as she opens them. They are pretty much what I told her. Marriage proposals. Invitations. Lewd propositions.

"Oh, my God." She covers her mouth with her hand. "This one sent a picture of her naked chest. Do you keep these in a drawer somewhere, you know, in case you need 'material'?" She giggles.

Man, I love the sound of her laugh. I could listen to it all day. "I don't have a drawer, Mal. Who needs crappy visual stimulation when I have you?"

She opens the trash can and deposits the letters inside. "I think I'll take that tour now. Why don't we start with the bedroom?"

I pull her body against me and wrap my hands around her back. I remember that she's without panties under her skirt and it has me getting hard again. "Have I told you how much I love you today?"

"Maybe," she says, nibbling at my ear.

"Well, how about I show you? Only this time, I plan on taking my sweet time with you." I grab her hand and lead her to my room.

~ ~ ~

"This is the life," she says, floating on a mat in my pool.

She's gorgeous in her tiny green shimmering bikini, making me glad there's a privacy fence around my backyard. Not because someone might see us together, but because I don't want anyone else seeing her like this. Lying back the way she is, her breasts all but spill out the sides of the small triangles trying to hold them in. And then there's her creamy skin and wet hair. *Shit*—I just want to cancel all plans for the week and stay holed up with her. I'm growing hard in my board shorts as I sit and watch her from my lounge chair. I set down what I'm reading and dive into the pool, swimming up next to her.

"It is now that *you're* here," I tell her. "I rarely even use the pool." I run my hand up the soft skin of her inner thigh. "But now I'm thinking of all kinds of ways we can use it."

"You're insatiable." She giggles.

"Only for you," I say, leaning over to place a kiss on her forehead.

"What were you reading over there?" she asks.

"Some scripts Paul sent over."

Her eyebrows shoot up. "Scripts? As in more than one?"

I nod. "It seems I pretty much have my choice of gigs these days."

"Do you mean you get to pick which parts you want? What about auditioning and stuff?"

"All those screaming fans; and the opening weekend numbers of *Defcon One*—those were pretty much my audition," I tell her. "I haven't had to screen test since I got the part in *Blind Shot*. Well, except when they want to see how I mesh with actors who are up for other parts."

"Wow," she says.

I huff through my nose. Sometimes I still can't believe it myself. "Yeah."

"So, what's on the agenda for the week?" she asks. "We're going to your parents, right?"

"I think they would kill me if I didn't bring you around. I was thinking we'd go for a beach day early in the week and then stay for dinner. You'll love it. Their house is right on the ocean and the beach goes on for miles."

"Sounds heavenly," she says.

"Ana Garner is having a party next week. I think you'll get along great. Hayden will be there and I'd like you to meet him, too. He's probably my closest friend here in L.A."

She looks up at me, using her hand to shield her eyes from the sun. "So you aren't going to keep me locked up here at your house?"

"Hardly," I say.

"But what about—"

"I don't give a shit about what people say or what they print in the tabloids, Mal. Paul will just have to deal with it. It's not like

I'm going to stick my tongue down your throat on Rodeo Drive or anything. But I'm sure as hell going to take my girlfriend out on the town."

She smiles. "You're taking me to Rodeo Drive?"

"Sure. If you want to," I say. "I thought you could join me next Thursday when I go in town for a pre-production meeting. It's a short one that day so we could do lunch and go shopping after."

"I'd love that," she says. "So what exactly happens at pre-production meetings?"

"A lot of things. I don't have to be there for all of them, though, because the studio makes the decisions about shooting locations, scheduling, and costuming. But they need me for the casting of supporting roles, legal agreements, training, fittings. Did I tell you I have to learn to rock climb?"

"Really? That sounds exciting."

"It is pretty fun, actually. I've only been training at inside facilities for now, but soon they'll be taking me on real climbs."

"Wait. Will you do your own stunts?" she asks, lines of concern etched into her forehead.

"Only the ones where there isn't the potential for me to fall to my death," I joke. "Maybe once I'm better at it, I can teach *you* how to do it."

She laughs. "There aren't many places to climb in New York City," she says. "Not unless you want to scale the side of the Freedom Tower."

"Well, maybe you'll have to visit me on location then. We'll be filming in Sedona, Arizona this summer."

"Maybe," she says, dipping her hand in the water and flicking it on me. "Will there be a private pool there?"

"There will be anything you want there," I say, reaching my arms under her and pulling her body off the floating mat. I cradle her in my arms and walk her to the side of the pool. "Let's get you out of the sun before you burn." I carry her up the steps of the pool and deposit her on a lounge chair, situating her under a large umbrella. "Can I get you a drink?"

"Water would be great." She uses a towel to dry her hair as I head to the kitchen.

I check my phone along the way, quickly replying to some texts from Hayden, Kyle, and Megan. I feel guilty that I haven't been to see Megan since I returned from my weekend in New York. Megan senses something, I can tell, and I don't want to hurt her, but seeing her would feel like I'm betraying Mallory. I can't tell Mal. Not yet. She wouldn't understand my having a relationship with another woman. And she especially wouldn't understand why.

I return with two bottles of water to find Mallory perusing some of the scripts I was reading. "This one sounds interesting," she says. *"Out of the Deep."*

"It's pretty sci-fi," I tell her. "Different from what I'm used to doing. Paul wants me to do it to show my range of acting ability."

"I'd think that should be pretty clear after seeing *Defcon One*," she says, with a prideful smile that makes my heart grow.

"Thanks, babe." I pull my chair next to hers and watch her page through the other scripts.

Her entire body tenses when she picks up the third one in the pile. "They want you to do a *Malibu 310* movie?" she asks, fear gripping the lovely features of her face.

"It's a possibility," I say. "But only if the entire original cast signs on."

"That would mean you'd have to work with Heather Crawford again," she says. "Do you really think that's a good idea?"

I narrow my eyes at her.

"Kyle told me she's the one who got you into drugs," she says.

"Kyle said that?" I ask, angry that my little brother is telling her shit about me before I get the chance. "That little cock-sucker. What else did he say?"

"Uh, that you liked to gamble and, um . . . that you stole money from your parents." Her gaze fixates on the patio pavers. She's disappointed in me. And she has every right to be. I fucked up so many times in so many ways.

I nod, taking responsibility for my sheer stupidity. "You must think I'm a terrible person. I guess I was afraid to tell you."

"Don't be," she says, reaching over to put her hand on mine. "You can tell me anything, Chad. I know it's all history, but I'd rather hear it from you than find out from anyone else. And I don't think you are a terrible person. You've proven to be quite the opposite."

Words collect on the tip of my tongue, begging to come out. She's given me an opening. I should put it all out there once and for all. Rip off the Band-Aid. She's here in L.A. in my house. She couldn't exactly run away. Well, not easily. I should do it now. "Mal," I thread my fingers through hers at the very second her phone starts ringing.

She glances at it and says, "Oh, shoot, I forgot to call my dad when I arrived last night. He'll be livid. I'll just be a sec." She glides her finger across the phone. "Hi, Daddy."

I point to the house and hold up my finger so she knows I'll only be gone a minute. I want to give her privacy. I also want to kick myself for being a damn coward, because all I feel is relief that her phone call robbed me of the perfect chance to tell her the things I know I should.

Samantha Christy

CHAPTER TWENTY

Mallory

I throw an arm over my head after I see the entertainment news on TMZ, frustrated over being tabloid fodder for the second time since I arrived three days ago. I hop off the bed, open the bathroom door and shout, "Chad, it happened again!"

"What is it now?" he asks, peeking around the side of the glass block shower.

Wow. My eyes quickly rake over his wet body, dripping with soapy suds. He looks good enough to eat. If I weren't so upset about the story, I might jump in with him. But I am upset, and he's got a meeting to get to, so I don't.

"They stood outside the gates of my school until they found someone who would talk," I tell him.

On Saturday, the story of the mystery woman broke and my name was plastered all over the tabloids and social media. I'm glad I was out here when it happened, cocooned away with Chad in our private little world.

"Is anyone even there? It's spring break," he says, his voice echoing off the shower walls.

"It was one of our janitors," I say. "He told reporters that it was my second year teaching fourth grade. And . . ."

When my voice trails off, Chad sticks his head out of the shower again. "And what, Mal?"

"And he said he can't understand why a celebrity like you would choose such a tawdry hometown girl like me."

"Tawdry?" he scoffs. "Did he actually call you that?"

I nod.

"He's an asshole, babe. You are the opposite of tawdry."

"He asked me out once," I tell him.

Chad turns off the shower and I hand him his towel. "The janitor asked you out? How old is he?"

"Not as old as you'd picture an elementary school janitor. I'd say he's in his thirties. He thought I turned him down because he's a janitor."

"But you didn't," he says. "That's not you. But why *did* you turn him down?"

I close the lid on the toilet and sit down. "Because he wasn't you."

Chad's mouth opens and closes as he tries to form words. "But . . . you've dated plenty of guys," he says, wrapping the towel around his waist before he leans against the vanity.

"Not in the last few years," I tell him. "I tried to date. After Julian, and when I went to college. I dated several guys, but none of them ever felt right. *I* didn't feel right dating them. So it just kind of got to the point where I swore off men."

"Swore off men?" He smiles. Maybe a little too big. "You said it had been a long time since you slept with anyone. Exactly how long are we talking, Mal?"

I roll my eyes at him.

He takes two steps over and lifts my chin. "How long?"

"I don't know. Close to three years maybe." I see the joy behind his eyes, so I add, "You don't have to look so darn happy about it."

He pulls me up so I'm standing before him. He cups my face in his hands. "Nobody else ever felt right for me either."

He kisses me until I forget my own name. Then he teases me by removing his towel and hanging it up, freeing his burgeoning erection. My mouth actually waters as I watch him walk across the bedroom to his closet.

He glances back at me, chuckling at my reaction. After he dresses, he turns off the TV. "No more television for you." He sits next to me on the bed. "I'm serious, Mal. You don't need to be actively seeking that shit out. It's out there now and we just have to let Kendra deal with it as she knows how."

I nod thinking of the statement she issued the other day when my name went public. The statement that branded me as 'a childhood friend and nothing more.'

"Sit by the pool. Work on your tan. I'll be back by four o'clock and then I'll join you." He winks. "This time in full daylight," he whispers in my ear, sending a shiver down my spine.

Oh! He wants a repeat of last night. When we were under the stars. In the pool. Naked.

He checks his phone. "Cole's here." He leans down to kiss me. "Don't answer the door. Call me if you need me and if I can't answer, Cole will."

"Yes, Dad," I tease.

"There is no way your dad would ever do to you the things I did to you last night." He laughs.

"Gross," I say, making a face.

"I'll see you later," he says. "I love you."

"I love you, too," I say, almost like it's an exchange we've shared for years. Maybe it has been. Maybe we just never said it out loud.

He stops in the doorway. "I think I like this," he says looking around his bedroom before his eyes fall back on me. "I think I like this a lot."

~ ~ ~

After floating around in the pool for an hour and then making a light lunch, I check my phone, replying to a dozen messages from friends asking if I'm Thad Stone's girlfriend. *Friends*. I use the term loosely. Some of these people are mere acquaintances who came out of the woodwork when the story broke. I'm beginning to realize why Chad doesn't have many true friends of his own. You just never know what some people's intentions are.

Other than his family, Hayden Keys and Ana Garner seem to be the only real friends he has here. We went out to lunch with them on Sunday. Ana is his co-star from *Blind Shot* and Hayden from *Defcon One*. But I guess they know each other because they travel in the same circles. Hayden brought Noreen Watkins, who played Chad's sister in his latest movie. She and Hayden are dating now.

Ana is having a party on Friday, but Chad wanted me to meet them beforehand. We hit it off. Ana is a relative newcomer to show business. Maybe that's why she seems like just a regular girl. She's someone I could see Mel and me hanging out with. I even had a thought that Julian might like her. Chad was all over that idea, even going so far as to show Ana a picture of Julian. All in all, it felt like a normal lunch with the exception of the fifteen paparazzi camped outside the restaurant. It's no surprise how the lunch spurred rumors of Chad dating either or both Ana and me, jilting Courtney once again.

My phone rings and I smile when I see it's Chad's mother. "Hi, Jackie," I answer, still a little uncomfortable using her first name. But she insisted on it when we were there for dinner Monday night.

"Hello, dear. Chad told me the other day how bad he felt knowing you'd be alone most of the day today."

"Oh, it's fine. I took a swim. He won't be gone that long," I tell her.

"Well, as luck would have it, my afternoon surgery got canceled. I thought I'd swing by and take you shopping. Maybe buy you a dress for Ana's party on Friday?"

It would be nice to have a new dress. After all, I'll be mingling with movie stars. "That would be wonderful," I say. "But you're not buying my dress, Jackie."

"I'm already on my way," she says, ignoring my statement. "I'll be there in twenty minutes."

An hour later, I find myself in another world, being catered to by not one, but two sales ladies as we drink champagne while they present me with dress options. I gulp down a swallow. I shudder to even look at the prices. Actually, I don't think the dresses even *have* price tags. Maybe they charge based on what they think you can afford. I wonder if it would be in poor taste to mention I'm just a school teacher.

Jackie really wants me to pick a dark green dress to match my eyes. They show me several and I end up trying on a skin-tight, cleavage-enhancing one and a flowy just-above-the-knee, conservative-yet-alluring one. I model both for Jackie as the sales ladies fawn over me. I break out into a sweat wondering if one of these dresses will breach the limit on my Visa card.

"You look stunning in both of them, Mallory," Jackie says when I come out wearing the conservative one. "Chad will simply drop dead when he sees you."

I smile, looking in the mirror thinking about his reaction. I have to admit; I look and feel great wearing it. I twirl around, watching the skirt show off a little more leg.

One of the ladies brings me a pair of black heels with matching green bows on the back that look amazing with the dress. Oh, screw it, I may have to work summer school to pay this off, but it will be worth it. I smile at Jackie. "This is the one," I say.

She sighs with relief. "Oh, thank God," she says, leaning back into the leather dressing room sofa. "I know you young girls like those tight dresses, but I still think you should leave *something* to the imagination."

I laugh. "I thought you liked the other one."

"I thought *you* liked the other one." She giggles.

"Oh, no. I only tried it on because your eyes lit up when you saw it," I tell her.

"Wishful thinking, dear. If only I could still fit into something like that. Actually, I'm not sure I ever could."

"You are gorgeous, Jackie. And you have a lovely figure," I say. "Chad's father is very lucky."

She pulls me in for a hug. "Thank you, dear. I think I'll keep you." Then she whispers in my ear so the ladies can't hear her. "Courtney Benson has nothing on you."

"You know her?" I ask, a little disappointed that he's brought other girls to their home for dinner.

"Oh, no. Not really," she says. "We met one time at his L.A. premiere. That dress you tried on? Hers was barely half of the material." She shakes her head disapprovingly. "Not to mention she spreads false rumors about my son. She better pray she doesn't use any of my friends for a nose job—which she needs, by the way—because I might just make sure they don't have steady hands during her procedure." She snorts at her own joke. "And just so you know, my son has never brought another woman home to meet us. You're the one and only."

I sigh with relief and then I smile. "He's *my* one and only, Jackie. I think he always has been."

"It's as it should be, Mallory. My son loves you very much. I can tell by the way he talks about you. By the way he looks at you across the room. You are the real thing for him, you know. Trust in that. And don't let all the hoopla distract you from it." She holds my arms out by my sides and looks at the dress again. "I hope you know CPR, dear, because his heart will stop for sure. Now go get changed so I can get you home before he even knows you were gone."

When I'm changing back into my clothes, Chad texts me, telling me he's going to be about a half hour late but that he'll make it up to me later, followed by a winky face. I smile as I exit the dressing room. One of the sales ladies puts the dress in a garment bag. The shoes go in their own bag that hangs along the side. "Let me give you my card," I say.

She waves me off. "It's been paid for, young lady. Have a good day."

I shoot a glance to Jackie, who's waiting for me by the front door with a big Cheshire cat smile. She shrugs. "Get used to it, dear. We Stones take care of our own."

"Jackie, it's too much."

"Hush now," she says. "You are worth every bit, Mallory Schaffer."

I smile at her, biting back tears. "I never really got to go shopping with my mom," I say. "I was always too busy to be bothered with it. But I imagine it would have been a lot like this. Minus the champagne."

She puts her arm around me. "You were the apple of that woman's eye, dear. She knew you loved her. You were a teenager. You were *supposed* to be out gallivanting with your friends. She would have been so proud of the woman you've become. Trust me."

"Thank you," I say, swallowing the lump in my throat. "And thank you for this." I hold the bag up. "So, so much."

"You're very welcome. Come, let's get you home."

~ ~ ~

I stuff the garment bag in the back of his closet, hoping Chad won't notice it before Friday. Then I realize I still have an hour to kill before he gets home. I pick up my phone and check social media. In hindsight, it probably wasn't a good idea to do that. I'm bombarded by tons of messages, posts, and tweets—by my supposed friends; the same ones who have recently come out of the woodwork—showing me pictures of Chad and Courtney together. They follow the pictures with sad faces and notes of condolences. I proceed to clean house, blocking, unfriending and unfollowing anyone who chooses to participate in the tabloid heyday. Part of me wants to post the picture I took of us cuddling on the couch yesterday. I want to scream at these people and tell them to mind their own business and quit assuming things are real just because they see a stupid picture.

But I realize I'm probably just taking my frustration out on them. Maybe if I weren't on the inside, I would believe everything I read, too. I mean, didn't I for all those years Chad was gone?

Granted, he did do a lot of what was printed, but it was made to seem so much worse.

The upsetting thing is that the pictures they're posting were taken today. I know because Chad is wearing the same light-blue shirt he put on this morning. The pictures show two 'love birds' eating lunch together. It's clear to me they aren't alone, the table is too big for that, but the picture is cropped to make it look like they are sharing an intimate lunch for two.

He's working, I know that. But deep down, I can't help but feel like I'm the dirty little secret hidden away in his house while he's out living his *real* life.

I can't help myself. I do a search of Thad Stone pictures.

Also a monumentally bad idea.

There are hundreds of them. Thousands maybe. Most of them pair him with Courtney or Heather. Although he looks quite a bit younger in the ones with Heather. *Wow*—Kyle was right, she really does look like me; I never saw that until just now. Chad also is clearly thinner and spaced out in those photos. I'm glad we weren't close then. It would have broken my heart to see him that way. There are some pictures with a girl named Nikki. My jealously radar peaks at full tilt. Nikki is the last girl he slept with before me. And she lives in New York City. She's gorgeous. *Splendid.*

There's another girl who shows up in several pictures, but there isn't a name. She's not insanely thin and beautiful like the others. She cute, with a long blonde ponytail in most of the photos, and I'd say quite a bit younger than he is. She doesn't even look to be out of her teens. The pictures with her are different than the others. They aren't so posed. They are more like the pictures I have of me and Chad. Fun. Spontaneous. Casual.

And that's what scares the hell out of me. That and the fact that it looks like she's been in his life for a while, at least a few years based on the ages Chad looks in them.

I throw my phone down on the couch. This is not helping. I go to the bedroom and pull a book out of my suitcase and lay down on Chad's bed to start reading.

The next thing I know, I'm being kissed awake by the man who I was just dreaming about. I smile before I even open my eyes. I could get used to this—him coming home to me.

"God, I missed you today," he says. "Do you know how hard it was to sit in meetings all day knowing you were back here? In my pool. On my bed." He kisses me again, hovering over me, but not leaning down to put any weight on me. "I'm going to make good on that promise to join you in the pool. I just want to take a quick shower first."

I draw my brows at him. "You need to shower *before* going in the pool?"

"Yeah. I was in conference rooms all day. I probably smell like Courtney's hideous perfume. And some of the producers were smoking." He kisses my nose and then empties his pockets onto the nightstand. "I'll only be a few minutes. Why don't you put on that green bikini of yours? Or better yet—just strip naked and save me the trouble of taking it off you." He winks on his way to the bathroom.

My body is humming knowing what he has in store for me. How did I ever get so lucky?

I'm trying to decide between nakedness or bikini when Chad's phone pings with a text. Then it pings again right after. I grab his phone and follow him. "Chad, your phone—" But the toilet flushes followed by the shower turning on. It'll have to wait.

I go to put his phone down on the nightstand but catch a glimpse of the text. And then my stomach becomes lodged in the vicinity of my throat. The picture of the person who sent the text is the same young blonde ponytail girl from the internet pictures. And her name is Megan. The Megan from his favorites list. The one he said he hadn't cleared out yet. I know it's horribly wrong and an invasion of his privacy, however, I can't help but tap on it and read the conversation as far back as it shows up on the screen.

Megan: I need you, Chad. Please?

Chad: Sweetie, I wish I could, but I'm in meetings all day.

Megan: Please? You said you would come whenever I need you. Well, I need you.

Chad: I did say that, didn't I? Okay. I may be able to stop by around 4, but I'll have to make it quick.

Megan: You're the best. I love you, you know that, right?

Chad: Love you, too. See you then.

Megan: Thank you for coming over, even though it was just a quickie. I feel so much better now.

Megan: See you Sunday night.

I don't bother reading back any further. I've read enough. With tear-blurred vision, I stare at her picture a moment longer and then I drop the phone onto the floor. I'm pretty sure I hear it crack but I'm too upset to care. My stomach turns and I have to concentrate to hold back the vomit. I don't even bother with my suitcase. I grab my purse and my phone and head out the front door. I summon an Uber on my walk to the front gate of the neighborhood and by the time I reach it, a car is waiting.

"LAX p-please," I tell him, trying to keep it together.

The whole way there, I wonder how I could have been so stupidly blind. He's not changed his ways at all. How could he even sit there and claim to love me when he is clearly in love with Megan? He stopped at her house for a quickie and then came home to me? What kind of man does that? A self-serving asshole, that's who.

I rip open the door before the car is even at a full stop. I start to run into the airport when I hear the screeching of tires behind me. I spin around to see what's what and see Chad's car. I quickly make a visual sweep but don't see Cole. He's here alone. He leaves his door open, running around the car in a t-shirt and board shorts as if he put on the first thing he found on his floor. "Mallory!" he yells.

He's twenty feet from me and that's close enough. I hold up my hand. "No," I say. "Stay back."

He pulls his shattered phone out of his shorts, holding it up for me to see. "It's not what you think. I swear."

I hear a crowd gathering, but don't have the energy to care. All my energy was spent on heartbreak in the cab ride over. "What I think is that you've been fucking someone else!" I shout. "It's pretty damn clear."

Chad looks around and I follow the direction of his eyes. Paparazzi are running towards us. They always camp out at the airport in hopes of finding celebrity photo ops. My heart fractures even further. We are about to break up in the most public of ways and it's going to make people salivate.

Chad takes a few steps forward, motioning to the gathering crowd. "Do you really want to do this right here, Mal?"

More tires screech behind us. I look over and see Cole running from *his* car.

"Get me a secure fucking room," Chad says to him through his gritted teeth.

I watch Cole run over and talk to a guy with a badge and not ten seconds later, they both come over to Chad. "Mr. Stone, right this way." The guy with the badge then turns to me. "Miss? Follow me, please."

My instinct is to keep walking into the airport. But I can see in Chad's eyes that he's not going to let this go so easily. He wants to win. Have his cake and eat it too. Part of me wants to let the whole bloody scene play out in front of the paparazzi. Let the carnage fall where it may. But then for just one second, I think of my job. My students. What kind of example would I be setting if I aired my dirty laundry for all to see?

I nod at the guy with the badge and let him escort me into a private, unmarked entrance. We walk down a hallway and into a small reception area. It looks like a ticket counter, but there is only one. I guess this is where the VIPs get to check in. We're escorted into a small room next to the counter. It has a couch and three chairs and I wonder what it's used for if not exclusively for asshole celebrities and their soon-to-be ex-girlfriends to fight in.

Chad whispers something to Cole and then Cole closes the door, leaving Chad and me alone in the room.

"I can explain," he says, sitting down and putting his elbows on his knees, fingering the broken screen of his phone.

"If you can explain that away, you'll earn a goddamn Oscar," I tell him, pacing the room.

"I'm not cheating on you, Mallory. I love you. I don't love anyone else—not in that way. I know what you read looks really bad, but I swear you'll understand once I explain it to you." He closes his eyes briefly and then focuses on the floor. "You'll understand, but you may still hate me."

I'm not sure there is anything else he could have said to grab my attention more. How could I hate him any more than if he were cheating on me? I take a seat in the chair farthest from him, wiping another tear off my sodden face. "I'm listening," I say. "Talk."

CHAPTER TWENTY-ONE

Chad

I hope Cole is quick about the errand I sent him on. Thank goodness he doesn't have to go far. I need all the help I can get on this one. When I found my shattered phone on the floor and read the texts on the screen, there was no doubt in my mind that Mallory had run. I would have run myself—after I hunted down and kicked some dude's ass, that is.

I don't think I've ever driven so fast in my life. It was a miracle I didn't get pulled over. But I had to get to Mallory. I don't even want to imagine what it would've been like for her if she'd gotten on that plane thinking I'd cheated on her.

"Can I get you something to drink?" I ask her, stalling.

"Don't beat around the bush so you have time to think up excuses, *Thad*. Just get to it; I have a plane to catch."

There was a time when I loved it when she called me Thad. Now it's just a reference to the asshole I once was and that she thinks I still am. And I hate that she had to spend her own money on airfare. "You already booked a ticket?"

"No. But I will as soon as we're done here."

"I hope that's not true, Mal. But if you still want to leave after what I tell you, I'll change your return ticket for you. You shouldn't have to pay for it."

"That's right, I forgot. You Stones are always buying stuff for people. How *generous* of you," she says sarcastically.

"What's that supposed to mean, '*we Stones*'?"

"Sorry," she says, looking guilty. "I didn't mean to put your mother in the same narcissistic group *you* belong to. She took me shopping today and bought an outrageously expensive dress for me to wear Friday night. It's in the back of your closet, by the way. Please have her return it for a refund."

I look at her, surprised. "You went shopping with my mom?"

She nods sadly, looking at the floor.

Damn it! Everything was perfect and I had to go fuck it up because I wasn't upfront with her about everything.

Her chin quivers and she swallows hard. "Chad, just say what you're going to say. Why did you even bother bringing me in here? Why did you come after me when you have *her* to go back to?"

"Megan isn't my girlfriend," I tell her. "She isn't my mistress or my fuck-buddy or even a one-night stand. Whatever you think she is, I assure you it couldn't be farther from the truth."

"I know what I saw on your phone. She said she needed you. She said she . . . l-loves you and . . . y-you said it back." Her voice trembles as more tears pool in her eyes. "She thanked you for a quickie. And she called you Chad. Nobody calls you Chad unless they are very important to you."

I nod. "She *is* very important to me, Mal. Besides you, she may be the most important person in my life."

She shakes her head. "You're confusing me. You say you aren't cheating on me, yet you've hidden her from me. Why would you do that? Who is she?"

"Check your phone," I say.

"Why?"

"I had Cole call my lawyer and he emailed you everything you need to read."

"Why can't you just tell me?" She eyes me skeptically.

"I could tell you, but I'm not sure you'll believe me. I want you to read about it for yourself."

She reluctantly pulls out her phone and checks her mail. I know it will give her the information she needs. I just hope once she's done reading, she doesn't get up and walk out of my life.

It takes her a while to get through the document my lawyer sent. I can see every emotion as it crosses her face. I can see the shock that lets me know she's reading about the accident I had when I was stoned out of my mind. I can see the sadness when she reads about a fifteen-year-old girl who was sent to the hospital in a coma because I had t-boned the side of her dad's car. I cringe when a hand flies to her mouth to stop her startled gasp as she reads about the leg the girl had amputated in the aftermath.

She finishes the article, looking up at me with red-rimmed eyes. "Oh my God. Why didn't I ever hear about this?"

"Probably because I have a damn good lawyer," I say. "He did a lot of damage control and the particulars of the accident were never released because Megan was a minor. Also, Megan's dad was sympathetic to me because he was drunk at the time, only he wasn't tested because the accident was my fault. It was a huge wake-up call for both of us. I went to rehab for four weeks, and then I paid all her medical bills."

"But why didn't you tell me?" she asks.

"You know why," I say, sick guilt rolling through me in punishing waves. "Your mom was killed by a drunk driver. I thought you'd hate me. I was sure you couldn't be with someone who'd done what I'd done."

She closes her eyes and I know she's thinking of her mom. "Why didn't you go to jail?" she asks.

"I almost did." *I should have.* I run a hand through my hair. "Ron, that's my lawyer, pulled some strings and got them to let me go right to rehab from the holding facility, putting off my arraignment in the process. And by the time I got out of rehab and met with Megan's dad, he'd had a lot of time to think about things. He said it very well could have been him. That he had driven drunk more times than he could count. That's why he wasn't going to sue me for everything I was worth. And believe me, they could have used the money. He's a construction worker and his wife is in retail management. He thanked me, can you believe it? He thanked me for getting him to quit drinking. It's then that I told him I wanted to pay for Megan's college education."

I shake my head still not believing how much that family has done for me. "Can you believe he showed up at my arraignment and asked the judge not to put me in jail? He asked him to sentence me to community service, taking Megan to all her rehab appointments and working with other amputees. It was hard at first because Megan hated me for taking her leg, but it turned out to be one of the greatest things I'd ever experienced. I think her dad knew all along that she'd come around. He once told me she'd watched every episode of *Malibu* a hundred times.

"Megan and I grew on each other. The kid is smart. Like rocket scientist smart. And that first year, during the time her stump healed but before she got the Cadillac of all prosthetics, she studied her ass off to try to get into a good college. Before the accident, she was a C student at best. Now, she's going to graduate with honors. And she's been accepted to both MIT and Harvard.

She wants to make advancements in the world of bionic prosthetics. Oh, and she took up running. She got a silver medal in the Paralympics last summer."

"You're kidding me?" Mallory says, looking surprised. So many emotions bleed from her eyes right now. Pain. Disbelief. Ambivalence.

She points to my phone. "Tell me about the texts. The *'I love yous'* and the *'quickie.'*"

"Prom dress crisis," I say.

"Come again?"

I nod. "She found a dress she loved, and the store let her bring it home for the afternoon before buying it so she could try on her various prosthetics with it. She has several. One for running, one for when she wears flat shoes, and one for heels. She even has one she can swim with. She wanted me to come over and make sure I knew the exact color tie to get. And also to get my opinion about whether she looked fat in it or not." I motion to my phone. "The quickie thing was just a poor choice of words on her part. But yes, I love her. I love her like a sister, Mal."

"Let me get this straight," she says. "You did cocaine and then drove a car, causing this girl to lose her leg. That prompted you to get sober and make friends with Megan, who then decided to go to college to change the world. College she couldn't afford unless you paid for it." She shakes her head. "And you're taking her to her prom?"

"Uh . . . I guess that about sums it up." I sit in the chair next to her. "Are you going to leave me now?"

"Leave you?" she says. She turns to face me and takes my hand. "Chad, I believe everything in this world happens for a reason. If you'd never had the accident, you might still be using drugs. You might even be dead."

"She lost her leg, Mallory. Because of *me*. There is no reason for it. I'd rather be dead myself than have put her through that." I hang my head down.

Mallory puts a finger under my chin and forces me to look at her. "If Megan hadn't been the one you hit, she never would be going on to college. She never would have won an Olympic medal. She never would have had this incredible friendship with you—her idol. And her dad might never have gotten sober. I'm not saying it was good that it happened, but look at the facts; despite her losing her leg, all of your lives are better off, wouldn't you say?"

For the first time since I saw the broken phone on my bedroom floor, I feel a glimmer of hope. "You're not leaving me?"

She smiles and it makes me want to shout in victory. "No, I'm not leaving you, Chad. But you have to promise me you'll never keep secrets from me again."

I kneel before her chair, taking her head in my hands as I crush my mouth against hers, tasting her salty lips. "I promise," I whisper into her mouth in between kisses. "I promise no more secrets. Ever."

There's a knock at the door and I stand up, pulling Mallory with me. "It's for you," I tell her.

"For me?" She walks over to the door and opens it.

Megan walks through, gracing us with her infectious smile. She looks at Mallory. "So you're the lucky chick who gets to have his gorgeous babies?"

~ ~ ~

Mallory comes out of my bathroom and my jaw hits the fucking carpet. *Ho-ly shit!* The dress she's wearing takes my breath away. It's not skin tight like most actresses I know would prefer.

This dress is so much better. The bodice is fitted and enticing, showing just enough cleavage to draw attention without being slutty. It shows off her slim waist, and the above-the-knee skirt displays her shapely legs while leaving what's beneath it to the imagination. Of course, I don't need to imagine. I've seen her. I've *had* her. More times than I can count now, yet it'll never be enough.

"God, Mal." I walk over to her and circle around her, my eyes taking in every inch of her gorgeous figure. "I didn't think you could get any more beautiful, but I was wrong."

She blushes. Making her blush is one of the highlights of my existence. If she weren't all dolled up and ready to party, I'd throw her back on my bed for another round of make-up sex. We've been having a lot of that lately. I've had a lot to make up for. And when we haven't been making love, we've been talking. Well, mostly *I've* been talking, telling her everything about my life from the minute I left her nine years ago until the second I saw her at the club.

"Thank you," she says, her hungry eyes looking me over. "You clean up pretty well yourself."

I'm wearing a pair of black jeans with a white shirt, tan jacket, and black tie. Mallory walks over to me and untucks my shirt. "There, you look very celebrity chic now."

"Since when did you become an expert?" I ask.

"You pick up a thing or two by watching Entertainment News Weekly," she says.

I frown. "Mal, I wish you wouldn't watch that shit."

"What?" She smiles innocently. "ENW is not a sleazy tabloid show, it's actually pretty good."

"Still, don't—"

"Believe everything I see," she says, completing my thought. "Yeah, yeah. I know."

I hold my hand out to her. "Come on, Cole's waiting."

Mallory is exceptionally quiet on the way to Ana's house. As Cole pulls into the circular driveway I ask her, "Is something bothering you?"

She shrugs. "I guess I'm a little nervous. After all, I'm about to walk into a room full of famous people."

"Well, you already met Ana, Hayden, and Noreen," I say. "That only leaves a few dozen people for you to meet. Don't worry, I'm pretty sure Ryan Gosling has other plans tonight." I wink when I say the name of her secret crush.

She gives me a look of annoyance. "Not helping," she says.

We're escorted through the front door and directed to Ana's back patio. It's decorated with tiki torches and large white paper lanterns. There's a summer kitchen that has been set up as a bar, tables and chairs under a pergola covered with vines, and attendants walking around with trays of champagne and hors d'oeuvres.

Ana spots us and comes over to say hello. "Hey, Mallory, nice to see you again." She kisses her cheek and then mine.

"You, too, Ana," Mallory says. "You have a lovely home and this is magnificent." She motions around the beautifully landscaped backyard.

"Thank you," Ana says with pride. "But I can't take all the credit. It was pretty much like this when I bought it last month."

Mallory flushes and she elbows me. Hard. "Oh, I'm so sorry, Ana. I didn't realize this was a housewarming party."

Ana laughs, putting a reassuring hand on Mallory's arm. "Don't worry, it's not." Then she motions for a waiter, grabbing a glass of champagne for Mallory. She tells him, "Please get a bottle of water for Mr. Stone."

More people arrive and Ana excuses herself to greet them. Mallory turns to me. "I really like her. She doesn't pressure you to drink."

"Yeah, she's one of the good ones," I say.

I introduce Mallory to several people. She impresses me with her ability to tamp down her nerves despite the fact that some of those people make much bigger headlines than I do. Easy conversation flows out of her as we make our rounds. She's no wallflower. Quite the opposite. And I somehow feel that having her by my side increases my worth—if that makes any sense at all.

I find us a table so we can sit down. She won't say it, but I can tell Mallory's feet are hurting in her new shoes. I haven't asked her yet, but I was hoping she might agree to keep them on later tonight. The little bows on the back, and the way they make her legs look—it's damn sexy.

"Thad, Mallory—good to see you," Hayden says, bringing Noreen over to sit with us.

"Hey, buddy, what's up?" Hayden and I get into a conversation about rock climbing. He's in training with me. He plays my arch enemy in the *Defcon* series and there's a great scene where he will chase me through a series of ropes and rock mazes. We both secretly hope they will let us do most of the stunts on that one.

I have one ear in the girls' conversation. They are talking about recipes. It's such a perfectly normal conversation that it makes me smile. I reach over and grab Mal's hand to let her know I haven't forgotten about her.

Hayden stiffens in his chair. "Oh, hell no," he says, looking behind me.

I whip around to see Heather Crawford standing in the patio doorway. She's wearing a fire-engine-red dress that leaves nothing to the imagination, especially about whether or not she's wearing a bra. Her long brown hair sparkles with glitter and her fuck-me heels make her look a lot taller than she really is. She sees me and smiles, dropping the hand of her date as she makes a bee-line towards us.

I glance at Mal, who looks about as green as her dress. Her desperate eyes meet mine and I feel helpless. I have no idea what's about to happen, but knowing Heather, it won't be anything good. All four of us stand up at the same time. Maybe we are all planning our escape.

Heather walks right past me and straight up to Mallory. "And you must be the new flavor of the week," she says, her eyes raking over Mal as if she's a parasite. She turns to me. "Who's your new toy, Thad?"

I put my arm around Mallory's waist, possessively pulling her against me. "Cut the shit, Heather. This is my girlfriend, Mallory."

"Your *girlfriend?*" she asks like it's a bad word. "Isn't she a waitress or something?"

"School teacher actually," Mallory says, extending her hand to Heather. "Isn't it you who should be waitressing? I mean, isn't that what all unemployed actors do?"

Hayden spits his drink out, laughing. I look at Mallory in awe. I've never been more proud. I didn't think she had it in her.

Heather scoffs at Mallory's hand, not bothering to shake it. "You don't know anything about me, honey, so keep your snarky comments to yourself," Heather spits.

"That's some good advice," Mallory retorts. "Why don't you take it?"

Heather rolls her eyes, turning her attention to me. "Have you read the script yet? Isn't it fabulous?"

I don't care to have this conversation here. I've all but decided not to do the movie. I know Paul will probably kill me, but after what happened earlier this week with Mal, I just don't want to put myself in that kind of position. It was a bad time in my life. I've no desire to dredge all that shit up again. "Not yet," I lie.

"Oh, you have to read it, Thad. It will be so much fun getting everyone back together again. Don't you think?"

The girl obviously needs a paycheck. And for some reason, she thinks she needs me. It's been over three years since I dumped her, along with every other bad habit in my life. "I'm not sure, Heather. We'll see."

"What, you think you're too good for us now? Lila, Caitlyn, and Joey have already agreed to do it. That just leaves you and Thomas—"

"I really don't want to talk about work tonight," I interrupt. "In fact, you'll have to excuse us, Mallory and I were just about to go grab a drink."

She leans into me. "I can get you something much better than a drink, Thad."

Jonah Bateman comes up behind Heather, wrapping his arms around her. "There you are. You disappeared on me."

She wriggles out of his arms. "Quit it, Jonah, you don't own me. I was just talking with Thad and" —she turns to Mallory, smirking— "what was your name again? I already forgot it."

"It's Mallory," I say through gritted teeth.

"Right. Mallory," Heather says in her direction. "It sounds so . . . industrial. But at least you smell good. What perfume are you wearing?"

Her unexpected compliment catches us both off guard. I put my nose in Mallory's hair and take a whiff. "Mmmm," I mumble. "It's *Desire Me,'* if I recall, right, baby?"

Mallory puts a possessive hand on my chest and smiles up at me. "That's right."

"If you'll excuse us now," I say, turning Mal and me towards the bar, Hayden and Noreen just behind us.

"Who let that bitch in?" Hayden asks.

Hayden always has my back. He didn't know Heather before, but he's come to hate her after some long conversations we've had. And after Hayden and I became good friends last year, Heather tried to use him to get to me. Luckily, he sees through all her superficial bullshit as well as I do.

"I didn't even know she was dating Jonah," Noreen says.

"She's probably not," Hayden tells her. "I'm sure she used him to get into Ana's party."

"Why would she do that?" Mallory asks.

Hayden and I share a look. "Because she can't seem to get it through her dense skull that I don't want anything to do with her," I say.

Mallory gasps. "She's still in love with you?"

"God, no," I say. "We were never in love." The thought of it makes me ill. *Love?* No. I'm not even sure I *liked* her. We enabled each other. We allowed ourselves to be out of control with one another. We lived in our own train-wreck of a world.

"It's more like a psychopathic obsession," Hayden jokes.

I shoot him a traitorous stare.

"She's *obsessed* with you?" Mallory asks in abhorrence, tightening her grip on my hand as if to protect me. "Is she stalking you, Chad?"

I stop walking and look down at her. "No. She's not stalking me. Please don't worry about her, Mal. She's of no consequence to us. Don't let her ruin our evening."

Ana comes over, looking apologetic. "Oh, my God. I'm so sorry, Thad. I had no idea Jonah was going to bring her here. Do you want me to ask them to leave?"

"No," Mallory says. "We don't need to cause a scene. We're all adults here."

Hayden snorts, looking over at Heather. "Well, most of us are anyway."

"Okay," Ana says. "But if I see any drugs, she's gone." She turns to Mallory. "Find me later, I want to show you those samples from the new clothing line I told you about."

I smile at their exchange. I'm happy to see Mallory getting along so well with my friends. And I love how they seem to be protective of her.

The rest of the night passes with only minor annoyances from Heather. She and Jonah end up leaving early. Probably because I failed to give her any attention. Why that girl keeps after me, I'll never understand.

Mallory leans her head on my shoulder in the car on the way home. "Ana says she wants to meet Julian," she tells me.

"Really?"

She nods sleepily into me. "Yeah. She said if he's anything like us, he's someone she wants to know."

I shake my head at the notion. "Can you imagine Julian with Ana?"

"I can, actually," she says, stifling a yawn. "I think it's a great idea."

"Well, she'll be in New York with me in May for our *Blind Shot* junket. I guess they can meet then."

"Ummhmm," she mumbles.

I run my fingers through her hair, massaging her head as I think about the days to come. Mallory leaves on Sunday. In two short days. I want so badly to go back to New York with her, but I've got meetings all week. I'm sure as hell not waiting six weeks until the press junket in May to see her again.

I worry about what she might be walking back into now that her name went public. I've made some arrangements that will hopefully make things easier. Still, it kills me to know I won't be there to help her handle it. Julian—he'll be there. *Shit.* I realize getting Ana out there might not be such a bad idea after all.

I look down at Mallory, peaceful and sleeping on my shoulder. This week has been perfect—take away the Megan debacle. I think back to the day Mal arrived, when I thought she would break up with me. No way am I giving her time to think about doing that again.

I pull out my new phone and text my travel agent. I tell her to book two tickets to JFK on Friday. And then I text Ana and ask her to clear her schedule.

CHAPTER TWENTY-TWO

Mallory

I got recognized in JFK. *Me.* Just walking from the gate to the luggage carousel. I'm glad Julian was there to meet me. He said Chad called him and asked him to come get me just in case anything happened. Nothing did, other than my being spotted by a girl as I walked through the terminal, and then some guy took a few pictures when Julian and I got into the cab.

Even though Chad's people still claim we're just friends, pictures of us kissing on the beach and holding hands in a restaurant went viral. One photo was a close-up and you could see the expression on Chad's face as he looked at me. Anyone could see it wasn't the way one friend looks at another. I took a picture of the photo and made it my phone background.

On the way home, I tell Julian all about Ana. "I'm happy to meet her, Mallory, but I'm not sure I want to date a celebrity."

"She's gorgeous," I tell him. "And nice. Nothing like his other leading ladies."

"I'm sure she is, I just don't want to have to deal with everything," he says.

We turn onto my street. "Deal with what?" I ask. As far as I know Ana doesn't come with the baggage Chad does.

We approach my house only to see several strange cars parked out front. When the cab pulls into my driveway, he can't even get close to the house because one of them is parked right in front of my garage. "Isn't it illegal for them to park in the driveway?" I ask Julian.

Julian tells the cabbie to wait while he walks me to the door. I eye the sleek white Lexus SUV in the driveway. "Geez," I say. "These guys must make a lot for their pictures."

"Mallory! Are you Thad's girlfriend?" a stout little man asks me from the other side of the white picket fence.

Another one asks, "Did you stay at his house in L.A.? Did you sleep in his bed?"

When we're almost at the door, the first guy shouts, "What about Courtney Benson? How do you feel about being the other woman? Do you really expect him to leave her for *you?*"

I can't help but turn around and spit fire at him with my eyes. *Bad idea.* I hear a hundred clicks of their cameras.

"Ignore them, Mal. You know they only say shit like that to get a good picture, right?"

I nod, putting my key in the front door. "I know. But he just said what everyone is thinking."

"Since when does Mallory Schaffer give a flying fuck what people think of her?"

"Maybe since I have twenty-one nine-year-olds looking up to me," I say, walking through the door. Julian puts my suitcase inside and gives me a hug as I thank him for bringing me home.

"You know I'm always here for you," he says.

"It goes both ways, you know," I tell him. "I'm here for you, too, Julian."

"See you Wednesday," he says. "Melissa is bringing Steve, so we need reservations for four."

"Sounds good. See you then." I close the door behind him and throw my purse on the coffee table, sinking into the couch where I can finally breathe. I can breathe again, but not easily. It's hard when I left a big piece of me back in L.A. I haven't seen him in seven hours and already it's too long. I miss having him come home to me. I miss eating breakfast and dinner together every day. I miss waking up next to him. Nine days with him wasn't nearly enough. How are we going to do this? I know I'll see him again on Friday, but right now, Friday seems like an eternity away.

There's a big box on the coffee table. I sit up and read the card on top.

> Mallory,
>
> I miss you already and I'm writing this before you're even gone. Please use everything in this box to keep the woman I love safe until I can be by her side—a place I will strive to be forever.
>
> All my love,
> Chad

My eyes mist up as I open the box. I laugh as I pull out an assortment of hats, sunglasses and even wigs. There is a hoodie inside that mimics the thought I had a few minutes ago. It reads *'I left my heart in L.A.'* I bring it up to my nose and smell it. God, it smells like him. Just like the pillow and blanket did for my movie night. I take off my coat and pull the hoodie over my head. There's another small box at the bottom of the big one. When I open it, I almost pee my pants. It's a key fob. And it reads: **Lexus**.

I run to the front window and peek out to admire it. *He bought me a whole car?* There is still a paparazzi outside, so I can't go out to see it. My emotions are at war with each other. I can't decide if I should feel like a giddy little girl on Christmas morning, or if I should feel like a kept woman.

I go back to the coffee table to find my phone when I see something else inside the key box. A sticker with numbers on it, but I don't know what it is.

I tap Chad's gorgeous face on my favorites screen. It doesn't even ring before he answers. "Did you make it home?"

I laugh into the phone. "I did. And it appears Santa came very early this year. You know it's too much, Chad."

"It's not too much, Mal. I need you safe. I didn't want you driving around in that little box of yours."

I contemplate arguing with him, but I know he's right. My small car offers little protection from anyone who might want to see inside. "I know," I say. "Thank you."

"Do you like it?"

I get up and peek out the window again. The photographer is still hanging around. "I'm sure it's wonderful, but I haven't had a chance to really see it yet."

"Why not?"

"Because there is a photographer standing in the road in front of my house," I tell him.

"Fuck," he huffs into the phone. "Did he say anything to you?"

"When I came home, there were two of them and they both asked me personal questions. I didn't talk to them, but they might have gotten a picture of me." *Or a hundred.*

"Call the police when we hang up. Tell them you were harassed. They'll make him leave."

"He isn't trespassing," I say. "He's on the other side of the front gate."

"But he made you uncomfortable with his questions. That's harassment, Mal."

"I don't want to get anyone in trouble, Chad. He's just doing his job."

He sighs into the phone. "My girlfriend. Always thinking of others," he says. "Just please make sure to keep your doors locked. You still have an alarm system, right?"

"Of course."

"Good. Use it. Have your dad move your old car out to the end of the driveway and put your new one in the garage so you don't have to go outside."

"My old car is still here? I thought you would've traded it in." Then I think about what I said and feel stupid for saying it. I doubt he would have gotten more than a few thousand for it. Not even enough to cover the sales tax on the Lexus.

"It's in your name, Mallory, I couldn't have done that. You can sell it yourself. Or maybe donate it."

His suggestion brings another smile to my face. "Oh, yes. I'll donate it to Hope. What a great idea. Thank you." I walk back over and eye the smaller box again. "What's the sticker with the numbers on it?"

"I leased you a parking space in a Midtown garage. It's only a few blocks from Melissa's place since you seem to stay there a lot. And it's close to many of the shops and clubs you like to go to. I don't want you taking the train or subway anymore. It exposes you too much. Use the Lexus or take cabs from now on."

I'm still stuck on *I leased you a parking space*. "What? You might as well have leased me a whole apartment for what that parking space must have cost."

"I will if you want me to. Just say the word."

"Lord, no. You've done quite enough already. I hate that you're spending so much money on me." I look around my familiar living room. "Plus, I'm not sure I could leave my dad."

"Stop it, Mallory. The only reason I have to spend that kind of money is because of who I am. It goes with the territory."

I sit on the sofa, getting a whiff of Chad's cologne every time I move around. "I love the car, but I think my favorite thing in the box was the hoodie. I'm wearing it now."

"You are?" I can hear the smile in his voice.

"Want me to send you a picture?"

"Hell, yes," he says. "Wait, is your dad home?"

"No. I don't know where he is actually, which is strange now that I think about it."

"Take your phone into your bedroom and lock the door," he says.

"What? Why?"

"Because I want to see you in the hoodie. And *only* the hoodie," he says, with a low growl. "And then I want to make you come while you're wearing it."

"Chad!" I squeal in surprise. I think my insides just melted, spreading warmth between my legs. Could I do such a thing knowing he could see me?

"We'll do it together," he says, reading my mind. "I'll be right there with you."

A bothersome thought flashes through my head. "Have you ever—"

"Never, Mal. You'd be my first," he says. "You'll be my only. And I promise you, you'll be my last."

I think he just made my heart flip over in my chest. How can I say no to him? And I might as well get used to this now. We'll be spending a lot more time apart in the future. I take the stairs two at a time. "I'm beginning to really like your promises," I say, locking my door behind me.

And then with his words, he makes the most passionate love to me.

~ ~ ~

Chad and I have spent a lot of time on the phone in the six weeks since I left L.A. *A lot.* He came out to visit every other weekend and for Kyle's med school graduation. Ana came with him on several of his weekend trips so she and Julian could get to know each other. They hit it off well, and now Julian is here with me at their press junket photo shoot. The four of us are going out to dinner after.

Julian and I are sitting in director's chairs, tucked away in a corner of the studio as Chad and Ana get dolled up for some *Blind Shot* promo pics while they are here promoting the upcoming release. Julian is tinkering around on his phone. "I wonder what shit they'll think up to print after they get pictures of the four of us tonight," he says.

I laugh. "Maybe that we're swingers?"

The press has been having a field day printing all kinds of rumors. First, I was stepping out on Thad with our longtime friend, Julian. They showed pictures of me hugging him at my door and pictures of our 'double date' with Mel and Steve. And when Julian escorted me to the *Blind Shot* premiere, we caused quite a stir. But

259

Chad's manager insisted Chad only show up with Ana on his arm, and since it wasn't Courtney, I told Chad not to bother arguing the point. Then one night, when I crashed at Julian's place, the pap even got pictures of me exiting his building early the next morning.

The second big story the press is salivating over is that Courtney Benson has been MIA for weeks. They say she's in hiding because she was dumped by Thad for 'the school teacher' and she's too heartbroken to make public appearances. We have no idea why she's gone off the grid, and I could care less. Chad is worried she's lying in a ditch somewhere after having OD'd on drugs. His only concern is that she be able to fulfill her obligations for the *Defcon* sequel.

I try not to think about the filming he'll have to do with her this summer. Eight weeks of filming, four on location in Sedona. Day in and day out they'll be together. They will have kissing scenes and sex scenes, and even though Chad has tried to tell me how it's not as bad as I would think, she will still have her lips on his lips and her hands on his body. The thought of it makes me ill.

"Whoa!" Julian says, grabbing onto my arm.

I look up to see Ana coming out of her dressing room. She's wearing a short red dress that barely covers her ass cheeks, and her legs look a mile long in the six-inch stilettos she's wearing. Her platinum-blonde hair has been made to look windblown and her flawless makeup screams that her face should be on the cover of every fashion magazine. "You get to have dinner with that tonight, you lucky man," I whisper to him.

"Holy shit, Mal. She's gorgeous," he says. "I mean, she's always beautiful, but . . . damn, is it wrong of me to want to take off my shirt and cover her with it? She's barely dressed and everyone will see her like this."

I stare at him, watching him watch her. "You really like her, don't you?"

They met the first time Chad brought Ana out last month. And she came out a second time with him a few weeks later. That was when they had their first official date. Julian can't stop talking about her. Chad says Ana is the same way. Julian doesn't even bother looking at me when he answers. "I do."

I smile. Maybe this one will stick. I've never seen him so giddy over a woman before. Not even when *we* were dating. It makes my heart feel good knowing that he's finally let his heart move on from me.

My own protective senses go into overdrive when I see Chad come out of his dressing room. My eyes bug out and I wipe the proverbial drool from my chin. "What was it you said about wanting to cover them up?" I ask Julian.

Julian laughs at me as my eyes are glued to my super-hot-and-sexy boyfriend. He's in black jeans. Jeans that are slung so low, I can see the beginning of his happy trail. And he's wearing a black leather jacket. With no shirt underneath. His perfectly ripped abs are showing. *Oh, God.*

"And *you* get to go out with *that*," Julian says. He elbows me. "Do you think they will let them keep the clothes?"

They pose Chad on a motorcycle and Ana next to him with her hand smack in the middle of his bare chest. She looks over and flashes an apology at both Julian and me. But somehow, neither of us seem to be bothered by it. This is Ana. You'd have to look far and wide to find anyone as sweet as her. She wouldn't hurt a fly. And she says she thinks of Chad as a big brother. Of course, it helps that they never dated. I wish she were Chad's *Defcon* co-star instead of Courtney. If I have to watch Chad stick his tongue down someone's throat, I'd rather it be her.

For the next hour, Julian and I stare at our dates as they make fuck-me eyes at each other, laughing and joking between photos. I have to admit, they look stunning together. They could even pass for brother and sister, both having gorgeous blonde hair and blue eyes.

Just before they wrap it up, Chad calls Julian and me over, having the photographer snap pictures of the four of us and then each couple. For our photo, Chad stands behind me, wrapping me inside his jacket as I gaze up at him out of the corner of my eye. His expression is even hotter than when he posed with Ana. There's so much emotion passing between us. Admiration, desire, love. I know these photos will become some of my most cherished possessions.

I walk Chad back to his dressing room, peering up at him in disbelief.

"What?" he asks.

I shake my head, smiling. "I just can't believe you're mine," I say, raking my gaze over him.

He pulls me into his dressing room and shuts the door. "Believe it, Mallory Kate. It's true. It's true now and forever," he says right before claiming my lips with his.

~ ~ ~

"That was the best meal ever," Chad says, rubbing his stomach in appreciation. "Thanks, bro."

I'm grateful Chad doesn't let his superstar ego get in the way of Julian paying for dinner. It's important for Julian to be able to do things like this. And although Julian's paychecks are hardly in the seven figures like Chad's, he does quite well and I'm proud of him. Plus, I think he wants Ana to know that he's perfectly capable of providing for her.

"Happy to do it," Julian says. "So, are you guys excited about going to Paris next?"

"Are you kidding?" Ana says, squirming in her chair. "I can't wait. It will be my first time out of the U.S."

Chad frowns. He wanted me to go with him so badly for the Paris *Blind Shot* premiere. But there are only two weeks of school left. There is no way I could go this close to the end of the year. "I guess," Chad says, shrugging a shoulder. "But it could have been a whole lot better."

"I'm sorry," I say. "If it were only two weeks later, you know I would do it."

"Are you saying that you'd go anywhere I asked as long as it falls over your summer break?"

"Of course," I say.

He points to Julian and Ana. "You guys heard that, right? She said she'd go wherever I asked her."

They both nod, looking at him strangely.

"What?" I ask, confused over where this is going.

"I've been wanting to ask you this all week, but didn't know how." He puts his arm behind me on the back of my chair, running his thumb in circles on my shoulder. "I would love it if you'd spend the summer with me, Mallory. I want you to come stay with me in L.A. and come with me to Sedona."

"You want me to go on location with you? While you're filming?" I look at Julian and Ana to see if they heard what I heard. They both smile at me.

"We talked about it once and you said you would," Chad says.

"I thought you meant a weekend, Chad. What on earth will I do while you're working?"

"A lot of actors bring their families on location. It's not that unusual. There will be plenty of things for you to do. You can go sightseeing. You can hang out in my trailer. You can come on set."

I smile shyly at him. "You think of me as family?"

"Only since you were six, Mal."

Then my face falls thinking of who I'd be leaving behind. "I can't go," I tell him. "Not for the whole summer. I can't leave my dad for that long."

Chad's eyes drop to the table. I know he won't argue with me. He knows how important it is for me to take care of my dad.

"Uh, Mallory?" Julian says. "I think there's something you should know about your dad."

"Oh, God, what?" I ask, scared by his declaration.

He makes some strange faces, as though he's trying to figure out how to tell me some deep, dark secret.

"Tell her," Ana says, nodding at Julian while she puts her hand on top of his.

What? How is it that Julian and Ana both know something about my dad that I don't?

"What is it, Julian?" I beg.

"Your dad should probably be the one to tell you this, Mallory. But he thought maybe it would upset you."

I look between him and Ana. "Is he selling the house or something?"

"Not that I know of. But um . . . he has been dating someone for a while now."

My jaw drops. Then for a few seconds, pictures of my mom flash through my mind. How is it possible to be so sad and happy over the same news? "Really? Define a while."

Julian motions between Chad and me. "Longer than you've been together. Six months, maybe."

I replay some of the moments with my dad in my head. I guess it makes sense. He's been able to talk about my mom without getting upset. He's been going out more than he ever used to. *Oh, my God. My dad has a girlfriend!*

"Who is she?"

Julian winces. "That's the part he thought you might have the most trouble with. She's a nurse."

I sigh. My mom was a nurse. Of course that's why he didn't want to tell me. I close my eyes and absorb the information. "No, it's fine. It makes sense that he'd date someone from the hospital. He's pretty much there all the time. How serious is it?" I ask.

He shrugs. "You'll have to ask him that. But I think pretty serious."

Julian and my dad have a great relationship. I never told my dad that he cheated on me, and they remained friends even when Julian and I weren't. What surprises me is that Julian has discussed this with Ana. I smile thinking maybe *their* relationship is more serious than I thought.

"So you don't have to stick around and take care of him, Mal," Julian says. "I have a feeling he'll be just fine if you leave for the summer."

"Maybe Julian could come out for a week and we can all hang out," Ana says, looking hopeful.

"I think that could be arranged," he says, putting his arm around her.

I smile, looking over at Chad. I don't need words to tell him I agree. He leans in to kiss me and then whispers in my ear. "Ten weeks with you will be like living in heaven."

My heart thunders. My body melts. My head spins. I'm not sure, but if I looked it up in the dictionary, that might be the definition of swooning.

CHAPTER TWENTY-THREE

Chad

I wasn't kidding when I told Mal it would be heaven having her live with me for the summer. Two weeks in and I already know this is what I want for the rest of our lives. But I know it's not always going to work out this well. Mallory works ten months out of the year. She won't be able to come with me when I film most times. What will happen then; when getting away for the weekend isn't an option? Filming is done on a very tight schedule. To stay within budget we sometimes work fourteen to sixteen hour days, six or seven days a week.

With Mallory's help, I picked two films to do next year. *Out of the Deep*, that sci-fi number Paul really wanted me to do; and another romantic comedy like *Blind Shot* called *Four Night Stand*. I told Paul no way in hell would I sign on for the *Malibu* movie. He wasn't too sore at me, though, because Thomas didn't want to do it either—and it was all or nothing. I'm hoping that will get Heather out of my life once and for all.

I'm showing Mal around my trailer in the studio lot where we'll be filming for the next few weeks before we head to Sedona. Kendra has made sure they provided all the comforts of home, especially since Mallory will be spending so much time here. Kendra even blew up a picture of the two of us and had it framed and mounted over the couch.

Mal opens the small refrigerator that has already been completely stocked. She pulls out a bottle of her favorite beer and examines it. "How did they know? Did you tell them?"

"It's Kendra's job to find out what we like," I say. "She submits a list of requests for our favorite things like food, drink or personal items. They're called riders."

She goes to the back, checking out the small bedroom. She opens the closet to see it's been filled with duplicates of my favorite shirts and jeans. She opens the drawers. She looks at me, red in the face. "Did you tell her to get these?" She holds up a box of condoms.

I laugh. "No. That's pretty much standard."

Mal's face falls into a frown and she puts the box back where she found it and sits on the bed. "So they will put them there even when I'm not with you? Do they expect you to use them?"

I step over to the bed and sit beside her. "Babe, they could put a naked Victoria's Secret model on my bed and I still wouldn't use them."

She gives me a sad smile. "What are we going to do when I can't come with you?" she asks.

"We're going to burn up cyber-space with our phone love." I push her back onto the bed and climb on top of her. "Don't worry, Mallory. We'll work it out. I promise."

There's a knock on the trailer door. "Ten minutes, Mr. Stone."

"Thanks!" I yell, still hovering over Mallory. Then I lean down to kiss her. I kiss her hard. I kiss her with everything I have. I've seen today's call sheet and I know it may be tough for Mallory to watch, so I need her to know without a doubt that she's the one I love.

After I've kissed her senseless, I lie next to her and pull her against me, cherishing these last quiet minutes.

I have no idea what will happen when I see Courtney. I haven't seen her in months, since the pre-production meetings back in April. I've purposely avoided her at all costs. Other than being concerned she might not be able to perform up to expectations, I don't give a rat's ass what she's been up to. But I'm not going to put up with any more of her shit. I made it perfectly clear to Paul and Kendra and the whole damn studio that I'm not going to pretend I'm with her. I'm not hiding my relationship with Mallory to sell a few more tickets to a movie. I told them in no uncertain terms if they try to make it look like Courtney and I are still together, I will issue a statement myself. It's pure bullshit what Paul and the studio wanted me to do. Maybe I was willing to go along with it before, when it seemed my career was riding on it. But now—when I can pretty much pick and choose what I want to do, and producers and directors are fighting over me—*I'm* going to be the one calling the shots, not them.

"We'd better get going," I say. We walk out to the front and I pick up the call sheets, handing her one. "This is the call sheet. I've told the AD to give me two of them so you can have one with you at all times."

"What's a call sheet?" she asks, looking over it. "And what's an AD?"

I laugh. Mallory has become such a big part of my life that I sometimes forget she's not in the business. "AD stands for Assistant Director," I tell her. "He prepares the call sheet from the director's shot list. The cast and crew get one to tell them when and where to report each day. It lists the order in which the scenes will be shot. This one is pretty basic, but when we're on location in Sedona, it will have additional information about transportation, safety, weather, and what meals are provided each day."

"So it's a daily schedule," she says. "Why not just call it a daily schedule?"

I kiss her on the nose, chuckling. But before I open the door, I tell her what I've been dreading. "Mallory, I'm going to have to kiss Courtney in a scene today. And I'll have to do it several times until they get the shot they want. If you don't want to watch, I'll understand. But it would be nice to have you there so you see how it's all very technical and not nearly as intimate as it looks on screen."

She nods sadly, looking at the floor. Then she smiles up at me. "I know you have to do this as part of your job, Chad. It's okay. You just go do what you need to do and then later" —she motions back to the bedroom— "we'll open that box."

Shit. She's going to send me out of the trailer with a hard-on. "You know," I say. "We've been together for a while now, and I've been tested more than once. And since you're on the pill, I was thinking maybe we could go without the box."

She smiles, looking all sultry and come-hither as she gazes at me through her lashes. "I would love to feel you with nothing between us."

Definite boner.

There's another knock on the door and I open it to see one of the ADs. "Mr. Stone, Ms. Benson would like to see you in her trailer before hair and makeup."

I give Mallory a look of annoyance. Then I turn back to the AD. "Can you please show Mallory the way to makeup, John. I'll be there in five." I kiss her on the top of the head. "Wish me luck, babe, I'm goin' in."

I walk over to Courtney's trailer and knock on her door. "Come in!" she yells.

I half expect her to be naked with bells on, but she's not. In fact, she doesn't look anything like what I expected. She's got on jeans and a t-shirt and her hair is in a ponytail. She resembles the Courtney I knew when we first met, the Courtney who hadn't yet been introduced to the black-hole world of drugs. "Uh . . . hi."

"Hi, Thad. Thanks for coming," she says, sitting on her couch. "I wanted to have a minute with you before all the craziness started."

"Okay, what's up?"

"Can you sit down for a second, please?"

Please? I'm beginning to wonder what she did with the real Courtney. I walk over and sit on the far end of her couch. "Will this take long? We're due in makeup."

"No. I just wanted to apologize to you, and I didn't want to do it in front of everyone."

"Apologize for what exactly?" I ask.

She shoots her eyebrows up like it should be blatantly obvious. "For the way I treated you, Thad." She shakes her head, briefly closing her eyes. "I've seen some of the press footage and the pictures. I was a self-centered bitch."

I stare at her for a minute. "You seem different," I say.

"Well, I should hope so. I'm clean now. Almost eight weeks."

My eyes light up. "Really?"

She nods.

"That's great, Courtney. I'm happy for you. You look well."

"Thanks. I feel good. I'm excited to get started filming. I was hoping we could start off on the right foot. Give them a performance to remember."

"I always try to," I say. "But, yeah, thanks for telling me. I think it will make things a lot easier for everyone."

"I hope so. Listen, I know you had to do what you did when you found out I was using. I'm not mad at you for breaking up with me. I just wish I would have realized how out of control I was a little sooner. Maybe then . . . well, maybe things could have been different between us. Maybe they still can be."

I shake my head. "I can hardly blame you for what you did when you were using, Courtney. That would make me a bit of a hypocrite, don't you think? But I'm not sure how differently things would have turned out. I'm with Mallory now. In some ways, I've always been with her. I'm not saying this to make you feel bad, but things would never have worked out between us in the long run. I could never be with anyone but her."

She nods sadly. "Well, you can't blame a girl for trying. I'm glad you're happy, Thad."

The stern knock on the door tells us we can't wait any longer. I get up and head across the room. "Thanks. You'll find someone to be happy with too, Courtney. See you on set?"

"Yeah. See you on set." I walk through the door, but she calls me back. "Thad!" She throws something at me and I catch it before it pelts me in the head. "Don't eat any onions today, okay?"

I look at the spearmint gum she threw at me and laugh. Then I smile back at her before walking away. Maybe this won't be so bad after all.

~ ~ ~

It's been a long day. The first day of filming usually is. All the bugs are getting worked out. Mallory has been getting quite an education watching everything. She's been careful to be nothing

272

more than a fly on the wall, taking great precautions not to be seen nor heard while still getting to hang out with me as much as possible. Which has been maybe ten minutes outside of lunchtime. Noreen and Hayden are on set today but don't have as busy a schedule as Courtney and I do, so they've been keeping Mal company.

I take a moment to be with her while they are setting up for our kissing scene. Our stand-ins are being used to make sure the lighting is good. I take a stick of gum from my pocket and pop it in my mouth. Mal watches my every move.

She sighs. "I think I'd prefer if you just have pizza breath."

I laugh. I pull her into a corner of the room. I tuck my body over hers and lean into her. "It's just acting, Mallory. You're the one who gets the *real* me." I kiss her long and hard so she knows every word is true.

"Places!" I hear called out behind me.

Mal smiles, popping the gum she just stole from my mouth. "Go do your job," she says. "I'll keep this for you until later."

Our set has been made to look like an old cabin we've found to hole up in. We've used all the resources in it and Courtney and I have a fight over whether to stay or find someplace new. Then Hayden's character comes barging through the door. He's my enemy and he's been following us to try and figure out where the safe zone is so he can rob it. We have to hide in a closet and that's where we kiss. I give the performance of my life. Hell, we might even end up winning best kiss of the year.

When the scene is over, I find Mal sitting outside the set on a curb. We've wrapped for the day so I've been cleared to leave. I sit down next to her, both of us silent.

"You didn't have to make it look so darn real," she pouts. "I mean, it was . . . wow, it was—"

"I know it was. I did it on purpose." She looks at me with confused eyes. "Do you want to know why?" I ask.

She nods.

"I only wanted to have to kiss her one time, Mal. I didn't want my lips on her any longer than necessary. So when I closed my eyes, I pretended she was you because you are the only person I ever want to be kissing. I knew that if I looked like I do when I kiss you, it would look incredible. Because every kiss with you is just that. So, yeah, I made it a good one. But in doing so, I made sure it was the *only* one."

She slips her hand around my elbow and leans her head into my shoulder. "Thank you," she says, relieved. "Now can you go wash that woman off of you so I can have *my* turn?"

~ ~ ~

We finally get a day off with a week of filming under our belt. As it so happens, Julian is in town staying with Ana this week. He was able to come on set for a day and hang out with Mal. I felt bad there wasn't more interesting filming for him to watch, it was mostly re-shoots of stuff they wanted changed.

Today I'm making up for a lot of lost time. Mallory and I picked up Megan and her friend, Alyssa, and then headed to my parents' place on the coast to meet Julian, Ana, Hayden, and Noreen for a beach day. Their house in Santa Monica has several hundred feet of coastline, with a long wooden stairway weaving down from their house through the rocks that line the dunes. It's a lot of fucking steps. One hundred and five of them. I've counted them more times than I can remember. And Megan navigated them all. She's a freaking rock star.

When we first moved out here, I was sixteen and Kyle was fifteen. It was pretty much a dream house for kids. My parents gave Kyle and me the guest house above the garage, so it was like we had our own little apartment. Hell, it's paradise here. And the only reason I moved out when I turned eighteen was that I had started using and didn't want my family to see everything that went along with it. I was a stupid shit.

I'm amused by Megan's friend, Alyssa, as she tries her best not to get all fangirl around me. Usually when I hang out with Megan, it's just us. Or now, us and Mal. But I didn't want her to feel left out today with all the couples, so I asked her to bring a friend. I see Alyssa trying to discreetly take a picture of me, so I get up and walk over to her. "Alyssa, how about having Megan take a picture of us?"

"Oh, my gosh, really?" she says, blushing.

"Sure. And I don't think the others would mind being in a few either."

Hayden, Ana, Noreen and I spend the next few minutes posing with Alyssa so she gets her pictures.

"That was very nice of you," Mallory says when I lie down on the towel next to hers.

"Sometimes I find it best to just get it all out of the way so we can try and have a normal day."

"Well, you just made that girl's year," she says.

I give her an incredulous look. "If that's true, it would be kind of sad."

She shakes her head at me. "You have no idea the effect you have on people, do you? Years from now, Alyssa will tell the story of how she got to hang out on the beach with Thad Stone and his movie-star friends. It will be one of the highlights of her life."

Before I grab the football to throw with Hayden, I kneel over her. "I only want to be the highlight of *your* life," I say, leaning down to kiss her.

"Get a room!" Megan yells.

I laugh and throw the football at her. She catches it, throwing a perfect spiral back at me. She comes over to keep Mallory company while I toss the ball with Hayden. I'm standing close to the towel they're on, so I hear their conversation.

"So, what's it like to be Thad Stone's girlfriend?" Megan asks Mal.

"I don't know, what's it like to be Thad Stone's best friend?" Mal asks her back.

They both giggle and I smile.

"You look great, by the way," Mal says. "I love your shimmering silver bikini. You amaze me, Megan."

She doesn't have to explain what she means. Not many eighteen-year-old girls with one leg would come to the beach. Her titanium prosthetic is more than obvious without pants to cover it. But Megan doesn't seem to care. Not anymore.

"What, this old thing?" Megan jokes. "It's the only one that matches my leg."

Alyssa and the other girls join them and they proceed to talk about girl shit I have no desire to hear, so Hayden, Julian and I throw the ball in the surf.

I haven't had much time to talk with Julian this week. "How are things going?" I ask him after we've worn ourselves out.

"Couldn't be better," he says.

"Ana's a great girl," Hayden adds.

Julian smiles, as he and Ana share a private look from a distance. "She is."

"Just how serious are we talking here?" I ask.

He shrugs. "We don't really talk about it. We're having a good time. We see each other when we can, but it's not like we're making long-term plans or anything."

"You don't think she's long-term material?" I ask, offended on Ana's behalf.

"No. It's not that," he says. "I'm just not sure this is the lifestyle I want to live. I know it can be hard. I'm the one who has to deal with Mallory every time she comes back from seeing you, and every time you leave. It's tough on her. And it's not like it will get any better, man. Not unless you expect her to quit the job she loves. And hell if I'm going to quit *my* job and follow Ana around like a fucking puppy dog. She's great. But I'm not sure it's worth it."

"I don't expect Mal to quit her job, Julian. That is completely up to her. We'll make it work either way. And it sure as hell *is* worth it if you love someone," I say, glancing over at Mallory who is laughing and having a great time with the girls. "Maybe you're just not there yet. Give it time. But if you still feel this way in a few months, don't string her along, okay? Ana is way too nice a girl for that."

He nods. "No way would I do that to her, Chad. I've hurt one too many girls in my life as it is."

My stomach growls and the sun is starting to set. "Come on," I challenge the guys. "Let's go pick up our girls and race to the top of the stairs."

"How can we race?" Julian asks. "They are too narrow to pass on."

I look up at the long stairway leading up to my parents' house. "Good point."

"We can have Megan and Alyssa keep time," Hayden says.

"Hell, yeah," Julian says, running over to scoop up Ana.

I laugh. We were always super competitive as kids. It's nice to know some things haven't changed.

We spend a few minutes making rules as the girls all roll their eyes at us. Then we send Alyssa to the top to time us on her phone's stopwatch. Megan will yell from the bottom to start.

After I watch Hayden struggle with Noreen, I decide to change my tactic. I throw Mallory over my shoulder in a fireman's hold. She fake screams at me while snapping me with the waistband of my board shorts. Megan is laughing and taking pictures. "What are you laughing at?" I ask her. "I'm coming right back down for *you*. All my girls get door-to-door service."

As I make my way up the steps, Mallory says, "I don't think I've ever loved you more."

I smile. And then I kiss her ass. Literally.

CHAPTER TWENTY-FOUR

Mallory

Dear Mr. and Mrs. Olive,

We at Canyon Properties truly hope you enjoy your stay. Cleaning will be done every Monday and Thursday. If there is anything you need, please do not hesitate to contact us at any time.

Next to the note, there is a huge basket of non-perishables along with several bottles of wine. And as I look around, I see Kendra has done her job fabulously, making sure Chad and I have everything we need in our home away from home. Or should I say castle?

I stand in the middle of the expansive home, circling around to take it all in. The impressive great room, the chef's kitchen, the breathtaking view of the red rock desert. The alluring pool with a waterfall that matches the picturesque landscape behind it. I turn to Chad and raise my eyebrows. "Is the whole cast staying here?"

He laughs. "No, but Cole is. Don't worry though, he won't bother us."

"Bother us?" I say. "He won't even be able to *find* us. How many bedrooms are here, six?"

He looks embarrassed. "Eight, actually."

Before I can pick my jaw up off the floor and scold him, he adds, "Well, you said you wanted a private pool, Mal. And don't get your panties in a twist, it wasn't any more expensive than the Presidential Suite in New York City." He comes up behind me and wraps his big arms around me, burying his mouth in my neck, sucking on a spot below my ear that makes me moan. "Just think of all the places we can—"

Cole clears his throat behind us and I quickly pull away from Chad as he chuckles that we got busted. "The place looks secure enough," Cole says, handing Chad a piece of paper. "Here are the instructions for the security pads, there's one by the front door, back door, garage door and in the master bedroom. The entire property is fenced in, but as the neighborhood is not gated, you'll have to be cautious when you're outside, just in case." He points to an electronic keypad on the wall. "There's an intercom throughout with a small panel like this in every room by the main light switch. If you need me, you can push the white button and it will broadcast in every room. There is also a safe room in the center of the house, through the kitchen pantry. Instructions for that are written down for you as well."

"Safe room?" I ask Chad. "What are you, James Bond?"

He shrugs. "Comes with the house. It's not like I requested it or anything." He asks Cole, "Did you find a bedroom for yourself?"

"Yeah, I took the one back by the mudroom, it's pretty out of the way. You won't even know I'm here."

"You don't have to do that, Cole," I say. "I'm sure there are plenty of nice rooms for you to choose from."

"That's okay," he says, shaking his head and smirking. "I'd prefer to be back there. You know, so I'm not near any of the places you will—"

"Okay," Chad interrupts, lifting his hand to cut Cole off. "Well then, we'll just go get settled." He grabs my hand, dragging me and my beet-red face behind him. "I'll meet you back here in ten, Cole."

We take a quick tour of the house before Chad has to go on location to do some last-minute fittings due to costuming changes. They are also going to try and get some shots of him and Courtney at sunset in the desert. "Are you sure you don't want to go with me?" he asks.

"No, that's okay. I'd like to get us unpacked. I'd like to call my dad, too. I haven't talked to him in a few days. And I thought you might like a home-cooked meal when you get back. The kitchen looked pretty stocked."

"That sounds great. I'll only be a few hours." He hands me the piece of paper Cole gave him. "Go over this. And Mal, don't go outside when Cole and I aren't around. I'm just not sure how secure it is. Can you do that for me?"

I look at the concern etched into his forehead. I was going to go for a dip in the pool, but I can see that would make him uncomfortable and I don't want him worrying the whole time he's gone. "Of course. There are plenty of other things I could do. Take up billiards. Or watch a movie in the theater room. The possibilities are endless."

"Good girl," he says, drawing me in for a kiss before he leaves. "See you in a few hours." He walks to the door and turns around. "I love you, Mrs. Olive."

No matter how many times he's said it in the past, it still makes my heart thunder. "I love you too, Mr. Olive."

I stare at the door he and Cole left through. Then I turn around and shake my head at the absurdity of it all. This home is massive. I'll bet it's ten thousand square feet. I hope he knows he doesn't have to do this to impress me. His heart is the only thing I'll ever want from him.

I realize I'm still holding the piece of paper he gave me. I glance over it, amused that the security code happens to be my birthday. I wonder if I share that day with one of the owners.

I head to the master bedroom to unpack our suitcases. We'll be here for a month so we may as well get settled. After I call my dad and text Melissa pictures of my new digs, I walk the house again, deciding what to do to keep myself busy. When I find myself in the kitchen again, I check out the pantry and cabinets, which are loaded with just about everything one could need to cook a gourmet meal.

I come across some pecans and chocolate chips. Once I confirm the rest of the ingredients are here, I commence to making Chad's favorite cookies. He's loved them since we were kids. He travels so much that I want him to feel the comforts of home. I smile thinking this should do the trick.

While they are baking, I recall the talk I had with my dad earlier. I wonder if Denise was there when we were on the phone. I could hear the TV in the background and he never watches TV.

Shortly after Julian told me my dad was dating someone, Dad brought Denise home to meet me. It wasn't nearly as weird as I thought it would be. She's nothing like my mother. Denise is petite with red hair. She's also ten years younger than my dad. And she's as quiet as a mouse. She lost her husband to cancer three years ago, so I guess she and my dad have a lot in common.

I think if I would have met her before Chad and I got together, I might not have been so accepting. It was always just my dad and me. I'd sworn off men and anyone who turned his eye would have just been an intrusion. But now . . . Now I think if Denise can bring him even a fraction of the happiness Chad brings me, my dad deserves that.

Before I know it, I've not only made Chad's cookies, but I've whipped up one of his favorite dinners as well. Chicken casserole with broccoli and rice. We didn't get a chance to eat anything healthy today while traveling from L.A., and it would be a shame to let any of the food they provided go to waste.

Chad and Cole come home just as I'm taking dinner out of the oven. I turn to see Chad leaning against the doorway to the kitchen, staring at me in awe. He closes his eyes, drawing in the aromas of my labor. "Are you for real, Mallory Kate?" he asks, not moving from where he stands.

"What?" I say. "I just feel bad that you have to travel so much and work such long hours. I wanted it to seem like you were at home for a change."

He pushes off the wall, taking long, purposeful strides over to me. His hand comes around me, pressing into my lower back as he pulls me against him. He puts his forehead on mine. "Wherever *you* are, that is home to me," he says.

~ ~ ~

I'm not sure which would be harder, watching my boyfriend do scenes with the queen bitch of Hollywood, or the sweet, nice woman she's transformed into after rehab. I mean, Courtney is someone I could see hanging out with Mel and me. If she hadn't been in Chad's bed, that is.

Funny thing, I had never met her before they started filming a few weeks ago in L.A. I'd only heard what Chad and Hayden and the others would tell me about her; and then there was everything I had seen on TV and read in magazines. But it's hard for me to picture *this* Courtney as that horrible person. She's nothing like the stories they would tell me. Stories about the diva who would throw a tantrum if her very specific kind of bottled water wasn't in her dressing room.

She wasn't always that way, though. Chad said before she started doing drugs, she was much more like she is now. Nice. Accommodating. Breathtakingly beautiful.

It makes me wonder if they would still be together if she hadn't gone rogue. What would have happened if she were still that person? Would she have been with him at the club the night of the premiere? Would he have even seen me that night; and if so, would he have bothered to look me up after?

Thoughts such as these plague me as I watch them have casual conversation between takes. As I see them laugh and banter the way Chad and I have always done.

Yesterday, after they wrapped up early due to technical issues, he invited her to go climbing with us. When we were in L.A., Chad took me to the place he trained for the movie. He taught me to rock climb so we could spend some quality time together on his days off in Sedona.

Well, I shouldn't say he invited her per se. More like she found out what we were going to do and showed such an interest it would have been rude not to ask her along. Still—rock climbing was supposed to be *our* thing. And since she hadn't been properly trained, Chad pretty much had to spend the entire time teaching her what to do even though he chose the easiest climb. It had me wondering if her nice-girl act is all for show. Is it some elaborate scheme to win him back?

"Whatever it is that you're thinking, stop it."

I turn around to see Noreen has snuck up behind me. "What is it that I'm thinking?" I ask.

"I see the way you're looking at them, Mallory. They are the leads in this movie, it behooves them to get along. Believe me, them hating each other would make this so much worse."

"For whom?" I ask, looking back at them.

She touches my shoulder, bringing my attention from them back to her. "I'm telling you, that man only has eyes for you."

I nod as if I agree with her. Sweat trickles down my cleavage as the sun beats down on me on this sweltering day. We walk over and sit down in chairs under a tent.

"Hayden tells me you're all Thad talks about when they are together," Noreen says. Then she laughs. "He says it's starting to get pretty disgusting. He calls Thad a love-sick puppy."

I try not to smile, but don't do a very good job of it. "Thanks, Noreen."

I look back to try and find Chad, wondering when they're going to do the cave scene. I saw it on his call sheet, and I could tell this morning at breakfast that he was nervous. In *Defcon One*, they spent so much time in a cave that he became claustrophobic.

"I'm worried about him," I tell Noreen. "You were there last time, right? When he freaked out in the cave? What if it happens again?"

She nods. "Hayden and I tried to convince the studio to make a set so he wouldn't have to actually film in a cave again. But when Thad found out about it, he told them not to. Said it would cost too much and take too much time. He said he was fine and he could do it."

"You didn't see him this morning," I say. "He's trying to be all big and brave about it, but I think it's a real issue for him."

"He'll be fine, Mallory. He's an actor. He can *act* like he's not claustrophobic."

"I hope so." The words are barely out of my mouth when John, one of the ADs, comes running over. I don't like the way he's looking at me. I don't like it at all.

"Ms. Schaffer, please come quickly."

I jump up out of my chair. "What is it? Is he okay?"

John pulls me along by my elbow, guiding me through the maze of trailers, tents, and cameras. "I think he's having a panic attack," he says. "He ran out of the cave and won't go back in. This could set us back days; weeks if we have to build a set. So if you think there is anything you can do, please help him."

I find Chad sitting on the ground next to a boulder, head slumped, elbows on his knees. The back of his shirt is drenched with sweat. It's hot here, yes, but this kind of sweat, it's from stress.

Everyone else is standing back. Nobody seems to know what to do. David, the director, looks pissed. He looks at me and then waves his arm at Chad as if to say 'deal with him, would you?'

As I walk over to him, Hayden, who is also in the cave scene, asks everyone to give us some privacy. I nod at him in thanks as the crew all back away and keep their distance.

I sit down next to Chad. I don't say anything, I just put my hand out to see if he wants to hold it. When he grabs onto it and squeezes it as if it's his lifeline, I'm not sure whether to be happy that he holds me in such regard, or sad that my man is in such distress that he even needs one.

"Hey," I finally say when I hear his breathing slow down.

He sighs so hard some dirt on the ground beneath his knees becomes displaced. "I'm a fucking joke, Mal. I thought I could do it. But once I got inside, it's like a goddamn tomb and I swear the walls started closing in on me. I don't know how they even got the camera in there. There's barely room in there to turn around let alone fit two grown men plus a cameraman."

"You are not a joke, Chad. Claustrophobia is a very real fear. Nobody is going to fault you if you can't do it. They'll just have to think of something else."

"Not fault me?" He motions behind me. "Did you see the look on David's face? He thinks I'm a pussy. I have to do this, Mal. I *have* to."

I think back on my teacher training. They gave us all kinds of tips and tricks to help kids get through difficult situations. "Okay. Um, can you remember a time when you were in an enclosed space where you weren't scared?"

Chad shoots me a look of annoyance. "Don't psychoanalyze me."

"Just humor me, okay? Was there ever a time like that?"

He takes a few deep breaths and I can feel his hand starting to relax in mine. Then he nods and his lips twitch with a half-smile.

"What?" I ask. "You thought of one?"

"Do you remember when we had that huge snowstorm when we were in middle school? School got canceled for a whole week and we had snow drifts as tall as your basketball hoop?"

How could I ever forget that? It's one of my favorite memories of him. But I don't want to recall the story for him; he needs to tell it. "Um, I guess so," I say, goading him on.

"Every time the snow plows would come by, more snow would pile up along the front yard. It must have been ten feet high out near the curb. Kyle, Ethan, Julian and I built something resembling an igloo. We just picked a spot by the driveway and started digging. We must have dug about fifty pounds of snow out and then someone suggested spraying cold water along the inside walls to solidify them as it froze. It was epic. You couldn't stand up in there, but two or three people could fit in at a time. We took blankets and snacks in there. We even had a lantern." He squeezes my hand. "You really don't remember?"

"I'm starting to," I say. "Didn't we get stuck in there or something?"

"Or something?" He laughs at the memory. "Mallory, we were stuck in there for like three hours one day. Kyle was pissed at me because I brought a girl into our fort, so when you and I were in there, he shoveled a ton of snow into the opening, giving us no way out. When I realized what he'd done, I didn't even care. I was happy, in fact, because we were forced to spend more time together. Man, was my mom mad at him. She said we could have frozen to death, but there was no way. When you got too cold, you let me put my arm around you. And believe me, I had a lot of body heat going on just thinking about how much I wanted to kiss you."

I look at him with wide eyes. "You wanted to kiss me? I was only eleven, Chad."

"And I was twelve," he says. "Hell yeah, I wanted to kiss you. I wanted to kiss you every time I was with you, Mal."

Chad closes his eyes and shakes his head. "Damn," he says. "You're one hell of a teacher, Mallory Kate. I think I'm ready to do this now."

I stand up and reach my hand out to him to help him up. Then when he goes to say something to Hayden, I walk over to the director. "Get everything set up in there and then give us a few minutes alone in the cave."

He looks at me like I'm crazy. "Who the hell is directing this film?" he asks, arching a mocking brow.

"Do you want the shot or not?" I ask, staring him down even though he towers over me by a good foot.

He scoffs, rolling his eyes at me before he calls John over and tells him what to do.

I watch Chad eye the mouth of the cave, taking a deep breath before he walks in. I hurry behind him, following him into the dark chamber that is illuminated by dim set lights. When he sees me coming in behind him, he balks at me. "Mal, you can't be in here." He looks at the entrance nervously as if David is going to reach in and pull me out by my collar.

"I can and I am." I put my hand against his chest, forcefully pushing him back into the cave wall. "I remember every single detail of that day," I tell him. "You're going to finally get that kiss, Chad Stone. The one you wanted in that igloo when you were twelve."

I press myself against him, reaching up to run my hands through the back of his hair, taking care not to ruin it for the shot. I trace my fingers across his broad shoulders, teasing him through his shirt. His gaze moves to my lips as my tongue comes out to wet them. His mouth moves closer to mine, pausing only to say, "I fucking love you," before bonding his lips to mine.

The heat of the cave only heightens my senses. I'm hyper-aware of how he tastes of mint and soda, how we both smell of sweat mingled with cologne and perfume, how the sounds of our kisses echo off the walls, and how his touch sends messages of want and desire straight to my center.

I don't know how much time passes. Seconds, minutes. But it doesn't matter because he's perfectly fine in this moment, making a new memory to add to his older one. He's perfectly fine being in this tomb of a cave. And when I pull away from him and hear someone clear their throat as they walk in behind me, I whisper to him, "Do this once, babe. Make it count. And when we go home, we'll finish the fantasy."

Hayden salutes me on my way out. Then I quickly go over to the monitor on the outside of the cave and huddle around it with five or six crew as we watch Chad and Hayden nail it in one take, Chad giving the performance of a lifetime in that one Oscar-worthy scene.

CHAPTER TWENTY-FIVE

Chad

"I think you just might be David's favorite person in the whole world right now," I say to Mal in the car on the way home. "He thinks you walk on water, you know. And David doesn't like *anybody*."

She shrugs as if it's no big deal.

"Seriously, nobody stands up to the guy," I say. "You just earned the respect of every person on the crew."

"He *was* a little terrifying," she admits with a smile.

"Do you know how good you are for me? I don't think an entire team of high-priced shrinks could have accomplished in a hundred hours of therapy what it took you ten minutes to do." I wrap my arm around her, pulling her close in the back seat. "You saved my ass today, Mallory."

She nuzzles her head into me. "It's nothing you wouldn't have done for me."

"And that's why we're perfect for each other." I look at Cole in the front, his eyes fully seated on the road in front of him. I take the opportunity to run my hand up Mallory's thigh. It's hot in

Sedona in the summer, so she's always wearing these short shorts and tank tops, making it damn hard for me to concentrate.

"Chad!" she whispers, scolding me with her stare.

"Just trying to make sure you don't renege on that promise you made in the cave." I plant my hand on her inner thigh and rub my thumb across her soft skin, repeating a pattern that sends goosebumps up and down her arms on this warm evening.

Her eyes are glued to the rearview mirror, making sure Cole isn't watching us. My eyes are glued to hers. And every once in a while she closes them, taking in a breath as her body quivers under my touch. The ride back home is too long. There are so many things I want to do to her right now, but can't. I remove my hand from her leg and she protests with silent, pouty lips, making me chuckle.

I pull out my phone and tap out a text.

Mallory stares at me, clearly annoyed. "You're sending a text? *Now?*" she whines.

I smile as her phone pings in her back pocket. I nod my head at it and watch as she pulls it out and reads the text.

Me: Do you know what I want to do to that tight, sweaty little body of yours?

She laughs when she reads it. Then she smiles a deviant smile and texts me back.

Mal: Why don't you tell me?

Damn. What did I ever do to deserve this girl? I stare at her and tell her with my eyes what I want to do. We don't need words. She knows what I'm saying without them. But what's the fun in that? She wants to play this game, so I go all in. Good thing I'm a fast texter.

> **Me: I was watching you all day. Every chance I got, my eyes were glued to you. You didn't know because you were busy making everyone on set fall in love with you. But you want to know my favorite thing about watching you today? It was when you took a drink of water and then someone made you laugh. A bead of water trickled out of your mouth and rolled down your chin. You tossed your head back, laughing, and that bead of water traced a line down your neck, across your collarbone, and into your cleavage, finally disappearing into your shirt. It was the sexiest thing I've ever seen. And I was jealous of a damn drop of water. I wanted to BE that drop of water. And tonight, when we get home, I'm going to follow the same path that bead of water followed. I'm going to kiss your beautiful lips and trace my tongue down your neck. I'm going to lick your salty skin and savor the sweet taste of you. But I won't stop there . . .**

I press send and then I watch her react as she reads the text. The more she reads, the faster her breathing gets. I'm already hard. Writing her the text was like reliving that moment. Her reaction makes me even harder. Her eyes close briefly before she taps out her reply.

Mal: How can you seduce me simply by talking about a drop of water? I want that. I want that and more. Every time your lips are on me, I'm in heaven. Every time you touch me, another memory gets added to my vault that chronicles my life's most cherished moments.

God. This girl.

Me: Oh, I plan to put my lips ALL over you. After my mouth gets its fill of your incredible breasts, I'm going to lick my way down your stomach. I'm going to kiss that sexy little scar of yours. And while my mouth is busy there, my fingers are going to explore how wet I've made you . . .

She squirms around in her seat as she reads my text. Her mouth hangs open slightly. I watch as she taps out a few short words with shaky fingers. I laugh when I read them.

Mal: Yes, please.

Me: God, Mal, you're going to be so wet for me that my fingers slide easily inside your tight walls. I move them around, massaging that little area that makes you groan every time I find it. Then my tongue is going to join the party and I'm going to taste how hungry you are for me. I'm going to flick your clit with my tongue and then I'll run it in circles, making you squirm so hard under me you'll want to explode. My fingers will start to work faster because I feel your thighs start to tighten around my shoulders. God, I love that moment right before you come, when I know it's going to happen and I'm the one who's going to take you there. I suck your hard nub into my mouth as your hands grip my shoulders so fiercely that your fingernails dig into me. They dig in so deeply it hurts a bit. But I love it because it means you are mine in every way, and while I'm making you come, you are marking me as yours. Your hips buck under me as I continue to rub that spot inside you, drawing every moan and shout out of your pretty pink lips. And when you cry my name, it's a prayer I want you to say every fucking day of our lives.

I hit send and watch her as she reads it. Her body language is spectacular. Her face flushes. Her lips form an 'O' as a long, slow breath leaves them. Her thighs press tightly together. She drops the phone onto her lap, and her head falls back against the leather seat, eyes closed as she tries to control her breathing. She steals a shy look at me, shaking her head as she smiles before she sends another short text.

Mal: I need a cigarette.

I laugh out loud, prompting Cole to look at us quizzically. *Fuck.* I'm hard as a rock. I can't wait to get my girl home.

~ ~ ~

It's difficult for me to sit across the table from Hayden and Noreen without a huge shit-eating grin thinking of what Mal and I were doing just an hour ago. What we were doing in the shower. What we were doing in the pool under the waterfall. My life is playing out like the best romantic film ever made. Better. Because the drama—it's all done. Over. In the past. We have only good times ahead. What we're doing now is just the very beginning of the rest of our lives. And I want it all with her. Marriage. Kids. Side-by-side burial plots. Everything.

"Have you even heard a fucking word I've said, douchebag?" Hayden asks when the girls get up to use the restroom.

"Uh, yeah. You were talking about tomorrow's scenes," I say. *I have no fucking idea.*

He laughs, shaking his head. "You truly are pussy-whipped, my friend."

I follow Mal with my eyes before responding to him. "If there's a better kind of whipped, please tell me," I say. "Maybe you should try it sometime."

"Um . . . no," he says, taking a swig of beer. "I'm perfectly happy doing casual. And so is Noreen. So don't go putting any ideas into her head with your sickening tales of young love."

"Hey, if Noreen is good with how things are, why rock the boat?" I say.

"Exactly," he says. "And speaking of rocking the boat, has Courtney been causing you guys any trouble? She really does seem different. Do you think it's an act or something? I mean, I didn't want to say anything earlier when the girls were here, but she was trying to extract an invitation to dinner."

"Thanks for not inviting her," I say. "Part of me feels bad that she isn't hanging out with us. Doesn't leave her many options, you know. But no way in hell do I want to be put in the position of having dinner with my old girlfriend and my current one at the same time. It was bad enough being strong-armed into taking her climbing with us. It was terrible, man. Courtney had no experience whatsoever and I had to keep helping her. She might just be trying to be friends, but there's enough crazy in my life, I can't take the chance of her hurting Mal in any way." I frown thinking of that afternoon. "I'm afraid it ruined rock climbing for Mallory and that was supposed to be our thing here."

"Well, I hate to tell you this, buddy, but if Mallory is planning on being on set this Friday, anything having to do with rocks, Sedona, or even this film, might be ruined for her."

I nod reluctantly. This Friday we'll be shooting the obligatory sex scene of the film. Even action films need to have one. Keeps the female fans happy or some shit like that. But this scene, it's going to wreck Mallory. Even if she's there, watching how technical and non-sexual it really is, it will have a lasting impact on her and that upsets me.

I think of what she did for me today. How she took a bad experience and made it into a good one. Maybe I can do the same for her. And suddenly it becomes clear to me. I pull out my phone and send a text to Kendra and then John, the AD I've become good friends with over the past month of production. I set the wheels of my plan in motion.

"I swear I just saw a light bulb go off over your head, dude," Hayden says.

"What's that about a light bulb?" Noreen asks behind us.

"Nothing," I say, shaking my head so only Hayden can see it. "It's just so dark in here, I can barely read the dessert menu."

"You want dessert?" Mal asks, rubbing her stomach. "I don't know where you boys put it all. I'm stuffed."

Our waiter comes over and puts a drink in front of me. I've already had my limit, so I'm not sure why he brought one when I didn't order it. "From the ladies at the bar," the waiter says.

I look over my shoulder and see three women huddled together, smiling and taking photos of our table. I'm glad it's dark in here; they won't get a very good shot. I raise the drink to them in thanks and then I put it in front of Mallory. Mallory smiles and takes a slow drink of it. Then she looks over at the girls, one of whom very blatantly raises her middle finger at her.

Hayden and I laugh while Mallory downs the rest of the drink. "Why don't good looking babes ever send *me* drinks?" Hayden asks. He looks at Noreen in question, motioning to me. "It's always this asshole. He's not even as hot as I am, right?"

Noreen stares him down and then points at her chest. "If you want *this* good looking babe to go home with your egotistical ass tonight, you'd best stop calling other women good looking babes."

I see commotion in my periphery and look over to where the three women were at the bar. About halfway between them and us, Cole is holding back two of the unruly and obviously drunk girls. "The drink was for you!" one of them yells at me. "Not that ugly bitch!"

The restaurant falls silent as Cole and the manager politely escort them to the front door. Before they are out of earshot, I hear Cole say, "Next time, best stick to asking for an autograph or a picture, Miss."

"I love Cole," Mallory says. "He needs a raise. I didn't even see them get up from the bar. He must have been watching them the whole time."

"That's why he's the best," I say.

"It must be hard for him, you know," Mal says, watching the door as he comes back in and resumes his perch at the end of the bar. "He probably doesn't have any time for a girlfriend. He has to follow you around all the time and be at your beck and call."

"I'm sure it is hard, but the pay is good," I say. "And they rarely do it for more than a year or so, taking long breaks between clients. Sometimes—like Cole did before I hired him exclusively—they work for multiple people on an as-needed basis. That allows bodyguards more time for a personal life because they can control when they work."

"Still," Mal says. "Maybe we should work on getting him a girl."

I roll my eyes at my uber-romantic girlfriend.

"It's just a shame all of our friends are taken," she says. "He's so handsome and fit. And he's very nice."

I raise my eyebrows at her. "Am I losing my godlike status here?"

She laughs and squeezes my leg under the table. "I just want everyone to be as happy as we are, that's all."

I lean into her so only she can hear. "Not possible."

My phone vibrates with a text. I think it might be Kendra or John, so I check it. It's my lawyer.

Ron: Settled the McIntyre case this afternoon for 2M. Think we should have kept fighting

**this one, but I guess you have your reasons.
I'll send final paperwork for you to sign when
you're back.**

I let out a deep, tension-relieving breath. That's the last of it. The very last shit from my past that has followed me around all these years. After the whole Megan debacle during Mal's spring break, I told Ron I wanted to clean house, get all my pending cases dealt with no matter what the cost. He was afraid I'd be seen as an easy target, a money train for anyone who files suit against me. I just wanted the shit done. I want to start my life with Mallory on a clean slate. This news couldn't have come at a better time.

"What is it?" Mallory asks.

I'll tell her later. I always do. I have no secrets from her anymore. She knows all about the fights I used to get into when I was using. The nights I spent in jail for breaking Lennie McIntyre's arms. The fact that I don't even remember it, but am willing to pay the guy an amount akin to him winning the state lottery.

I shake my head, telling her I don't want to get into it here. She understands the message behind my eyes. She always has. "Nothing to worry about, babe. Nothing at all."

When we leave the restaurant, we're followed out by some teenage girls who were dining with their parents. They are giggling behind us, each trying to get the other to ask me for an autograph. I also notice the drunk girls from the bar sitting on a bench out front. The ones who called my lovely girlfriend an ugly bitch. I decide to teach them a bit of an etiquette lesson. One that says: don't try to hit on a man when he's obviously on a date with his girl.

I whisper my plan to Cole and he makes sure to plant himself between me and said drunk girls. I turn around and ask the shy ones, "Would you like to get some pictures? I could have my girlfriend take them, she's really nice like that."

The sisters squeal at each other. "Oh, my gosh, yes," the younger one says. She turns to Mallory. "You would do that for us?"

"Of course," Mal says, smiling. "Why don't you get on either side of Thad and I'll get you all in one picture and then we'll get you each with him separately."

"That's so nice," the older one says, handing Mallory her phone.

Mallory spends the next few minutes posing us in pictures that will surely make these girls the talk of their school. She's laying it on thick for the drunk girls and I love that we're on the same wavelength.

After our impromptu photo shoot is done and I sign one girl's shirt and the other girl's hat, they thank me profusely and politely walk away.

I can see the drunk girls bouncing around on the bench, getting out their phones. They think they're next. I pull Mallory over in front of them. "Got your phones ready?" I ask them.

They nod with excitement and hold up their devices.

I dip Mallory back and plant a long, hard, wet kiss on her. I try to make it romantic but we both have a hard time not breaking into hysterics, so it doesn't go quite as planned at first. But then as we taste each other, our kiss turns real, and everything around us becomes of no importance as we slip into our own little world. Like the cave. Like the igloo. Like every time the two of us are together.

When we finally pull our lips apart, I turn my head to the girls, still holding Mal's languid body. "I hope you got that, because it's the only picture you'll be getting tonight."

Then I take my thoroughly-kissed girlfriend and walk away.

CHAPTER TWENTY-SIX

Mallory

As if this day weren't bad enough already, Chad's manager had to call him on the way to the set and tear into him for the kiss that went viral this week. Chad looks at me apologetically as I listen to his side of the conversation.

"I told you I wasn't going to hide Mallory anymore, Paul."

"Because I wanted her here."

"No. *You* listen. That's *your* shit, not mine. This is the way it's going to be."

"Nobody else fucking cares."

"Listen, I'm on set," he lies. "There's nothing we can do about it anyway. It's out there. It's done. Now let me go do my job so you can continue earning your inflated fucking paycheck." I can hear Paul say something else when Chad pulls the phone away from his ear and hangs up on him.

"Sorry," he says.

"It's fine." I'm not letting Paul ruin what was not only a fun night out with friends, but quite possibly the only intimate moment that will ever be recorded between Chad and me. Unlike the dozens of intimate moments he gets to record with beautiful actresses.

I frown, once again thinking about what will happen on set today.

"Hey," Chad says, putting his hand under my chin and forcing me to look over at him. "Don't let Paul get to you, Mal. Everyone else has accepted this. He's a selfish prick; a whiny little kid throwing a tantrum because he didn't get his way."

I shake my head. "I know. It's not that." I look down at my lap.

He nods in understanding. "You're worried about today."

"I'm sorry," I say. "I'm trying not to be a stick in the mud, but it's hard knowing your boyfriend will be making love to another woman."

"I'll hardly be making love to her, Mal."

"I saw *Defcon One*, Chad. You did it then. With Courtney— who you actually *have* made love to." I can't even help the tear that escapes my eye and rolls down the side of my face.

"Stop the car, Cole. We need a minute, please," Chad says.

Cole pulls over to the side of the road and gets out of the car, giving us our privacy.

Chad removes our seatbelts and positions us so we're facing each other. "You are the only woman I've ever made love to, Mallory Kate. I promise you that with all my heart." He takes my hands and rubs his thumbs across my knuckles as he tries to put me at ease. "Let me tell you exactly what will happen today. And it's not what you might think. First of all, acting is hard. We get nervous before every take. All we're thinking about is how we can deliver our lines to make everyone believe we are who we're pretending to be. And most of us are terrified over doing sex scenes. Don't think men aren't afraid of having their naked bodies displayed for all to see. I mean, what if I have a zit on my ass today?"

I laugh half-heartedly. "You don't," I say. "I checked thoroughly in the shower earlier."

My joke makes him smile. "Let's just say I did have a zit on my ass. I'd be in makeup for an hour just so they could cover it up. Actually, I'll be in makeup anyway just so they can put goo on my ass to make it look perfect. And then they'll have me put on a cock sock."

My eyes widen. "A what?"

"A cock sock. It's a flesh-colored bag that holds all my junk. And Courtney will wear a similarly colored G-string. But it's not what you think. It's not as if we'll be spending hours naked and smashing our bodies together. Most of our shots will be done with our pants on. There will only be a few takes when we have to strip down and, um . . . grind into each other."

I cringe when he says that. I close my eyes and wonder why I even decided to come on set today. I should have stayed at home, drinking heavily. "I shouldn't be here," I tell him. "Maybe it would be easier if—"

"If you were at home imagining the worst?" he asks. "Fuck that, Mallory. I need to have you here. You need to see for yourself there is nothing sexual about a sex scene."

"But what if you . . ." I nod to his lap and sigh. Of course he'll get an erection. Not only will he be kissing and touching a beautiful woman, but one he's been with before. Will he remember what it's like to be with her? Before she turned to drugs? His body may respond to hers even if he doesn't want it to.

"It's not going to happen, baby," he says, tightening his grip on me. "It didn't even happen when Courtney and I were dating. You'll see how it is. There will be people around, telling us what to do and how to do it. Where to put a hand or mouth. We'll have to do the same thing over and over until we are so bored with it we could scream. And when it comes to actually stripping down, they will have two cameras filming everything so we don't have to do a lot of takes."

I nod. I know he's trying to make me feel better. But I still can't get it out of my head that he'll be touching her. And for a minute, I hate myself for wishing Courtney were still using. If she were still doing drugs, she wouldn't be this perky, nice, uber-friendly woman. The kind of woman Chad is drawn to.

I know it's his job. And I know this won't be the last time he has to make love to someone on set. But it doesn't make what's about to happen any easier. "Still," I say. "You'll be touching her boobs. And she has pretty nice ones."

He laughs. "Not really," he says. "I'll be touching silicone." He draws me onto his lap and takes my face into his hands. "I don't have any feelings for Courtney. I *won't* have any feelings for her. I love *you*, Mallory."

He kisses me so softly and tenderly, how could I be anything but putty in his hands? When he pulls away, I beg him, "Please don't kiss her like you just kissed me."

"Kissing her will never be like kissing you," he says. He traces my lips with his finger. "This mouth; these lips. I dream about them. They belong to me. And I promise you, mine belong to you. For as long as you want them."

"I'll never stop wanting them," I tell him.

He smiles proudly. "I'm glad to hear you say that." He motions for Cole to get back in the car. "Now, come on, we have a big day ahead. Both of us."

I'm not sure what he means by that. Usually, big days are reserved for big things. Good things. There's nothing about today that is good. I'd just as soon go to sleep and wake up in tomorrow.

~ ~ ~

"Thad, move your hand up higher," David says. "You need to cover her nipple. Yeah, that's good. Now tilt your shoulders to your right so we can get a clean shot. Okay, good. Courtney, lean your head back against the rock a little more; expose your throat. Nice. Okay. Let's go people. Let's get it this time. Stand by."

"Cameras rolling," Jonah, the lead camera operator says.

The clapboard makes an appearance and then David calls, "Action."

And then I watch my boyfriend, my love, my life, kiss and grope another woman for the third take today. And this isn't even the worst part. They're not naked yet. They still have their pants on. They've been shooting close-up shots of their heads and chests for the last two hours. Unfortunately for me, they left these scenes to do last thing, and all I've been doing today is obsessing over how it would go.

The cast and crew have been giving me strange looks all day. I guess they feel sorry for me, having to stand around and watch this. Chad tells me it's quite common to have significant others watch love scenes. I don't know how they handle it. Because I just want to vomit.

I close my eyes and hope it will be over soon. David yells, "Cut! Nicely done." Then makeup and costume rush to them before the next scene. They spray beads of sweat on Chad's back and fix Courtney's hair to look more mussed up.

When David calls action again, I watch Courtney and Chad tear each other's pants off and then Chad presses her into the rock, grinding against her while kissing her once more. The scene ends and makeup comes over to brush something across Chad's ass. I guess they don't think it's perfect the way it is. Stupid, stupid women. I bet they love their jobs right about now.

Chad looks over at me while his hands are still on Courtney. He knows what's coming next. *I* know what's coming next. He gives me the biggest, brightest smile I've ever seen. He holds my stare, telling me with his eyes all the things I need to hear. Then he tells me with his lips as he mouths, *I love you.*

Then he closes his eyes and takes a deep breath. When he opens them, I can see the transformation from Chad Stone to Lt. Jake Cross. He's not my boyfriend anymore, he's a superstar. He's a man doing what he was born to do. And despite how I feel about what he's doing right this minute, I have an overwhelming sense of pride when I look at him.

"Let's do this in one take, people," David says as John looks at me with sympathetic eyes.

I move off to the side so I can barely see what they are doing. The more obscure I can make this, the better. I don't watch the monitors; those make it look too real. I watch the actors. I watch Chad lift Courtney into his arms, pressing her back against the massive boulder as he simulates moving inside her. I listen to them moan with pleasure. I watch his lips move down her neck like they have a hundred times on mine. And when it gets to be too much, I look over at the cameras and the microphones and the tents and trailers just to remind myself it's not real.

Then I watch Courtney throw her head back in ecstasy as my boyfriend makes her come. I hear Chad shout into the canyon as he simulates his own orgasm. I feel my heart lurch in my chest as a vise grips it, getting tighter and tighter until it almost snaps me in two.

I feel hot tears stream down my face as I watch my boyfriend make love to his ex.

I double over and put my hands on my knees, embarrassed that I'm having this visceral reaction. I've never been so happy to hear the words, "Cut. Print that."

I discreetly wipe my eyes as I watch Chad and Courtney put their robes on. I take a breath for what feels like the first time in hours. Finally, Noreen comes up behind me. She's left me alone this afternoon. I think everyone knows I didn't want to be handled. I needed to get through this myself.

Chad is watching me, clearly needing to get to me, but someone has pulled him aside. Courtney is walking back to her trailer but stops when she sees me. We haven't talked much over the course of filming, but when we have, she's been nothing less than professional and insanely nice.

She smiles at me, but it's a sad smile. "He's all yours now," she says. "You are one lucky woman. I hope you know that."

There's no ill intent. No malice in her words. Just sincerity. I wish she and Chad hadn't dated. Not just for obvious reasons, but because I like her. I think we could have been great friends. I watch her walk back to her trailer. And I'm almost positive I see her wipe a tear off her face when she gets there. She loves him. She loves him like Julian loved me. She gets to pretend Chad is hers, but at the end of the day, he goes home with me. And for the first time, I feel sorry for her. I feel sorry for her because I know what she's missing. And I'm pretty sure she does, too.

There's some commotion by Chad. He's being put back into costume which confuses me because I thought they were done. Usually, when David goes off set, that means they call it a day. But

John asks everyone to get set up for one last shot over at the rock formation they used for Chad's climb scene last week. As everyone scrambles to get the cameras and the gear, John walks over to me. "We need to re-shoot the climb. It shouldn't take long. You can wait over there."

Chad shrugs at me and walks over to take his place.

There isn't much pomp and circumstance, they don't even go through all the normal motions of shooting a scene. I guess if they just need some extra footage to work into what they already have, it's not such a big deal.

Chad easily scales the rock that is only fifteen feet high where they have him climb. It looks much higher from the viewpoint they get on camera. When he gets to the top, he looks down on me with a huge smile. "Mallory, you have to see this," he calls down to me. "The sunset will be awesome from up here."

I look around at the crew, embarrassed that he's spoken to me when he should be filming. Nobody else seems as surprised. I give him a 'WTF' look and he laughs. John's assistant comes over, bringing me a harness. She kneels down and waits for me to put my feet through. "What's going on here?" I ask her.

She shrugs. "I just work here," she says. "I do what they tell me."

She secures me into the gear and I put on rock-climbing shoes that just happen to be my size. She escorts me to the bottom of the rock formation. I look up at Chad, still freaked out by what he wants me to do. He wants me to climb up to him. In front of everyone. I've only done this a half dozen times. I'm awkward and unskilled. They will laugh at me. If he wanted to go climbing, why didn't he just send everyone away?

"Come on, Mal," Chad yells down at me. "Live a little."

I look at the crew just standing about. And I think someone left the camera rolling. "Uh, you guys don't have to hang around."

"We know," John says, but nobody moves an inch.

I guess they don't think I can do it. Or they plan to catch me if the rope breaks and I fall. I find my footing and climb as fast as I can. Faster than I've ever done it before. The last thing I need are people staring at my ass longer than necessary.

When I make it to the top, Chad pulls me into his arms. I reluctantly let him, after all, there are people watching us. And I'm pretty sure the crowd grew bigger on my way up.

He smiles down at me, gently removing my helmet before he removes his own. "I know today was really hard for you. I can't even imagine having to watch you do what I did. You are so strong and brave and I thank God every day that you came back into my life." He shifts his weight nervously from foot to foot. "I wanted you to have a good memory," he says. "Of these rocks. This place. I want to wipe everything you saw today from your thoughts. Because none of that is real." He motions a finger between us. "This is real. You and me. This is all that matters."

The sun starts to set and the sky behind Chad is a perfect mixture of orange and yellow. It takes my breath away. "It's beautiful up here," I say.

"It sure as hell is," he says, not bothering to tear his eyes away from mine to look behind him. He reaches into the pocket of his pants and pulls out a small velvet box. My heart thunders harder than it ever has. My breath catches and I feel faint. *Is this really happening?*

As if he can read my thoughts, he nods at me. Then he drops to a knee and takes my hand in his. "I hope you won't let the fact that I just had sex with another woman dissuade you from giving me the answer I desire."

I laugh, tears rolling down my face in streams of pure happiness.

"Mallory, I love you. I've loved you since the first day I met you at the bus stop when you were only six years old. I loved you even when I moved away and we lost touch. I loved you the second I saw you at the club. And I'll love you until I draw my last breath. My life can be crazy sometimes, you've seen a lot of that these past months. And I have to travel much of the time. But there's nobody I want to come home to more than you. There is no one else I want to be holed up in hotel rooms with. There's nobody else I want to eat pizza with and play HORSE with. There is no one else I'd rather go through life with. And I'm not giving any other guy the chance to keep me from the promise I made you at your aunt's wedding. It was you and me then. And it's you and me now. We were put on this earth to be together."

He drops my hand to open the box. I squeeze my eyelids together to get rid of the tears clouding my vision. Inside the box is the most beautiful ring I've ever seen. The diamond is tear-shaped. Big, but not too big. It's surrounded by smaller diamonds lining a platinum band. He clears the frog in his throat. "Mallory Kate, will you marry me?"

My throat stings so badly I can't speak. My heart gets so big my chest hurts. My eyes spill over and bleed my love for him. All I can do is nod and mumble, "Mmmhmm."

He smiles, still on his knees. "I'm sorry," he says. "I didn't quite hear that. You'll have to speak up for the cameras."

It's now I realize he's having this filmed. By professional cameramen no less. He orchestrated and pre-planned this so one of the worst days of my life would become one of the best. "Yes," I say. "Yes, yes, yes!"

He slips the ring on my finger and hugs me where he kneels. He wraps his arms around me and picks me up as I look down upon him. He gazes up at me as he twirls us in a circle. The sunset has turned into a brilliant mixture of red and orange hues. The claps and cheers from below echo off the rocks and canyon walls. There couldn't be a more perfect moment than this if we searched a million moments in a million lifetimes. He lets my body slide down his until our mouths meet. Then he kisses me like it's our first. Like it's our last. Like this kiss matters more than any other because it's sealing our fate. Solidifying our bond.

And I know right in this moment that this rock, this canyon, this place, will never be anything but a perfect memory. Chad knew that. He knew exactly what to do to make it this way.

He steps back, still holding my hand, admiring his ring on my finger. "No take backs," he says, reminding me of the phrase he used often when we were kids.

I laugh and shake my head. "No take backs. Never. But what I want to know is, how are you going to top this? If I remember correctly, you have a few more movies coming up. What are you going to do the next time you have a love scene?"

His face falls. "Shit, Mal. I didn't think of that. I've just set a big fucking precedent, haven't I?"

CHAPTER TWENTY-SEVEN

Chad

Mallory's head is propped against my shoulder in the car as Cole drives us home from the airport. She's been staring at her ring, looking at her hand from all different angles. She thinks the surprises are all done, but they're only just beginning.

"I was going to wait until we got back in L.A., you know," I confess to her. "I had the ring all picked out and I was going to ask you on your last night here, before you went back to New York."

She looks up at me. "What changed your mind?"

"It was something Hayden said when we were out to dinner one night. He said you would never like Sedona because of what I was going to do there with another woman. I didn't want you thinking of that place as somewhere I cheated on you or anything."

"I would never," she says.

"I know. But still. My hope is that whenever your schedule allows in the future, you will join me on location. But if you'd had a negative experience, you might not want to. So I had Kendra get the ring from my house and overnight it to me."

She giggles. "Well, you certainly accomplished your goal, Mr. Stone. I'll be happy to join you on set whenever I can."

I kiss the top of her head. "Mission accomplished, future Mrs. Stone." Then I frown thinking maybe I shouldn't be so assuming. "Uh, are you going to take my name?"

Her face breaks into a shy smile and she wrinkles her nose in embarrassment. "Do you know how many times I've written my name as Mallory Stone? Thousands. I used to doodle it in my notebooks in school. I was always afraid you'd see it but you never did."

Hearing that makes me want to pound my chest and high-five someone. "So you'll take my name?"

She nods. "Of course I will."

"Mallory Stone," I say, testing out the sound of it. "I think I like it. I think I *love* it."

"We have a lot to figure out, you know," she says. "I'm not sure I'm ready to leave New York. My job is there, my family. Mel and Julian. What are we going to do?"

I smile big. Because she couldn't have picked a better time to ask that question. Cole pulls into my driveway. I get out and run around the car to open her door. When she exits the car and sees what's in my front yard, she covers her mouth and squeals. "Chad, is that what I think it is?"

I look at the sign in the front yard. "If you think it's a For Sale sign, then you'd be right. But I figured with you being a school teacher and all, I wouldn't really have to spell it out for you."

She slaps my arm playfully. "Not that, silly. Does this mean . . . ?" She looks at me hopefully.

I nod. "I can live anywhere, Mal. I know I'll have to be on the west coast quite a bit, but I can crash with my parents. I don't want home to be anywhere but where you are."

"You're moving to New York?" she yells, jumping into my arms.

"Where else would I possibly want to be?" I say right before her lips crash on top of mine.

I carry her to the front door. I have no choice; she's wrapped around me as snugly as a latex glove. I try to put her down when we get to the door, but she won't let me. "Don't you want to carry me across the threshold?" she asks.

"I thought that was *after* we get married," I say.

She laughs. "I think you need to practice."

"You think I need to work out more, babe?" I tease.

"No. I just don't want you to take your hands off me right now unless it's to remove every stitch of my clothing."

I laugh knowing what's on the other side of the door. "You might change your mind in about five seconds," I say.

I open the door and walk through, carrying my bride to be. Then she jumps out of my arms, startled when everyone yells, "Surprise!"

"What? What is this?" She looks around my living room. Everyone we know and love is here. My parents and brothers. Megan. Ethan's wife, Charlie. Mallory's dad and his girlfriend. Julian and Melissa. Kendra and Ana. Even Hayden and Noreen are here even though we just left them thirty minutes ago at the airport. I also invited some of the crew we hung out with in Sedona. There's a huge banner hanging on the back wall that reads 'Congratulations.' Mallory turns around and looks at me, her mouth hanging open. "A surprise engagement party? Are you serious? When did you even have the time?"

"Kendra and my mom did most of it." I pull her against me and whisper in her ear. "I'm holding you to what you said earlier, you know. As soon as they all leave, you're mine."

I feel a shiver run through her. Then she looks at me and her eyes tell me I'm in for one hell of a night once we're alone.

Her dad comes up behind her, picking her up and spinning her around. "Congratulations, pumpkin." She hugs him for a long time, eliciting tears from both of them. Then Richard holds his hand out to me. "I can't think of a finer man for my daughter." After I shake his hand, he pulls me in for a hug.

His girlfriend, Denise, congratulates us as well, and then my parents follow suit.

My mom fawns over Mallory's ring, tears welling up in her eyes. "I must be the luckiest mother-in-law in the world. My sons sure do know how to pick 'em," she says. "Welcome to the family, dear."

We make our way through family and friends, taking time to be congratulated by every one of them. Then the caterers circulate with trays of finger food and champagne.

"I hear you're a movie star, Mal," Julian says to my fiancée.

She shakes her head. "I still can't believe he did that," she says, elbowing me. "But I can't wait to see it. I wonder how long it will take for it to be ready."

I pull a DVD case out of a bag Cole left by the front door. "It's not a good party without entertainment."

She covers her mouth. "Oh, my God. Is that it? Can we really watch it? I was so nervous," she says. "Everything you said was beautiful and perfect, but I can't remember it exactly, because . . . well, because you were proposing and I was about to pass out from shock I guess."

I laugh. "You bet your ass we can watch it. We can watch it a million times if you'd like. And whenever you forget how much I love you, I'm going to strap your beautiful behind to my La-Z-Boy recliner and make you watch it over and over."

After everyone has some food and a few drinks, we get settled and watch the DVD. I normally don't like to watch myself on screen. But this is one time I don't mind it. I don't mind it because it's Mal and me. And it's not me I'm watching. It's her. I'll never get tired of watching her reaction. Of seeing the excitement on her face. The love in her eyes.

"Well, shit," Kyle says, when it's over and all the women in the room are crying. "You've pretty much just ruined any chance the rest of us have at an epic proposal. How in the hell are we going to beat that?"

Everyone laughs. "I like to set the bar high, little brother."

Julian corners me in the kitchen when I'm grabbing a bottle of water. "So I take it Courtney wasn't invited. What's going on with all of that?"

I think back over the past eight weeks of filming. How she never even made a pass at me after that very first comment in her trailer. She *has* changed. And I catch myself hoping she can find someone to make her happy. I know it must have been hard for her to see Mal and me together. And she was conspicuously absent for my proposal. However, she gracefully congratulated both of us the next day.

I shake my head as it dawns on me. "What's going on is I think all the crazy is finally out of my life."

Julian pats me on the back. "Well thank God for small favors. Or huge ones." He laughs.

I look across the room at my gorgeous fiancée. "Yes," I say, agreeing whole-heartedly. "Thank God for those."

~ ~ ~

Mallory pulls the covers up to her chin as I spoon her from behind. "I don't want to leave you," she says, sadly.

"Then don't," I tell her.

I know her job is important to her and I'd never ask her to quit for me. On the other hand, it will keep us apart more than it'll keep us together. The reality of it is sinking in now that she has to go home and prepare for the new school year.

She cranes her neck around, rolling her eyes at me. "You know I have to, Chad. School starts in a week and I have to get ready."

I pull her tightly against me. "I know. I just want you with me all the time."

"I want that, too. I wish there were a way to have you *and* my job," she says.

"You can have both," I tell her. "You *do* have both. We'll make it work. After the next few weeks of voice-overs and L.A. reshoots, I'll have a long break until *Dark Tunnels* filming starts." I rise up on an elbow and rub my hand down her arm. "I just have one request, babe."

"Anything." She smiles over her shoulder at me.

"If by some miracle, I ever get nominated for anything, I'm going to need you there with me. I know the awards shows all fall during the school year. But I'm not sure I could handle—"

"Chad," she interrupts. "That goes without saying. Wild horses couldn't keep me away." She turns around to face me. "And it won't be by some miracle that you get nominated. It will be because of your talent. You're a genius in front of the camera, Chad Stone. I don't make many promises. But I promise you this: if you continue to perform like you did for this film, we'll have to get a pretty big display case for our new pad because you'll be filling it with all kinds of awards."

"It's you," I tell her. "You bring out the best in me, Mal."

She smiles. "We bring out the best in each other."

I kiss the tip of her nose. "I'm glad you think so. But you were perfect *before* me."

"There wasn't a before you, Chad," she says, her eyes glistening in the morning light. "I don't even have any memories of a time you weren't either in my life or in my heart. The day you walked up to my bus stop was the day I began living."

She snuggles into the crook of my neck. "It'll be strange, you know, not living in my dad's house. There are a lot of memories there."

"I'm sure he won't mind if you visit a lot," I say. "Maybe we could make it a thing. You know, Sunday dinner in the old 'hood. I'd like to get you back on the court from time to time. I'm not sure we can find a place in the city where we can have one."

"Do you want to live in the city?" she asks.

"I want to live wherever you do, Mal."

"Really? Because I want to live there so badly," she says, her voice perking up. "All my friends live there. I've always been so jealous over how they can just walk out their front doors and go shopping. Or get coffee. Or walk home from clubbing."

"Then it's settled," I tell her. "We'll live in the city."

After looking downright giddy for a few seconds, her smile turns into a frown. "Are you sure that's wise? I mean, you'll get bothered all the time. You won't be able to walk down the street, Chad."

"I'm not sure I'll be able to do that no matter where we live."

"We'll have to live in a place with good security," she says. "That can be expensive."

I stare at her with raised brows.

She rolls her eyes. "Right. Sorry," she says. "Sometimes I forget you have more money than God."

I laugh. "*We* do, babe. *We* have more money than God," I joke. Then I trace the outline of her face with my finger. "Everything I have is yours."

"And everything *I* have is *yours*," she says. Then she winces, forming a wrinkle in her elegant nose. "Sorry. I know you're getting the short end of the stick."

I shake my head looking at the incredible woman lying next to me. "No. I'm definitely the winner here. I promise you that."

My phone vibrates on the nightstand for the third time, so I roll over to check it.

> **Richard: I didn't want to alarm Mallory. When I got home last night, there was something for her at the front door. I can't even explain it, so I sent a picture.**

I tap on the attached picture to expand it and my heart stops. There on the front steps of her house is a life-sized teddy bear with its insides ripped out and spilling down the front porch steps. It looks like it has blood all over it and it's holding a sign that reads, "Die, bitch."

The news of our engagement has spread quickly what with the cast and crew all witnessing it. It was never my intention to keep a lid on it. I'm glad it's out there. I want the world to know I'm with her. And I did expect some backlash, but I sure as hell didn't think it would come in the form of an eviscerated teddy bear on Mal's front porch.

I read his other text.

> **Richard: There were also a dozen or so cards stuffed in the front door and several**

photographers out front. I know she comes home tomorrow. I know you'll do whatever is needed to keep her safe. Let me know what I can do to help.

I quickly scroll through the rest of my missed messages. They are mostly from Paul, who is pissed at me that I didn't clear things with him first. As if I need his permission to propose to my girl. And my lawyer, Ron, is already bugging me about a prenup that will never see the light of day.

"What is it?" Mal asks, sitting up in bed when she reads my body language.

"Nothing," I say. *You have to tell her.* "Well, not nothing, but I don't want you to worry. We pretty much expected this with the news of our engagement."

"What happened?" she asks. "Are women protesting in the streets? Are they mourning the loss of the world's most eligible bachelor?" She giggles and I feel terrible that I'm going to ruin her good mood.

"Funny, but no. It seems you've gotten some, um . . . hate mail back at your house."

She laughs. "Already? Wow, that was fast." Her face falls. "Wait, how do you know about this?"

"Your dad texted me."

"Why did he text you and not me?" she asks. "They didn't egg his house or anything, did they?"

I shake my head. "No. They didn't egg his house." I reluctantly hand my phone over and show her the picture Richard sent.

Her hand comes up to cover her mouth as I watch horror cross her face. "Oh, God, Chad. How can people be so cruel?"

323

"I'll have the police look into it. But I'm going to send Cole home with you."

"What?" She gives me a crazy-eyed look. "That's ridiculous. Cole is needed here, with you."

"I need to keep you safe, Mal."

"I need *you* to be safe, Chad."

I blow out a sigh. "I'll hire you your own bodyguard then."

"I don't need a bodyguard," she says. "It's just a jealous fan."

"A jealous fan who could be psychotic for all we know. I'm not taking the chance. Either move out of your dad's house to someplace more secure, or I'm getting you a bodyguard. Take your pick, Mal."

I've never been so stern with her before. I hold my breath to see just how hard she's going to push back. I watch as she processes what I've told her. I can read her eyes. She doesn't know whether to be pissed at me for being an over-protective prick or relieved because I'll do anything to take care of her.

"But what about my dad? If I leave, he will be left to deal with things. I want him safe, too. And where would I go?"

"First off, your dad is a big guy. Nobody is going to mess with him. And it won't take long for word to get out that you aren't living there anymore. I was thinking that maybe you could stay with Ethan or Kyle until we can find a place. I don't think Melissa or Julian would have enough space for you to comfortably stay with them longer than a day or two."

She shakes her head. "I'm not staying with Ethan and Charlie. They have a baby and don't need me hanging around."

"What about Kyle?" I ask. "He's never home. He's at the hospital pretty much all the time now that he's an intern. His apartment is close to Melissa's, so you and she could ride to work together."

"I don't know," she says reluctantly. "It's such an imposition."

"You know as well as I do that he'd love to have you. He's always thought of you as a sister, and soon you'll actually *be* one."

She shrugs. "That might work. But only if you don't have to strong-arm him into it."

"Strong-arm him? Hardly," I say, laughing. "As soon as he tastes your cooking, he'll never let you leave."

My doorbell rings so I hop out of bed and pull on some sweatpants. Walking down the hall, I pray I don't open it to find the eviscerated Teddy's twin on my doorstep. But when I open the door, I see it's even worse than I feared.

"Is it true?" Heather asks, plowing past me and into my living room before I can stop her.

"What the hell are you doing here, Heather?"

She crosses her arms and looks at me sadly. "How could you do this to me, Thad?"

"Heather, I don't know what you're on these days, but it's made you delusional. I'm not doing anything to you. I haven't *been* with you for almost four years. I'm engaged to Mallory and you need to respect that."

"Respect that?" she scoffs. "You're with a school teacher, Thad. It's just wrong." She walks over to me, getting too close for my liking. She puts a hand on my bare chest, violating me with her eyes. "We were good together once. We can be again."

Mallory walks around the corner wearing her short robe, clearly looking like she just rolled out of bed with her mussed-up hair. Two things happen. Mal looks at Heather's hand on my chest—hatred seeping from her eyes. And Heather scowls melodramatically at Mal, eyeing her from head to toe as if she's a mangy stray, a pauper off the street.

I quickly step aside, out from under Heather's touch and walk back to my front door which is still wide open. "Thanks for stopping by to congratulate us, Heather. I wouldn't want to keep you any longer. I know how busy you are."

Heather sneers at Mallory. "Congratulate," she says dryly. "Whatever." She walks past Mal and toward the door where she doesn't even bother to lower her voice. "When you tire of her, I'll be waiting."

"You'll be waiting forever, Heather. Because I won't leave her."

"Huh," she says. "That's not how I see it. You did it once, Thad. You'll do it again."

I point to the porch. "Out," I tell her.

She walks through the doorway and I slam the door after her. Then I turn to Mallory. "I'm so sorry. I had no idea she was coming. I'm going to call the gate and have her banned."

"It's okay," she says, sadly. "I know I'm going to have to deal with women who want you. If it's not Heather, it will be someone else. It's just . . ."

I step over to her and cup her face in my hands. "It's just what?"

"Well, you and Heather were together for years," she says. "And when I saw her hand on you. It just makes me wonder if you miss it sometimes."

"Miss it?" I say incredulously. "Miss Heather? Are you kidding?"

She shakes her head. "Maybe not miss Heather, per se, but the fun you two had when you were together. I've seen pictures; read stories. You were young and wild. Do you ever miss the drugs, Chad? Do you crave them?"

"Oh, wow." *Deep fucking question.* I take her hand, leading her over to the couch where I sit her down next to me. "To be honest, the answer is yes and no. Intellectually, I know drugs are bad for me and they lead to destructive behavior. But physiologically, my body does still crave the feeling I'd get from getting high. It's why I never drink much. I don't ever want to be in a position where I'll make a stupid choice. I'm not sure drug addicts are ever fully recovered."

She grips my hand, seemingly terrified.

"You have nothing to worry about, Mal. I'm not doing drugs again. Ever. If I do, I give you permission to publicly flog me, shame me, string me up by my testicle."

She shakes her head and then looks at me with serious eyes. "I wouldn't do any of that, Chad. But I would leave you."

I smile at her and nod. "I know you would. I would expect nothing less. But I'm not going to fuck this up by being a . . . what did you tell me never to be that first night we made love?"

"Stupid bastard," she says.

"Right. I'll never be a stupid bastard." She relaxes into the couch causing her robe to gape open, allowing me to see the curve of her bare breasts. "But I will be a horny one if you keep teasing me with what may or may not be under that robe."

She smiles seductively at me. "I'll let you in on a secret. There's nothing under it."

"Oh, there's something under it, all right," I say, peeling it away from her body like layers of an onion. "And I plan to explore every exquisite inch."

As soon as my hands touch her skin, she moans. God, I'm going to miss this when she leaves tomorrow. I plan on spending every waking minute until then touching her body. Kissing those lips. Feeling her writhe beneath me. I am a composer and she is my muse. And we're about to make beautiful fucking music together.

CHAPTER TWENTY-EIGHT

Mallory

"Thank you so much, Kyle. You really didn't need to go through all the trouble," I say.

He brings my last suitcase into his guest room. "You're family now, Mallory. It's what we do for each other."

I laugh. "I almost forgot. You are ever the philanthropist. I bet you don't stop until you've cured the world of homelessness. And cancer."

"And hunger," he adds.

"You and your brother," I say. "Do you know he feeds almost every homeless person he sees?"

"Really?" he asks, narrowing his eyes at me in surprise.

I nod. "He does," I say. "But he doesn't think it's very tough-guy of him so he keeps it on the down low."

He laughs, shaking his head over what I've revealed about Chad. "And what about you, Mallory? I've heard you do good work at Hope For Life."

"I try," I say with a frown. "But I haven't been very good at it lately, traveling the country with the movie star."

"Didn't Charlie tell you?" he says, looking confused. "She not only took over your Tuesday-night shifts, but now she has Piper Mitchell volunteering there as well."

My jaw drops.

"Don't look so surprised," he says. "You have this way about you that makes everyone want to be a part of your world. Most of all, my brother. He's a lucky guy, Mallory."

"I'm the lucky one, Kyle."

He hands me a key. "Stay as long as you like. Just don't scream my brother's name in bed when he visits. That might be more than I can handle."

I feel my cheeks heat up. "Duly noted," I say. "And, um, when you want to bring women home, I can go crash at Melissa's or Julian's."

"Ha!" he says. "Who the hell has time for that? Being an intern is kicking my ass. Hey, did you know your dad came by over the summer to congratulate me for getting an internship at his hospital? I always liked him, you know. His new girlfriend seems nice. Young, too."

"She is, on both counts. She's not quite forty yet while he's pushing fifty. I think they're afraid to say anything to me, but I saw some of Denise's things at the house when I was packing up today. I wonder if she's been staying there. Oh, my God, maybe she's going to move in now that I'm pretty much gone."

"Would you be okay with that?" he asks.

I think about how happy my dad has been these past months. Then I think of all those miserable years he spent after my mom died. He deserves this. He deserves it more than anyone. I nod. "I think I would."

"Then you should tell him, Mallory. He's probably scared shitless to say anything. I'm sure you giving him your blessing would mean the world to him."

I smile, thinking of all the happiness my dad and I have been lucky enough to experience this year. "I will. Thanks, Kyle."

"I'm off to work now. I won't be home for forty-eight hours, so don't worry."

"That must be awful," I say. "I don't know how you do it."

"I wouldn't do it if I didn't love it." He leans in to kiss my cheek and then picks up his keys off the entry table.

I get his attention before he walks out the door. "What's your favorite meal?" I ask.

"Lasagna. Why?"

I shrug. "After working for forty-eight hours, I think you should be able to come home and eat something you love."

He winks at me. "How about you just blow off my brother and let me keep you?"

I laugh as he closes the door behind him.

I get started unpacking my clothes. I can't help but smile. I feel like Chad must feel a lot of the time, a nomad without a home, wandering from rental house to guest house to hotel room. But I'm so happy to finally be living in the city. And in as little as a few weeks, Chad will be living here right along with me.

~ ~ ~

It didn't take long for the vultures to come out. It's all over the tabloids that Chad and I have split, and only a week after they were announcing our engagement. Don't these people have better things to do?

There's a picture of me someone must have snapped in the airport. It shows me sad and alone. Of course I was alone; Chad didn't have a ticket so he couldn't go through security with me. The good news is at least now I don't have to go through the main entrance anymore, so the only paparazzi we run into are at the curb. A fellow passenger must have taken the picture of me at the gate.

More pictures entail Kyle hugging me when I arrived at JFK and him escorting me home to pack my things and go to his place. So now I'm mending my broken heart by sleeping with Thad Stone's younger brother. Do people really believe this crap?

And since Chad and Courtney are still wrapping up last-minute filming, they are being rumored to have reconciled. Paul must be salivating over that story.

The hate mail has subsided since I moved in with Kyle last week. I suspect either people have moved on, or Kyle and my dad are running interference for me.

I try not to think about the tabloids as I lie on my bed and put together my first week's lesson plans. I'm excited to meet my new students on Monday. I think fourth grade is the best grade to teach. For the most part they sit still when you tell them to, and they haven't yet developed attitudes.

I had a hard time putting my classroom together last week with the constant interruptions. A lot happened over the summer and I swear each of the fifty-five teachers at my school plus all the staff had to come and grill me about it. I think I should have just held a school press conference to get it all over with at once.

My phone rings and I look at it to see Chad's handsome face on my screen. My heart skips a beat. I think it has done that ever since I was a kid. Every time I look at him it happens. It's like he has this invisible tether to my heart and when I see him, or even think about him, he pulls the strings like I'm a puppet under his control. I never understood what 'pulling heartstrings' meant until Chad. Now he is the very definition of them.

"Hi!" I answer excitedly.

"Hey, you," he says, the low timbre of his voice resonating through my entire body. "What's up with you today?"

"Just making my lesson plans. You?"

"Enjoying the day off," he says. "If I'd known we were going to get the whole weekend off, I'd have flown out."

"It's fine," I tell him. "I've been super busy getting ready for school. I'll still see you next weekend, right?"

"Yes. And I think I'm about to make it even better." I can hear the smile in his voice and it makes me sit up on the bed in anticipation.

I'm afraid to even hope what he means by making it better. I know what I want it to mean. I know what I need it to mean. And I want so badly for him to say it. "Really? Why?"

"David thinks we'll be pretty much done by Thursday. So, although I might have to fly back to L.A. a few times in September, I'm pretty much good to go."

"Oh, my gosh! Really? Did you sell the house?"

He laughs. "No. It's only been on the market for ten days, Mal. But I don't care if I sell it or not, I'm moving to New York. And now comes the even better news. At least I hope you think so."

"What could possibly be better than you moving out here next weekend?"

"God, I love you," he says. "Do you know how much you pump up my ego?"

"Chaaaaaad," I whine. "Tell me the better news."

He chuckles into the phone. "I know we were going to go apartment hunting together, and if you don't like it, I'll just forfeit the deposit. But a place came available in Ethan's building, and since they sell like hotcakes there, I went ahead and put money on it this morning."

"That's a nice building. Of course I don't mind. But, uh, Ethan owns the only penthouse. And while I in no way think we need something that big, won't your sibling rivalry get in the way?"

"In Ethan's mind, he'll always be older, richer and better looking than me. It wouldn't matter if we owned the fucking Freedom Tower."

"As long as you're fine with it, I'm fine with it," I say.

"I looked at the apartment online. I'll send you a link to it as soon as we hang up. Charlie said she would go down and walk through it with you today if you have time. The best part is that it's a quick sale. The owner doesn't even live there and wanted to unload it fast. We can even keep whatever furniture you want and replace the rest. He said we could move in right away and close at the end of the month."

I smile from ear to ear. I know the apartment will be great, but I couldn't care less what it looks like. I could live in a cardboard box with this man if it meant we'd be together. "We can move in next weekend?"

"I'll fly in Friday. How does Friday night sound?"

Being without him is like missing a part of myself. I haven't felt quite right. I feel like I'm a clock that has a broken second hand, and it just keeps ticking away in the same spot over and over. Nothing is the same when he's not with me. I look down at the ring on my finger. The ring that says he's mine. "I think Friday just might be my favorite day ever," I say.

"I think we're going to make so many favorite days you won't be able to pick just one."

God, this man.

"I love you, Chad Christopher."

"I love you, Mallory Kate."

~ ~ ~

I stand in the foyer and look around at the open-floorplan apartment. If I could put two words together, I might be able to thank Charlie for meeting me here. But I can't. I thought Chad might feel inferior to his brother not being in the penthouse like Ethan is. But I can already see, the penthouse has nothing on this place.

"There are two bedrooms and an office down that hall," says the manager who let us in. Then he points to another hallway off the living room. "The master suite is over there." He hands me two Post-It note pads, one green and one red. "Put the green stickers on the furniture you want to keep and the red tags on the furniture you want gone. You can return the key to the concierge desk when you're finished."

I still can't speak. I'm too busy taking in the twelve-foot ceilings, the quartz countertops, the incredible view.

"Thank you," Charlie says to the manager before he closes the door behind us. She walks around in front of me, laughing. "Would it surprise you to know I had the same reaction when I first saw Ethan's place? I believe I called him Richie Rich."

I finally put my eyes back into my head and stare at her in confusion. "But you grew up with a famous mom, didn't you live in places like this?"

She shakes her head sadly. "Besides her Oscars, my mother won the award for crappiest mom to ever live. And she pretty much snorted most of her earnings up her nose. So, no, I never knew what it was like to live like this. It's one of the reasons I was eager to help out over at Hope."

"Thank you for that," I say. "I'm so relieved they didn't have to find a replacement for me over the summer."

"I'll be happy to do it anytime. In fact, Piper and I liked it so much, we're going to keep volunteering. And she's been in contact with Mason's people over at the Giants organization to see if they'll sponsor a fundraiser."

"Why would she do that for me? We don't even know each other all that well."

"She's not doing it for *you*, Mallory."

The way Charlie looks at me makes me understand that maybe Piper has some deep dark secrets in her past, too. I'm beginning to think one way or another, we all do.

Charlie spends the next three hours going through all the rooms with me. I end up keeping most of the furniture with the exception of the master bedroom. I want our bed to be ours and only ours. The people who lived here have good taste. Modern-contemporary. I think it suits us.

"I can't believe we'll be neighbors," I tell Charlie. "You know, I'll babysit whenever you and Ethan need a break. I love kids. And Eli is adorable."

"Thanks," she says. "I might just take you up on that. Have you and Chad talked about kids yet?"

I shake my head, not wanting to reveal we'd talked about my teen pregnancy. "Not really. But I know he loves kids. He's always holding babies of people he works with, and he can't say enough about his nephew."

"What about you?" Charlie asks. "Do you want them?"

I think about her question. "Oh, yes," I say. "But until earlier this year, I never thought I'd have to even consider that possibility. I'd sworn off men." I look down at my ring and twist it around on my finger. "And now here I am, engaged and moving in with Chad. I'm twenty-four years old, so I have plenty of time. But I guess when I really think about it, I would like to be a young mom like you. Maybe it's because I lost my mother when I was seventeen and I would just want as much time with my kids as possible. So the earlier I have them . . . But I think Chad will probably want to wait because of his hectic schedule."

"I think you will make a great mom, Mallory. No matter when you decide to have kids."

"Thank you. I certainly have you as a role model."

Charlie hugs me before we part ways. Then she goes back up to the penthouse, and I go down to return the key before going home to Kyle's.

The walk back is about four blocks. Along the way, I realize that despite my earlier concerns, living in the city may just be the best place for us. New York is crowded and busy. People are always in a hurry and they rarely look at you much less make eye contact. It really is the best place to be anonymous, and that's exactly what Chad needs.

As I wait for the elevator in Kyle's building, a lady from the front desk walks over to me with a package. "You're Kyle Stone's houseguest, yes?"

"That's right," I tell her.

"Would you be so kind as to take this up? It's marked perishable and I'd hate for it to go bad."

"Of course." I take the package from her noticing it's been addressed to: The Stone Residence.

I text Kyle along the way.

Me: You got a package marked perishable. Do I need to just put it in the refrigerator, or is there anything else you need me to do?

He texts me back a few minutes later.

Kyle: I didn't order anything, but my mom is always sending me stuff. Go ahead and open it and do what you need to with it.

I get a knife and work my way through the heavy packing tape that surrounds all the edges of the package. Geesh, she must have used a whole roll of tape. As I slice through one side, a sickening smell escapes the box and I frown thinking whatever's inside has long since spoiled. But when I open the top, I cringe at what I see.

There's dried blood everywhere, and I'm not sure what kind of rodent is inside, but it might be a rat. Sadly, though, that's not the most disturbing part. It's the torn-up pictures of me scattered around the deceased creature that makes me gasp.

I check the label of the box and see it was mailed locally. Then I close it up tightly and try to decide what to do.

A half hour later, Ethan is examining the contents. After all, he's a private investigator, so who better to call? "Jesus, there are some sickos in this world," he says, using a pen to rifle through the package. "What did Chad say about this? Does he have any known stalkers?"

I shake my head. "I haven't told him yet," I admit.

He raises his eyebrows, giving me a stern look.

"I will," I say. "But he has a lot going on this week. They have several days of re-shoots at the L.A. set. He needs his focus to be on that, not this. If he knew about this, I don't know what he'd do."

"He'd lose his shit, Mallory. That's what."

"Can I count on you to keep this quiet until he gets here on Friday?" I ask.

He looks down at the box and runs a hand through his hair. "I don't like it. But I get why you don't want to tell him." He uses latex gloves to close the box and put it in a large plastic bag. "We'll still have to get the police involved. Chad told me you had a similar delivery at the house last week. They could be related. And he'd have my head on a fucking stick if I didn't make sure you were safe this week, so I won't tell him—on one condition."

"What's that?"

"You don't leave this apartment without someone with you. Me, Kyle, Julian, your dad. And if we're not available, I'll get someone from my agency to escort you."

I shake my head. "I start work tomorrow, Ethan. I can't miss the first week."

"What time do you need to leave in the mornings?" he asks.

"Seven."

"I'll be here at six forty-five," he says. "I like my coffee black. And if one of us can't be there to get you home safely after, I'll send someone from the office. You've met Levi, right?"

I nod. "Thank you, Ethan."

I'm relieved he's willing to keep a lid on this even though it means lying to his brother. I hate lying to Chad. It will mean no video chats with him this week. He'd be able to tell just by looking at me that I'm not telling him something.

Instead of dwelling on negative things for the rest of the day, I decide to use my pent-up energy for a better purpose. I start planning a party. A welcome home party, so to speak. I call Kendra to ask her if she can get me some phone numbers. Then I get started on the guest list. I'm amazed at how many people are willing to fly across the country just for a party.

Against my better judgment, I even invite his manager. I think it would be good for Paul to see that Chad and I are moving forward with our relationship. He's an integral part of Chad's career which means he'll be in his life for a long time. I'm determined to win the guy over come hell or high water.

I send an email to Skylar to see if Mitchell's can cater on short notice. I call the manager of our new building to see if he'll allow me to have new bedroom furniture delivered on Thursday, the day before we move in. Then I text Mel and ask if she's up for a shopping trip to West End this week. Fully chaperoned by Julian, of course. I laugh to myself thinking of how he'll love that— furniture shopping with the girls.

By the time I go to bed, I've put the wheels in motion for the surprise party, excited to be doing something nice for *him* for a change. And I fall asleep wondering—desecrated rodents notwithstanding—how my life could possibly get any better.

CHAPTER TWENTY-NINE

Chad

It's been two weeks since I've held her. One since I've seen her gorgeous face. She didn't want to video chat this week. She said it would make it all that much better when we saw each other today. And damn, my proverbial balls are bluer than a whale in the pacific. I can't wait to get her alone.

She's spent a better part of this week making all the arrangements at our new place. I was happy to have her make the choices as far as decorating. It's the least I could do after not consulting with her about the quick purchase. But I couldn't care less how it looks; the only room I want to see is the bedroom.

I look at my watch. Four o'clock. I stare through the tinted windows of the back seat, eagerly waiting for her to emerge from the school. Every time the front door opens and someone walks out who isn't her, I pout.

Cole laughs quietly in the front seat, amused by my childlike impatience. I'm glad he decided to come to New York with me. I know it's not permanent; he's a certified west-coaster. But he said he'd stay on until I could find a replacement. I'm hoping I won't necessarily need one. Mallory got me thinking on our talks this week. She said it's refreshing being somewhere she doesn't get recognized. When she was in L.A. with me, she couldn't even go into a grocery store without someone taking her picture. It's different here, she said; everyone is anonymous. I intend to test that theory before I go hiring anyone new.

Five minutes go by and then I see her. She exits the school with Melissa and another teacher, and then I notice a familiar guy walking up to the three of them. I could swear he works for Ethan.

More teachers are spilling out of the building behind them, so to prevent causing a scene I ask Cole to fetch Mallory for me. I watch her eyes when she sees him. Her face lights up with excitement and her eyes scan the cars lining the curb in front of the school. I crack the window so she can see me. She squeals and runs to the car. I open the door for her and she pile-drives me into the back seat, planting a long-awaited kiss on me.

I laugh. "Are you going to greet me like this every time I pick you up?"

She pushes up on her elbows. "Will that be a problem, Mr. Stone?"

"I'm gonna go with *no*." I bring her lips down on mine and kiss her once more.

She giggles. "I thought we were meeting at Kyle's."

"Couldn't wait," I mumble between kisses. When I come up for air, I ask, "Was that one of Ethan's employees out there? Is he dating one of your co-workers or something?"

She shrugs, pulling me back to her. "Less talking. More kissing."

She doesn't have to ask me twice. Cole gives us another minute before getting back in the car. When he opens the door, Mallory quickly extricates herself from on top of me and sits over on her side of the back seat. I ask Cole to take us to our new place.

"Actually, Cole," Mal says, "can you swing by Kyle's first? I'd like to pick up my things."

"Sure thing," he says.

Damn. I'm going to have to wait that much longer to get her alone. On the way to Kyle's place, Mallory sends a few quick texts and then relaxes back into her seat. Except she's not exactly relaxed. I study her for a minute. Her body language is all wrong.

"What?" she asks, turning to look at me.

I look into her eyes. "Something's not right."

She shifts uncomfortably. "What do you mean?"

"You." I motion my hand up and down her body. "What aren't you telling me?"

"Nothing," she says, trying to make her face look all innocent.

I give her my best *you're-full-of-shit* stare.

"What? Nothing," she insists.

"Mallory, how long have I known you?"

She shrugs. "Eighteen years, on and off."

"I've been able to read you since we were kids. Now spill."

She rolls her eyes, looking guilty. I can tell she's battling with herself over what to say to me, and quite frankly it's starting to make me a little scared. "Fine," she says, blowing out a deep sigh. "But don't tell me *I'm* the one who ruined the surprise, Nosey Nellie."

"Surprise?" My eyebrows shoot up. "What surprise?"

"I may have invited a few friends over to welcome you to your new home."

My face cracks open with a smile. "You planned a surprise party?" I ask.

She nods. "Well, not so much surprise anymore."

"Shit, Mal." I take her hand. "Sorry I ruined it. I promise to act surprised. Is that why you wanted to go by Kyle's first, to stall?"

"We're not supposed to show up at our new place until after six," she says. "I was going to take you back to Kyle's and, um . . . distract you."

I laugh. "Distract me, huh?"

"Yeah. But now that you know about the party, I really need to take a shower and get ready. I didn't think this through very well. I've got kid germs galore on me and I'd like to straighten my hair and—"

I bury my face in her neck, licking her throat and stopping her train of thought. "I vote for distraction," I whisper in her ear.

She moans silently. "I promise you all the distraction you can handle later. Maybe we can even sneak in a quickie at the party. But I really need a shower. One of my students was pretty sick today."

"Okay, fine," I pout. I realize she's probably put a lot of effort into this party and the least I can do is let her look her best for it. "But I'm going to hold you to both. All the distraction I can handle *and* a quickie."

~ ~ ~

I'm not sure how one woman could have pulled it all off, but she did. Mallory somehow managed to make this place ours in a matter of a week. She told me she sweet-talked the manager into letting her have the keys so she could get started putting her touch on it. She even outfitted our master bedroom with brand new furniture. She gave everyone a quick tour when we got here. When we got to the bedroom, I was sure to hold her back and tell her exactly how I planned to break in our new bed.

"So you planned a party, went shopping for bedroom furniture, and got our new house in order—all during the very first week of school." I shake my head in awe. "I'm marrying Superwoman."

She laughs. "I prefer Wonder Woman, actually."

The only people who couldn't make it are my parents. With the exception of the *Defcon* crew who were at our engagement party, everyone else who was there is here tonight. Even Megan. Her parents moved her to Boston a few weeks ago so she could start at MIT. Mal sent her a train ticket and Ethan and Charlie graciously agreed to house her for the weekend. Smart girl, my fiancée. We wouldn't want anyone around to hear me make her scream my name later.

The women are all fawning over baby pictures. Skylar and Baylor, two of the three Mitchell sisters, both had little girls in May. They gave birth to cousins who are only two days apart. Mallory told me all about them this summer. She's going to make a great mom, I know it. We probably should've had a conversation about kids before getting engaged. I know what she went through at sixteen. And I know she wants kids someday. I just hope we're on the same page about it.

The doorbell rings and I look around the room, confused. Everyone I know is here. I open the front door and see my manager on the other side. "Hi, Paul." I look behind me. "Uh, sorry. I didn't know you were in town. My fiancée threw me this surprise housewarming party."

He rolls his eyes. I'm assuming at the word *fiancée*. "I know," he says. "She invited me."

I look over my shoulder at Mal, but she's busy with the women. "She did?"

What that woman will do for me never ceases to amaze me. She hates Paul. She knows Paul hates her. But she's trying to forge an amicable relationship between them. Damn, I love her.

345

"Don't look so surprised," he says. "I can be a decent guy sometimes."

I hear heels click on the tile in the common hallway and stick my head out the door. "Oh, hell no." I push Paul out the door and shut it behind me so we're standing outside in the hall. "What the fuck, Paul?"

Heather and Lila walk up to us. "Sorry," Heather says. "I got stuck signing autographs in the elevator. Can you believe I got propositioned again? By a fan, no less. When will they understand things never work out between actors and regular people?"

I find myself shaking my head at how uncanny the similarity is between Heather and Mallory. Of course, their physical appearance is where the similarity ends. And I'm certain now that's what drew me to Heather in the first place. But the two women couldn't be more different in personality. I swear to God if I were to Google 'bitch,' Heather's picture would show up under it. I sure as hell knew how to pick 'em back then.

I give Paul a look of death. "Why would you bring her here?"

Paul shrugs like he has no idea I hate the pretentious she-devil standing next to him.

Then I greet Lila, who is an old friend of mine from *Malibu* whom I dated briefly before Heather. "Hey, Lila. Nice to see you."

Lila pulls me in for a hug. "Oh my gosh, Thad, it's been so long. I hear you're engaged. Congratulations! And you're moving to New York? How exciting. I can't wait to meet your fiancée."

I always liked Lila. I should never have broken up with her for Heather. But Lila wasn't into drugs and Heather and I were. And my priorities were all fucked up back then. She was and still seems to be a great girl. "I'm glad you could come," I tell her.

I turn my attention to Heather. "Surely there is something better you can find to do with your time than hang out with my fiancée and I in our new home," I say, with no uncertain meaning.

"Oh, come on, Thad. We happened to be in town and Paul invited us," she says. "He's Lila's manager now, too."

"Really?" I'm a little surprised at that, but also happy for Lila. Paul is a highly sought-after man in the entertainment business.

"That's right," he says. "I'm going to shoot her straight to the top, just like I did you."

Paul likes to take credit for everything. Well, not everything. He takes credit for successes. Failures will land you right out on your ass in his book.

"I'm sure Lila could do that with *any* manager," I tell him. "Can I talk to you for a second, Paul?" I walk to the end of the hallway by the stairwell. "What are you thinking bringing Heather here? You know I don't get along with her. Do you have some ulterior motive?" I look back over at Heather and Lila and it dawns on me. I lean against the wall and let out a sigh. "Thomas changed his mind, didn't he?"

Paul just stares at me.

"Of course he did," I say pacing back and forth. "And you've brought reinforcements to try and talk me into signing on, too. Am I wrong?"

He shrugs a smug shoulder.

I walk back to where Heather and Lila are standing and address them all. "I'm telling you right now that I'm not doing it. So if you've come here to beg me to do the *Malibu* movie, you can leave now and not waste your breath."

The door to my apartment opens and Mallory spills out of it, obviously tipsy from the free-flowing champagne. "What's going on out here?" Then she sees Heather and her smile falls. "Oh."

Shit. I really wish she wouldn't have opened the door. Mal is too nice to send them away. Even though she despises Heather. I walk over and put my arm around Mallory. "I was just telling Paul that they might be more comfortable somewhere else."

As anticipated, Mallory looks at me in horror. "Uh, I invited him. You can't send him away."

"Yes," I say, smiling while speaking through my tightly closed jaw. "But he's brought unexpected guests, babe."

"I can see that," she says, looking embarrassed that I'm not being hospitable. She holds out her hand to Lila. "Hi, we haven't formally met yet, Lila. I'm Mallory. Thad has told me very nice things about you."

Lila shakes her hand. "It's good to meet you, Mallory."

"Heather," Mallory says in the driest of acknowledgments. After all, the last time she saw her, Heather's hand was on my bare chest in the living room of my house. She motions them all in. "I trust you will all respect that this is our home and this party is to welcome Thad to New York."

Heather scoots by us before Mal has a chance to change her mind. Lila thanks her and ducks in as well, followed by Paul, who doesn't seem to give a shit what Mallory or I think.

I pull Mal close. "Just say the word and they're gone."

"It'll be fine," she says. "Do you know how many people in there have our backs?"

I look in the apartment, feeling damn lucky to have these friends and family in my life. And it's all because of Mallory. She brings out the best in everyone. She brings out the best in *me.* "You're right. Come on." I pull her behind me. "I think I'll have my drink now."

She giggles and offers to get me one. But before she leaves, she whispers to me. "I'll let you in on a little secret. I've already had three. My judgment is not the best right now. Obviously," she says, giggling again while motioning to Heather. "And I might just let you feel me up in the bathroom. But, shhhhhh, don't tell anyone."

I laugh as I watch her walk away. I'm one lucky motherfucker.

I notice Heather heads straight for the bar. Nothing ever changes with her. I swear if she brought drugs into my home, I'll call the goddamn police on her myself. She's trying her best to mingle when most of my guests want nothing to do with her. "Who are you?" she asks Julian, pointing at him rudely.

"I'm Julian, Thad and Mallory's friend from way back. I've also escorted the lovely Ana Garner to this fine party." He smiles at his beautiful date.

"Oh . . . my . . . God," Heather says dramatically. "Not again. Is there something in the fucking water here?"

"Shut up, Heather," Hayden says, coming over to run interference. He pulls me aside. "For the love of God, why did you let that woman in?"

"I didn't, Mal did," I tell him. "She didn't want to be rude."

"Well, I have no problem being a prick. I'll kick her ass out where it belongs."

I shake my head. "No, don't do that. Not unless she does something stupid."

Mallory comes up behind me, kissing my neck. She's definitely feeling good right now. She never gropes me in public. I reach my hand behind her head and press her lips further into me. God, she smells so good.

"Here's your drink, babe," she says, putting it down next to me.

I see Heather watching us from across the room. I realize what I'm about to do is probably not the best move, but it's my house so I really don't fucking care. I pull Mal into my lap and kiss her. *Hard.* Cheers erupt around the room from everyone here. Well, almost everyone.

Mallory's dad beckons me over to him. *Shit.* Maybe I shouldn't have done that. "I think I'm about to get scolded by your father," I tell her.

She giggles. "That man worships the ground you walk on, Chad."

"Still. He's big and I just had my tongue down your throat."

I help her off my lap and make my way to Richard. He asks me to join him on the balcony. He hands me a small box. "In this box are the rings I gave to Mallory's mom. I don't know what you have planned for her wedding ring, and if you don't want them, I'll understand, but I thought maybe you could somehow use the diamonds . . ."

"Yes. Of course, yes, Richard. I know Mallory would be honored to have something that belonged to her mother." I take the box from him. "Thank you."

"There's one more thing," he says, looking nervous.

"What it is?"

He looks around uncomfortably. "I'm not exactly sure how to give Mallory some news."

I can't help my smile. I had suspected as much. "You're getting married, too, aren't you?"

He nods. "Yes. But that's not the news that might be hard for her to hear." He nods inside to Denise.

It takes me a minute to wrap my brain around what he's trying to tell me. "She's . . . you're . . . ?"

I'm not sure if he's happy or terrified. Maybe a bit of both. He releases a long sigh. "Denise is pregnant. Mallory is going to be a big sister."

"And this is a good thing, right?" I ask, just to be sure.

He smiles and pats my shoulder. "This is a great thing," he says.

"She'll be over the moon, Richard. She tells me all the time how happy she is to see you living again."

"Will you be there when we tell her?" he asks.

I nod. "Of course. How about Sunday at your place?" I ask. "Just the other day we were talking about making it a weekly thing. If that's okay with you."

"I would love that," he says. "Now go back to your party, son. Quit letting this old man monopolize your time."

"Old man my ass," I say. "You're about to remember what it's like to wake up for 2 a.m. feedings. That'll keep you young."

Back inside, I hunt down my drink. After all, I better enjoy the heck out of it since I get only one.

Lila asks Mallory for a tour of the place since the rest of the guests already had one before she arrived. Mal is all too happy to show off our new digs.

Julian comes over to sit next to me, looking all serious. "What is it?" I ask, studying him. "Oh, hell, you're not breaking up with her, are you? Ana really likes you. I think she might even love you. You guys are great together. I know you don't think you want this life, but Julian, it's no big deal. You'll work it out. You see how good it is for Mal and me. With your background, you can get a job anywhere. Or Ana can move; she can live here in New York. You can't just throw it—"

"She's pregnant, Chad."

What the fuck? I take a large swig of my drink, tossing it back in a single swallow.

I glance over at Heather, who's looking at me but talking with Paul. Then I look over at Richard and Denise. I say to Julian, "I guess there really *is* something in the water."

"What?" he asks in confusion.

"Nothing. So, uh . . . I'm not sure what you want me to say. Are you asking me what you should do?"

He shakes his head. "No." He looks over at Ana as she laughs with Noreen, Megan, and Charlie. "I think I might want to marry her."

This night is turning into the most surreal night of my life. I'm starting to feel a disconnect between my mind and my body, like all of this is a dream happening to someone else.

"Is that what she wants?" I ask.

He shrugs. "I'm not sure. She just told me yesterday. But look at her," he says. "She looks happy, doesn't she?"

"She looks happy, Jul-ann. You shuuu go fer it."

He scrunches his eyes at me. "Are you sure that's your first drink, bro?"

"Uh huh," I say, laughing. But the laugh comes out of my eyes, the sound swirling into the room in brightly colored hues. "Somethin's goin' on."

A loud crash comes from behind us. I turn to see one of the distraught caterers who had dropped a glass of champagne.

"I'll deal with that," Julian says. "Go drink some water."

I get up and float to my bedroom, walking through to the bathroom so I can splash some water on my face. When I lift my head up, I look in the mirror and see Mallory behind me. Actually, I smell her more than I see her. Because at this point, everything I see is little more than a blur. I need to lie down.

"How strong a drink did ya make me, Mal?"

She comes up behind me and whispers into my ear. "Let's get you into bed, Chad."

I turn around and bury myself into her. She smells so damn good I can see it. I can actually see her smell. It's like pink and purple flowers are coming out of her pores. I want to grab them. I reach out and feel her hot flesh under my hand. She's so soft and welcoming. I let her lead me to our new bed. I'm already getting hard. I know what she promised me earlier and she's about to deliver.

When she guides me to the bed, I feel like I'm not even moving but that I'm stationary and things are moving around me. Every object has a tracer feel to it. Not trails like when you move a flashlight quickly, more like paths of liquid, like wormhole trails in sci-fi movies. Oh, yeah, I'm doing research for that film. That's what this is. I should thank Mal for helping me.

When she pushes me down on the bed, it's in slow motion, the bed swallowing me up when I hit the soft duvet. I hold my arms out for her to join me, but when I do, my hands are white static, like I'm in a virtual reality game.

Mallory leans down to kiss me and it's like no kiss I've ever felt. Not only can I feel her kiss; I can see it. And when she puts my hands to her breasts, I can hear them as well as feel them. And I surmise this is the best fucking dream I've ever had in my life.

She rips off my shirt and I rip off hers, seeing the sounds of her buttons as they fly through the air. She leaves me as I watch them float and suspend above my head. When Mal comes back, she sits beside me, holding something up to her nose as she laughs in delight. She holds something out to me, telling me I should sniff it and it will make all this even better.

I just want to be inside her so I push her hand away, watching the wormhole trail as it moves. "Just need you . . . now."

She climbs on top of me, grinding herself into me as I try to touch as much flesh as I can, but our damn pants are getting in the way. I reach down to fix the situation.

And then, I hear voices. Many voices behind me. But mostly I hear Mal. Which is strange, because Mal is on top of me. But when I turn my head to see the voices, I see Mal. She's everywhere in the room. She's yelling at me but I see her words more than I hear them.

"Stupid bastard," I see floating through the air. Then I hear something small hit the top of my head.

More images appear in my bedroom, floating around me.

"Can I kick her ass now, Thad?" I see someone say. "Or maybe I should just kick *yours*."

My body bounces off the bed along with Mal's as she screams to be let go. Then I think I see Julian say, "you'll have to wait in fucking line," right before I see red wormhole trails before my eyes. And then . . . nothing.

CHAPTER THIRTY

Mallory

The sun set long ago and my behind hurts from sitting on the hard wooden planks for hours. Every time I think there aren't any more tears for me to cry, I picture Chad underneath her in our bedroom—on our bed—and the waterworks start all over again. I've gone over it a thousand times. Why would he do that to me?

There's only one explanation and it breaks my heart almost as much as the fact that he cheated on me. Cocaine. He's told me before the addiction is still there. The draw is still strong. I guess he wasn't strong enough to resist it after all.

The thing is, I know he hates her. He would have never been with Heather if he hadn't gotten high. But it really doesn't matter anymore. Even if he wouldn't have been with Heather, I would still have left him. And he knows it. Yet he still did it. Stupid bastard.

He promised.

"There you are. Jesus," I hear someone say behind me, following an exasperated sigh. I close my eyes, squeezing more tears out. I don't want to see anyone. Not even my best friend.

Julian climbs the rest of the way into the treehouse and sits down next to me. "We've been looking for you everywhere,

Mallory. Everyone has been worried about you. Chad was right. He knew you'd be here."

I shake my head in anger. "Don't, Julian. Don't even say his name."

"It's not what you think, Mal. It's not even close. You ran out so fast," he says. "Shit hit the fan after you left. In more ways than one." He holds up his hand for me to see, using his phone to illuminate the inside of the treehouse.

His hand looks bruised and swollen and I'm hoping the stupid bastard's face looks a sight worse. The last thing I remember—other than Chad's hands all over Heather—is Paul asking us to come quickly and then Julian and Hayden rushing past me into the bedroom.

I look at Julian like he's crazy. "Not what I think? It's obvious to me what happened, Julian. They had their shirts off." My throat stings and my heart hurts as I say the painful words. "He . . . He was *touching* her. They were both high, I'm sure. If that's what he wants, fine. She can have him. I don't want him anymore. Not after that."

But the thing is, that's all a lie. Even though he's betrayed me in the worst way, I keep hoping it's all just a terrible joke. Some big misunderstanding. Because I *do* want him. I *love* him. I'll never love anyone but him. And I'll never be the same without him. But that's exactly what I am now—without him. And there is no way it can ever be any different. I won't take him back. Not ever. Not after what he did.

"I know that's what it looked like, but Mallory, I need you to listen to me. I need you to hear what I'm telling you. Chad didn't use cocaine. He didn't cheat on you."

I scoff at him. "I suppose you're going to tell me that wasn't Chad. Does he have some evil twin I don't know about? Because that would be the only explanation that would even come close to making any of this okay."

Please, oh please, let him have an evil twin.

"The whole night was orchestrated so you'd walk in on them, Mal."

"What? What do you mean?" I shake my head and then look up through the hole in the ceiling, catching a sliver of the moon. "It doesn't matter if I was meant to see it or not, the fact is it happened."

"Look at me, Mallory. Listen." He cups my chin and moves my head towards him so I have no choice but to watch his face as he speaks to me. "His dickhead manager set it all up. He didn't want you two together. And he wanted Chad to do the movie he kept turning down. So they came up with a plan. Heather drugged him. It wasn't cocaine, although it looked like she tried to get him to do that, too. She put PCP in his drink. Angel dust. Kyle said it's a quick-acting hallucinogen that loosens you up and makes you feel invincible."

I stare at him in disbelief. "How do you know all this? How can you be sure Chad isn't trying to cover up his actions by blaming everyone else?"

"Lila told us," he says. "She was beside herself after everything went down. She just thought they were there to convince Chad to do the movie. It was her job to distract you so Heather and Paul could corner him and talk him into it."

I blow out a deep breath. "The tour of the apartment," I say, remembering how Lila seemed overly interested in everything I showed her.

I nod. "Yup. Lila had no idea about the drugs. Or at least that's what she told us before the police came."

I snap my eyes to him. "The police?"

"After I punched Chad, I realized he would never do that to you, Mal. He loves you more than I've ever seen a man love a woman. And then it all started to make sense. I mean, why would Paul tell you that you were needed in the bedroom? And why would he call the rest of us along? So I pinned Paul against the wall until he cried Uncle. He said he had no idea she was going to drug him. But at the time, nobody had said anything about Chad being drugged. Then Ana dumped Heather's purse on the floor and saw a tiny non-descript bottle of liquid along with a bag of cocaine. We asked her what was in the bottle. She wouldn't say, but she insisted Chad took it willingly. That's when we called the cops. I stayed at your place while Kyle and an officer took Chad to the hospital. A urine test confirmed the presence of PCP."

I gasp. "Oh my God!"

"They tested his blood, too. Nothing else was found in his system, not cocaine—nothing. Paul, Lila, and Heather were all taken for questioning, but Heather was the only one arrested. She's been charged with possession, not to mention assault and battery."

My hand comes up to cover my mouth, trying, but failing to hold in the cries that pour out of me. She drugged him? Assaulted him?

"Ethan thinks the hate mail you got was probably from her as well. She's been obsessed with him for a while now, so it makes sense." He scolds me with his punishing stare. "He told us about the package you got last week. You can't keep that shit from us, Mallory."

I sniff back more tears and then wipe my nose with the back of my hand. "I was going to tell him after the party. I didn't want to ruin it for him."

"Chad is a wreck," he says. "He's physically okay, and the drugs are out of his system, but he's scared of what you must think of him."

I get on my knees, wanting to plow past him to go find Chad. He must be out of his mind with worry. I can't imagine if the tables were turned and he was the one to find out *I* was drugged. "Where is he? I have to find him."

Julian grabs my shoulders, settling me back down where I was. "*He* found *you*. He's here." He nods out the door of the treehouse. "Right down there. We came straight here as soon as they released him from the hospital. He wanted to come up first, but I thought hearing the truth from someone else might be best. He's already been punched once tonight," he says, raising his injured hand. "I was afraid you might give him a second shiner before he could tell you everything."

"Thank you," I say to the person who knows me almost as well as the man standing at the base of the tree.

"Are you ready to see him?" he asks.

I nod over and over as tears well up in my eyes in anticipation.

Julian touches my hand in support before he backs out and climbs down the rope ladder. My heart is beating so wildly I can hear it pounding in my head. Never in my life have I been so happy and so sad at the same time. He didn't use drugs. He didn't cheat on me. We're still Chad and Mallory. But at the same time, he's been violated. And I've never wanted to kill someone as much as I do right now.

I feel the treehouse shake as Chad climbs up the ladder. Before he gets all the way up, he pushes a sleeping bag through the entrance. I wipe away the tears that spill over my lashes when I realize it's the same old sleeping bag I brought up here as a kid. He must have asked my dad for it. When he completes his ascent, I push the rolled-up bag out of the way and catapult myself into his arms.

"I love you," I say at the same time that he says, "I'm sorry."

Then he says, "I love you," when I say, "I'm sorry."

Then we simultaneously ask each other if we're okay. Then we laugh through our tears. Then we kiss through our tears. Then we hold onto each other like we're the lifeboat that will save us from drowning.

When I can finally get myself to pull away, I take in his face in the moonlight. "Can I see?"

He pulls out his phone and turns on the flashlight. I trace my fingers lightly across the red and purple bruise that surrounds his left eye. "Does it hurt?"

He shakes his head. "Not nearly as much as my heart does. I'm so sorry this happened. It's all my fault, Mal. If I had never gotten mixed up with her. With drugs . . ."

I take his whole face in my hands. "This is not your fault, babe. If anyone is to blame, it's me. I'm the one who insisted they come into the party. I invited Paul. You did nothing wrong. And you know if this wouldn't have happened tonight, she probably would have found some other way. At least this way, Julian was there, and Kyle, Ethan, and my dad. They had your back. If they hadn't called the police and figured this all out, it could have turned out much differently."

"It scares the shit out of me to think how this could have turned out. What if I'd . . . God, Mal, what if I'd slept with her? I thought she was you. She smelled like you. She looks like you. She was in our bedroom. *Our* fucking bedroom."

Tears stream down his cheeks at the thought of what that would have done to him. To me. To us. "Shhhhh," I say, pulling him close to me. "I'd still love you, Chad. Even if that happened. I promise you I'd still be here."

"It was like I was in a dream," he says, holding me tightly. "I knew everything that was happening to me, but it was like my mind was disconnected from my body. Reality was altered. The laws of physics didn't exist. I remember all of it. Every detail. You offered me coke, but I wanted *you* more, so I pushed it away. Then when you came in the room, there was two of you, the one on top of me and the one yelling at me. And then I was being punched by Julian, but I didn't feel a thing. I didn't even know it was Heather until they told me later at the hospital."

I shake my head in utter disbelief. "I can't believe she did that. Did she think she'd get you hooked on drugs again?"

"I guess so," he says. "She was desperate for work. Desperate for the pathetic life we once shared. Paul was in on it, too. Although he claims he didn't know about the drugs. I don't believe him. Not even Paul would be so dense to think that bitch could seduce me."

"So what's going to happen to him?" I ask. "Julian said he wasn't arrested like Heather was."

"There wasn't enough evidence to hold him."

I frown in disgust. "He should have to pay for what he did."

"Oh, he will," he says. "If nothing else, at least he'll feel it in his wallet."

"You fired him?" I look at him with a reluctant smile.

"Hell yes, I fired him. So did Lila. And I've called two other people who I know he represents. So I'm pretty sure by this time tomorrow, the only clients he'll be able to get are the small, furry, four-legged kind."

"What will you do? Who will be your manager?"

"Kendra is already putting together a list." He sees the concern etched across my face. "Don't worry. I'll be fine. If Paul knows what's good for him, he won't fight me on this. I'm fairly confident a few of our party guests recorded the whole thing, and Julian tells me Paul cried like a fucking baby."

I can't keep my hands off him. I want our bodies close, so I can protect him.

He points to the sleeping bag. "Let me set that up for us. We can lie here and stare at the stars like when we were kids."

"Good. I think I'd like to sleep here," I tell him, as he spreads the bag open. "Because there is no way I'd be able to sleep in that bed."

"Of course you wouldn't," he says. "I'll burn the damn thing. Hell, we don't even have to go back there if you don't want to. We can find a new place."

"I love that apartment, Chad. But the bed has to go. I'd never be able to look at it again without picturing how she was leaning over you and how you were touching her."

"And the perfume," he says, cringing. "It has to go, too. While I love it on you, it'll always remind me of what happened."

I pull away and look at him in confusion. "She was wearing my perfume? Did she steal if from my vanity? Wait—it's still packed. How . . . ?"

He shakes his head as if in pain, still clearly affected by tonight's events. "Do you remember last spring at Ana's party when Heather asked about your perfume? I thought it was strange and completely out of character."

My hand comes up to cover my gasp. "Oh, my God. Was she planning this all along?"

362

He shrugs. "She was planning *something*," he says. "But it just goes to show you, she would have gotten to me one way or another. You can't beat yourself up over the Paul invitation."

Another tear rolls down my cheek. "I thought I'd lost you," I tell him. "I wanted to die, Chad. I wanted to lie here and rot away so I didn't have to feel what I was feeling. But I knew that would never happen. I knew I would always love you even if you betrayed me."

He lies down and pulls me next to him as I rest my head on his chest. "I will never betray you, Mallory. I know it may seem like I did, but I would never willingly break my promise to you."

"I know you wouldn't. I know you *didn't*." I rest my head on my hand and peek up at him. "I promise I won't jump to conclusions again. I've done that twice now."

"With damn good reason both times," he says. "I promise I will do everything I can to make sure we're never put in a position like this again."

"I promise to throw away every bottle of 'Desire Me' that I own."

He kisses the top of my head. "I promise to buy you a whole damn magnum of any other perfume."

"I promise to always let you know when I get dead rodents in the mail."

He laughs and my head bounces up and down on his chest. "I promise to never use tongue when I kiss other women."

"Any other fiancée would be offended," I say, giggling. "But I think that's very romantic of you." I kiss him through his shirt. "I promise to be the best wife I can."

He wiggles beneath me and pulls something from his pocket. "Give me your hand," he says. I hold it up, sad that for a few hours the ring I threw at his head was missing. He slips it back onto my finger. "I promise to never be a stupid bastard."

I admire the ring back in its rightful place. "I promise to never take it off again."

He pulls me on top of him. "Did we just write our vows, future wife?"

I laugh. "Those are some pretty crazy vows," I say.

"To go with our pretty crazy life," he says. "But it's *our* crazy, and I love it. Just like I love you." He threads his hands into my hair and pulls my lips to his. "I promise to make you scream my name every damn day of our lives."

Right before our lips meet, I make one last vow. "I promise to let you."

His lips capture mine, gently at first and then demanding. Almost like how a whisper becomes a shout. We taste each other knowing after what we've endured, nothing can tear us apart. Our kisses are salty reminders of the bond we have that can never be broken.

His hands come up to unbutton my blouse. He reaches inside to cup my breasts and I quiver. I want to remember every touch; every kiss; every sound of our love. Because it was almost taken away from us in an instant.

"Mal, I want you so much," he says. He turns to his side, spilling me off of him as his hand reaches down to unbutton my pants. "I promise to fulfill your every fantasy," he says, looking at my bare chest. "Because right now, you're sure as hell fulfilling one of mine."

My eyes mist up thinking of the time he told me he used to fantasize about what we would do in this very treehouse. I wanted him, too. Even way back then. Even when I couldn't comprehend that the tingles running down my spine meant I was falling for a twelve-year-old boy. Even when I didn't understand that the butterflies in my stomach meant my heart belonged to a sixteen-year-old man.

Our clothes become a heap on the clapboard floor of the old battered treehouse. He peels my panties slowly down my thighs, inhaling my scent along the way. He spreads my legs and buries his mouth in me making me writhe and buck beneath his expertly placed tongue. I grab his hair, weaving my fingers through it, holding him tightly to me until his name rolls off my lips in pleasurable waves.

He climbs up my sweat-slickened body, kissing my scar, my breasts, my neck, as he works his way on top of me. And as he enters me and we become one, his hot whispers caress my ear. "I'll promise you anything. I promise you everything. Just promise me you'll always be mine."

I moan at the feeling of him filling me so completely. At the feeling of his hot flesh on mine. "I've always been yours, Chad. Since the day we met. Maybe even before that. I was made for you."

He rocks his body into me, faster and faster with every delicious thrust. "I need to hear you say it, Mallory," he begs, as he works a hand between us, bringing me once again to the precipice of ecstasy.

I lift my hips and squeeze my thighs, my stomach tightening with my impending explosion. "I promise," I say breathily, just as he shouts into the night, emptying himself into me as I pulsate around him.

~ ~ ~

Dawn wakes us, our backs sore from sleeping on the hard wooden floor. Our bodies battered from the love we bestowed upon each other time and time again. Pain has never felt so good. Chad wraps our naked bodies in the sleeping bag as we hold on to this moment that will be etched into our memories until the day we die.

I feel a wave of heat cross my face when I hear my father yell from the back door. "Coffee and pancakes in ten!" he shouts.

"Oh my gosh," I say, burying my head into Chad's shoulder. "Do you think he heard us last night?"

He laughs. "Babe, I think New Jersey heard us last night."

He hands me my clothes and we get dressed before climbing down to the ground. On our way to the house, we pass the driveway. Chad grabs my hand and pulls me to a stop. He nods at the basketball. "One last game?" he asks.

I smile before I tell him, "But I have everything I could possibly want. There's nothing left to play for."

He stares me down. His brilliant blue eyes are thick with determination. He wants something. He wants it bad.

"Fine, I say, walking over to pick up the orange ball. HORSE?" I ask.

He shakes his head, smiling deviously. Maybe he's hungry and wants a shorter game.

"PIG?" I ask, with the bounce of the ball.

He shakes his head again.

I'm confused. "Well, what game do you want to play then?" I ask.

He walks over and steals the ball from me, setting up for his first shot. Then he turns and stares into my eyes. It's then when I see it. I see what he wants. I see our entire future as he's mapped it out. And I know with one hundred percent certainty that everything he wants—I want. I'm not even surprised when he tells me the name of the game we're going to play. "BABY," he says with a crooked smile, right before perfectly netting his first shot.

Tears cloud my eyes as I go to retrieve the ball. My blurred vision makes it almost impossible to sink my shot. But that's okay. Because I'm fairly certain no matter what I do next—we're both going to win this game.

EPILOGUE

Chad

Seven years later . . .

I can't wipe the huge smile off my face. I look over at Mal and know she's feeling exactly what I'm feeling as we watch the kids on the basketball court in our backyard.

Brayden, Julian's son, and Mallory's brother, Ryan, who are both seven years old, are teaching Kiera, our six-year-old daughter how to play.

Mallory reaches over to grab my hand. We know all too well what's in store for them. The fun they will have growing up together. The bad times they will help each other navigate. The memories they will make. The incredible friendship they will all share.

"Do you think one day Brayden and Kiera will be sitting here watching *their* kids do the very same thing?" she asks.

I squeeze her hand. "They could only be so lucky."

I look around the patio and see Mal's dad and step-mom sipping lemonade on this warm summer day. I glance over at Ana, who is bouncing a laughing toddler on her knee. I look at my beautiful wife and place a hand on her growing belly. This is what it's all about. Not the awards lining the shelves of my study. Not the houses we own or the numbers in our bank account. *This*— family and friends—this is what makes life worth living.

Kiera squeals in delight when she finally makes her first shot.

We all clap and smile with pride. Mallory turns to me with tears in her eyes. "I don't know where we'll end up or what the future holds," she says. "But I'm telling you this right now—we will *always* have a basketball hoop."

I smile and nod, swallowing the lump in my throat. "And a treehouse," I say. "Definitely a treehouse."

Coming soon, Kyle's story

Stone Vows

If you've enjoyed Stone Promises, I would appreciate you taking a minute to leave a review on Amazon. Reviews, even just a few words, are incredibly valuable to indie authors like me.

Acknowledgements

I can't believe this is my eighth novel. I'm still pinching myself. When I started this journey a mere three years ago, I questioned my ability to publish one book let alone eight. It has been an incredible ride. And for that, I have my readers to thank. If it weren't for you, loving my characters and encouraging me to write more (and write faster), I wouldn't be able to do what I do.

Thank you to my editors, Ann Peters and Jeannie Hinkle. Editing is boring, repetitive, tedious work and for all that and more, I thank you from the bottom of my heart.

To my beta readers, Laura Conley, Heather Durham, Tammy Dixon and Angela Marie: thank you for your tireless work that surely made this book a much better read.

My family has stood by my side and watched me become a full-time writer. They've taken over the housework and the cooking, allowing me to follow my dreams. None of this would be possible without you.

About the author

Samantha Christy's passion for writing started long before her first novel was published. Graduating from the University of Nebraska with a degree in Criminal Justice, she held the title of Computer Systems Analyst for The Supreme Court of Wisconsin and several major universities around the United States. Raised mainly in Indianapolis, she holds the Midwest and its homegrown values dear to her heart and upon the birth of her third child devoted herself to raising her family full time. While it took time to get from there to here, writing has remained her utmost passion and being a stay-at-home mom facilitated her ability to follow that dream. When she is not writing, she keeps busy cruising to every Caribbean island where ships sail. Samantha Christy currently resides in St. Augustine, Florida with her husband and four children.

You can reach Samantha Christy at any of these wonderful places:

Website: www.samanthachristy.com

Facebook: https://www.facebook.com/SamanthaChristyAuthor

Twitter: @SamLoves2Write

E-mail: samanthachristy@comcast.net

Made in the USA
San Bernardino, CA
01 July 2017